THE BALLAD OF JOHNNY ARCANE

ↄ

Publisher: Inkwater Press | www.inkwaterpress.com

Publisher's Cataloging-in-Publication

    Nail, Jim, 1948- author.

        The ballad of Johnny Arcane : a novel / Jim Nail.

        pages cm

        LCCN 2015917300

        ISBN 978-1-62901-309-1 (pbk.)

        ISBN 978-1-62901-310-7 (Kindle)

        1. Musicians--Fiction. 2. Dystopian fiction.
      3. Science fiction. I. Title.

    PS3614.A555B35 2016   813'.6
                    QBI16-600012

Scan this QR Code to learn more about this title

Paperback
ISBN-13 978-1-62901-309-1 | ISBN-10 1-62901-309-9

Kindle
ISBN-13 978-1-62901-310-7 | ISBN-10 1-62901-310-2

Printed in the U.S.A.

1   3   5   7   9   10   8   6   4   2

THE BALLAD OF JOHNNY

ARCANE

A NOVEL

Jim Nail

JIM NAIL

INKWATER
PRESS

PORTLAND•OREGON
INKWATERPRESS.COM

This is for David West, who has always believed in Johnny Arcane

and for my beloved sweetheart Claire, who has always believed in me.

THE COLLECTED POEMS OF THE KNOWN WORLD

t some point on the continuum of space and time, certain works of poetry from your world, dear reader, passed through a permeable membrane into the world in which the events of this novel take place. They were compiled and printed in a volume during the era known as *No Time,* and given the title *Collected Poems of the Known World.* How many copies were printed is unknown, and only one copy has actually been documented. This was the one Johnny Arcane rescued from the trash heaps outside the city of Cantankerberg.

No doubt the integrity of the poetry was compromised in the transition between the worlds. Regardless, I would be amiss if I were to neglect to cite the authorship of the original works. The two poems printed—whole or in part—are:

The Feet of the Young Men by Rudyard Kipling.

The Lake Isle of Innisfree by William Butler Yeats.

In addition, Curvy Greyroad, the hermit-king of Hermit Town quotes William Blake when he remarks: *let the slave grinding at the mill run out into the field and laugh in the bright air!* It is a little-known fact that King Greyroad was an avid reader of poetry and probably kept a copy of *The Collected Poems* somewhere in his shack in Hermit Town.

PROLOGUE

hree cowboys are sitting around a campfire roasting a cat. In the distance the restless coyotes are setting up their cacophony, and the pungent aroma of sage permeates the warm night air. Up close, wild cats are skulking about in the underbrush, guttering like off-key harmonicas and complaining about the injustice of their lives. The cats have become a problem. So many of them, they hole up in abandoned barns and they hide under the floorboards of inhabited houses, permeating the ductwork with the stench of their feces. Sometimes you come across a dead cat in the woodpile, or a live cat may jump out at you all claws and snarling, when you open the broom closet. Cats get into the grain silos and their trampled carcasses are often seen on the roadbeds.

But they make good eating.

Aramis, the youngest cowboy, leans back on his knapsack and watches the stars. He watches a blinker crossing the sky. Blinkers look like stars but they move slowly, yet visibly across the sky, and they blink. Nobody knows what the blinkers are. Aramis wonders about this. Why don't people care? Why aren't people more curious about the blinkers?

"Look at that," says Climber as he turns the spit. "Did ye ever see a more delicious looking thing? Don't that just make yer mouth water?"

Birdleg takes a swig from his bottle of corn liquor. "Yes, I have." he replies.

"Yes, you have *what*?"

"Yes, I have seen a more delicious looking thing. In fact, I have tasted a more delicious looking thing."

Climber lets go an exasperated sigh. "Birdleg, I'm just using a figger of speech. There are lotsa delicious looking things. And delicious *tasting* things too. But this is the one what's set before us tonight."

Birdleg makes the kind of smile you make when you remember something. "It was a pie," he says. "Just three weeks ago, before we left. Annabelle made it. She got a holt of some beet sugar and she used them fresh blackberries from behind the grange. It were sweet."

Climber turns the cat and some fat drops and sizzles on the coals. "Sweetness. That ain't something we taste much of these days."

Birdleg nods. "You know 'bout the theory of the flavors, don't you? There's only three flavors in the Known World. There's sweet and there's bitter and there's sour. Everything we taste on our tongues is made up of some permutation of them three flavors."

"So, you're saying mostly these days we just been tasting bitter and sour."

"Well, I don't know 'bout that. I mean I'm not sure I agree with the theory of the flavors. On account of I'm not sure what sweetness is a flavor."

"Oh yeah? Well then what is it if it's not a flavor?"

"Can't say for sure. I think there's lotsa flavors, like there's salty and there's spicy, like peppers. But sweetness don't seem like a flavor to me. Seems more like a feeling, like you get when you remember something sweet. Like just now, when I remembered Annabelle's pie. It felt like sweetness."

"Nah, I don't think spicy's a flavor neither," Climber

says, after a pause. "I mean one winter, when it was cold, this old medicine man told me I should put peppers in my shoes, and I did, and I walked in the snow, and my feet were warm. That weren't a flavor. That were a feeling."

The two men are quiet for a while, and the young cowboy, Aramis, remains quiet, watching the blinker as it disappears behind the tree-lined western ridge. Then suddenly there's a change in the air, a kind of shimmering, like a pebble dropped in a pond, and a little breeze seems to rustle itself out of the fire, and the tent flaps rustle. And suddenly there's another man standing there, a tall, thin man in a shredded buckskin jacket, shaggy mop of hair, a grizzled beard.

Birdleg startles, but Climber remains calm, still turning the cat. "Evenin' stranger. You hungry? Want some cat?"

"No, thank you," the stranger replies. "Maybe just a little warmth from your fire. I was going to pass on by in the night and not bother you, but I overheard what you were talking about, and I was interested."

There's a moment of quiet. Birdleg regains his composure. "We was talking about sweetness. We was talking about the theory of the flavors, how there's only three flavors, but we're not sure that sweetness is a flavor."

Climber coughs. "We're not sure spicy's a flavor, neither."

"So what's your take on it, stranger?" Birdleg says. "Sweetness. Is it a flavor?"

The stranger laughs. His laughter is warm and melodious, and rich with overtones. The cowboys are a little shaken by it. "No," he replies. "Sweetness isn't a flavor. Sweetness is just sorrow that has been transformed."

Aramis shakes his head suddenly as if waking from a dream. "Sorrow?" he says, but Birdleg interrupts. "I know sorrow. Our little Ivy, just last winter. She died of the fever. We were all in so much sorrow."

The stranger considers this for a moment. "Your sorrow is real, and I can tell by the sweetness in your voice, it is being transformed. But I must tell you something difficult. Outside the four directions of the Known World, there is *great* sorrow— unimaginable sorrow, and it is moving in. The cornmeal that seals the borders is blowing in the wind. But there are places here and there where the sorrow is being transformed. The Known World is only one of those places. Sweetness is just sorrow that has been transformed."

Then again there was a shimmer in the air. This time it seemed like the wind blew back from the tent flaps into the fire and a tongue of flame circled up and disappeared into the coals, and the stranger was gone.

For a long time nobody said anything. Climber let go of the spit and turned the coals with a poker. Birdleg took another swig of his corn liquor. Cats gurgled and cackled in the underbrush and branches snapped. The restless coyotes sang another distant chorus.

Aramis shivered, then spoke. "That was Johnny Arcane, wasn't it?"

Climber threw his poker down decisively into the dirt. "You shut up! That weren't Johnny Arcane. Johnny Arcane is dead!"

Aramis rallied. "No, he's not! They say he's dead but he's not. I know he's not."

"He's dead. He died when Frankie took the photograph. We all know that. It's just true!"

"He didn't die, he just disappeared, like all the others. Like the people from the camp. They went into the side world so you can't see them anymore. But they can come back any time."

"Aramis, you talk shit and it's not good for you. You can't ride with us if you're going to keep talking shit like that."

But Aramis was now crying, softly, in soft little sniffles with a voice like a child's. "He's not dead. I know it. Johnny Arcane's not dead."

CHAPTER ONE

JOHNNY ARCANE
SETS OUT

A messenger appeared on the afternoon of the owl moon in Johnny Arcane's seventeenth summer. Johnny was out working the garden, thinning the carrots, when he saw the stranger round the crest of the western ridge, no more than a speck from that distance, like an oak tree walking.

The stranger stomped the road dust off his boots when he reached the house. He was mostly dressed in rags, but he had the distinguishing red armband of a messenger, and he wore a fine leather hat. He came inside and sat at the table. Mother gave him a tall tumbler of water and a slice of homemade bread.

"The news I bring weighs heavy on my heart," he said. "About ten days ago I was at the midsummer fair in a place called Archer's Bale. There was a man there. He was playing concertina for some children, but when he saw me, he stopped, and said '*messenger.*' He took me into the roadhouse and we drank some beer, even though it was only mid-day. He told me what he needed me to do. He drew me a map and he gave me a letter."

The messenger reached into his pocket and produced a tattered envelope. The seal was clearly broken.

"He said it was ten days walking should I start out in the morning. He said the letter was for a woman who was the mother of his son."

Mother took a short breath and reached her folded hands across the table. Johnny sat down quickly and took her hands in his, but she pulled them away. Her expression revealed nothing, except that she appeared to be looking into something large and deep, like a cavern.

"The hard part is this:" the messenger continued. "That night was midsummer and at Archer's Bale they build a large scarecrow out of straw, and they light him on fire. The man was playing his concertina when they lit the scarecrow. People were dancing a ring around it, especially the children. Dancing to the man's music. The scarecrow began to topple over and the dancers moved away, but the man stayed where he was. And the scarecrow fell on him and covered him in flame. The people rushed to him but they couldn't get close—it was too hot. When the fire burned out there was nothing, just a pile of ash. The man burned up completely, even his bones."

Mother stood and walked to the stove. A pot of soup stock was simmering and she stirred it with a wooden spoon. She did not turn around when she spoke.

"We weren't close. He left before Johnny was born and I haven't heard from him since. But it's always sad when a life is lost."

Ↄ

That night, Mother fixed the Messenger up with a bed of straw in the hayloft. It was a warm night and the owls were restless. The moon was nearly full. It wasn't until the dogs were quiet and the hens were clucking quietly in their sleep that she lit the carbide lamp and set it on the table, and she and Johnny sat down there, and she opened the letter.

She fingered the broken wax seal. "Corn damn messengers!" she said. "No purity these days. Why do people always want to *know* things?" Then without further comment she spread the parchment on the table and read in a flat-sur-faced voice.

My dear Calendula,

The memory of the time we spent together is like a beacon shining in a dark night. In all my seasons of sojourning there has been no other, and Johnny is my only child. Now I must tell you this.

Tonight I plan to leave my body. In my travels I have learned many things, more than you could imagine, were you prone to imagination. One thing I learned is that it is possible to choose the time of one's own depar-ture. I won't go into the details except to say that tonight is my chosen time.

Sojourning is not a choice one makes; it is in the blood, and surely there is some sojourning in Johnny's blood. He is, after all, my son, and your father too was a sojourner. If Johnny is to be a sojourner, you will have recognized it by now. You must let him go, and if he is reluctant, you must encourage him. I believe the sojourners are a new kind of people in this world. They bring something new, something inevitable. Whether or not it is a good thing is yet to be seen, but its inevitability cannot be denied.

But I don't need to tell you this. I remember the clarity, almost disin-terest, with which you let me go, such a short time before our son was born. To be honest, for the first few months my heart was broken, until I realized the rightness of your approach. Now that I have seen and learned so much, affections and yearnings are no longer part of my vocabulary.

So tonight I will leave the body. I will have finished my travels. I will have done my work. I only regret that I will not know if this message has reached you. I can only trust that it will, and the circle will be closed.
Yours in solitude,
Caspar Arcane

There was a long silence. Mother remained at the table, stone-faced. Johnny got up and walked about the kitchen. A green winged beetle crawled across the tabletop, courting the cold white glow of the carbide lamp.

Johnny turned. "Mother ... does everything ... does everything everywhere happen at the same time?"

"I don't understand your question, son."

"Well, my question is this. The messenger said it was a ten-day journey. That means it was eleven nights ago when the scarecrow fell on father. At that time we were probably sitting at this table eating supper, or playing runes, or shelling beans. If everything, everywhere happens at the same time, we should have been able to know what was happening to father. Perhaps we could even have stopped it from happening."

"Johnny, that is foolishness. Even if you knew what was happening somewhere else, you couldn't do anything about it. You have to be there. You have to *be* someplace to do something about it."

"But you could be wrong. What if you knew what was happening somewhere else, you *could* do something about it? You could send a message, one that doesn't need to travel over distance. It could be possible, Mother."

Mother sighed and stretched one hand across the table as if she were reaching for her son. But Johnny was pacing the other side of the room. Mother sighed again, and then she made a little far-away smile.

"And that's why I know your father is right. You're a sojourner, Johnny. Only a sojourner would think such thoughts."

☽

In the days and nights that followed, while the moon slowly dwindled to a crescent fingernail, Johnny and Mother quarreled incessantly, bitterly. At first it was over trivialities. He left the root cellar door open when he brought in the parsnips. She didn't like the way he stacked the firewood with the big logs on the bottom. When she stood at the door in the evening and wrung her hands, as she did every evening, it drove him crazy, but he didn't know how to say it. Instead he scolded her for allowing the fire to grow so warm on a summer day.

One morning Johnny sat at the table in front of a stack of pancakes while Mother performed her daily ritual, emptying the water from the sconces on the four walls of the house, refilling them and sprinkling into each a pinch of ash from the fireplace grate. Johnny straightened his back. "Mother, that is so foolish."

Mother scowled. "It's not foolish, Johnny. You have to appease the four directions. Otherwise, things could change."

Johnny slammed the palm of his hand on the table top, making the plates jump. "It's foolish! In the first place, it doesn't do anything. It's just a superstition. And besides, why don't you want things to change? Change is necessary. Change has to happen."

"The time of change is over, Johnny. You know that.

Don't turn your back on what you've learned in school. We have good things to eat, and plenty of wood. People are kind and gentle now. The fire and the bandits are gone. The weather is fair. As long as we appease the four directions, things will remain as they are."

"You don't even know the four directions, Mother. You only know the four walls of this house. Let me tell you what I know about the four directions. I've been outside. I've wandered the four directions. In the west there are the rocks. They look like faces with ears. A trail winds through them but I have never seen anyone walk this trail. At night the blinkers rise up from the snowy mountains in the north. They move through the stars and set in the flatlands of the south. There's a house on the southern horizon, with a palm tree and a windmill. On a hot afternoon it shimmers in a lake of shallow water. I walked there once. There was no water. The house was deserted, falling down. The ground was dry and barren. Sometimes in the night, from the south, I see flashes of green light. A road comes down from the scrub hills in the east. That's the way the messenger came and it's probably the way he left. It's the way I will leave."

After that, their quarrels were far less lucid. They quarreled over the number of strokes to churn butter, or the proper bedtime for dogs. Mother cooked her meals with a noisy clatter while Johnny sat on the floor scribbling pictures of mountains on the parchment tablet, then ripping them off, crumpling them up and hurling them in the fire.

One warm night, Mother got her squeezebox down from the shelf and sat by the fire, playing through the old melodies, the stovepipes, the cotillions, the meringues, the strathspeys. Johnny took down his mandolin and strummed the strings, but he could not get his fingers to play. On so many other evenings they had played, he and his mother, sometimes late into the night, working through the familiar melodies and then deconstructing them, making brand new tunes that they would give funny names like *The Caterpillars of Peril,* or *Your Hand Brushes the Midnight Crumbs From the Table.* But tonight the reeds of the accordion were too sharp for his ears. He took his mandolin and left the house, first to the woodshed where he set it down next to the cutting block and split twelve large cherry stumps, all the while saying to himself, *I won't feel the heat of this wood. By the winter I will be gone.*

Then he took his mandolin up to the top of Gravestone Hill where Huxley and Vermillion and Rug-Chomper were buried. He played to the stars and the blinkers and the crescent setting moon, the coyotes on the eastern ridge joining in harmony. Suddenly he had a revelation.

She's doing this on purpose. She's just following father's orders.

He stopped playing then, returned to the house quietly, and put himself to bed without another word.

The next morning, Johnny Arcane got up early and left his house and his mother, and set out to take on the life of a sojourner.

Mother was ready for this. She had filled his backpack with necessary items, some clean shirts and pants, a good sharp whittling knife, a canteen full of fresh water, a tin of oat flakes and a sack of dried cat meat. She hooked the mandolin in its case to the strap on the side of the pack. It was a chilly morning and he wore a light jacket. She straightened the collar. Her eyes were dry.

"You will send a messenger from time to time to tell me

how you're doing, won't you Johnny? Not just on the day before you leave your body."

Her words cut him, and for a moment he thought, *she's making me do this. This isn't my idea. She's driving me out.* But at the same moment his legs told him *no. We want to be on our way.*

"I will, Mother,' he said. "Perhaps I will even pass this way again."

He turned abruptly to hide the tears. His back to home, his face to the world, Johnny Arcane set out on his journey toward the unknown.

CHAPTER TWO

JOHNNY LOSES HIS VOICE

nd then there it was, simple strong and merciful, the wind-swept, rain-washed, sun-dried bracing freedom of the open road!

It ambushed him slowly as he rose from his anxiety and despondency and ascended into the scrub hills on the northbound road, the very path on which the messenger had arrived. Involuntarily, his steps grew lighter, his heartbeat stronger. At the crest, he stopped and caught his breath.

He had been here before, but it had never looked like this. On the other side of the ridge the eye-view opened into a rich, green valley, bound in the distance by a range of powder-blue mountains. Rolling hills covered with healthy orchards, apples, pears, hazelnuts, grapevines heavy with purple fruit. Occasional small, thatch-roofed houses nestled among shade trees. Wisps of fragrant smoke curled from chimneys.

A new kind of joy overcame him. He didn't have a name for it. It propelled him down the road and into the valley. His thoughts grew light and skimmed the surface. Things once commonplace were imbued with a surprising beauty. A pond with ducks, where a rowboat sat idle. A fence leaning under the weight of morning glories. A water tower completely engulfed by a quilt of wild, pink roses. Patterned rays of slanted sunlight through the ordered columns of an apple orchard. Beehives between the trees—the hum of bees. Johnny had no thoughts, only the delight of impressions. Dogs barked at him from porches but did not approach.

Midday he came upon a table and a bench by the side of the road. He sat here and drank some water and ate some of the dried cat meat Mother had packed. Ahead on the road, a figure approached, a man, walking with a stick. A discomfort seeped into Johnny's stomach. At first he thought it was the food he had eaten, but no. All day he had spoken to no one. No one had approached him on the road, passing from either direction. So deep had been the quiet of his mind and the joy of his traveling that the thought of conversing with another person felt like a heavy burden.

The man stopped in the road and looked at Johnny while his dust swirled up behind him. Then he continued. He walked with a limp. One leg dangled lifelessly and touched the ground only with the cadence of the stick. He wore khaki clothing and a beret. On his arm: the distinctive red band of the Messenger. He halted in front of the table, smiled, but said nothing.

Johnny spoke. "Messenger."

"Sojourner." The word fell like an ice cube in Johnny Arcane's soul.

"I just started today." he replied.

The man nodded, then pointed his stick to the bench by the table. "Move over, let an old man rest his bones."

Johnny moved over, offered his canteen. "Water?"

The Messenger drank deeply, wiped the slobber off on

his sleeve, then turned and looked Johnny straight in the face. "It's a lonely lot this life has dealt you, son. The world as we know it don't shuck much corn with the sojourner. They don't want to know what the sojourner knows. There's a veil o' ignorance what keeps us happy. You got anything there to eat?"

Johnny offered him some cat meat. The man chewed it silently, his eyes fixed on the vineyard across the road. "I respect them, though. Sojourners. I just couldn't be one. Goin' home to Honeydew now, to see my sweet Harmony, and my little Melody. It's good work, *messengering*. You learn just enough to know, but not enough to grieve. Lots a sojourners start out by being messengers. You memberize the lay of land, and the borders. Masticate on that sometimes, son. Might do you good."

The Messenger rubbed his hands together and spat something brown and viscous into the dust. "Much obliged for the vittles. Let me give you something in return." He dug in his coat pocket and produced a small, amber vial sealed with wax. "Keep it hid," he said. "Only take it if the pain is so strong you can't go on. Powerful medicine, but it don't last forever."

Then he hobbled to his feet, tipped his hat, smiled a toothless grin, and continued on his way.

Ↄ

At nightfall Johnny came across a roadhouse nestled in a stand of willows on the shore of a river. He could tell by the color of the light, they were burning corn oil, and there was music from within, fiddles and guitars, and the sound of drunken voices. Two separate herds of goats mingled about untethered on the grounds. Johnny knew there were two because of the brands burnt on their haunches, one the trident, the other the hourglass.

He was hungry, but the encounter with the messenger had left him shaken, unsure of any further human contact. Yet he had to eat. Cautiously he pushed on the heavy wooden slab of a door. The air inside was warm and redolent with spices, especially coriander. Corn lamps flickered in wall sconces. The musicians stood on a raised platform at the other end of the room. Two fiddles, three guitars. He recognized the melody: *The Shoe Becomes the Foot That Wears It.* Perhaps he might join them on his mandolin. Perhaps that might untie the weight from his heart.

He eased his way in. Long heavy tables filled the room, and people sat at all of them, men and women; goat people with their colorful rags; farmers in their bib overalls; woodcarvers with sawdust in their hair; mummers, male and female, in white robes. Beer steins, full and empty, cluttered the tables, and heavy stone bowls ladled with some kind of stew.

People looked up as he passed between the tables. A few eyes lingered. There was no place to sit, until at last he saw a tiny booth off in a corner, away from the musicians, the only single table in the house.

A stout woman appeared with a tray. "You'd be wantin' some supper I suppose," she said. "Tonight we be servin' goat stew with parsnips and rutabagas. And a fine pale ale."

The stew was warm and flavorful, and the ale was strong and quickly went to Johnny's head, but it only served to tighten the conspicuous cloak of silence that enshrouded him. Everyone was conversing; everyone was together, laughing, singing. Stories were everywhere.

He was the only person who was alone. How he wished

he were invisible! How he wished he could join them, for to join them would be to become invisible. But the force of his silence was like a repellent shield. Several times he almost got up and bolted for the door. But he had to eat. His body demanded it. So he settled back and listened to the conversations that surrounded him.

"Rudder, you got a onion in your beard." The speaker was a scrawny goat man whose rag shirt was mostly crimson and gold, signifying the flat grasslands of the north. The man named Rudder did, indeed, have an onion in his long curly beard, or more correctly, a dried purple shallot tied to the beard hairs with a piece of twine.

"Well, yes, I do have a onion in my beard. I put it there just this morning. Had to come through Bastard Pass and there's horn pigs there. Horn pigs won't go near a man with a onion in his beard."

The goat man snorted. "Huh! Never heard of that before. I allus thought that horn pigs was afraid a carbide."

A woman spoke. Broad-shouldered, small, callused fingers, she wore the frilled vest of a dressmaker. "You silly men! You know there's no such thing as horn pigs."

"Oh yes, there are! I seed 'em!"

"What you see are javalinas, not horn pigs. There's only one thing that javalinas are afraid of. You know what that is?"

"No, what?"

"You. They're afraid of you."

A great round of laughter circled the table. "Ha, ha, Rudder!" the goat man cackled. "I'm gonna grab that onion out of your beard and throw it in my stew!"

"No, you're not!"

"Yes, I am!" and the goat man thrust his hand into the folds of Rudder's beard. Rudder swung his muscular arm and the goat man clattered to the floor. There was applause and the music swelled.

The dressmaker turned to another woman, also a dressmaker, seated next to her.

"Rittles vary from place to place, you know. They don't put sheep skin on the roof tiles down in Beggar's Bog. And they burn their stalk fires on the full moon."

The other woman chewed on a corncob pipe. "Makes more sense to burn them on the dark of the moon," she replied. "That's when you need the light."

"Well, it innit always about making sense. Sometimes it's just about doing things the same. Like you always sleep on the same side o' your husband. Or you sit at the same place at the table."

The other dressmaker set down her pipe and lifted her stein. "I knew a man that had these terrible fears, like he was afeart of the sky, cause it was so big. He thought it was gonna swaller him up. Couldn't even go outside lest he was in the forest where you couldn't see the sky. The doctor made him take all the herbs, but it didn't do any good. Then one day this man, he got the toothache, and his tooth swelled up so big it just popped out of his head, and then all of a sudden he didn't have any fear anymore. So he took the tooth into the doctor. The doctor said, *the roots of this tooth is full of blasting salt. Did you ever chew on bat shit?* The man said, *Yeah, well, I did when I was young, cause I heard it would make me, uh, you know...virile.* Doctor said, *you should never chew on bat shit. It goes right to the roots of your tooth, and it gets into your brain.* You never know. What you're doing right now—might be good— might be bad."

The first dressmaker leaned far across the table. "It's allus good to get up early and watch the full moon going down. It fixes your speech. Not so good to watch it comin' up, though."

The second dressmaker, "You should rub your feet in the morning afore you get out of bed. That way the sickness can't get in through your feet."

Rudder slammed his stein down so quickly the beer stayed in the air and then fell like rain on the tabletop. "It's poison what makes you sick!"

"Of course it's poison," said the goat man. "What else would it be?"

The second dressmaker leaned across the lake of spilled ale. "Well, some people say it's little bugs so small you can't even see 'em gets into your body. Like they be on the floor when ye set yer feet down."

Rudder folded his arms across his chest. "No, no, it's poison. You heard about Doctor Clearwater didn't ye? He did a experiment with small doses a different poisons to determine the qualitative difference between the discomforts."

"What, did he give them to pigs?"

"No, he took them himself. He wanted to experience it first hand."

The goat man scratched his chin. "Sounds like a sojourner to me."

At that moment Johnny felt a pair of eyes upon him, not the eyes of anyone who had been speaking, a man further down the table, wearing no distinguishing uniform of any trade, just a plain white shirt and a brown collarless jacket, no hat. The man held Johnny's stare for just a moment, then turned back to conversation with someone next to him.

All the uneasiness rushed back into Johnny's body, as the voices around him swelled into an unintelligible staccato, like locusts at a window. He felt a throbbing in his temples and in his legs. He looked down at his empty bowl and stein. Time to go, then! I am but a bruise in this place. I am a lobelia to be expelled. I am a hairball.

He stood slowly and scanned the sea of faces between the table and the door. So many shoulders to jostle and toes on which to tread! But there was another door at the nearby corner, a short, rounded one, perhaps for the children or for the dogs. He dropped to his hands and knees and slipped unnoticed between the feet and the table legs until he burst into the bracing cool of the night.

Ↄ

For the period of two full moons, Johnny Arcane wandered alone and lost, trapped in a prison whose walls were his skin and the only door was his mind, his thoughts opening to a rich inner world, populated with phantasms and memories, drawing him further and further into himself and away from the landscape through which he traveled.

For a while he stayed on the roads, but he kept encountering people, women gardening or drawing water from wells, men hauling carts full of vegetables, bands of mummers practicing their dances in open fields. They tried to speak to him but he only mumbled a few words and hurried on his way, anxious to be forgotten. He grew hungry. All the food Mother had packed him was gone in a day, and his canteen was empty. The first night he slept between the rows in a cornfield and gnawed on the half-ripe kernels of corn. The second day he filled his canteen from a roadside well, but he found no food and he slept cold and famished like an outlaw, in a barn loft after the farmer and his wife had extinguished their lamps and the dogs were quiet.

But oh, his thoughts!

He thought of Mother, how she honored the four directions each morning, and what he had told her. *You don't know anything about the four directions, Mother. You only know the four walls of this house.* He had described the attributes of the four directions—the face-like rocks to the west, the snowy mountains to the north, the shimmering flatlands to the south, the western scrub hills with the road winding through them. All this, only a few days ago, and yet now it seemed so far away. He could visualize the four directions as they appeared from the summit of Gravestone Hill where Huxley, Vermillion and Rug-Chomper were buried.

He thought of his father, Caspar Arcane. In the letter his father wrote, *to be honest, for the first few months my heart was broken, until I realized the rightness of your approach.*

Had his father carried this heartbreak longer than he cared to admit? What other heartbreaks had he uncovered in his sojourning? *One thing I learned is that it is possible to choose the time of one's own departure.* Johnny had heard stories of this before, of people who had simply sat down and stopped breathing. He had even heard of people who had left their bodies in a moment of great joy, as if the joy was so great their bodies could not contain it. But he had never heard of anyone who had willed his death through an external event, such as the fall of a flaming scarecrow. It didn't harmonize for him. There was no resonance. His father was not an old man. A shudder of sadness passed through him. *Oh! If only you could know of something happening far away, a peril or an opportunity. Oh, if you could only change things from a distance!*

And this, said Mother, *is how I knew you were a sojourner.*
In the morning there were more people on the road,
all moving in the same direction, pulling carts festooned
with colorful banners, laden with carvings of improbable
beings, tureens steaming with savory concoctions, stacks of
pottery and garlands of flowers. Donkeys pulled some of the
carts. Children, both boys and girls, skipped and cavorted
in brightly colored dresses. Bands of mummers progressed
in twirling motions, trailing bright ribbons. There must be
some kind of fair in the next village. Johnny watched it all
from behind a blind of firs. He could not join them, although
the aromas made him tremble with hunger. If he could make
himself invisible he would slip in among them, snatch a few
pastries, perhaps a handful of persimmons for his pockets.
But he couldn't bear the thought of being seen, of speaking
to anyone.

A path led into the forest. It was a dense forest of firs
standing shoulder to shoulder, limb to limb. Johnny took
this path. Immediately he was engulfed in a shadow almost
as dark as night. He was comforted by its arboring shelter,
and he recalled the story the dressmaker told of the man
who was afraid of the sky and could only go outside if there
was a forest.

The moon swelled to ripeness and shrank to a dried rind.
His body grew weak but his thoughts in their increasing
strangeness propelled him on his way. Through the sky of his
mind flew objects, cooking utensils, ladles and multi-tined
forks, butter churns, hinges and hasps, nail sets, keyhole
saws. He heard melodies and recognized their names. *The
Onion Skin, The Baker's Misfortune, Many the Days I Count
My Fingers.* The path ascended continuously and the climb
weighed heavily on his legs. Hunger and thirst were his two

relentless pursuers. He ate tree fungus and salmon berries, but water was scarce. When the trail skirted a spring-moistened cliff, he sucked on the rocks like lozenges. At night the darkness was impenetrable. He slept where he was, on the trail. Each night was a little colder than the night before. His stomach shrunk to the size of a child's fist, and he stopped defecating entirely.

Late one afternoon, after many uncounted days and nights, he glimpsed something flickering among the trees. A precipice rose from a small clearing, and behind it, the round, dark mouth of a cave. Directly in front, a shrine had been built, its wooden platform thickly covered in bright green moss. Seven corn lamps burned on the altar and in between the lamps were plates of food, oat cakes, baked apples, yellow melons, roasted parsnips and rutabagas, strips of dried cat meat. To one side of the altar was a glass pitcher sparkling with clear water, and next to it, a tumbler, waiting to be filled.

Johnny fell to his knees and his eyes met the image carved on the arched niche of the shrine. Winged creatures circled a woman seated on a golden cushion. She was completely naked. Her long black hair trailed behind her, lifted aloft by the beaks of tiny red winged blackbirds. Before her face, wisps of incense rose from cones nestled among the moss.

An utterance rose from Johnny's chest, like a river breaking through a log jam, and he lunged for the pitcher, filled the tumbler, and poured the water down his throat. Then he grabbed at the food, thrusting several oatcakes into his mouth at once. He downed another tumbler of water and fell back in the dirt, exhausted. The sensation of food and water coursing through his limbs was almost unbearable. He couldn't move, and he felt his consciousness spiraling like a whirlpool. He keeled onto his back and collapsed into a deep sleep.

He opened his eyes. It wasn't completely dark. A yellow glow slipped in and out of the branches overhead. He sat up and saw the corn lamps still burning on the altar, casting a pale illumination on the image of the woman. In the lamplight she looked more like a real person. Her naked skin had a velvet sheen and he thought he saw beads of perspiration on her breasts and shoulders. Her body swayed from side to side in the flickering light, but her dark eyes remained immobile, fixed on his. He held their gaze as long as he could, until the weariness overtook him. Flat on his back in the dirt he slipped into a shallow slumber, waves of bliss and pleasure radiating through his limbs, his torso supported by many tiny, soft and supple hands.

A pale sun flooded his face. He woke, refreshed but weak. He knelt at the altar, drank the rest of the water, and ate some of the food. He ate all of the melons, a few more oatcakes, some of the cat meat. Then he gathered up all the rest and dropped it in his backpack.

He stood. On the ground were two stone jars full of corn oil. He took them both in his hands. *Who keeps these lamps lit, and who refills these plates with food?* The food was not an issue. He needed it to survive. But with one of the jars he refilled all the lamps. He took a few flints from the pile and placed them in his backpack with the other jar of oil. He took one last look at the altar.

Refreshed with the oil, the lamps danced happily and the carved woman smiled. Johnny stared at her face. He found it hard to believe she had seemed so real to him in the dark of night. Her paint was chipped and her skin was rutted with the grain of the wood. *Enough of these silly rituals, these fool-*

ish beliefs, based on nothing but ignorance! He had to know what was really out there, beyond the boundaries of the four directions. It was the burden of the sojourner.

There was no trail beyond this place, but he found some footholds in the cliff. His fingers were bruised and his knees were shaky by the time he reached the open space at the top. There was a rocky summit with view in all directions. Everywhere, trees, mostly firs but some deciduous maples and alders gilding the green with streaks of early autumnal gold. Bands of different shades of color layered the receding distance, brush stroked by mist and shadow, and on the far horizon, a single, magnificent mountain, cloaked in white.

He found the faintest suggestion of a path tunneling down into the low clinging vines to the south. It could have been made by people or by animals, but he set out on it nonetheless. He couldn't tarry here. He had to be on his way.

And so began the second leg of Johnny Arcane's journey through solitude, this one lasting twenty days and nights. The path led ever downward and continually branched. He didn't stop to decide. He just plunged in the direction his body fell. Gravity chose his course, again and again. For a while, the freefall exhilarated him, but soon his joints and muscles began to recoil with each impact. Branches slapped his face and thorns scratched his arms. He slowed a little. He stopped to rest. It was dark and cool but he was drenched in perspiration. He ate some food and continued.

The first night he slept uneasily. Owls whooped, bats whistled and moths fluttered against his ears. Nights after that he sank like a stone, exhausted. In only a few days he ate all the food from the altar, and he had no water. He heard water everywhere, phantom rainfall in the high canopies, cascading streams in gulches far below. The sound of water haunted his dreams.

He ceased to feel his legs. His body slammed into trees and tripped over vines. His foot snagged on a rotten stump and he tumbled like a log down a ravine of gorse bushes, barbed leaves puncturing his skin. He saw something like smoke rush out of his mouth when he struck the hard ground, and above him a crow dropped a silvery object and he watched it fall. Before him was a dark, brackish pool. He flung himself at it and drank deeply of its bitter offering. He felt his blood explode and a burst of sparks peppered his vision, followed by a gulf of darkness.

He awoke sick. His stomach knotted in pain and his arms and legs thrashed like branches in a storm. He rolled onto his side and vomited out the entire contents of his body. In the vomit he saw creatures, like cockroaches, scurrying away into the underbrush, and armies of maggots waving at him from the bile. A spasm ripped through his bowels and they unleashed a burden so putrid he rolled over and vomited again.

He lay there feverish, puking and crapping, moaning in pain and then contracting into a stillness as solid as ice. Shadowy figures approached. Each one offered him something but he did not know who they were or what they offered. Sometimes he was able to rise in the air above his body, but he didn't have the strength to fly.

All at once his vision congealed, and he was staring into the face of a creature, its eyes fixed on him intently. It was not a dream or a phantom, and at the same time he felt warmth, rushing back into him from all directions.

The creature was a weasel, and it held in its mouth the body of a large quail, its topknot a quivering banner in the wind. The weasel had been waiting for this moment. It dropped the bird in the dirt and nodded toward it several times. *This is for you.* Then it disappeared.

Johnny sat up suddenly. The sun was shining and his body felt whole and solid. But thirsty. He regarded the pond. The water was new, clean, rippling in a gentle wind. Cautiously he scooped some up in his hands, sniffed it, touched his lips to it, then swallowed it ravenously. He dropped his face into the surface and drank deeply.

He regarded the gift, the quail, with curiosity. He desired it. With bare hands he plucked the feathers and pulled the body apart, dumping the intestines out on the ground. Memory rushed in. He got up on wobbly legs and groused about in the bracken for twigs and small pieces of wood. He opened the backpack and found the jar of corn oil and the flints. He drenched the damp wood with oil, struck the flints, and soon had a crackling fire. He skewered the bird, roasted it, and devoured it. Then he lay on his back and stared into the blue of sky for the rest of the morning, slipping between sensations of great joy and great sadness.

Sun broke through the trees. With a lightened heart, he continued on his way. His tumble down the mountain had deposited him at the head of a well-worn trail, winding downhill through the forest at a gentle slope. Birds serenaded him from branches, and here and there the trees parted to allow beams of sunlight to warm his shoulders. In time, the trail joined a small brook of clear water. He drank from it freely. He came across a meadow lush with wild green mustard, and stuffed a handful of its leaves into his mouth. It was a tonic to his nerves and sent a jolt of power into his limbs. At nightfall he found a small cabin with no windows and no bedding, only a hard wooden platform, but he slept there like a baby.

He began to discover other signs of human presence. Small stone cairns marked the places where the trail made a bend. There was a bare footprint in a mud puddle, a goatman's rag tied to a branch, the remnant of a fire. Further along, he came across stick figures and undecipherable runes scratched in a stone wall, and once, a magnificent apple tree, laden with yellow fruit, standing next to a broken down windmill. He could feel the weight of his solitude lifting.

People! The thought flooded him with apprehension and longing. Mostly longing, though. He remembered the altar with the food and the carvings and the flickering flames. In this dark forest filled with creatures that sought his attention, this was the one thing that filled him with comfort and warmth. A road, then, and people on the road, their smiles, their voices, their laughter. The touch of a hand. The sparkle in an eye. The thought made his legs quicken and his heart thump with a nervous joy.

But there was a problem.

CHAPTER THREE

LUCY

e was filthier than a javalina in a pig sty. His hair and beard were bristle-stiff with dried mud and leaves, and to his encrusted fingers his face felt like the basin of an arid desert lake. Down the front of his shirt the remnants of his vomit clung—bits of oat cake, melons, cat meat, all in a sauce of green bile. His pant legs were glued to his skin with dried feces. He must have reeked like a skunk but he couldn't smell it. He only knew that if he met a stranger on the road they would flee in revulsion, even before they saw him. The trailside creek bed was too shallow to scoop. He had to bathe.

Night fell. He slept briefly in a spinney of blackthorn, and woke to the sound of music. In his dreams it was a mosquito, but the melodies were so lovely that he sat up suddenly and opened his eyes to moonbeams streaming through branches, and fireflies flickering in the underbrush.

It was a fiddle for sure, but far away. The tunes were haunting, and wholly unfamiliar. He got up at once, threw on his pack, and started down the path. The moon guided him and soon there was another light, a golden glow, moving in and out of the trees.

He stood before a building like none he had ever seen before.

First he saw the fires. Four enormous iron furnaces stood against a backdrop of trees. Orange flames danced in the chambers and smoke rose from the stacks. Around them wound a maze of pipes and steaming caldrons. The building itself was old board in a bungalow style, broad steps leading up to a porch, lit with a string of colored globes. Johnny couldn't identify the source of illumination. Wherever there was wood, it was carved or painted. The ceiling of the porch was a dazzlement of color–sunspires and spirals, faces, winged creatures, starbursts, spiders, smiling moon-crescents, ringed orbs. Lattice work framed the porch, each slat painted a different color. The partitions leaned inward under the weight of honeysuckle vines. A heavy iron door, red with rust, slouched open on bent hinges and a curtain of wooden beads dangled from the stoop. There were no windows, but through the doorway Johnny could see a pale blue glow. Above the door a single word was carved in large blocked letters: BATH.

On the porch, seated on a high-backed chair, plush with colored cushions, a plump man was drowsing. He was dressed in a robe, like a mummer's, except it was the color of a cantaloupe. Johnny stared at him in wonder. Never before had he seen a person with skin so dark, night-sky dark, almost black, but when the man stirred, opened his eyes and smiled, his white teeth glowed like pearls.

"You must be a god," said the man, in a strange, thick accent.

Johnny stood perplexed. "I don't know what you mean." His own voice startled him. It had been so long since he had heard it.

"You ate the food offered to the gods, and you took the oil."
Johnny did not move. "I need a bath."

"Indeed." The man clapped his hands twice. "Lucy! Bather!"

The bead curtain parted with a rattle, and a girl stood there, wearing a short blue linen robe tied at the waist with a sash. Barely older than a child, she was small and thin, with long, shiny black hair tumbling down the sides of her face and out behind her, as if lifted by the beaks of tiny red-winged blackbirds.

She glanced at the dark man with a twinkle in her eye. "He *is* a dirty one, isn't he?"

The dark man smiled. "Stinks, too." He started to laugh. The girl laughed, and soon they both were laughing, a light, lilting, musical laughter, like tinkling bells. Johnny almost laughed himself, but before he could, the girl reached out her arm.

"Come then, quickly. We will make you clean." Her tiny fingers curled around his filthy hand and she dragged him, stumbling, though the curtain of beads.

It was hard to make out the features of the room because of the steam. Mist rose and curled in all directions, not the cold mist of waterfalls, more like the vapor from a teakettle just before it boils. There was a blue glow at the center of the room and patterns of pastel hues behind it.

"Take off your clothes!" the girl commanded. "We will wash them!"

Too weak to formulate an argument, Johnny threw off his backpack, unlaced and kicked off his boots, dropped his pants, tore off his shirt and stood there naked. Then the girl did a startling thing. She pulled the sash on her robe. It fell to the floor and she, too, stood there naked before him.

"We'll have to rinse you first. You're too dirty for the pool." She guided him to the far end of the room where something like a mountain aqueduct jutted from the wall and poured a cascade of water onto a jumble of rocks. The rocks were dotted with candles, some burning, some extinguished, and a curvature of molten wax poured over them, like flowstone in a cave.

"Quickly! Get under! Breathe deeply! It's cold!"

Indeed it was cold. Johnny gasped as the water dashed over him. It almost knocked him down with its weight. The girl jumped in beside him. She had some kind of sponge in her hand and she covered his body with fragrant lather, all the while singing a quick little song.

Be gone! Be gone! The mud of sorrow
Be gone! Be gone! The filth of sorrow
Be gone! Be gone! The stink of sorrow
Come on! Come on! Into the pool!
Into the pool! Be clean!

Then she thrust him out of the water with such force that he landed on his back on what turned out to be a soft, matted floor.

"Not clean yet, Mr. Stinky Beard! Come on! Come on! Into the pool!"

The waters of the pool were hot. They made him gasp even more than the cold from the shower. But quite soon he found himself surrendering to the deep massage of the currents. The girl slipped in after him. She did not approach him, but swam circles around him.

"Stinky Beard! Go under!"

He sank beneath the surface. Everywhere there was a

pale blue glow. He swam to the bottom and ran his fingers along the smooth tiles, but he could not locate the source of the light. The water itself seemed to be lit.

Out of the pool, she put her robe back on. It clung to the contours of her body like a second skin. She helped him out, handed him a similar robe, and led him to a mound of cushions where a dark green bottle stood on a low table. From the bottle she poured something fragrant into the palm of her hand, pungent like juniper, yet sweet like honey. On the cushions she straddled him and began applying the oil to his hair, his face, his neck. She slipped the robe off his shoulders and massaged his arms, his chest. She ran her fingers down his belly. Johnny clutched the crumpled robe to his lap in embarrassment, for now the shaft of his sex was iron-hard and throbbing.

"What do you have there, Mr. Smelly Beard? Let me see!"

She pulled away the robe and giggled teasingly. "Ah! What I thought! We can take care of that!" Helpless to the moment, Johnny surrendered to her oiled fingers as they drew from him, slowly, stroke by stroke, a pleasure he had never even imagined.

Some time later he felt himself rising from something that was not quite sleep, more like a waking dream. There was a candle flickering, and something was rustling in his hair. Fingers. Lucy's fingers. She was leaning over him, sifting through his locks, smiling at him, a playful smile.

"Haven't you ever done that to yourself before?" she asked.

He sat up suddenly and looked around. He was still on the cushions. In the distance the pool performed its pale blue dance.

"I never knew I could!" he said in astonishment.

Lucy giggled. "Ha! I wonder what else there is you never knew that you could do." Her words made Johnny sink back into the cushion in silence. Lucy resumed stroking his hair. There was a sound like steam venting from somewhere in the building, followed by a clicking and banging of metal pipes.

"I just started out," he said at last. "I was going to be a sojourner, but something happened."

"What's a sojourner?"

He stared at her in puzzlement. Who *was* this girl, and where was she from? "A sojourner is something that you are. You don't choose it. It's passed down to you from someone in your bloodline. The sojourner doesn't stay home and tend to a profession. He wonders what's out there. He leaves his home. He goes to find out. But the first thing I found out was how alone I was, completely cut off from people. I couldn't be with them. So I escaped into the forest. I got lost. I fell. I drank poison water. I got sick. And then when I got well, I came here."

Her smile became suddenly knowing. "There's more to it than that. You're forgetting. You ate the food offered to the gods, and you took the oil. Then later you were fed by one of the creatures. If those things had not happened, you wouldn't have come to me."

"But who are you?"

"I'm Lucy. I'm not important. I'm just a bather."

"But then who is the man? The man at the door?"

"Oh, that's Bow Wow. He builds the altars and commands the creatures. He knew you were coming. Bow Wow knows everything. He's a Seer. Listen! Do you hear that?"

Johnny listened. He heard many things. There was a soft continuous humming. No, there was more than one. There were harmonies and dissonances between them. There was an occasional sibilance, like air escaping from a reed. In the distance the cascade from the aqueduct plashed, and he heard small waves lapping at the rim of the pool.

"It's raining. I hear it on the roof. Stay with us, Johnny. Until the rain stops. We can teach you things to make you a better... what you call it?"

"Sojourner."

"Sojourner, yes. We can give you back your voice."

He felt a desire to weep, and tears filled his eyes. *When had he lost his voice?* Was it back on the road when the messenger told him of the lonely lot this life had dealt him, or was it before that? Perhaps he was born without a voice. He imagined all the elements of his being, flying together from all directions to converge upon the place where he was to be born. But his voice lost its way and didn't make it in time, and now it was hovering somewhere, perhaps over this very bathhouse, and it was about to descend at last into his throat and complete the process of his birthing. He blinked and the tears fell away.

Lucy. He kept his eyes open, staring at her, against the prompting of his mind to turn away, and he felt a force moving toward him, like a storm rolling in over the northern hills. Her skin as white as a cloud, her hair black and shiny, like obsidian, and she was so thin, but she was not frail; there was strength in her arms and her face, delicate, but strong with emotion, shifting, complex; her face was a lake full of reflections. He looked at her hands and recalled the pleasure they had drawn from him and he felt this pleasure all over again, not just his sex, but everywhere, and especially the center of his chest. There was nothing here to deny. There was only surrender.

They went outside, each wearing nothing but identical linen robes. The heart of night was approaching and the rain spoke whispered words on the leaves and branches. She led him through the maze of kettles and furnaces to a flight of steps carved in the fern-covered hillside above the bathhouse. A simple structure clung to the slope; one room, a porch, many window openings, but no glass, an iron woodstove now cold, an unmade bed with a patchwork quilt, a table, two chairs. Everywhere there were bells hanging, and from the porch stoop a series of tiny metal ladles descended on a knotted cord, catching the rainfall. As each ladle filled, it tipped and dropped its water into the ladle below, sending a clear bell tone as it struck. Each ladle was pitched differently, and the result was a shimmering cascade of liquid melody.

Lucy set about building a fire while Johnny sat at the table. She talked to him incessantly but he couldn't make out what she was saying. It was as if she had slipped into another language, or a baby's babble. Mostly he just watched her, amazed by the delight she gave him. Soon there was some warmth in the room, although not enough to dispel the damp cold through the open windows.

There was a knock on the porch. Lucy got up and returned with a tureen of something steaming and fragrant.

"It's our supper," she said. "Please forgive poor Bow Wow. He can be so private."

Because they were cold they sat at the table shoulder to shoulder, with Lucy's quilt wrapped around them as they ate their food directly from the tureen with bare hands. Johnny had no idea what it was. The sauce was yellow and spicy and there were some kind of soft and crumbly curds, and sweet strips of a fruit or vegetable he had never seen before. They drank mugs of rainwater direct from the cascading ladles on the porch. When the food was gone Lucy fetched an amber glass bottle from under the bed and filled the mugs with a strong and fragrant brew.

"This will help us stay warm," she said. It was sweet and thick with spirits. It tasted like herbs, especially woodruff and damiana. While they drank Lucy lapsed back into her other language. It sounded almost like singing, and it was clear she didn't care if he understood her. He let the sounds wash over him as the drink went to his head. Then suddenly she drained her glass and looked directly at him.

"Come, sleep. It's been a long day and we can keep each other warm." She pulled the quilt away and tumbled into the bed, between the rumpled sheets. Johnny slipped in beside her.

But of course, they did not sleep. The moment their bodies touched, they entered into a ritual established at the beginning of time, a sequence of precise motions starting with fingers, then hands and mouths, then arms and legs, and finally the thrusting of whole bodies and the litany of cries and whispers, bursting at last like ripe dandelions, then release, the gradual slowing of breath, the calmed fingers curled lightly around the chalice of bare skin.

They repeated the cycle seven times throughout the night. There was no need for sleep. No activity of the mind was required. No decisions were made. Through the open windows the rain broke down the divisions of time into one continuous moment, and from the porch the ladles chimed their rain-filled melody until it was completely forgotten.

Somewhere before dawn they fell asleep in earnest. A knocking on the porch woke them. Lucy stumbled out of bed and threw on her robe but by the time she got outside, Bow Wow was gone.

She returned with Johnny's backpack. "Look! He washed your clothes and cleaned your bag. Johnny, what's this?"

It was the mandolin. He stared at it in wonder, as if it were a relic from a former life. How could he have carried it all this time without thinking of it, without playing it? He had not played it since he left home.

"It's an instrument. A mandolin. It makes music."

Lucy frowned. "It makes music all by itself?"

"No, no, you have to play it. Here, let me show you."

Johnny took the mandolin by the neck and strummed the strings. It was completely out of tune, but without hesitation he launched into the first melody he could think of. *The Ashes of Last Night's Fire*. It could have been anything or nothing. It was just a series of atonal plunkings in six-eight time. But Lucy clapped her hands in delight.

"Oh! Music! I love music. I can make music. I play the fiddle."

Johnny stopped his fingers. "So, it was you then I heard that first night in the forest, when I came here."

"Of course it was me. Who else do you think? Bow Wow?" She reached under the bed and pulled out the most dilapidated old violin Johnny had ever seen. The wood was completely flat, the color of ebony, and there were notches carved up and down the neck and a sloppy picture of a yellow rose painted on the fingerboard. The chinrest was missing and there were two small holes bored completely through the wood where it used to be. When she took the bow and rasped it across the strings he knew at once it was no more in tune than his mandolin. But still she seemed to make something that sounded like music with it, closer to the music of a coyote than that of a human voice.

"Play with me! Play your mandolin!"

So he played. He didn't know how to improvise in this strange tuning, so he played a familiar tune. *Maggots in the Cornmeal*. She didn't even stop to listen. She just started playing something else alongside it, but there was a drift to her cadence that attached itself to the phrasing of the melody and pursued it, like a swarm of hornets. Their eyes met and she smiled. It was a kind of lovemaking. He launched into the bridge, the key change completely lost to the dissonance of the strings. He returned to the A section and repeated the form several more times, finally executing the coda with a flourish.

"Keep going! Keep going! More music!"

They played together all that day, and every day into the days that followed. Johnny dug into his memory bag of old standards while Lucy plowed ferociously through a stream of angular riffs that always seemed to compliment the spirit, if not the tonal center of the moment. After a while he began to loosen up and experiment with the melodies, to sharpen a fourth or flatten a seventh, or even shift into a different key entirely. It didn't matter. Nothing was what it seemed to be.

And once, something strange happened. It was mid-afternoon. They were working their way through *The Shepherd Calls the Sheep* when suddenly a great sadness overtook him and a string of sad memories flooded his mind. The morning he found the remains of Huxley and Vermillion in the wire pen, devoured by wild pigs, only their ears and entrails left in the dust. The day his friend Osterman fell from the olive tree and broke his neck, and died. The letter from his father, Caspar Arcane, brought by the messenger—how Mother broke his father's heart with her indifference, and later, his father was killed by a flaming scarecrow. Johnny's eyes filled with tears but before he could shed them they dropped, inexplicably, into the music itself, and the music became first sad and then sweet, a tender sweetness, like maple sugar, full of longing that hovered continuously on the brink of fulfillment. The tempo slowed, the harmonies blended, the moment passed and he found his eyes dry and sparkling.

At nightfall Bow Wow left food on the porch. Lucy kindled a fire. They wrapped in the quilt, sat at the table, ate and drank the rainwater from the ladles. Then she uncorked the amber bottle and they repeated the ritual of the night before, although this time with a little more sleeping.

ɔ

It rained for seven days and seven nights. Something brand new woke up in Johnny's heart. He had never felt anything so constant—a person, beside him, always—not like mother, not like any of the girls in school, someone small and vulnerable, yet strong and sturdy, like a crocus pushing through the snow. He felt his arms around her always, even when she wasn't beside him. He wanted to shelter her and protect her, now and into the dark future. At the same time he felt a power growing in his arms and legs. He felt like a giant walking on the land. He felt the boundaries of his body extending into the Known World.

The days became rituals. Lucy was always the first to wake. Johnny felt her warmth slip away as she rose to stoke the fire and prepare the tea. He lingered, half suspended in slumber, until she called his name. Their morning conversations were formless, single words and phrases, bits of poetry, fragments of last night's dreams. Sometimes she lapsed into her other language. When she did this she pulled away. She moved about the room drawing pictures with her arms, making little leaps and catching invisible things from the air. But every now and then she glanced at him to see if he was watching. He was.

Then they got out the instruments and played. They never tuned. Johnny didn't even mention the concept. The music they made was so far outside the conventions of melody and harmony, he gave up trying to call upon the old songs, and followed her lead, emptying his mind of all content, pursuing the sound wherever it took him. Often it drove him straight into Lucy, the shape of her body, the fall of her hair, the bliss in her closed eyes as she pulled the bow across the strings, and then suddenly he would penetrate her; through the thin membrane of her skin he would fall into the vast, heart-shaped kingdom of her soul, where there were provinces of pleasure, preserves of mystery, and small, shadowy pockets of foreboding and despair.

Evening. Bow Wow brought food, and while they ate, they talked in earnest, about real things. Johnny told her everything he could think of. He told her about his childhood, about the schoolhouse where he and seven other children learned how to write words and make pictures. How to care for animals—how to kill the ones you ate and nurture the ones that gave you wool and eggs and milk. How to grow food from seeds and to chop wood and build a fire. He learned all the songs, first to sing, and later to play on the mandolin. In the summer there were dances. Sometimes as many as fifty people would gather from the neighboring villages, and there were often as many musicians as there were dancers.

"In school they taught us there was once a time of fire and bandits," he said. "But the fire killed all the bandits and then burned itself out. Still, we had to learn the rituals. We had to perform them every day. To keep us safe. Mother honored the four directions, emptying the water from the sconces and refilling them with a pinch of fire grate ash. At night she swept all the floors, all the dust and bug bodies and cornmeal into a pyramid, and she whisked it into a platter and tossed it into the fire. It drove me crazy. It was foolish superstition. I had walked in all the four directions. She knew nothing about them, only the four walls of the house."

Lucy made almost no mention of her past. She mostly spoke of the here and now, of her life at the bathhouse. There was a family of foxes in the woods above the cabin. The baby foxes had eaten pumpkin seeds from the palm of her hand. Once a man with only one leg came to bathe. Lucy had washed the stump below the man's knee. It felt like leather. Bow Wow was teaching her how to carve wood. She showed Johnny the snakes and faces she had carved in the legs of her bed. The hills were full of caves, all connected. She had explored them with a carbide lamp. Wherever the caves opened up to the air, Bow Wow built an altar and he spent days moving through the caves, refilling the altar plates with food. There were all kinds of creatures you couldn't see, but you could talk to them if you learned their language. The creatures you couldn't see were all connected, the way that mushrooms are connected in the forest. She knew of one mushroom, deep in the forest, that covered a whole hillside. It looked like hundreds of mushrooms all peeking through the moss, but they were only one, all connected, under the ground. She once watched a puddle of slime in a shadowy glade pull itself together and form a creature with tentacles and legs, and it crawled across the forest floor until it came to a patch of sunlight where it dissolved back into a puddle of slime. She watched the whole thing. It took all day. In the winter it snows and everything falls asleep. Once a very old woman came to take a bath in the winter, and after the bath she fell asleep, and she died.

One morning Johnny woke and found her standing in the center of the room going through a series of slow movements, shifting her weight from side to side, reaching and grabbing invisible objects and moving them about, setting them on the floor and lifting them, rolling them into balls, stretching them out like taffy, spreading invisible veils over her head and shoulders.

"Johnny, look. You can tell your mother. This is how you honor the four directions." She kept moving, making large circles and caressing them into small circles. "Bow Wow told me. There's something in the air. You can't see it, but messages can travel through it. He called it *dough,* you know, *dough,* like you use to make bread. You can play with this *dough.* You can move it around. It helps to make you strong and happy. Get up! I'll show you how."

He got up, stood beside her, and tried to follow along. She had words for different actions, things like *rocking the baby, calling in the lambs, sending out the falcons.* He was awkward and clumsy, frequently stumbling. Once he bumped into her but she just kept on moving. Still he began to feel something, a kind of firmness, like a tree, branches reaching for the sky.

On some days she had clients at the bathhouse. Then Bow Wow rang a bell and she would have to go. The first time she left he felt himself gutted with uneasiness. When she returned he said, "These people you bathed, were they men or women?"

Oh, this time there were two men and a woman."

"The men. Do you...do you do to them what you did to me?"

A twinkle came into her eyes and she giggled. "Johnny, you're *jealous*! Don't be jealous! It's just a function of the body. It doesn't mean anything. It's not like what we do, me and you, together, in the night. I don't do that with anybody but you." She shook her head. "Not now."

Ↄ

On the seventh day the rain dwindled, and the ladles stopped singing. Big drops plopped from branches, and rivulets gurgled through the fern and moss. Lucy sat on the porch, staring at a patch of blue sky above the distant hills. Johnny sat beside her, took her hand, and held it there in silence for a long time.

The music they made that morning was slow and mysterious, the harmonies purer, less prone to flights of ragged wildness, fewer storms, more quiet yearnings. It was as if the strings of the fiddle and the mandolin had come into tune of their own accord, as if they had stretched and relaxed until they found a brief, common tonality. Johnny tried a few of the old songs, *Woodpecker's Dilemma, Softly Breaks the Baker's Egg*. Lucy followed him obediently, like a schoolgirl, first tracing the melody directly, then in octaves, then in thirds and open fifths. There was great beauty and tenderness in the sound. Once he caught sight of the glint of a tear in her eye.

Midmorning the bell rang from below. There were clients at the bathhouse. Lucy put on her customary silk robe and excused herself. She was gone for a long time, leaving Johnny alone in the cabin with a gnawing restlessness in his arms and legs, and a soft ache in his heart. He went outside. Birds were singing, and there was a constant murmur of wind at the top of the trees. He walked around behind the cabin and found a village of birdhouses made of bark, overflowing with seeds. On the ground was a blue ceramic bowl full of some sort of soggy meal. Above it, on a plank of wood, words were scrawled: FOR RACCOONS ONLY.

He went back in the cabin, found the amber bottle under the bed, poured a goodly portion into a mug, and drank it down. Then he went back outside and stood on the porch. He heard sounds from the bathhouse, the hissing of steam and the roiling of the kettles. Then he heard voices. You couldn't usually hear voices from the bathhouse. Someone was shouting, then a bang, like a door slam, then shouting again, higher pitched this time, a girl's voice. It was Lucy. She was using her other language, but it was different. It was jagged and harsh, and wobbling in the high register like a chicken on the chopping block.

He heard the branches on the trail snap and the plod of her feet on the steps. She burst into the clearing in front of the cabin. Her robe was untied and flying open; her naked-ness was everywhere. When she saw Johnny she shifted languages but she did not appear to be speaking to him.

"He's not a good man! He's a bad man! He shouldn't have come!" She stumbled into the cabin, her arms flailing. She grabbed the quilt from the bed and threw it on the floor. Her eyes glazed the room wildly as if she were looking for something to break. Then she saw Johnny and she ran out and fell into his arms.

"Oh Johnny, he's a bad man. He wants to hurt me. Johnny, what am I going to do?"

Johnny pulled her close and pressed her head to his chest. "Who wants to hurt you? Is it Bow Wow?"

"Oh, no, no, no, no, no, not Bow Wow. Bow Wow would never hurt me. Bow Wow saved me."

Then she just started crying, and she cried for a long time, her tears and her slobber soaking his chest. Slowly her sobs subsided into whimpers, then sniffles, and she dropped her shoulders and slumped her weight into him. He thought she was going to fall asleep, but at last she spoke.

"A man came. He said he wanted a bath. But he didn't want a bath. He came for me. He kept asking me questions, bad questions, the kind you shouldn't ask. I know what he wanted. He wanted to take me back. They sent him to take me back."

Johnny pulled himself away, held her at arm's length, and stared into her face.

"Where? Why would they want to take you back?"

She cast her eyes down. "Johnny, I'm a fugitive."

He was perplexed. "I don't know the meaning of the word."

"A fugitive is a person who is running away from someone who wants to hurt them. Sometimes a fugitive is running away from something they did wrong. But I didn't do anything wrong."

He tried to pull her back against him but she had made herself stiff and unmovable.

"Lucy, who wants to hurt you?"

She shook her head. "I can't tell you everything, Johnny. There are things I can't tell anybody."

"Tell me something, then. Anything. Tell me something I don't already know."

They went back in the cabin. She picked up the quilt and wrapped herself in it. He kindled a fire. He made her a cup of tea and she sat on the edge of the bed, cradling it in her hands.

"The man who came for you. Is he still here?"

"No, Bow Wow sent him away. He used magic. He can do this thing where he erases your mind. Not forever. That would be too cruel."

"Will he come back?"

"I don't think so. Bow Wow's magic is very strong, but there may be others. Johnny, I'm afraid. I'm so afraid."

"You could come with me. I can keep you safe. We could be sojourners together."

"I don't want to be a sojourner." There was a whimper in her voice. "I want to stay here, with Bow Wow. I want to stay here for the rest of my life." She started to cry. This time she let Johnny comfort her. He sat on the bed and stroked her hair. She rested her head on his shoulder.

"Why is it like this?" she sighed. "Why is it like this? Why is it so beautiful? It would have been better if it had never been so beautiful."

Ɔ

Bow Wow brought dinner in his usual fashion. After they ate they lay together on the bed and finished the elixir in the amber bottle. They talked. Johnny tried many ways to get her to tell him more of her story.

"I didn't want to bring any of it here," she said. "I wanted to forget it all. I don't even remember what my name was in the other place. It wasn't Lucy."

"Where did you get the name Lucy?"

"Bow Wow gave it to me. He said it means the Morning Light."

Johnny told her of a story he learned in school. In the time of fire and bandits, the hero, Borderbinder, stole a bag of cornmeal from the bandit king, Deathbridge. With minions of bandits in pursuit, he circled the four directions, spreading a line of cornmeal everywhere he went. When he came full circle and wound up where he started, the bandits caught him and cut of his head. But immediately the fires swelled and killed all the bandits, and burned themselves out. Ever since then, the people inside the circle have been safe and happy, but they must remember to honor the four directions, and practice the rituals.

"That story is true," she said. "Except for one thing. The fires didn't really burn themselves out. They just moved further away. They're still burning."

There was something different in her voice when she said this. It was like she had slipped away from his grasp into somewhere he couldn't go. He reached out to touch her but she stood abruptly and her face changed back into that of a child.

"I want to show you something," she said. "It's very beautiful." She knelt by the bed and pulled from under it a tarnished copper box with engravings on the lid. Inside were many bright shiny things, but what she selected was a piece of parchment folded in half. "Look!" she exclaimed as she unfolded it.

The ply was thin and wrinkled, unlike the sturdy parchment used for messages, and it had a little shine to it, like a bayberry leaf. It was a picture unlike any he had ever seen. A waterfall plunged over a jagged cliff and mist rose from the pool below. It wasn't the subject that was so extraordinary.

It was the way it was made. Every detail was so sharply etched, yet blended together, the shadows in the cascade, the tiny young tendrils of the moss clinging to the stone. But there were no raised cakes of pigment on the surface. It was flat and glossy. He ran his fingers over it. It was like looking at the image of a waterfall in a mirror.

"How could this be?"

Lucy clapped her hands and laughed. "You like it! I knew you would. It was given to us when..." She caught herself and drew a quick breath. A cloud crossed her face. But then she laughed. "I think it was made by wood sprites with tiny little pots of paint. Two or three of them could have fit on it at once. It probably took them days. You can have it. You can take it when you—" Her words halted momentarily, and her eyes changed color. "—when you go."

There was a moment of silence, then they fell into each other's arms, and a tear escaped Lucy's eye. They spent that night wrapped together in the bed, caressing, kissing, drifting in and out of sleep. They did not repeat the ecstatic ritual of the body. Sometimes they cried together openly. Other times she buried her head in his chest and sang little songs in her other language. Mostly he wanted to memorize her, the hourglass of her waist, the pout of her lips, the wild extravagance of her hair. He followed her breathing, especially when she drifted off to sleep. He synchronized his breath with hers and found, to his surprise, he couldn't get enough air. Her bellows were so small, his so wide and thirsty. For Lucy, these four walls would suffice. She wanted to be protected, sheltered, enclosed, *enwombed*. He stroked her shoulders and she stirred. He rested his palm on her cheek. Inwardly he knew why he did these things, but he did not articulate it. Tonight these four walls would suffice.

In the morning there was a knock on the porch. Bow Wow stood there in his melon-colored robes. "Lucy, your friend must leave now. The rain has stopped."

Lucy took a short, sharp breath and stared into Johnny's face for a moment. Then it was as if something descended upon her from within. Her eyes went wild and her voice broke open in a wail. "No!" she cried. "No! No! No! You can't take him! You can't take him!"

She rushed at Bow Wow and shoved him hard on the chest. But he was like a mountain. He didn't even tilt. His face remained calm and serene.

She turned to Johnny. "Johnny, don't let him take you!" Johnny tried to hold her but she pulled away. Thrashing about the room, she threw herself at the walls. A string of bells tinkled to the floor. Finally Johnny was able to get her by the arm. He pulled her up and pressed her to his chest.

"He's not trying to take me, Lucy. He's just telling me it's time to go. It's what I'm called to do. You knew this. We both knew this."

He stroked her hair. She pulled against his arms, but he held tight and finally she gave in and sank into him, weeping.

"I don't want you to go, Johnny. I want you stay with me forever."

"I could take you with me. I told you that before. We could be sojourners together."

"No, no, that can't be." She pulled away and wiped her arm across her eyes. When she spoke again it was with a tone of flat resignation. "I'll help you with your things."

She turned and started gathering up Johnny's clothing and his tools and placing them in the backpack. She did not speak. She seemed to be performing a series of routine tasks. But when she picked up the mandolin, she held it for a while, stroked its neck, ran her fingers over the strings. Then she handed it to him, bowed, turned, and fell onto the bed.

As he followed Bow Wow down the steps toward the bath-house, Johnny heard her voice, singing in the other language, an elegant yet mournful melody, part blessing, part lament. His heart was torn in two. He wanted to run back to the cabin and draw her entire body into his arms. *Lucy! Lucy!* So small! He could put her in his pocket. All of her! No. He would come back. He would send messages. It wasn't over. At the same time he knew he was being propelled toward a destiny that was beyond his control. He felt a great restless-ness in his arms and legs. Above, small white clouds moved with purpose across a clear, blue sky.

CHAPTER FOUR

CORNFEST

ut on the open road, his heart lifted. He could feel the lonesome tug of what lay behind slowly give way the welcoming pull of what lay ahead. Lucy stayed with him, a warmth at his side, a second body inside his body. He carried her flame in his chest, her mysterious language murmuring in his ears. But he was free. A strange thing, this freedom. For the second time since leaving home, it rushed in to fill the void left by the act of parting.

Down from the bathhouse, a short wooded trail opened to a broad road through fields and hills, morning mist curling around summits, rising from low, boggy places. Gravity was his guide. He took the direction that led downhill, only partially aware of his deeper motives, for he no longer feared his aloneness in the company of others. In fact, he welcomed it. He longed to tell his story, and listen to the stories of others. And something in his arms and legs intuitively knew, if he came down out of the hills and into the valleys, he would find the people.

Mid-afternoon, a long, straight stretch of road, flanked on both sides by overarching cottonwoods, curved to the right where the trees parted, and there was a field of corn, goldening in the autumnal afternoon light. A man sat at a table piled high with ears of unshucked corn. It was the first person Johnny had seen all day.

"Greetings, stranger!" The man wore a hat of woven cornhusks, and there was a bright red bandana tied around his neck. "You be goin' to the festival?"

"What festival?"

"Down the road a few bends, the town of King Corn, they pobble their full moon Cornfest tonight. I be goin' there myself, soon's the sun gets low."

"Well, I'm just a sojourner myself. I go where my feet take me. Cornfest sounds as good as any."

The man nodded at Johnny's backpack where the mandolin in its case was hooked to the shoulder straps. "You play that turtlebox?"

"Yes, I do, sir. Pretty well, I think."

"Well, go to Cornfest, then. They be lookin' for musicians. Here, take an ear to nibble on your way."

Further down the road, nibbling on an ear of corn, Johnny felt an excitement kindling in his belly. A festival! Musicians! And surely there would be food and dancing!

It wasn't long before others joined him. People came out of their houses, some of them pushing carts piled with corn and apples. Some wore colorful costumes. Some were dressed entirely in cornhusks. There were many children.

Johnny fell in with a group of children who were escorting a pig. The tallest boy had a willow switch that he snapped on either side of the pig to keep it straight on the road.

"What's the pig's name?" Johnny asked.

"We call him Fat Man," said the boy, "but not for long. Tonight we eats him and then Pink Baby gets the name, so we can eats him next fest."

"Do you know any magic?" asked a pigtailed little girl who was skipping along beside him.

"No, I don't. Do you?"

"Yes, I do!" she cried. "Watch!" And she ran ahead until she reached a rise in the road where she leapt into the air with her knees bent so that she kicked her own rear end. She turned and laughed. "Did you see? I was flying!"

"Oh, that's not magic! I can do that!" Johnny took off at a trot and when he reached the girl he tried to exercise the movement, but with his heavy backpack it was harder than he thought. His ankles barely left the ground.

"Ha! Ha! You can't do it! I'm the only one who can do it!"

Around a grassy hill with a single oak tree at its summit, the village of King Corn came into view. First there were smells, then sounds. The smells were roasty and smoky, like nuts about to split open and animal fat dripping on glowing coals. The sounds were voices, young and old, excitement, enthusiasm, laughter, the strumming of strings and thumping of drums, the cawing of crows.

It was a wide clearing of dry grass, bales of hay, some kind of mill with a tall silo. Faces and landscapes were painted all around the silo. The houses and dispensaries of the town nestled at the foot of a forested rise. A yellow sun, shining in the blue sky, was making its descent toward the tips of these trees. The field was filled with people in motion—children skipping and dancing; men erecting colorful carved poles, and then climbing them to string banners, women laying out tables, covering them with cloth, lading them with pots and pies and piles of corn and cakes of cornbread.

An old woman caught Johnny's eye and cast him a toothless grin. "Come, quick, boy! They be climbin' the silo!"

Johnny hurried after her. People were gathering around the base of the silo. A circle of young girls were unrolling a swath of canvass and stretching it taut between them.

"I can do it!" came a voice. A man jumped up on a platform. He was as skinny as a stork and his gray hair was wild and frizzy. He tore off his shirt and started jumping up and down, chest-naked on the platform. "I been workin' on this!"

People in the crowd laughed and hooted. "Bagman, you couldn't climb a goat, even if he had cream on his nose!"

"Oh, yeah? Well, watch!" Bagman turned to the silo. Up its side there were handholds, cleats and brackets, but they were randomly spaced, some further apart than a man's arm span. Bagman pulled himself up onto the closest one, then swung his leg over the next. A chorus of ascending ululations rose from the crowd and the girls tightened their grip on the canvass hoop. Bagman reached a narrow ledge about a third of the way up. His next hold was a knoblike protuberance just out of reach and across the painted face of a smiling, doglike creature. But he lost his balance. His stable leg slipped and he let out a yelp as he plunged sidelong into the air. The girls lifted the hoop and uttered a shrill syllable in unison. He struck the canvass like a stone in water and all the girls fell over backwards, laughing. Bagman laughed the loudest.

The next to try was a woman. She had a muscular body and a sureness in her voice. People in the crowd called her Maggie. She wore pants, and a shirt greasy with pigfat, great ovals of sweat under her arms. She circled the silo in a spiral from hold to hold. The girls had to keep tracking the hoop after her, to stay in falling range. But after three rotations she realized she had gained no altitude. She was merely following a groove. She did not fall. She simply climbed down. When her feet touched the ground, she was greeted by a burly, bearded man who threw his arms around her and handed her a stein of beer.

The burly man himself was the next to try. He climbed with skill and cunning. There was strength in his biceps and balance in his legs. He executed several daring leaps, making the people gasp. But near the top, his arms grasping a conduit above, he lost his footing and the weight of his body pulled him loose. Halfway down he bent at the waist and the side of his head struck a metal bar. There was a scream from the ground. The girls lifted the hoop and he tumbled into it with a gentle bounce, but when they lowered him to the ground there was blood running down the side of his face from his ear.

Much commotion, people running. Someone brought a damp cloth and the woman named Maggie sat with the burly man's head cradled in her lap, daubing his wounds. He looked around, lifted his shoulders. "Where's my beer?" he said.

All this time Johnny had been looking at the silo, studying the holds, and processing the steps the others had taken. At last he was certain. He jumped up on the platform. "I'd like to try it!" he announced.

Nobody heard him at first. Everybody was busy, attending to the burly man's wounds. The burly man himself was the first to notice. He pulled himself up on his elbows, lifted his arm, and pointed his finger. "That kid wants to go. Let the kid try it!"

A few people looked around to see what the man was talking about. Johnny felt his courage propped up by the attention. He stomped his foot on the platform. "Right here! Me! I want to try it!"

Reluctantly the girls picked up the hoop. Johnny threw off his backpack and faced the silo. A few voices began to chant. "Let the kid try it! Let the kid try it!" Intentionally he chose different handholds than any of the other three contenders. Mostly he focused on the paintings. There was a picture of a sun cresting a hill with beams of golden light streaming out. Birds were flying through the beams. The birds were not flat. They were carved objects protruding from the wall, and the beams themselves were furrowed deep enough to get a foot in.

Up the ladder of sunbeams he climbed, pulling his weight by the birds. Above the sunbeams: clouds. These were definitely painted, but there was a hatch cover handle, and above that, a seamed rim where perhaps portions of the silo had been welded together. He scrambled with the ease of one crawling along the ground, while below him, the chanting voices faded further and further away. The easiest part was the last. There was actually a short wooden ladder extending above the silo's lip. He tested the rungs. A little soft—he would have to be careful. Putting as much weight on his arms as on his feet, he pulled himself up, step by step. At the crest he heard the crowd go wild below. "Bring down the honey!" someone cried.

At the top was a flat floor of wooden boards, several short chimneys protruding. He stood up tall and waved to the crowd of cheering people. They waved back. He scanned the horizon. The sun had almost reached the trees. All hills and buildings cast long blue shadows. He could see the road he had arrived on, and in the distance beyond that, the rise of deep, forested mountains where somewhere Lucy sat in her cabin on the cliff. He wished he could wave to her. *Lucy, look where I am!*

Then he saw the beehive.

It was right at his feet, a traditional single tiered wooden box hive with a metal plated lid and a screened bottom board. He had worked with this kind of hive many times before. A few bees were buzzing around but they didn't bother him. He took the side handles and lifted the hive slowly. Standing, he raised it above his head and held it out to show the crowd below. People were waving their arms, whooping and whistling. Then someone shouted, "You've got to jump with it!"

Johnny gasped, and a wave of dread shot up his spine. Below him the girls raised the hoop. It looked like a small grey eye widening in astonishment. His knees weakened and he thought he would have to sit. But no! He had come this far! He pulled the hive securely to his chest and let his crumpling legs do the work. He didn't really jump. He just fell.

In the rushing of the air, the bees became agitated and started swarming from the hive. He felt some stings on the side of his face, and one under his arm, and he almost lost his grip. But before that happened he landed in the hoop, hive first. The girls held on, but his momentum was too great. The canvass bowed and the hive struck the ground and split apart under his weight. He sank into a cushion of soft, wet honey.

The next thing he knew he was being lifted up by arms, and raised high in the air. He was carried aloft, floating on a sea of bodies while voices shouted, "The kid! The kid got the honey!" A woman leaned into him. "What's your name, sonny?"

"Arcane. Johnny Arcane." He gasped. Honey dripped from his arms and his bee stings throbbed.

"Arcane!" she shouted. "His name's Arcane!" And soon they were all yelling, "Arcane! Arcane! Arcane got the honey!" The woman leaned into him again. "It's been seven fests since anyone's brought down the honey."

They took him to a large, covered area where tables were spread. In the shadows, smoke rose from spits where pigs were roasting and ears of corn lay on the coals. Someone plomped a stein of beer in front of him and soon he was cradling a slab of pork slathered in some kind of dark sauce. The hoop girls appeared and surrounded him. Two of them started stroking his hair and daubing their fingers in the honey on his shirt. Another kissed him on the cheek. "Arcane," she said, "How did you do it?"

Johnny's face flushed with pleasure. "Well, it was easy. I just followed the sun. I climbed the sunbeams and held onto the birds." The girls laughed and laughed. Word got around. Soon everyone was saying it. "He climbed the sunbeams and held onto the birds!" And everywhere, people repeated his name. "Arcane! Arcane!"

A strum of strings and a rattle of gourds; musicians were setting up on a low platform at one end of the shelter. Johnny looked around. "Where's my backpack? I left my backpack at the silo."

"We've got your backpack," said one of the hoop girls. "Here it is!"

"I have a mandolin in there. I want to join the musicians." Johnny could almost feel the melodies streaming like light out of his fingers. He stood up so quickly the hoop girls had to steady the chair to keep it from falling over. "Here! Is this a mandolin?"

There were two guitarists and two fiddlers. One of the fiddlers was a girl. Another girl was playing with a selection of gourd shakers and seedpod rattlers. A young man had a gut string fastened to a metal bucket and secured at the top to a broom handle. He twanged the string and pulled the handle, changing the pitch of the thumping bass notes.

"Let me join you!" Johnny jumped up on the platform.

"Arcane!" exclaimed one of the guitarists, a broad-shouldered man with a wealth of beard on his chin but only a scrub of hair on his head. "Hey, look! Arcane plays the turtlebox! What do you know, Arcane?"

"I know everything. You name it, I'll play it!"

"How 'bout *The Cabbage Moth?* Goes like this." But before the guitarist could play a single note, Johnny launched into the opening strains of *The Cabbage Moth*.

And they were off. They rambled through *The Cabbage Moth* at a leisurely pace, the gut string thumping, gourds rattling like a pepper of hailstones. People turned, started to clap and sway from side to side. Someone shouted, "Look! Arcane plays the turtle box!"

"The Wind in the Cornrows!" called the guitarist, who was clearly the leader. This was a jig tune and they played a little faster. Lines of dancers began to form. The gut string player, a skinny, curly haired boy, beamed a big smile at Johnny and picked up the pace. The girl on the fiddle started to laugh, and the guitarist called out, *Down the Drain!"* as they swerved into a stovepipe rhythm. Johnny felt his fingers and spirits lift with joy. Never before had he played with such able and good-hearted musicians.

They played late into the night. They played *Piggy With a Whistle, Up the Ladder and Down the Chute, Here Comes Trouble, The Quilt With no Corners, The Dog That Licked the Platter Clean, The Milky Mountain, Don't Touch Me With Your Dirty Hands, All We Have is What We Know, The Perils of Pig Dancing, The Blushing Seamstress, Borderbinder's Retreat.* Soon the field was full of dancers, each dance appropriate to the tune: line dances for the reels, squares for the stove-pipes, and couples danced the waltzes and the jingle-jangles. Lanterns were lit, slabs of pork were passed around, and steins of ale were raised and drained. But the musicians did not eat or drink. Fueled by the music, they pressed on from song to song, laughing each other in the face as they swapped changes and solos and navigated through the keys.

The girl on the fiddle watched Johnny intently. It seemed like her eyes were only for him. But the skinny gut string boy was all over the place, his smile as wide as a river, some-times throwing his head back in a swoon, while the guitarist dictated the rhythm with his beard bobbing over the strings, and he was the one to call out the name of each new tune.

It was well past midnight when it ended. The crowd had thinned, but the energy of the music had not dwindled. It just stopped, abruptly. They were climbing through the last chorus of *The Bandit's Repentance*, and into its precipitous coda, and when they struck the last high note it just ended, like that. Silence. It was because the guitarist failed to call another tune, as if he had exhausted his entire repertoire of titles.

After a moment of recognition, the remains of the crowd broke into a weary but heartfelt applause, and the musicians melted into laughter, handshakes, hugs, back-thumping and foot-stomping. All except for the lead guitarist, that is. He just sat there staring at his fingers in puzzlement.

"Let's get something to eat!" cried the gut string boy. "Yow! Yow! Yow!" the rest agreed, and they tumbled off the platform, leaving the guitarist, still bewildered on his bench.

Presently they returned with meat and beer, and some for the guitarist as well. He was still sitting in a sort of stupor, running his fingers silently over his guitar strings. But when he saw the meat, his face lit up.

"There's one we didn't play!" he beamed a smile. *"From Pig to Pork!"*

The fiddler girl sat on the floor next to Johnny and after a while she became bold enough to rest a hand on his knee. It was a strong, freckled, sunburned hand. He looked at her face. A farm-girl's face, round as the moon, hair the color of corn. She was older than he.

"What's your name?" he asked her.

"Ant," she replied.

"What, you mean like your mother's sister?"

"No, *Ant*, like the bug that lives in the ground. It's short for Antelleramine. But that name is very hard to say."

The gut string boy slapped his gut string. "We can't stop now. Look at that moon!" All heads turned to observe an enormous, bone-white full moon climbing above the open field where the dancers were gradually dispersing. "We got to play that moon clear across the sky!"

The man-fiddler and two of the three guitarists were already packing up their instruments, and the gourd-girl had never returned from the food-gathering. "Gotta work tomorrow, Jocko," said the man-fiddler. "Not too loud, OK? Don't be waking the children."

Soon there were just the four of them, Johnny, the lead guitarist, Jocko the gut string boy, and Ant, who was now resting her head on Johnny's shoulder.

"I know how we can do it," said Johnny. "I know a way we can keep playing without having to know any more songs."

The guitarist sat up abruptly. He looked puzzled. "What do you mean? We know lots more songs."

Johnny chuckled. "I don't think I do. But listen to me. Do what I say. Believe me, I promise this will work. Untune your instruments."

"Untune? How do you untune?"

"Like this." Johnny grasped the mandolin and skewed each of the eight pegs, randomly, in either direction. He strummed the strings once. It sounded a little like a table full of kitchen utensils falling over. "You do that. With your guitar."

The guitarist just gaped, dumbfounded at his fretboard. Johnny grew impatient. "Do it!" He reached out for the neck of the guitar and twisted three of the pegs. The guitarist pulled away and hunched his shoulders with his back to the others. But after a moment he raised his left hand and untuned the rest of the strings.

"Can't untune my instrument," said Jocko as he thumped the string. "Got no pegs."

"Well, you're lucky, then. You can go anywhere." Johnny glanced at Ant. Her chin to the fiddle, she was plucking each string and cocking her ear to it, as if to make sure it was properly out of tune.

"Jocko, just start. Play something." Jocko launched into a slappy rhythm, unanchored to any tonality. "Forget the songs. Just listen, and play what you feel." The guitarist kept his back turned, leaning into his instrument, brushing the frets, trying to comprehend the concept. Ant was the first to join in. Obediently she drew her bow across the strings, producing a dissonant squawk against Johnny's tentative plucking.

Johnny smiled at her in encouragement and admiration, and also something like desire, but an image quickly rushed in to replace it. Lucy. Lucy, whose fiddle was always untuned, who sometimes spoke and sang in a secret language and knew how to move the *dough* through the air with her fingers. Lucy, who was a fugitive from some kind of cruelty she would not disclose, and who would not leave the shelter of the bathhouse for fear this cruelty would catch up with her. Lucy, whose small body fit so perfectly in his sheltering arms. At that moment it became clear to him. There was a tether between them that would never be cut.

His reverie was broken by a loud clang. The guitarist had figured it out. There was something defiant about his announcement, like a boast or a challenge, and there was a grip of resolution on his face, but all the while he was staring straight at the fiddler's freckled fingers. Johnny quickly answered with a strum of equal force. Jocko kicked the bucket with his foot. Ant jumped back, startled, then she grasped the bow and struck the strings as if she were beating a rug. For a moment it looked like there was going to be a battle. The cacophony was anything but harmonious. But then Jocko found a rhythm, a soothing canter, and it wasn't long before everyone was anchored to it. The guitarist tried to race ahead for a while, but the backbeat was too infectious. Eventually he relaxed his shoulders, widened his fingers, and turned his ear to the strange and wondrous sound that was being born, something like wind and rain and laughter, the call of swans flying over, the rush of rivers.

Ant played her fiddle deftly. She was clearly more rooted in tradition than Lucy ever was, but as the night moved on her melodies veered into more and more unfamiliar territory. The guitarist just played it straight, fingering the chords and strumming the strings, as if it were any other day. But he was moonstruck, for sure. He craned his neck to the shared space between them, his attention rapt. After a while he got up and walked around, weaving between the other musicians, listening to the interplay.

And indeed, they did play the moon clear across the sky. Perhaps it was Johnny's experience with Lucy that kept him going, and goaded the others on. But the guitarist himself had opened up, his hands once bone-stiff, softened like candlewax. Ant was willing, and Jocko just lifted his face in trancelike bliss while he made love to his single string.

Very late, the music slowed and stilled, but did not diminish in intensity. There were crickets singing. Everyone heard them, and left silences between the notes to welcome their songs. It was then that Johnny looked out across the field and saw the dancers. Men and women, twirling in white gowns lit by moonglow, six or seven of them, moved slowly, at distances from each other; they held their arms aloft, dipped and swooned, swayed, joined hands in circles, pulled apart, leaping and folding until the moon sank below the western ridge, and suddenly they were gone.

ↄ

He had no memory of it ending. He woke on a rumpled bed of canvass behind the platform. There was a warm body pressed against his, Ant's body, her arm across his chest, her face nuzzled in his neck.

Slowly he pulled himself free, stood and shook off the slumber. Jocko was stretched out on the other side of Ant, his arms extended above his head as if he were reaching for the long departed moon. The guitarist was nowhere to be seen.

Johnny walked out on the meadow. Morning mist was scattering. Most of the tables were still up and a few people were milling around, half awake. In front of a steaming kettle, a man was passing out cups of some hot, dark roasted brew. Johnny took one and nodded his thanks. He strolled over to a table where a woman had spread out items of clothing. There were bib overalls for the farmers, dressmaker's cloaks, goat herder's colorful rags, even a few white mummer's robes.

"Morning, Arcane," said the woman. She had stern eyes, like Mother's, but there was something melodious in her voice.

Johnny fingered the lapel of a shoemaker's jacket. "Who makes these?" he asked.

"Well, the fabric is milled in Stubblefield. Mostly flax. Some corn silk. Hardly any cotton these days. I make the clothes myself, right here. Did you ever see such a pretty baker's bonnet?" She held up something blue and embroidered.

"Well that's right nice. But tell me this. Last night, everybody wore something different. Nobody wore the uniform of their profession."

"Oh, well, the Cornfest, we leave our work behind. Then in the morning people come up and pick new work clothes. Sometimes they even pick new work."

On a rack of pegs above the trapper's ties and the butcher's aprons, hung a row of red armbands. Johnny took one in his hand. "Is there much demand for these?"

The woman shook her head. "Nope. Not at all. It's hard to find a good messenger anymore. Leastwise an honest one."

Johnny stretched the armband and let it snap back together. The words of the messenger on the road rang in his ears. *Lotsa sojourners start out by being messengers. You memberize the lay of land, and the borders. Masticate on that sometimes, son. Might do you good.*

"I think I'll take one," he told the woman.

The woman nodded and smiled. "A smart boy. You must be new at this sojourning thing. Lots of sojourners start out by being messengers."

Johnny slipped the armband up his sleeve and onto his shoulder; then he walked across the meadow to the town proper, where smoke was rising from the chimney of a grey stone log house.

Inside was where most of the townspeople had gathered, sitting at log tables, groggily slurping from bowls of porridge and munching on bits of crunchy bacon. A few people hailed him. "Arcane! Arcane!" One man shook his hand. One of the hoop girls reached up and stroked his arm. He got himself some food and sat down. Immediately he felt a presence beside him.

It was the burly man. Half his face was wrapped in gauze, and his right arm was in a sling. They regarded each other.

"Thought you might," he said.

"Thought I might *what?*"

"Was hoping you would, actually. I got a message to send. Wrote it last night. There hasn't been a messenger come through here in weeks."

Awkwardly, with his left hand, he retrieved a sealed envelope from his vest pocket and slapped it on the table. "Gonna be hard for me to draw you a map. But I'll try." He fished through his pocket and produced a piece of parchment, which he flattened on the wood surface. "It's for the mayor of Stubblefield, about five days walking from here, mostly to the south. I'll note the roadhouses for you on the map, since you're new to this."

"What's a mayor?" asked Johnny.

"What's a *mayor?* Well, you *are* a small town boy, aren't you? A town gets big enough, it needs a mayor—you know, to make sure everything runs smoothly. We could never have a Cornfest at King Corn, if we didn't have a mayor." While he talked he drew the map with a stub of charcoal. There were all sorts of things on it, hills, houses, orchards, barns, lakes and rivers. His whole arm was shaking with the effort. "You start out soon, you'll get to the first roadhouse well before sundown."

So that very morning, Johnny Arcane set out in his new role as a messenger. He studied the map carefully over breakfast, thanked the burly man, stood, left the long house, and left the town of King Corn on the road heading south.

Just past the first bend he heard muffled footsteps, and a voice called his name. "Johnny! Johnny, don't go!"

He turned. It was Ant. She was wearing the same dress as the night before, and she was running in bare feet.

"Ant!" he cried. She flung herself into his arms. "Don't go, Johnny! We made such beautiful music. We could be a band—me, you, Jocko, Bearclaw. Don't go, Johnny. I love you!"

He stroked her shoulders and cradled the back of her head. "Ant, Ant, *Antelleramine*! No, Ant, I have a job to do. I have a message to carry. This is my destiny."

"Then I'll come with you. I can be your companion. Your helpmate."

"No, I have to go alone. I'm a sojourner. Sojourners go alone."

Ant sunk her head between her shoulders and made her mouth into a pout. "You're so cruel!"

"No, I'm not cruel. It's just my destiny, and yours." He pulled away from her embrace. "I'll come back someday. My path will bring me back. We'll make music again."

As he walked away, listening to her sobs in the road behind him, he thought, *this will be a pattern, then. Everywhere he goes, Johnny Arcane will leave a trail of broken hearts...*

CHAPTER FIVE

TROUBLE IN STUBBLEFIELD

he sun rose and fell five times before he stood at the foot of a gently sloping hill, the entire summit commanded by the house of Miles Castorbean, Mayor of Stubblefield. Johnny had never seen a domicile so big before. It was twice the size of any normal house, and it was made of milled boards, the kind no longer fashioned in the Known World. Two enormous round columns framed the porch, and white lace curtains hung in the upstairs windows. The house demanded respect, but at the same time it elicited a sort of pity. The paint was discolored, and in places, completely chipped away. The front porch slaunched downward to the left, and the entire right side was covered in creeping ivy. Like a bad birthmark the ivy stretched its fingers over the wallboards, curled around the drainpipe, and covered half the glass of the rightmost window.

The hillside was planted in vineyards, old vines, long ago espaliered on wires and posts, now overgrown and mounded up in phantasmic shapes, resembling bears and giant shaggy badgers. This afternoon, the vineyard was full of people, running about with baskets full of purple grapes, and snapping grapes off the vines with little hand sickles.

A man noticed Johnny and approached him. "Welcome, messenger! You be lookin' for the master?"

"I'm looking for Miles Castorbean."

"Well, that be the master, then. He's up to the house. Think they're uncorking last summer's vintage."

On the porch, two orange cats appeared, both remarkably tame. Johnny jumped back in revulsion but they continued to approach, and one of them rubbed its head on his ankle, causing a shudder to shoot up his spine. The door was a large slab of oak with an oval window of beveled amber glass, moss-stained at the edges. Before he could knock, it opened. A child with long, unkempt locks, stood there. Boy or girl, Johnny couldn't tell. The child turned and ran. "Bapa! It's a messenger!"

"Well, let him in!" crackled a crusty voice. "Where's yer manners?"

The mayor of Stubblefield sat at a table set with an array of unlabeled green bottles. Johnny thought he'd never seen a man who looked so old. He was wearing a robe of some kind of shiny gold fabric that glinted in the light of the corn lamps. On his head was a conical hat with tassels at the tip. From the hat floated a cascade of white curls that framed his smiley round face, and seamlessly joined a curly white beard. Two men sat, one on either side of him. They were equally old, but they were clean-shaven and wore conventional workingman's clothing.

"Apples and berries!" Miles Castorbean clapped his hands. "We haven't seen a message in so long. I hope it's a good one. Give me at once!"

Johnny handed him the envelope. The man grabbed

it, ripped it open, and read it voraciously in a matter of seconds. Then he set the note down on the table and closed his eyes for a moment, as if to process the news.

"Arcane," he said. "What's yer first name, m'boy?"

"How did you know I was Arcane?"

"Oh, Burlyman mentioned you in his note."

"Burlyman is his name? He never told me. I called him the burley man in my head."

"Ah, well, it suits him. Youngfellow! The boy needs some wine. Start him on the tour!"

"Indeed, sir," said the old man, Youngfellow, hefting one of the dark green bottles. He spoke as if reciting something by rote. "We begin with a pringleback varietal. It has a loamy interface, with a finish of carbonate and toad." He splashed a puddle of purple liquid into a dirty, tall-stemmed glass.

Johnny had never seen or tasted wine before. If anything, there had been a little ale at the summer dances, and nothing strong had ever crossed his lips until the night Lucy had brought the amber bottle out from under the bed. He sipped cautiously. Indeed, it did taste loamy, like the earth, but once past his tongue, the flavor changed to something both heavy and light, walnut husks or woodsmoke.

"You look a little green around the ears, master Arcane," said Mayor Castorbean. "You been a messenger for long?"

"No, sir. This is my first assignment."

"Well, then I'll be givin' you yer second assignment in the morning. But tonight we wine and dine. Next, Mr. Youngfellow?"

"Indeed. Next we have a robust sharbonazz, with a fine fruited approach, and a coarse, vegetative retreat."

There were five more rounds, seven in all, and by the time they were finished, Johnny was feeling something he had never quite felt before. Different from the slow sleepy sensuality of Lucy's amber elixir, this intoxication was more active. He wanted to get up and move. He wanted to see things.

"Would you like a tour of the grounds?" asked Mayor Castorbean. "My man Caraway can show you."

The other old man on the mayor's right stood. "At your service."

He took Johnny out and up to an arbor on a hillside overlooking all the vineyards. The sun was getting low, the shadows were long, and the worker's were coming in with their baskets of grapes, dumping them into a series of wooden bins. Some of them were young girls. With their peasant blouses and their hair pulled back, they kindled an energy in his limbs, a conquering spirit driven through his blood by the purple power of the wine.

Caraway rattled on about the different varieties of grapes, their seasons and their reasons, but Johnny couldn't pay any attention. Eventually he noticed a line of low buildings in the east, their stacks pumping out billows of grey smoke. He asked about these.

"Ah, the textile mills. Yes, I dare say everything you're wearing comes from fabric woven in those mills. The machines run on steam. Everybody in the town of Stubblefield works in the mills. The vineyard workers come from far away, during the harvest and the pressing."

"How do they get here?"

"They come on a boat. Can't you see the river? Look out past the mills. It's the only river there is, in all the four directions. That's why they call it the River Only."

Yes, there was a river, just a glint of it, snaking in a

bend around the other side of the mills. A curious thought fluttered through Johnny's head.

"Well, how could that be? A river can't just keep going. It has to start someplace, and end someplace."

"Well, of course it can. It comes out of the big cave in the north Skybird Mountains, and it drops into the big hole in the south salty flatlands. They should teach you more geography in school, sonny boy."

Ɔ

Back at the big house, a feast was being prepared. In a massive stone hearth at the far end of the long hall, a fire brightly blazed. The room was full of people, both vineyard laborers from far away and local millworkers. You could tell them apart by their uniforms. The vineyard people all wore white gauzy tunics with colorful embroidery. The women had puffier sleeves and lower necklines. The local millworkers, both men and women, dressed in sturdy khaki, and each wore a darker khaki vest with many pockets. Some still had their tools in their pockets, little ball peen hammers, punches and awls.

Mayor Castorbean had changed his costume. He stood at the head of the long table garbed in a robe of iridescent green, the color of the wingfeather of a male mallard duck. A real duck beak was strapped to his nose, and with his open hand he pounded rhythms on a big skin hoop drum. People nearby swayed from side to side, and the heartbeat of the drum echoed throughout the hall.

"I know many secrets, young Arcane," he said to Johnny who stood at his right. "Would you like me to tell you one?"

Johnny's face flushed with the radiance of the wine.

"Maybe one," he said. "I'm not sure I could handle more than one new secret at this time."

Castorbean laughed and pounded the drum. His cheeks were red as raspberries. He leaned over and spoke in a hushed voice. "Some of the people you see are not people. Even some of the people you see here tonight."

Johnny felt the hair stand up on the back of his neck. "Then what are they?"

"They're messengers, like you, but they don't bring messages from this world. They bring messages from another world. Do you know what I mean, young Arcane?"

"What other world is there?"

Castorbean pulled the duck beak off his nose to reveal his full face. "I think you know what I mean, young Arcane."

Johnny's heart began to pound, his hands to sweat. "Do you mean the world beyond the four directions?"

The mayor stared at him for a moment with wide, round eyes. Then suddenly he broke out in loud laughter, as if the whole thing was just some big, crazy joke. He put his beak back on and clapped his hands. "Look! The food is coming!"

Men were weaving their way through the crowd, bearing trays. Wearing starched white suits, they were neither mill-workers nor vineyard laborers. Castorbean pulled out a chair for Johnny to sit, and a steaming plate was laid before him.

It was a whole, roasted quail in a bed of yellow rice framed by a halo of sautéed turnip greens. Johnny immediately remembered the weasel's gift. He heard Lucy's voice as if conducted from the murmur of voices in the room. *You ate the food offered to the gods, and you took the oil. Then later you were fed by one of the creatures.* So many things were falling into place, but there were missing pieces. Mostly he was famished. He lit into the food like a hungry wolf.

Old man Caraway approached with something in his hands. He held out a curved briar pipe with a metal lid and a chain.

"Our master Arcane is an inquisitive boy," he said to Castorbean. "Perhaps he would like to try a little of the *Illumination?*"

"Well, damn it, Caraway, I will have some of that!" Castorbean snatched the pipe into his mouth and flipped the lid. "Young Arcane can decide for himself." By some trick of magic, Caraway flicked his hand and a tiny flame jumped from his fingers into the pipe. The smoke that rose was blue and smelled like rotting wood. Castorbean inhaled deeply, then handed the pipe across the table.

"Try it, Arcane. It might open you up a bit."

In drunken carelessness, Johnny reached for the pipe and took a deep drag. The smoke was harsh but its first effect was to calm him and center him. Centered, as if he were the center of everything, and everything he saw was emanating from his eyes. He liked this feeling. He wanted more. He inhaled again.

"Give it back now," mumbled Caraway. "Don't be a horn pig."

After that all the sounds in the room began to pulsate. He looked at Castorbean who said something to him, but the words made no sense. They just merged with the rhythm. He looked at the hoop drum sitting on the chair. It seemed to be beating of its own accord. Before he realized what he was doing he had snatched the drum up to his chest and started pounding on it the primal heartbeat he felt coming at him from all directions. Caraway frowned, but Castorbean laughed and clapped his hands.

"Open up, young Arcane! Tell us who you really are!"

Johnny stood, as if addressing an audience. The sensation persisted: he was the center of everything. Some vineyard workers at the end of the table began to clap to the beat. He stepped out and approached them. They stood and followed.

The pulse of his drum seemed to exert an attraction from all directions. All the sounds, the clinking of glasses, the clacking of plates, the shuffling of feet, swirled around and came together in alignment with its thrust and release. More people stood, their bodies swaying to the rhythm. Johnny glanced back at the head of the table. Mayor Castorbean was clapping his hands and nodding in time with his beak, but Caraway sat with his arms folded, his face in a scowl.

Then the force became irresistible. Johnny moved out into the crowd, working his way between the tables. People stood and followed, all of them vineyard laborers, come on a boat from far away. Not a single millworker joined the dance.

One of the vineyard girls jumped out in front of him. She had bright red hair, freckled skin, and a full figure. She raised her arms in the air and began shimmying from side to side. Then she turned and beckoned him to follow. A human serpent, they coiled through the aisles and into the clear space in front of the open fire. There the line broke into clusters of dancers, faces glowing in the firelight, moving to a music without melody, only the throbbing of an ancient cadence, like the repetitive phases of the sun and the moon and the heartbeat of life itself.

The red-haired vineyard girl stayed close to Johnny. She engaged him with her eyes and entreated him with her arms. He liked it, and when the tempo of his drumbeat quickened, all the others followed.

After a while, the girl moved away and approached one of the millworkers at the table, a woman who had been smiling and nodding her head in enjoyment, unlike all the others who sat stone-faced and grim. The redhead girl grabbed the woman's hand and tried to coax her to the floor, but she shied and pulled away.

A man sitting next to her stood, scowling, and shoved the red-haired girl on the shoulder. She took it in her stride and twirled back into the sea of dancers. But another vineyard man had been watching. He advanced upon the millworker and stood before him, dancing, taunting. *Loosen your starched collar! Come and embrace!* The millworker snarled out some words that couldn't be heard. The dancing man answered back in a lilting voice and then millworker jumped to his feet. He grabbed the man by his embroidered shirt and thrust him backwards, hard, into the crowd.

A circle of dancers broke the vineyard man's fall. There was shouting and clenched fists. The rhythm began to fall apart. A few of the millworkers stood and pressed their way into the crowd, to be met by the faces of angry dancers. Words were exchanged, then shouts. The shoving began. The rhythm collapsed entirely, as more and more dancers became aware of what was happening.

A millworker delivered the first real blow—a moist thud, and a vineyard woman went reeling sideways. Several vineyard men tackled the millworker and brought him to the floor where they began kicking him without mercy. A wine glass flew overhead and smashed. Across the dance floor fists scudded into flesh, arms flailed, voices bellowed.

Suddenly a loud blast pierced the chaos. Everyone stopped what he was doing. Some dropped to the floor.

Mayor Castorbean stood at his table, a huge, curly ram's horn in his hand. He had removed his duck beak, and had donned a helmet of antlers sprouting like a tree from the roots of his head. This emblem commanded some kind of fearful respect. All the voices went silent and most everyone sat. There was some sobbing and some sniffling. The fire crackled.

"My people, my people, my *people!*" he pronounced, his voice resounding through the hall. "I am ashamed of you! You behave so badly, always, you behave badly! Do you not know what has come? Do you not know what is moving among you?"

He paused, lowered his head, and shook it from side to side. "No, you don't," he said, more quietly, his head still down. "How could you?" He lifted his face. "This banquet is over. Everyone go home!"

The people picked themselves up and began gathering their things. They did not look at each other. There were a few murmuring voices. Some people were wounded and others were attending to their wounds.

Johnny pressed through the battlefield and approached the table where Mayor Castorbean now sat alone.

"Ah, young Arcane, I am so sorry you had to see that. But I am not surprised. My people have much to learn." He folded his hands and a tear slipped from his eye. He looked up. "We have a room prepared where you will sleep comfortably tonight. Your things are already there. Come to me in the morning and I will dispatch your next assignment. Youngfellow, show Arcane to his chambers."

Old Youngfellow appeared. "Indeed, sir."

In the lobby by the front door, Youngfellow opened a cupboard and began rummaging through the linens, leaving Johnny standing idle. On the plain of the very desk where he had first met Castorbean earlier that day, Johnny saw the envelope he had carried all the way from King Corn. And there, next to the envelope, the letter itself lay open, the writing boldly scrawled. Johnny did not intend to read it but the words were so few. They entered his eye before he could stop them.

CASTORBEAN
I BELIEVE BORDERBINDER HAS RETURNED. HE
IS THE ONE WHO BRINGS THIS MESSAGE. HIS NAME
IS ARCANE.

He dizzied. His head spun. Perhaps it was just the wine and the smoke. No, it was not. Another piece of the puzzle was falling into place.

Youngfellow turned from the cupboard, an armful of towels. Johnny placed his back to the table to conceal the note.

"Right this way, sir." The old man led him up a flight of creaky stairs and down a long, dark hallway. A cat disappeared into the shadows at their approach. The walls were stained with mildew and a threadbare runner of rotting wool clung to the floor.

Youngfellow shoved open the last door at the end of the hall. "Here you are sir. These are your towels. The bath will be warm if you let it run for a while. Is there anything I can get you? More wine, perhaps?"

"No, no thank you." Johnny shook his head. "I think I will just sleep."

"Very well, sir."

The bed had an iron frame and stood directly under the window. Johnny knew at once which window, because it was partially covered with ivy. He looked out on the mounded vineyards, indistinct in the dark. He turned back to the room.

A large, clawfoot tub sat in the corner. He wondered

how it could be filled up here on the second floor, far from any well or stove. Then he saw the pipes protruding from the floor, and the small silver knob. He turned the knob and jumped back in surprise as the water gushed into the tub from the spout.

Soon he found himself soaking in a tub of warm water, pondering the strange events of the day. He found nothing he could moor himself to. Superstition was everywhere. How could he ever distinguish the facts from the beliefs? Yes, he had learned the story of Borderbinder, how he sealed the four directions with cornmeal and ended the time of fire and bandits. And yes, he had listened to the tales around the campfires, believed by few, but often told, that Borderbinder did not really die, that he had slipped into the side world where he had been transformed into a different kind of being, one that could pass through walls and barriers, one who would someday return to reopen the gates of the four directions. But this was childishness. Nobody really believed it. Nobody except the fools who lived on the fringes and ate the flesh of lizards. Life would go on as usual. The four directions would stand, and contain all their laws within them.

But what if you were to go there? What if you were to walk north and north and north, until you came to the cave from which flowed the source of the River Only, and then you kept walking north. What would you find? How could it not be possible to keep going? What would stop you?

He climbed from the bath and dried himself with Young-fellow's towel. He did not dress, but slipped into the bed, naked, pulled the blankets up to his chin, and fell immediately asleep.

He dreamt of Lucy. She was on a boat, on a river, the River Only. He was on the shore, running along the shore, trying to keep up with the boat. Lucy was crying to him, *Johnny, Johnny, stop them! They're going to take me back!* At the helm of the boat a dark figure hunched, cloaked in black. It did not place a hand on the tiller, but seemed to steer the boat by magic. Just before the boat rounded a bend and disappeared from sight, the figure lifted its hood to reveal a helmet of antlers.

Johnny woke with a start. It was icy cold and his body was shivering. A shadow was moving across the window. It was just the ivy, lilting in the wind. Outside a pale half moon was rising through a quilt of clouds. He felt himself gripped by a fist of terror beyond his comprehension. The old house was creaking and breathing and out in the hall he heard whispering voices. The door opened and someone entered.

She stood there at the center of the room. He recognized her at once. It was the red-haired vineyard girl from the dance. The moonlight lit her white tunic like phosphorescence. She looked around, adjusting her eyes to the dark.

"There you are!" she cried. "I thought you'd be there!" She scampered across the room, threw back the covers and jumped into the bed, then gasped at the touch of Johnny's naked skin.

"Oh! You're so cold!"

"I'm afraid. I'm so afraid. Hold me please. Hold me."

"Well, of course I'll hold you. That's what I came to do." Her voice was full of warmth. She pressed her body against his and threw her legs over his legs, her arms around his neck. Then she kissed him on the face, on the chest, and began to run her mouth down his belly.

"No, no, don't do that. I can't do that. I belong to another. I'm just afraid. Hold me, that's all. Just hold me. I'm so afraid."

Ɔ

Morning. Johnny sat at a big oak table in the Castorbean kitchen, eating a bowl of porridge, while at a nearby desk, the mayor made inky scratches on a piece of parchment with a feather quill pen. Old man Youngfellow stood in the corner, as still as a wooden statue.

Earlier, when Johnny awoke, the red-haired girl was gone and the morning sun was streaming in through the ivy-clad window. He heard the songs of the vineyard workers as they moved through the vines and his mind was calm and still; gone was both the fear and the elation of the night before. The day was a blank slate on which he would write.

"There!" said the mayor, breaking his reverie. "That should do it. Pan Clangbanger is a metal worker in the town of Sputum, three days walk, north along the river road. I've prepared you a map as well. But I've recompensed you nothing for your labors."

"On the contrary," said Johnny. "Last night was one I'll never forget."

Castorbean looked around the kitchen. "There must be something, anything. Look around, from where you're sitting. Anything you can see without standing, you can take with you on your journey."

These words surprised him, for he had already been looking at something, and thinking of what use he might make of it. He stood and walked to the counter where a flat metal container rested on the tiles. He picked it up. Only as thick as a finger, and just wide enough and long enough to slip into his backpack.

"What do you use this for?" he asked.

"Oh, that's nothing. I put documents in it when I have

to carry them from place to place. Keeps them dry if it rains. I have several."

"Well, I'll take this one, then. I think I can use it."

"Whatever suits your fancy, young Arcane. You are a strange one, but I knew that when you came. And even more so after you'd been here for awhile. Here is your burden, and your map. Tell my man Clangbanger that time is shorter than it is long. He'll know what I mean." He handed Johnny the message and the map. The envelope was sealed with red wax embossed with a letter C. "We shall meet again, there is no doubt."

Youngfellow took one step forward. "Your pack, sir," he said, and handed Johnny his backpack. For a moment Johnny thought he saw a ripple pass across the old man's face, like the surface of a lake in a breeze. Perhaps not. Perhaps it was only his imagination.

CHAPTER SIX

THE DOLMENS

rue to the map, the northbound road followed the levee of the River Only upstream as it flowed to the south. Here the Only was so wide the groves on the opposite shore looked like shrubs, and there wasn't a bridge in sight.

He hadn't gone long before he came to a fallen tree, blocking any passage except for foot travel. Here he sat and drank some water from his canteen. Then he pulled the metal container from the backpack and opened it. There were a few scraps of parchment inside, with nothing on them. He scattered these to the wind and laid the opened container on the ground.

In the backpack he found the map that Burleyman had drawn, depicting all the landmarks on the road between King Corn and Stubblefield. Castorbean's map was much simpler, basically a curved line that stayed on the west side of the river, with two roads departing westward, words indicating their destinations: TO CHOKEBERRY, TO FOOTBALM. About two days out there was a single square on the river side of the road with the words: THE DOLMENS.

He straightened the edges of Burleyman's map and flattened it into the metal box. Then he produced something else from the pack. Folded four times, it was the picture Lucy had given him—the waterfall with its unimaginably fine detail. This, too, he pressed flat into the metal box. He replaced the box in the pack and drew out the message he was carrying from Castorbean to Pan Clangbanger in the town of Sputum.

What could it possibly say? He burned with curiosity. Pieces of the puzzle were falling into place, and surely one piece was sealed in this envelope. But he dared not open it. He slipped the message back in his pack and continued on his way.

That night he stayed with a ferryman and his wife in their hut on stilts above the river. The ferryman had a boat that he used to ferry people across to the town of Candlewax on the other side. After supper, Johnny spread Castorbean's map on the floor and scrawled the word FERRYMAN at the bend where the ferryman's hut stood, and across the river: CANDLEWAX. Then he took Castorbean's message out and padded it with his fingers, as if he could read its contents by the contours of the parchment.

The next day was hot, and the river flowed under an open sky with barely a tree in sight. To the west, endless fields of corn and turnips. To the east, only the River Only, so wide, he had no idea what lay beyond it. As he walked he scrolled through the events of his night in Stubblefield. Miles Castorbean in his strange robes, flanked by old Youngfellow and Caraway; the tour of wines, and Caraway's detachment on the hillside as he described the comings and the goings of the River. Later there were the mayor's mysterious words about the people who weren't people, and then the crazy smoke and the rhythm that drew him into the crowd, into the dance that led to the fight between the vineyard people and the millworkers. And that night he dreamt of Lucy and woke in fear, and the red-haired girl came in and comforted him. But of all the memories, none obsessed him more than the words he had brought from King Corn to Stubblefield:

I BELIEVE BORDERBINDER HAS RETURNED. HE IS THE ONE WHO BRINGS THIS MESSAGE. HIS NAME IS ARCANE.

And all the while the envelope he was bearing from Stubblefield to Sputum burned like an ember at his back.

Far ahead on the river's wide curve, he saw a building dancing in heat mirage. This would be the Dolmens. If lacking in detail, Castorbean's map was at least accurate. A crow leapt from the branch of a dead tree, touched briefly in the road, cawed at him, then flew on as if beckoning him to follow. But of course he had no choice. There was only the road and the river.

As he drew nearer, the form of the building took shape, a log house with a steep, barnlike roof and a stone chimney. One lone willow. And to the left, on the river side, there were three strange objects—towers several times taller than a man, upright and branching into a series of arms at the top, segmented appendages hanging down from the fingers. They were too regular to be part of the natural world. They could only have been made by humans.

Only as he approached the steps of the establishment did he notice something else. Across the river, obscured by the haze, stood three more towers, identical to those beside the log house. For a moment he thought he saw threads, like spider webs spanning the river from tower to tower. But then the light shifted and they disappeared.

In the gloom of the log house two men sat at a table

drinking beer and playing a game of barn nails. The house-mistress leaned on the counter in a dirty apron. "Welcome, traveler," she said in a lazy voice.

"I need a meal and a bed," Johnny announced.

"We got that, if you don't mind a little cat in your food."

Johnny threw down his pack and sat with the men at the table. "How do you play this game?"

They showed him the moves and allotted him a pile of square nails. They filled him a glass of beer from the pitcher. The housemistress brought him a bowl of cold stew, then sat down and joined the game.

"So what are the towers outside?" Johnny asked, after a few moves. "What are they for?"

"Oh, them be the Dolmens," said one of the men. "That's why they call us the Dolmens. Because of the dolmens outside."

"What are dolmens?"

"Dolmens are things made by people long ago, back in No Time, before the fire and the bandits. There's hardly any dolmens left in this world anymore. And we got 'em."

"Yeah, that's right, Jimson," chided the housemistress. "People flock from miles around just to see our dolmens."

"Well, they do!" said Jimson. "It's an extinguishing feature. Hereby lies a mystery. Sometimes at night I hear 'em talking at each other, right across the river."

"Oh yeah? What do they say?" asked the other man. "Maybe they say, hey over there! I want to have your baby!"

The housemistress let out a husky, masculine chuckle. "You fellas are full of beans."

"But where are the other dolmens?' asked Johnny. "You suggested there were others."

"Hell, I don't know. I don't care, though. We got the Dolmens."

"What about the blinkers? Do you suppose the blinkers are dolmens?"

"The blinkers? Nah, the blinkers are just stars that blink."

Johnny poured himself another glass. It took three beers to wash down the fetid taste of the stew. He got a little tipsy and started telling stories. He said that there were all kinds of wonders in the world. There was a slime that lived on the forest floor, and when it needed light it turned into a creature with legs, and it crawled across the forest to reach the light, and then it broke back down into a slime again. Once when he was hungry a weasel brought him a quail to eat. He told them that once he saw a man produce flame from his fingertips, and he described how people traveled by boat at harvest time to work the vineyards of Stubblefield.

"Oh, we seen them all the time," said Jimson. "They stop here and make a mess of things with their crazy antics. But they're not near as bad as the Blackcoats."

"Blackcoats?"

"Yeah, the Blackcoats, they don't talk at all. They come here and they eat and they sleep and afterwards they leave a stink so bad we have to throw away the sheets. They're up to no good, them Blackcoats."

Johnny drank one more beer after that; then he picked up his pack and stumbled off to his room.

There was a little desk next to the bed. On this he flattened Castorbean's map and with his scratch pen he wrote the word *dolmens* in tiny letters, across the river from where he sat. Then he took out Castorbean's message to Clangbanger, threw it on the table, and stared at it for a long time.

The room spun slowly in his drunkenness. A candle by the bedside flickered. He got up and took the candle over to the desk. The sun went down and still he sat there, staring at the letter.

Another piece of the puzzle. Some things were more important than others. What if he had a destiny to fulfill, something higher and loftier than just the delivery of messages or the strumming of mandolins at harvest dances? Do some codes carry more weight than others? What if it was necessary to know, at any cost, what waited in the road ahead? And who was he really, and why was he placed here? It was his imperative to find out.

He lifted the letter and held it over the candle flame. Slowly the wax seal began to soften. He picked at it with his fingernails until at last it broke loose, intact, the insignia unblemished. With great care and trembling hands he lifted the flap, extracted the parchment, and unfolded it onto the desk. His heart beat wildly as he read the words.

MY DEAR CLANGBANGER,
THE EAST GUTTER OF THE HOUSE IS SAGGING BADLY AND THE DOWNSPOUT IS CRACKED. I CAN PROP THE GUTTER WITH BOARDS BUT THE SPOUT MUST BE REPLACED. PLEASE FASHION A NEW ONE AS SOON AS YOU CAN AND SEND IT DOWN BY BOAT. THE RAIN WILL SOON BE HERE. REMEMBER, TIME IS SHORTER THAN IT IS LONG.
CASTORBEAN

Johnny closed his eyes. He felt himself falling into a great abyss. He felt his heart, so recently throbbing with potency, suddenly break open and empty itself of its contents, like the bowels of some hideous creature in a dark and boggy swamp. He heard two voices, audibly, one directly after the other. First his mother, fingering the broken seal on the envelope: *Corn damned messengers. No purity these days.* Then the woman who gave him the armband at the Cornfest: *It's hard to find a good messenger anymore, leastwise an honest one.*

"What have I done?" he cried out loud, and he flung himself onto the bed and wept.

CHAPTER SEVEN

JOHNNY ARCANE, MESSENGER

ive summers passed. Johnny Arcane grew a long beard and gradually settled into his role as a messenger. For a while at least, he lost sight of that which first drove him away from his home and onto the open road, the power that ran through his bloodstream and kindled his earliest stirrings: the call of the sojourner. It was partly due to his shame. From his moment of triumph at the top of the silo at King Corn, through the resonance of the crowds following his drumbeat into the dance at Castorbean's great hall in Stubblefield, he had begun to imagine himself as some sort of legendary figure, Borderbinder returned to open the four directions; or maybe someone more than Borderbinder. "Arcane! Arcane!" they cried as they carried him aloft into the crush of bodies at the Cornfest. He began to hear his name as more than a name.

In the dingy room of the log house at the Dolmens, everything fell apart. When he read the words of the message he was delivering from Stubblefield to Sputum, he was overcome by two waves of remorse. The first was the banality of the message itself, and the recognition of his foolishness, how he had thought he was bringing some great heraldry of which he himself was the portent, the one who was to come, the deliverer. But far greater was the wave of shame when he realized what he had done. He had broken the seal, and so deceptively, melting the wax, carefully, to keep the insignia intact. And all because of pride. In a single fall of an envelope, his pride was severed.

He presented the message to Clangbanger at Sputum without apologies. The metal worker appeared to suspect nothing. From Sputum, Johnny was dispatched on his next assignment, carrying a thick envelope, dusty with flour, from a baker to a woman of interest in the town of Fairheart, ten days walking to the west.

And so it began. Johnny accepted his duty with a sense of willingness at first, but little by little he began to take pleasure in the feeling of a job well done. And there were other pleasures as well.

At roadhouses he sampled the variations of local cuisine, from cats to goats, rutabagas to thistleberries. He made friends with the locals and the fellow travelers. They often shared stories late into the night, and if there were musicians, they would soon be pulling out the fiddles and squeezeboxes and swapping stovepipes and slip jigs, the instruments always fully tuned.

And there were women who liked him, and he liked them, too. Sometimes they kissed him, and he always kissed them back, but he never let a woman into his bed. His heart was decided. He could not go back to Lucy. She was from the time of his innocence, before he broke the vow. But he would stay true to her fading memory.

And he did not touch intoxicating drink again, nor did he indulge in the crazy blue smoke that was sometimes passed around. He knew where it would lead, and he would not go there.

But the blood of the sojourner was never far beneath his skin. It moved through his veins and cycled rhythmically through his heart. He memorized the lay of the land and he paid attention to the roads not taken. Often, later, an assignment would take him down these very roads, and another piece of the puzzle would fall into place.

He saved every map that was drawn for him. They soon strained the closure of Mayor Castorbean's metal box. He especially liked the ones that were rich in detail. Sometimes at night, in the solitude of a roadhouse room, he got out the maps and pieced them together, trying to match the boundaries and build a bigger map, one that encompassed the entirety of the world through which he traveled. In the beginning it fit on a table, but quite soon he had to spread it out on the floor.

The River Only did in fact bisect the map down the middle, from north to south. You had to know where the bridges were if your destination was on the other side. The Only formed the bed of a valley so broad there were places where you could see nothing but a horizon of cornfields in all directions. Neither the valley's head nor its foot was on his map. The northernmost village he had seen was Cabbage, at the foot of the blue hills; the southernmost was Arden's Plain, where the Only fanned into a delta, creating many small islands and bogs where rice was grown.

Mountains rose slowly to the west, the east, and the north, but he saw no mountains to the south. South, the map ended at the delta. The sky above the delta was always hazy and brown, and smelled like smoke. Johnny's home was northeast of there, about four days walking through the scrub hills, where the scent of sage was strong. He had not seen his mother, nor did he wish to, although once an assignment had taken him along the scrubhill ridge road, past a bluff to which he had occasionally climbed as a child. He paused here and looked out over the familiar terrain. Off in the distance he saw the rise of Gravestone Hill where Huxley, Vermillion and Rug-Chomper were buried.

"Someday I'll be able to see you again," he said. He wiped a tear and moved on.

Sometimes walking, especially in the morning, he began to notice the cadence of his steps. It was never something he chose. It was a quality of light or a condition of his heart, seasoned, perhaps, by the events of the night before, or simply by what he had eaten for breakfast. The division was always two or three; the two could be the stately tread of a promenade, or the lively strut of a reel, or the jingle-jangle stutter of a stovepipe. The three would be a jig, slip or double, but slowed down so that the nuance and tenderness of the melody could be heard. He didn't make these things up. They came to him. He listened to them. He named them. *The Stream That Hugs the Shore, Dry Leaves on the Road, Red Clouds Holding Hands, The Wind in the Thistles, The String Plucked by Memory...*

Ɔ

At the end of his Johnny's fifth summer as a messenger, a young woman in the south central village of Belltone dispatched him to bring a message to her father, Curvy Grey-road, the Hermit King of Hermit Town. Hermit Town was an encampment in the woods of the blue mountains, six days walking southeast, crossing the River Only on the Rickety-back Bridge.

Curvy Greyroad was its king only by default. He had gone there to live out a life of solitude, but soon others followed, mostly ragtag people who were born with hollow places in their heads, people who couldn't spell their own names or count past the number of their fingers. They lived in tents in the woods around Curvy's cabin. They came and went. In spite of his thirst for solitude, Curvy had a heart that needed to beat. So he organized these people in a loose-fitting political body. He found small tasks for each one, and he created a simple set of rules that everyone was willing to follow. He showed them how to forage for food and prepare meals, and how to bathe in the creek. For these reasons they called him the King of Hermit Town.

Johnny found him in his cabin on a cool, crisp evening. The King ripped open the letter without ceremony, and read its contents out loud, but in such a muffled voice that Johnny understood none of the words.

"Damn my daughter and her empty-headed mother!" he exclaimed, as the letter fell to the ground. "They think it possible I could be a town person again. Never! Never! Let the slave grinding at the mill run out into the field and look up into the heavens and laugh in the bright air! Let the unchained soul rise up and look out. His dungeon doors are open!"

The old man became quite agitated, shaking his arms as if there were chains attached to them, his long white hair leaping like a flame of phosphorus from his head. But soon he ran out of steam. His shoulders slumped and he just stood there for a long time, nodding his head in agreement at some undisclosed truth.

"If you want to eat there's some snake meat. But you can't sleep here. You have to find yourself a place in the woods."

◯

After dark, a few of the residents of Hermit Town were drawn out of curiosity to Johnny's little campfire in a remote corner of the forest. They hovered in the shadows like shy deer, shifting their weight from side to side, sometimes making soft, cooing sounds.

"Come on over if you want to share the warmth," he told them. "You got anything to eat?" He had not been able to stomach King Greyroad's snake meat.

They crept forward, slowly, cautiously. There were five of them, four men, one woman, as best as he could tell. They were dressed in filthy rags. One man held up a burlap sack. There was something moving in it. "I got frogs," he said.

Johnny eyed the sack. "They're alive. They're moving."

The man nodded. "They stop when you put them in the fire. Watch." He reached into the sack and pulled out a large bullfrog with fat legs and a throbbing glottis. With a grunt he tossed the creature into the flames.

Of course the frog tried to escape, but the man caught it and threw it back in, then cradled the fire with his hands so it couldn't get out. When it let out its death croak, everyone laughed. It was not a cruel laugh. It was more like children laughing at a clown.

The man held the charred remains up in Johnny's face. "Here," he said.

So Johnny ate the frog. He had no choice. It did not taste bad. Several other frogs were roasted and eaten. The hermit people sat on the ground. Johnny asked them their names. Most of them did not know. The man with the sack said his name was *frog*. This made everyone laugh.

All night long, curled in the womb of a rotten stump, he was troubled by a whistling sound, high in the canopy of trees overhead. Every time he drifted to sleep it pierced the darkness and shook him from a dream of frog ghosts with translucent green wings. At the first tinge of dawn he got up, hefted his pack and took the path through the woods to the main road where he expected he would be dispatched on his next assignment. An autumn rain was beginning to fall; the drops drizzling down through the branches. Johnny kept seeing things from the corners of his eyes, movement in the underbrush, like he was being trailed on both sides. In the path behind him he heard branches crack. He quickened his pace. The distance seemed longer than it had the day before. Had he lost his way? But no, ahead loomed the road, at the base of a series of switchbacks.

Suddenly there was a voice behind him. "Wait!" He wheeled around. A person stood in the bracken. It was one of the frog-eaters from the night before, and gradually he realized it was the one he took to be a woman. In the plain light of morning she didn't look so crazy. She still wore the same filthy rags, but there was something clear about her eyes.

"You're a messenger, aren't you?" she said.

"I am," he replied. In the silence that followed the woman raised her arms and lowered them several times, like she was trying to pick things out of the air. Her lips quivered around words she was unable to form.

"You're not one of them," he said.

"No. No, I'm not. It's complicated. I can't explain. I need

you to send a message for me." She was holding a stained piece of parchment, folded unevenly, no envelope.

"That's what I do. Where's it going?'

"It's for the mayor of King Corn. His name is Burleyman."

Johnny felt his knees go weak. *Burleyman!* Memories flooded up from a deep well inside him, voices that had been silent for so many seasons. "Arcane! Arcane!" they cried as they carried him aloft through the crowd. "Can't untune my instrument," said Jocko as he thumped the string. "Got no pegs." "Then I'll come with you," said Ant, on the road out of town, "I can be your companion. Your helpmate." And then something else rose up from a deeper place and overpowered all the other images. One day's foot travel south of King Corn: the bathhouse. Bow Wow. *Lucy!*

"You'll have to draw me a map."

"You don't need a map. Surely you know how to get to get to King Corn!"

"King Corn is where I started out as a messenger. I saved every map that was ever drawn for me. If I retrace my steps it would take me five summers to get there."

"You don't have to retrace your steps. Just head north, on the forest road."

"How many days walking?"

"I don't know how many days walking." She looked around, behind her, on all four sides of her. "Please, just take it. I have to get back before they miss me." The woman thrust the message into Johnny's hand, then turned and fled.

Johnny found the forest road and followed it north most of the day, meeting no one. It was a lonely road, hugging the shoulder of a fir-covered mountain where his only companions were scrub jays and the occasional circling hawk. From a clearing he glimpsed a lookout tower perched on a rocky bluff to the east. He waved at it. There was no response.

Midday the rain stopped and the sun broke through the clouds, igniting the gold and crimson alders hiding among the firs. A tumbled-down little cabin stood in the lower woods and he reasoned this might be the last chance for shelter before nightfall. So he shoved open the door, shooed away the mice, and dropped his backpack. On the floor he spread out his composite map and studied it. The map had grown so big it barely fit from wall to wall, but at its center there was an empty space. It had always been there. It was where his journeys had not yet taken him. It was a piece of the puzzle that had not yet fallen into place. It was the road back to King Corn.

Darkness fell. He folded the map, taking care not to crumble the brittle corners. He ate a little cat meat, lay down on the hard floor and slept.

He dreamt of Lucy. In the dream she was only a shadow cast on a grey stone wall, but he recognized her hair, the way it fell on her shoulders. The shadow spoke. *"Johnny!"* she cried. *"They've captured me. They're taking me back! I don't know what they did to Bow Wow. Oh, Johnny, what will happen? Will I ever see you again?"*

As she spoke the shadow came into sharper focus and color began to develop. Soon he could recognize the features of her face and even the embroidered design on her silk robe. But then the image changed. It became a waterfall tumbling over a cliff into a deep pool, bright green moss clinging to the rocks. Gradually the picture disappeared into the mists, and there was nothing.

In the morning, the fog was heavy. It was like walking through a cloud. Shadowy creatures scampered out the path before him. His step was slow and labored, his legs stiff from sleeping on the hard wooden boards.

Something materialized at the side of the road, slowly, feature by feature. His heart leapt when he recognized it. It was an altar, nestled among a cluster of rocks, its chipped paint radiating warmly through the fog. He quickened his pace. Details came into focus—the pastel faces of cherubs, carved vines and blossoms, a congregation of figurines winking at him from nooks and niches. But as he drew closer his gait slowed and he became troubled.

There was no food laid out, and many of the plates were broken. The kibbled scat of animals littered the flat surface, and all the corn lamps were extinguished. He stood there with a pounding heart and a sinking feeling in his stomach. On the ground under the altar a blue glass oil bottle was smashed. There were no others.

He did not know what kind of ceremony he could offer to this scene. He removed the broken plates, hurled the shards into the forest, and swept away the dried feces with his bare hands. He took all of the dried cat meat out of his backpack and spread it out on the one intact plate. He poured the last of his remaining bottle of corn oil into a lamp, and lit it with his fire stick. Still it did not seem like enough.

Eventually he drew out his mandolin and began to play. The mandolin was untuned, so he played the music he had learned from Lucy and shared with the people of King Corn. He played for a long time and he danced a little, swaying from side to side. It was a dance full of sadness and dread.

The sun grew curious in the sky and burned a hole through the fog to see what was happening. Johnny packed up his instrument and hurried on up the road, his legs wobbling with anxiety, following the patches of sunlight

THE BALLAD OF JOHNNY ARCANE

that rolled like water, always forward. The terrain began to appear more and more familiar. As much as anything, it was the way it sounded, the particular songs the wind sang in the branches, and the smells, the saps and resins of certain trees. A thrush rendered a bit of melody and another answered, deep in the forest.

And there was the path, and the sign, painted on a bare board, nailed to a tree, with an arrow pointing, and a single word: BATH. He broke into a run, his legs brushing the ferns and the vines that had grown over the trail. "Lucy!" he cried her name out loud, hurling his voice into the ominous silence that waited in the clearing ahead.

The bathhouse was deserted. The furnaces and boilers were still. Bow Wow's wicker chair lay in pieces on the porch. Johnny dashed up the steps and threw open the door. It broke from its sagging hinges and crashed to the floor. In the dim light he could see that the pool was empty and littered with debris. Part of the roof above had caved in, and flies were swarming everywhere. From the dry rocks where the aqueduct once tumbled, a grey cat snarled and fled.

"Lucy!" Johnny turned and ran back outside, through the furnaces and the empty vats, up the fern-clad steps to the cabin. His feet crunched on something on the deck, shards of broken glass, and something else, some metal bits—the ladles! They were strewn about on the boards and the cord lay crumpled in the corner.

Inside the cabin was chaos. Figures had been blackened onto the walls by torches, strange runes in an alphabet he had never seen before. The woodstove was gone, the metal chimney pipe dangling from the ceiling. The mattress had been torn from the bed and lay slaunchways on the floor, its batting ripped open where mice had nested. Frantically

Johnny threw over the mattress, looking for any signs of Lucy. Under the bed frame he found the battered violin case. The moment he snatched it up he could tell by its weight, it was empty.

Craziness overcame him. He threw himself about the room, grabbing anything his hands could reach and hurling it any direction it would go. He smashed the table and used one of its legs to batter down the dangling stovepipe. In the corner behind the pipe a hornet's nest clung. He smashed this too, but the hornets were long gone. With his bare hands he ripped open the mattress, releasing a haze of moldy spores.

There was nothing left of her! Nothing! Twice she had come to him in a dream and pleaded for her rescue. His thoughts ripped through his brain like fire. How could he have traveled through five summers without returning to this place? He had walked as if through a waking dream, her memory dwindling into a mere concept, a belief, like the rituals that kept the borders sealed. He had given in to the lure of the boundaries that kept her out. *Oh, oh, Lucy, I would save you, again and again! If only you had come with me. What made me think I could go alone? Oh, Lucy! Come back to me! Tell me where you are — send me a message. I will save you, again and again. I will save you! Lucy, Lucy, I will find you. I will save you!*

Spent with exhaustion his arms and legs folded and he fell onto the moldy mattress. His tears flowed like the waters of the River Only, and he moaned her name over and over, until it became a song, and the song became a lonesome lullaby and he drifted off to sleep.

He dreamt nothing. The first thing he saw on waking was his backpack propped against the wall, and he remembered.

He had a task to complete. He had a message to deliver to Burleyman, the mayor of King Corn. Once he had done this, the circle would be complete, the map finished. This buoyed him a little and he felt spent of all his emotions from the night before. He wanted to be out of this place. He wanted to be moving. He wanted to be on the road.

Still, he thought, there must be something he could take from here, some talisman of the moment, something to mark his resolve. Or perhaps there was something he should leave here, a dolmen of sorts. Yes, a *dolmen*, but what? He had nothing.

He scoured the room but he could make no sense of the chaos and the rubble. Out on the porch the rain ladles lay scattered. He picked one up. It had a loop at the top where the cord once ran through. He found the cord in the corner. It was patterned with a series of tiny knots. He gathered together the ladles. Each was a different size, and he remembered the sequence from the long rainy nights, lying in bed next to Lucy, listening to the tuning, from the highest note at the top to the lowest at the bottom.

He could do this. He lined all the ladles out on the porch railing, and then sorted them according to size. Beginning with the largest on the bottom he looped them onto the knotted cord. The work was painstaking, and halfway through the morning he grew impatient. Why had he started this? He had to be going! But then the rain began to fall. Its gentle pattering from the high fir branches to the low sagging eaves brought back a flood of memories, the watercourse melody a continuous underscore to everything they had done together, the music they had created, the words they had spoken in both his language and hers, the tears they had cried, the love they had made under the soft, patchwork quilt. It may take a long time to find her. He would not give up.

By the time he tied the last ladle, the rain song was full and mournful. He hung the cord from the peg on the porch and the cups began to fill. He recognized the first note, and the second, and then the third. Just after the fourth note struck, the first repeated, and so began the fugue that had filled the seven days and nights he had spent with Lucy. He sat on the porch stoop and listened through seven full cycles. Then he hefted his backpack and started out into the rain.

CHAPTER EIGHT

RETURN

ohnny shouldered the road like a burden, the memory of that warm, late afternoon, five summers ago, so indelible that the present almost felt like the past, like two leaves of reality overlaid, today's grey and troubled journey, shrouded in mists, while the sun shone bright on the clarity of the earlier time. He shared the path with the ghosts of happy people in bright costumes, children herding pigs with their sticks, a little girl who made magic happen by leaping over potholes.

Ahead and around the grassy hill, King Corn came into sight. He felt a quickening in his limbs; even his fingers tingled as if they yearned for something to grasp. Everything was still and quiet, evening shadows closing in. Faint lamplight glowed from windows. A stratum of fog over the meadow and made a halo around the silo. There was no one in sight, but small wisps of smoke curled from some of the houses, and a welcoming plume rose from the chimney of the log house.

He shoved open the door against the musty warmth of body heat. The place was packed. He recognized a few faces in the dim corn lamp glow—a couple of the hoop girls, and the woman who first gave him the messenger's armband. A few heads turned. "It's Arcane," said someone in a muffled voice. He heard his name whispered as he moved through the crowd toward the table where Mayor Burleyman sat gnawing on a chicken bone, one hand around a stein of beer.

Burleyman looked older than a man should look after only five summers. He was plumper, softer around the middle, and a network of wrinkles branched from his eyes. On his left cheek he still bore the scar of his fall from the silo.

"Well...well." said the mayor, eyeing him up and down, neither smiling nor frowning. "If it isn't the long lost prophet, home from his quest. Sit down, take a load off your feet. We'll get you some food."

Johnny dropped his pack. "I'm not a prophet. I'm just a messenger. Remember, you were the one who first sent me out."

Burleyman waved to a girl with a tray. "Chamomile, look! Johnny Arcane has returned! Bring him some food and some ale!"

Johnny welcomed the plate of chicken and greens with gusto, but he waved away the ale. "Just water, please," he said. From his backpack he produced a folded bit of parchment. "I came on business. I bring you a message from a person at Hermit Town, but she wasn't King Greyroad, and she wasn't one of them."

Burleyman took the letter. "Aha, that be old Darcy Dinkum, then. Poor girl's lived among those fools for so long she's startin' to think like them. What's she got for me today?"

The mayor took a long time reading the message, even though it appeared the words were few. The silence made Johnny uncomfortable. Eventually Burleyman set down the parchment and stared at Johnny, his face expressionless except for the tiny pictures flickering inside his eyes.

Suddenly he seemed to come to his senses, and he threw out his arm in an expansive gesture.

"Well, Johnny Arcane, look around. You'll see King Corn hasn't changed much. Your name's still spoken, but I think many can't recognize you behind that long beard."

Johnny nodded. "Do you still have the Cornfest?"

"Ah, yes, it been two moons ago, and I tell you something. Every fest since you were here, someone has climbed the silo and brought down the honey. Always a different person. It's like you broke the spell, or wove a new one."

"Oh, I just climbed the sunbeams and held onto the birds, that's all. I showed them how. But where are the musicians? Bearclaw, Jocko, Ant."

"Well, that's something else you set in motion. They're on tour. They formed a band. Now they're playing festivals all around the countryside. Tonight they be playin' the Alderball in Bentbranch."

"Will they be back here?"

"Within the moon, I think. Ant and Bearclaw married. Now they take young Chestnut on tour with them."

Johnny's heart jumped, then settled back into a steady beat. He felt a mixture of sadness and relief. Ant. Bearclaw. *Married*. "Chestnut. That be a boy or a girl?"

"Sweet little girl, curly hair. Why you not be drinkin' the ale?"

"Oh, it's not my friend anymore. It made me do some things I regret. Tell me...tell me...tell me..." His thoughts grew dark. "There's a place, a bathhouse, about a day's walk south of here. I spent some time there that summer, before I came to the Cornfest, and I went back last night. The place is in ruins. What happened?"

Burleyman squinched up his mouth, as if tasting something unpleasant. "Yes, I heard it had been abandoned. Some folks from King Corn used to go there, Frankie for one, but I never encouraged it. They always came back with strange ideas."

"But why was it abandoned?"

"Well, some Blackcoats came through here a few summers ago."

"Blackcoats?"

"You know, Blackcoats. People say that the Blackcoats are the descendants of the bandits, but I don't shuck much corn with that. There can be bad people without some kind of crazy mythology attached to them. Blackcoats are just no-goods that weren't raised right."

"What do they do?"

"They don't do much. They don't bathe, that's for sure. You can tell they're coming before they get here, just by the smell. That's why some people think it was the Blackcoats that messed up the bathhouse."

Johnny felt his heart sink. This conversation was only stirring the trouble in his heart, and he didn't know what to do about it. He would have to change the subject.

"I think I'd like to take off the armband for a while, before someone dispatches me somewhere else," he said. "I'd like to stay in one place till I find out what's next."

Burleyman eyed him with a wry grin. "Or maybe your legs are just worn out from all that walking. There's a room in the back, behind the kitchen. It's Jocko's, but you could stay there till they return. Maybe you'll join the band. Maybe that will be Johnny Arcane's next big adventure."

ɔ

Indeed, Johnny found Jocko's room directly behind the longhall kitchen, and well past midnight he could hear the scullery workers scouring the pots and pans on the other side of the clapboard wall. No bed, only a pile of soiled and lumpy pillows, no furniture of any kind, but shallow shelves lined the walls, and on the shelves languished a collection of many small, handmade dolls fashioned of cornhusks, cloth, woven straw or carved wood. They were mostly people, a few animals, carefully arranged, some standing, some sitting, some reclining on miniature beds. Some sat at little tables set with tiny plates and bottles.

As Johnny examined them he began to suspect the people-dolls were replicas of actual people. He found a little Burley-man seated on a high-backed chair, wearing an odd little cap snipped from the skin of a mouse. Mayors always wore strange hats. And there was Bearclaw sitting with his guitar, Ant standing behind him with her fiddle, one hand resting on his shoulder. Three straw girls held up a miniature hoop, and on the shelf above, a bare-chested man grasped a beehive, his knees bent as if he were about to leap. And in a corner all by itself Johnny found an image of his own likeness. It was carved from a plug of cedar, but the mandolin itself was constructed out of the abandoned shell of a sow bug. Directly on the wall behind the figure, a flourish of golden sunbeams was painted, and above it, a small flock of birds.

Johnny lay on the pile of pillows, his eyes big as saucers, his mind blazing with thoughts and sub-thoughts, everything tangential to everything else, every memory, every impression connected by tendrils to every other memory and impression. He knew he was not going to sleep tonight. He felt like a fire in a hall of slumbering giants. He felt like the last glowing coal in the darkened ash of a dying campfire.

Out in the longhall he heard voices, muffled, quiet; they sounded thoughtful, like they were discussing something deep and wondrous. A man's voice mostly, orating, as if explaining something, and then women's voices chiming in, questioning, inquisitive.

Johnny got up and opened the door. The longhall was dark, all the corn lamps extinguished; only a single candle flickered at the central table where a heavy man sat, flanked by two young women.

The talking stopped. They stared at him. He stared at them. Then one of the women spoke. "I know him. It's Johnny Arcane."

The other woman gasped, then clapped her hands in delight. "He climbed the sunbeams and held onto the birds!" she cried. It sounded like a lyric to an old song. "Come over here Johnny Arcane and see what Frankie is showing us."

Johnny approached the table cautiously, more out of respect than fear. Immediately he saw that the man was missing a leg. His pant leg was tied below the stump of his left knee, his right foot planted firmly on the floor, a pair of crutches leaning on the table. On the table was a strange object. It appeared to be a rusty vice with a threaded stem. Two small square paddles were positioned facing each other, vertically, about a hands-width apart. And there between them, glinting in the candleglow, a shiny gold ball hung suspended in mid-air.

"Johnny Arcane, at last." The man's voice was deep and resonant. "I have *longed* you here." He stretched out a meaty hand. "Frankie Fulcrum. We have *so* much to talk about."

Johnny lowered himself slowly into the chair, his eyes fixed firmly on the floating ball, his mind awhirl. "How does it work?" he said at last.

"Two separate attractions of equal strength," replied Frankie Fulcrum. "Case in point: you'll notice I have two equally attractive young ladies, one on either side of me, and I am unable to move from this spot." The attractive young lady on his left giggled while the other on his right punched him in the shoulder. "But now, observe. I will decrease the strength of the lower attractor."

Frankie tweaked a knob at the base of the contraption. The gold ball wobbled for a moment, then fell, striking the paddle with a thud. It did not roll off, but clung, a fixed appendage.

"Ha! Ha! I win!" cried the girl on the right.

"Ha! Ha! You are the lower attractor!" cried the girl on the left.

"Watch again," said Frankie. He reset the knob and replaced the gold ball in the air between the paddles. "Now I will increase the strength of the upper attractor." He tweaked the knob this time in the opposite direction. The ball wobbled again, then began to ascend, but soon its movements became erratic, and suddenly it spun out of control and flew sideways, striking the tabletop and rolling onto the floor. The girl on the left plunged after it while the girl on the right clapped her hands and laughed. "Loser! Loser!"

"Thus demonstrating a simple principle," continued Frankie. "There is always a third attractor. It's the one that attracts us downward, toward the earth. This is why you always fall down. You never fall up."

Johnny pondered this. "Well, that much I understand. I'm always falling down, all the time. But the other two attractors—I don't understand them. Where do they come from?"

Frankie folded his hands and smiled. "I don't understand them either, but I think it has something to do with the poles."

"The poles?"

"Yes, the poles. I didn't make up the term, but the old man who told me was half out of his mind, and I doubt he understood what he was talking about. My research has suggested that there are two attractors that have an effect on everything we see. One comes from the north, the other from the south. This is why the sun rises in the east and sets in the west. It's also why the seasons shift from winter to summer and back again."

Johnny sat with his spine flush against the back of the chair. His mind was spinning. The pieces of the puzzle were falling into place, so rapidly he couldn't process them.

"Who are you and why do you think about these things?" he asked.

The left-hand girl took Frankie's arm. "He's a magician, Johnny Arcane," she said.

Frankie patted her hand. "No, no. Magic is just what you call something when you don't understand it." He turned to look at Johnny. "When I was young I was like you. I had the blood of a sojourner in me. The curiosity. I was only twelve summers old when I fell into the grain auger and it chewed off my left leg. I had to rethink everything. I wasn't going to be able to wander. It hurt for a while, but finally I figured it out. I could wander through the bones of things. The breath. I think it might have started one night when I was lying in bed, listening to my own breath. Why do I breathe? Does anything else breathe? Animals breathe. Do trees breathe? What about rocks? What about houses? One day I hobbled up to the top of Pickett Butte and yelled my name as loud as I could. FRANKIE FULCRUM! My voice came back to me three times, each a little softer. It got me thinking about the way forces—sound and light and heat, travel through time and space. I started building devices and I performed many experiments—hundreds of experiments. I have learned so much, but not enough. It doesn't all fit together. People have listened to me talk, but inevitably, their minds wander." He glanced at the left-hand girl who was digging dirt from under her fingernails with a toothpick. "Very few people have anything new to offer. That's why I longed you here, Johnny Arcane. I think maybe you can help me fill in the pieces."

Fill in the pieces. The words hovered in the air like smoke. At that moment the candle guttered and looked like it was going to go out. Then, suddenly, the flame leapt from the dying wick and danced a quick arc across the table, landing on the taper of another, younger candle, where it flickered happily. Johnny, Frankie, and the two girls all stopped what they were doing and stared at it in silence. Nobody said anything for a long time. Johnny found himself troubling over something Frankie had said. The voice. The echo. The time it takes for the voice to return. He shook the thought out of his mind and spoke.

"I was here, five summers ago. I left wearing the armband of a messenger, because I wanted to see everything, in all the four directions. I made a map of everywhere I went, until it became a map of the Known World, everything there is within the borders. Now I think it's time. I want to know what is there outside those borders."

Frankie leaned back in his chair and nodded his head over and over in some kind of mysterious silent agreement. The left-hand girl tugged at his sleeve. "Hey, Frankie, we be working in the morning. This was fun, though. Let's do it again, tomorrow night. You can make some more magic for us."

The right hand girl wiggled and hopped up and down. "That was funny what the candle did, wasn't it?"

Frankie seemed to come out of a trance. "Oh, yes, yes of course. You girls get some sleep now. Come back tomorrow night. Lot's more fun. Magic."

The girls both kissed Frankie on his balding head; then they scampered out of the longhall. Frankie shifted his weight, painfully. He tried several positions until he found one that seemed to work, leaning forward, his elbows on the tabletop, his fingers splayed on its surface.

"Not every sojourner wants to go outside the four directions, Johnny Arcane." Frankie moved one hand across the table, searching for something invisible. "Try the north first. That's where you'll find the closest attractor, at least by my calculations. I want to see your map. Do you have it with you?"

The map wouldn't fit on one table; Johnny had to push two together to accommodate it. Leaning heavily on his crutches, Frankie followed Johnny's tracing finger across the lay of the land, the way the River Only carved the central, vast, bedded valley and spread the fingered foothills of the high northern mountains. Johnny identified each village and what it was known for—the beehives of Candlewax, the sand mines of Belltone, the textile mills of Stubblefield. The Only poured out of a cave somewhere in the northern mountains, and disappeared into a great sinkhole somewhere in the southern flatlands, or so they told him. He had seen neither of these things. They were off the map.

Frankie traced every road on the map with his finger. He was traveling all the places his body would not let him go.

He said he was born forty-seven summer's ago in the town of Sunnybelly, four days to the north, and he had never left that town until just three summers past, when Mayor Burleyman, informed of his intellectual prowess, had summoned him to King Corn to design a system of cisterns that would deliver clean water to every home and dispensary in the town. In exchange the mayor would provide him a laboratory equipped with whatever apparatus he desired, within its availability, to continue his research into the nature of things. Burleyman wanted to know the nature of things so he could use them. Frankie just wanted to understand. They sometimes quarreled about this.

"The Dolmens," said Frankie, pointing to their mark on the map. "What are they?"

"Well, these dolmens are towers, with arms, and something that looked like glass lamps hanging from the arms. There were identical towers across the river. The people there said dolmens were things left long ago, by those who lived before the time of fire and bandits. Those who lived in No Time."

"Ach!" Frankie coughed up a bit of displeasure into his mouth. "No Time, No Time! I'm tired of hearing about No Time. I have a theory about No Time, Johnny. Would you like to hear it?"

"Yes."

"I will tell you then. In the time of fire and bandits there was something in the smoke that poisoned people's thinking so they stopped wondering, what's ahead, what's behind, what's before, what's after. It got in their blood so it was passed down from children to children's children. But there are some people whose blood is so strong they are impervious to the poison. These people are the sojourners."

For a moment Johnny glimpsed a ring of flame, circling him, and he smelled the ash of smoke in his nostrils. But it quickly faded. "The dolmens," he said, "and the people who made them ..."

Frankie thought for a while. "Johnny, dolmens are everywhere. We eat dolmens. We live in them. Did you know there is no one in the Known World today who knows how to make glass? All the glass that exists has been there from some time that no one can remember. No Time. That's why it's such bad luck to break glass. And don't get me started on metal. The textile mills in Stubblefield are dolmens. Oh, yes, some trees were cut. Some stones were quarried. They added on. But the original structures, nobody knows how they got there. Tell me this: the messages you carry, what are they written on?"

"On parchment."

"Yes, parchment. And do you know what parchment is made of?"

"Yes, I think it's made from goat skin, isn't that right?"

"Yes, any message that has ever been sent was made from goat skin, cured into parchment in the textile mills of Stubblefield. But what about the envelopes? Do you know what the envelopes are made of?"

"I don't know. Sometimes it's called vellum. Not all messages are delivered in envelopes."

"That's correct. And no one in the Known World knows how to make vellum. So it's a dolmen, too. All the vellum there is, comes from a cellar deep beneath the Stubblefield mills, where it was found in a time so long ago that no one can remember it."

Johnny let this sink in as far as it would go. "The people at the Dolmens. I asked them about the blinkers. Are the blinkers dolmens?"

"What are the blinkers?"

"The blinkers are stars that blink and move. They said no, the blinkers are not dolmens. They're just stars that blink and move."

"Hmmm ..." Frankie said it several times. "Hmmm. Hmmm." He made little chewing noises with his jaws. Then he reached into the pocket of his ratty leather jacket and produced something, a tapered metal cylinder, with a bit of curved glass on either end.

"Do you know what this is?"

"No."

"It's a spyglass. A dolmen in itself. But I think we need to get up and go outside. There's something you need to see. You'll have to help me."

Johnny helped Frankie to his crutches and they lumbered to the door, Frankie clutching Johnny's arm and occasionally wincing in pain. Outside, a rosy aura was forming around the grassy hill, but overhead the sky was pitch black and vibrant with stars. They rested against a table at the center of the meadow and craned their necks toward the heavens.

"There's one," said Johnny at last.

"Yes." Frankie lifted the spyglass. "Yes, yes. Look quick, while you can." He handed Johnny the spyglass.

The first thing Johnny noticed was that there were more stars in the spyglass than there were in the sky—tiny stars, stars everywhere, stars between stars. Then he saw the blinker.

It was a perfectly round shadow passing in front of the stars, briefly obscuring their light. Then it blinked. The blink was much smaller than the shadow. It was like a prick of light, shining through a window.

"Do you see what I mean?" asked Frankie. "The blinkers are dolmens. They are machines in the sky."

As they found their way back to the longhouse their bodies became heavy with fatigue. "We've talked enough," said Frankie, "Although there is much more to be said. We need to sleep a little before the work day begins. Find me in my workshop in the afternoon. Ask Burleyman. We will continue."

He left Johnny by the log house door and started his laborious trek toward the houses beyond the meadow. Overhead the stars were fading and the morning sun was opening its single round eye above the curve of the grassy hill.

C

Johnny woke. The room was dark, but he could tell it was day by the chink of sunlight filtering in through a wide horizontal crack where the wallboards did not meet. For a while he lay there on the pile of pillows staring with disbelief at what his eyes insisted was happening. Jocko's dolls had come alive. They were strolling about on the shelves, exchanging casual greetings, shaking hands, conversing soundlessly, or in voices too soft to be heard. But something wasn't quite right. It took him a while to discern what it was. They were upside-down, walking on the ceiling of the shelf above. He sat up abruptly and the scene vanished, everything dark and still, the dolls as stationary as they had been the night before.

One quick move to the side and he realized what had happened. His torso had blocked the penetration of light from the wall crack. Now the phenomenon reappeared as what it was—shadows projected on the wall through an aperture so narrow they were sharpened into shapes, even colors. It was a moving picture of everything that was happening outside in the meadow, the people of the village going about their daily business. He even recognized some faces, and the uniforms of the various professions. *"Wait till I tell Frankie about this!"* he said to himself.

ɔ

Winter moved in swiftly, and with it the traveling musicians returned to the village of King Corn. It was the morning of the First Snow Cornmeal Pancake Breakfast, and almost all the townsfolk gathered in the longhall of the log house. Stacks of pancakes piled on platters floated about the room like pipe smoke, and the sweet, slightly burnt aroma of birch and maple syrup permeated the air. Suddenly the big door flew open with a flurry of snowflakes, and there they stood, the four of them, Ant cradling the child, Chestnut, against her breast, Bearclaw leaning over them protectively, while Jocko, in a long wool coat, peered expectantly into the smoke-filled room.

Shouts of joy, a wave of applause; people rose to their feet to welcome the travelers. But Ant locked eyes with Johnny's immediately and pressed through the crowd until she reached him and threw her one free arm around him, rousing the sleeping child at her breast.

"Oh, Johnny, we were *so* hoping you would be here!" Bearclaw drew up behind her and shook his hand vigorously, his eyes clear and shining. Jocko, on the other hand, did not make it that far. He was brought down by a bevy of young women who smothered him with kisses and caresses.

Plates of pancakes were produced. "Eat before dance!" someone shouted. Bearclaw winked at Johnny. "Go get your turtlebox!" he urged.

They wolfed down their pancakes and clambered up on the longhall platform to tune their instruments, all except Jocko, of course, thumping on his gutstring and grinning like a long-eared donkey. The moment little Chestnut's bare feet touched the floor she snatched up a tambourine and began pounding on it, belting out a wordless melody in a gravelly voice. Bearclaw strummed a rich minor chord.

"*Happy to Meet, Sorry to Part!*" he called, and they were off.

Johnny's joy was immediate, a warm beam of sun pouring into his heart. It was like the last five summers had never happened, and yet every memory contained in them still intact, not as a memory, more like a very old story, first learned in childhood and preserved through countless tellings. The melodies leapt from his fingers. The music was bracing and rapturous. Ant and Bearclaw stood close together, their ears cocked, their fingers trading melodies, harmonies, counterpoint. Jocko threw his curly head back in the way that Johnny remembered so well, as if he were drawing the rhythm down from thunderbolts in the sky. And little Chestnut just beat her tambourine and sang with abandon, her voice remarkably in tune. Some people got up from their pancakes and danced. Others banged out the beat with spoons on plates. Every now and then the door flew open and more people blew in, stamping off the snow from their boots and staring with delight at the scene that was unfolding.

They played all morning. They play all the Soybean Variations, and both versions of The Humors of Vellum. They played through Captain Baxter's entire collection of Forbidden Stovepipes, and then moved on to the Winter Waltzes and the Summer Strathspeys. But they made a mistake when they launched into *The Boatman's Lullaby*. It is, after all, a lullaby, and halfway through it Ant began to yawn and Bearclaw started doubling over his guitar until his forehead nearly touched the frets. Chestnut had long since dropped the tambourine and now was playing in the corner with a pile of knotted twine. Most of the townsfolk had left to attend to their labors.

Bearclaw strummed one last chord, then looked up with a grin. "We are tired," he said. "It has been a long journey,"

"We'll get some sleep," said Ant. "Let's meet here again tonight. We can play untuned."

☽

With a head full of fiddle tunes, Johnny made his way through the snow-drifted meadow back to Frankie Fulcrum's workshop, where he had spent every morning and afternoon since his return to King Corn.

Frankie's workshop also served as his house, where he slept in a cot in the corner and hung his other set of clothes on a nail, but he took all his meals in the longhall, and stayed there late in the evenings, drinking beer and entertaining the scullery maids after every pot and pan had been scrubbed.

Johnny stomped the snow off his shoes on the gravel path out of the meadow. He felt a lingering in his legs and a longing in his heart, sparked to life by the sweetness of the music. In the turning of a morning, everything had changed. For many days he had been swept up by Frankie's spell, the strange ideas that spewed from Frankie's mouth, and the wondrous phenomena Frankie could conjure from the potions and contraptions overflowing the countertops and shelves, and littering the floor. Frankie could elicit pure tones from iron rods and make shifting patterns dance on the surface of water by resonating the sound over deep filled basins. He could make small objects rattle from across the room by changing the pitch of vibrating strings. "They're called wavelengths," he said. "Things you cannot see travel along wavelengths." On one occasion Johnny had asked him about the machines that cluttered the room, how did Frankie make them.

"I didn't make them," answered Frankie. "These are *dolmens* as you would call them, just like so many other things. That's the problem with my work. It's all been done before me, by others, at a time before human memory. No Time. All I have are these remnants, these clues, these *dolmens*. I send out scouts to places I can't go myself. They scour abandoned buildings, warehouses, especially the cellars. They dig through trash heaps. Sometimes they bring me trash, sometimes treasures. My job is to sort it all out, to sift through the properties and potentials."

A few days after that Johnny mentioned the model of the cisterns Frankie had been commissioned to make by Burleyman. The model had been collecting dust in a corner since the day of his arrival.

Oh, there's no mystery to that," Frankie replied. "They're already doing it at Stubblefield. It has nothing to do with my purpose. You just build a tank on a hill and use the third attractor to bring it down to the people."

Johnny shook off the memories as he stood on the porch of Frankie's house. From inside, he caught the familiar scent of burning sulfur. It brought back a trace of his childhood summers when Mother burned sulfur in the smokehouse to preserve the sliced peaches before drying them in the sun. He shoved open the door.

Frankie looked up from the bench, his hair and clothes in their usual dishevelment. "Ah, Johnny." he said. "Do you remember the night you first arrived? Do you remember the candles, what they did?"

"The flame jumped."

"Watch this!" Frankie moved aside to reveal two candles on the counter, one burning, the other extinguished. Two identical devices flanked them, short rods on low platforms, with square paddles fastened to the tops. Johnny immediately remembered the attraction machine in the long hall the first night he arrived.

"Keep watching! Keep watching!" Frankie did something to the base of one of the platforms. The flickering candle flame twisted and pulled, like a dog on a tether, until suddenly it broke free and jumped across the space, landing with a splat on the wick of the other candle, while a whirl of smoke rose from its absence.

"Damn!" Frankie slammed his palm on the counter. "Corn damn! It works! Watch this now!" He touched the other platform. The flame, still swaying from its landing, curled in a ball and leapt again, riding the rising smoke back down into its original wick.

"Your turtleback. Get it out. Set it over there!"

With some reluctance, Johnny pulled the mandolin from his pack and set it on the counter. "There's more!" Frankie intoned. "Hold very still and listen." He turned the paddles down and positioned them outward, facing the room. He held a finger to his lips as he twisted the knobs.

There was a moment of silence, only the soft swish of snow falling outside. Then slowly, almost imperceptibly, something began to hum. The harmonics were familiar. Gradually it dawned on Johnny, what it was.

His mandolin was playing itself. It wasn't a strumming, just a mere vibration of the strings, as if they were being caressed by a gentle zephyr, a drone in perfect tune, resonant with every other sound in the room. The tuning was open, fiddle tuning, fourths, fifths and octaves, overtones hidden like distant voices, voices from the past and the unseen corners of the present, and the inevitable call of the future.

"The attraction itself is a substance," said Frankie. Johnny struggled to make sense of these words. "Like sound. When Jocko plucks his catgut it makes a sound. The sound travels through the air until it reaches you. Most sounds are made by something so close you don't notice the time it takes for it to get to your ears. But when lightning strikes, you have to wait to hear it. Or when you shout your name from a mountaintop. Substances are moving all the time, from place to place. Substances we can't see."

"You mean like the *dough*?" said Johnny. The words just spewed from his mouth, unbidden.

"I don't know what you're talking about."

"The *dough*. I knew this girl that said there was something called *dough*. You can't see it, but messages can travel through it. You can play with it. You can move it around. It helps to make you strong and happy."

Frankie grew agitated. His hands began to tremble. "Where is this girl?"

"I don't know where she is. She worked in a bathhouse a few days south of here."

Frankie caught his breath. His eyes grew wide. The silence made Johnny uncomfortable. But he pushed on.

"I stayed there," he continued. "We became close. But I left her because I was a sojourner and I had to keep moving. I asked her to come with me but she would not. She was afraid of the world outside of the bathhouse. She told me she was a fugitive. Sometimes she comes to me in dreams. She says she's in peril; she's being taken away by someone. On my way back to King Corn I stopped at the bathhouse. It was in ruins, abandoned. This grieves me."

Frankie sat in thought for a while. Then he pulled himself up on his crutches, hobbled across the room and back. "I know her. I went there once. She bathed me. Burleyman was upset. He didn't want any of his people to go there."

Johnny remembered something Lucy had told him. Once she bathed a man with one leg. His stump felt like leather. Lately, when a piece of the puzzle fell into place, he could almost hear a sound in his head, a metallic clink, like a nail falling into a pile of nails.

"Lucy." he said.

"Yes, Lucy. And the man."

"Bow Wow."

"Bow Wow. He knows something. I could tell. We have to find them, Johnny. I think they can help us."

Johnny took a deep breath. "You said you can see something before you hear the sound, like lightning. You said your voice leaves your mouth and comes back to you in time—" He halted his words. He couldn't find the connection between his thoughts and the present moment. It was something he had once expressed to Mother. *If you can know something that happens far away, at the time it happens, can you change the way it happens?* He said no more, and Frankie didn't seem to notice.

They devised an experiment. It was mostly Frankie's idea. They assembled ten clear glass beakers on the counter and filled them with different levels of water. Frankie moistened a finger and ran it around the rim of one of the beakers.

His hand was trembling, but eventually he was able to elicit a clear, shining tone, like something Johnny had once heard a woman produce by drawing a fiddle bow across the edge of a carpenter's saw.

"It's a pure frequency. No overtones," said Frankie. "A simple frequency will travel farther and faster than a complex one. Especially if there's an attractor of the same wavelength. I'll show you what I mean."

He placed two of the beakers side by side, then he used a pipette to adjust the water levels until they were roughly equal. With his fingers he sung the glass and adjusted the water until the two pitches meshed in unison. Something strange happened then. The song of the beakers continued, and did not fade, and seemed like they would continue singing forever, until he pinched the beaker walls and stopped the vibration.

"There! You see! Mutual attraction. Frequencies passing between. Johnny! This girl. Lucy. Do you *love* her?"

The words were so uncharacteristic it was like somebody else was using Frankie's voice to speak. Frankie blushed and he swiveled on his crutch. He coughed, then cleared his throat.

"I need to look at everything," he said. "I need to consider everything that might send out frequencies. Human emotions could send out frequencies."

Johnny smiled. He could feel the answer in his heart. "Yes, I love her. She comes to me in dreams."

Frankie ignored this. He set about tuning the other beakers, the second set a whole tone above the first. His innate sense of pitch was surprisingly accurate. It wasn't long before he had two sets of five beakers, each tuned to the same pentatonic scale. He had Johnny carry one set to the window ledge across the room. Then he set his beakers to ringing, while Johnny turned his ears to his own.

Nothing happened. Set by set they strummed pairs of beakers simultaneously and waited for the decay. As soon as their fingers left the glass, the sound began to fade. Frankie situated his paddles of attraction behind the counter beakers, hoping that its unidentified magic might ignite the process. But it did not. He became irritated. He tried other things. He refilled all the beakers with fresh water. He put a drop of soap in each beaker. They moved the beakers around, away from the window, on the floor, on a shelf, in the washbasin. Nothing happened. No response. A sense of defeat crept in, and the shadows of evening pulled themselves like curtains across the wall.

Frankie's stomach grumbled. He scratched his stubbly chin. "I'm hungry," he said. "Enough of this. Let's go see what Burleyman's fixed up for supper."

◠

That night, full of fried catfish and steamed rocket greens, Bearclaw, Jocko, Ant and Johnny untuned their instruments. At first they seemed a little shy, even after the morning's rousing success with more traditional fare. But little by little they melted together, warmed by Jocko's thumping rhythms, and the deep-set smile on Johnny's face.

The music they made gradually deepened into mysterious channels of movement, attractions drawing them this way and that, patterned ripples on water, belltones struck from beakers, chimes ringing from falling ladles.

Chestnut slumbered in a basinet. Occasionally she stirred and sung a few notes. The only other people in the long hall were Frankie and the two scullery maids, sitting center table at a corn lamp. Frankie had brought another of his contraptions, his *dolmens*, to impress the girls. It was a sealed glass globe with colored liquids inside. Frankie could make the colors swirl in patterns by holding his hand over the globe. Tonight he was drinking heavily. There were three green bottles on the table; one lay on its side. The tabletop was spattered with purple puddles. Frankie's voice was loud and sloppy, but whatever he said, it made the girls laugh. Johnny caught a few of the words in between the music.

"Impossible to prove."

"There is no such thing as magic."

"I can unbutton your blouse without touching you."

Sometime past midnight the music modulated into a dark forest full of owls and hanging vines. Spores of mold were organizing themselves into a footed organism to crawl across the humus in search of light. Suddenly Ant lifted her bow and directed her attention outward.

"Wow!" she said. "Look at that!" All the music percolated into silence and everyone turned to the center of the room.

Frankie was still hunched over at the table, the corn lamp flickering. The scullery girls were gone but he continued to mumble as if they were there. From all the front windows, shafts of bone-white light were streaming across the tables and onto the walls, seeking out the corners, shifting in slow shadow play.

"The moon is up! We have to go and say hello!"

No questions were asked. They set down their instruments and moved quickly off the platform toward the door. Frankie raised his head as they passed. "What is it? Is the house on fire?"

Outside in the meadow a billowing quilt of snow drifted

under a sky of brilliant black, in which, directly overhead, the full moon reigned Queen Supreme. The houses, the trees, the silo, everything was frosted like a cake, or covered with a curtain of calcite, flowing, sparkling, softening every sharp edge into female forms, shoulders, breasts, rolling bellies.

Ant ran on ahead. Each footstep made a deep crunching sound. She squealed with delight, lifted drifts of snow into her arms, and flung them into the air. Jocko just raised his hands, lifted his head, and walked forward, slowly, drinking the sky. Bearclaw stood at the meadow's edge, his arms folded, smiling.

"Hello, moon!" cried Ant. "Johnny, come out and dance!" Johnny started into the snow. Ant ran toward him, grabbed both his hands, and spun him around like crack-the-whip. Her force was powerful. They flew apart and both fell backwards, laughing, into the soft drifts. When Jocko saw them fall, he fell backwards too, of his own accord.

Smoke rose from a fire circle near the open shelter. Bearclaw trudged over to it and dutifully poked and prodded until he had teased up a tongue of flame, which he quickly fed from the tinder pile. "Come over here and warm your bones!" he called.

The four of them gathered in a circle around the fire, rubbing their hands and stamping their feet. Bearclaw stoked the fire until he had a brilliant blaze, higher than their heads, throwing sparks up to the stars. Johnny looked at the sky.

"Do you know how many more stars there are than you can see? Frankie showed me in his spyglass."

Bearclaw chuckled. "Ha! Frankie Fulcrum and his famous spyglass! 'Fore you know it he'll be building us a wagon that we can fly in to the moon."

"Like a bird!" said Jocko. "Johnny, do you think birds fly to the moon?"

Ant slipped a hand around Johnny's arm. "Johnny you—you won't be leaving us any time soon will you?"

Johnny sighed. "I don't know. Not soon, I don't think. Maybe I'll stay here the winter. But there's someone out there I've got to find."

Ant pulled her hand away. "You mean *Lucy.*"

"How did you know about Lucy?"

"Everyone knows about Lucy. It's part of the story. The legend of Johnny Arcane."

Johnny felt a quiver in his stomach, as if one of the embers from the fire was turning there. *Who had he told about Lucy?* No one. Frankie, he had told Frankie. No, not just Frankie. There had been others. She had been with him constantly in his twenty seasons as a messenger. The attraction had never weakened. There had been times when the burden was so heavy; he had no choice but to get it off his heart. But there was no legend of Johnny Arcane. That was ridiculous! He wanted to say it out loud. He almost did say it out loud, but suddenly, there came a sound from far in the distance, deep in the northern hills. It was a melody, long slow, mournful, rising. At first it was solo, but then another voice joined, and another, and another. It wove the intervals in counterpart, harmonies strange, untuned.

Ant scurried over to Bearclaw and grabbed his arm. "It's the winter wolves!"

Bearclaw laid a hand on her shoulder. "Yep. That's what it be. The winter wolves."

Jocko's voice was trembling. "The winter wolves are good, though. They scare away the ghosts!"

For a while they stood and listened while the fire crackled a staccato percussion.

"We have to go back inside," said Ant. "They might wake Chestnut."

Back in the longhall Frankie was sound asleep and snoring, his head buried in his arm. Indeed, Chestnut was awake, but she was happy, singing and chuckling. The bigger concern was Frankie. "How are we going to get him home?" asked Ant. "We can't just leave him here."

"Certainly not!" laughed Bearclaw. "One one-legged man is no match for four strong musicians. Come on, old horn pig, wake up! We're dragging you back to your nice comfy bed."

But it only took three strong musicians to carry Frankie home. They wrapped him in a blanket. Johnny carried his crutches and supported his legless side, while Bearclaw and Jocko held his right leg and shoulder. Sometimes they lifted him clear off the snowy ground, like a sack of potatoes. "I can walk on my own!" he complained.

Ant followed, holding Chestnut's hand. Chestnut was wide-eyed with wonder. She wanted to pull away and run through the drifts, but her mother wouldn't let her. In the distance, the song of the winter wolves was receding, deeper and deeper into the hills.

Bearclaw and Ant's house stood directly next to Frankie's workshop-home. They dragged him up the steps and shoved open the door. Immediately inside, they heard the sound. Frankie snatched his crutches from Johnny's hand and hobbled to the center of the room. "Shhh!" He brought his finger to his lips. Everyone was silent.

It was a single, pure, pitch, ringing steadily, constantly, like something you might hear if ran your finger around the rim of a crystal wineglass. Frankie advanced to the counter and bent his ear to the beakers. He shook his head and pulled himself across the room to the window, where he began pinching the wall of each beaker with his thumb and forefinger. On the third beaker the music stopped.

"It was this one! Something was making it resonate!"

"Well, that...that's interesting," said Bearclaw, "but it's late, and we have to work tomorrow."

Frankie stumbled back across the room and began fiddling with the attractors. "No, no, don't go, stay with me. Johnny, stay with me. I've got to figure this one out."

"Really, Frankie, it is late. We're taking Johnny home with us. He needs to sleep. You can tell us how it turns out in the morning."

Frankie was beside himself, twisting the knobs, tapping on beakers with rods, rummaging through drawers. Jocko stepped up to him and spoke quietly. "It was the wolves, Frankie. The winter wolves."

ɔ

Back at Bearclaw's house, Ant had kindled up a cheery fire and Chestnut was coaxing soft melodies from a small vibraphone. It was just the four of them. Jocko had drifted back to his little room at the log house. Bearclaw produced a decanter of brandy and three stone mugs.

"Little nightcap for you, Johnny."

"No, no I don't drink anymore. It makes me do bad things."

"Ah, but tonight you will. Just tonight. We'll keep you from doing bad things. This is a momentous occasion. You've come back to us."

So Johnny accepted the brandy and they settled in, the fire shadows leaping off the bare wood walls, Chestnut's sleepy music, Ant's hands dancing with a skein of yarn and a pair of curved spokes, a ribbon of purple, streaked with green, rolling out from her fingers.

"I want to tell you how it was," Bearclaw began. "When you first came here so long ago. That one night. I was jealous of you. I was in love with Ant, but she didn't know it yet, and she was in love with you. I could see it in her eyes and hear it in her voice. It drove me wild. But then we made that crazy music and—well, I don't know, nothing else mattered, anymore. I felt like everything was going to be all right. And the next day, after you left, she came to me in tears. She threw her arms around me. She told me you loved another. I said, 'I love another, too. Can you guess who it is?' It took her a whole two summers to figure it out, though. We were married at the next Cornfest. Burleyman did the ceremony."

Chestnut climbed onto the chair and buried her head in her mother's lap. Ant did not stop knitting. The yarn tumbled down liked caresses onto the child's curls. Bearclaw got up and fed another log to the fire. On the windowpane a rime of frost was forming. Johnny felt himself falling under the spell of the sweetness of the drink. He scratched his beard and pondered the events of the day.

"I feel like I've come home," he said at last.

Bearclaw leaned back in his chair and sipped from his mug. Slowly he shook his head. "No sojourner feels that way for long. You be walking away soon enough. But stay awhile."

Ant stroked Chestnut's curly locks as the child turned in her lap. "There's more to the story, Johnny," she said. "To the legend of Johnny Arcane."

"There is no legend of Johnny Arcane."

"Oh, but there is. Ask the hoop girls. Ask Burleyman. Ask Frankie. There's never been more than two or three sojourners in the Known World at any one time. And there's never been one known to go beyond the four directions, not since Borderbinder."

Her words made the brandy turn sour in Johnny's stomach. He tried to direct the focus outward. "Frankie would, if he could."

"This is true," mused Bearclaw. "Things will change because of what Frankie does. For better or worse, I'm not sure. But Frankie knew you were coming. Like all of us did. He knew he would be part of your destiny."

"I have no destiny."

Ant sighed. "You know that's not true, but you don't know it very well. Why can't you see it? Why did it take you so long?"

Johnny shifted his weight nervously. "So long—for what? To return to you?"

'Not to us. To Lucy. You say you loved her. Five summers passed. You never went to find her. We heard the stories—all the girls you left behind. Sometimes I think you just like to leave us behind. That sweet sad freedom."

There was a trace of discomfort in Bearclaw's chuckle. "Be careful, now darling. We don't want to scare the boy." He looked up at Johnny. "Besides, we all know you're still in love with him. We can see it in your eyes."

CHAPTER NINE

WINTER IN KING CORN

So Johnny Arcane spent that winter in the town of King Corn, sleeping nights at Ant and Bearclaw's, spending most of the daylight hours with Frankie in his workshop and retiring in the evenings to the longhall for food and companionship with the townspeople.

Evenings in the longhall, the musicians gathered when they could. Sometimes Ant stayed home with Chestnut, and Bearclaw would sink into deep conversation with someone at a table, or join in a game of barn nails or flatstones. Jocko was a wanderer. He might not be seen for days, and then suddenly he was there, usually with the hoop girls, telling very short stories, once about an abandoned hornet's nest where tiny mice had moved in, once a fat tree in the forest with a door and a bed inside, once a footbridge over a pond which reflected a face other than your own. But his words were always few.

That winter, a craze of arm wrestling broke out among the men, and some of the women too. The reward for a pinning was usually a kiss from a scullery maid, but when two women wrestled, there was no reward. After a victory, the women contestants would embrace and laugh. Very few of them regarded a kiss from a man as any sort of prize.

All in all, the winter began, wearing a dress of quiet drowsiness, especially in the daylight hours when there was no one in the longhall, and very few people in the meadow or the dispensaries. Smoke curled from the chimneys of most houses, but the people inside were hidden, sleeping or daydreaming, or drinking, or making love. Who knows what they were doing, or if they even existed at all behind their snowdrifted doors?

But mornings and afternoons in the workshop, Frankie kept busy, and Johnny followed behind, picking up the crumbs of mystery that the man dropped as he went about his work. Frankie obsessed over understanding the attractions. "Burleyman wants me to harness them," he said, "to make our lives more comfortable. That doesn't interest me. It only keeps us here. I want to go outside of here, but without leaving. I want to arrive without traveling."

He was quite certain this had been done before, in a forgotten time, and he was always on the lookout for dolmens that might harbor this power. But every now and then he let down his guard and suggested that the power might reside in the attractions of human emotion.

"Do you have anything that belonged to her?" he asked one afternoon. "Did she ever give you anything?"

Johnny thought for a moment. "Yes, I do. In the box with the map. I've been meaning to show it to you." He fumbled through the parchments until he found the picture of the waterfall, still folded. He handed it to Frankie. Frankie's eyes grew bright and his hands trembled a little on the edges of the page. His mouth curled into a smile.

"It can be done," he said.

"Lucy said she thought it was painted by tiny people, no bigger than your finger, with very small brushes."

"No, of course not. There are no such people. Listen. Remember what you once told me—about the magic lantern in Jocko's room?"

"Yes." *The magic lantern.* That was what Frankie had called it when Johnny first described the projected people walking upside down on Jocko's wall.

Frankie set himself to hauling down vials of powders and pots of colored liquids from the shelves. In beakers he prepared potions of various hues and viscosities. With a brush he painted blotches on any flat surface he could find— plates, saucers, bits of vellum. He set these things in the pale light of the window ledge and placed objects on them, nails, bracelets, tufts of lichen, acorns.

"I don't know what these substances are," he said. "My scouts bring them. They find them growing on trees or crystalized in caves. Some of them are pollens. Some are minerals. Some of them are dolmens, hiding in glass jars in hidden cellars. I play with them to see what happens. I have learned a few things."

The next morning Frankie carefully removed the objects from the surfaces to see what he would find underneath. On some he found nothing, just the dried paint, maybe a little chipped or crumbly. But on others there was a perfect, darkened imprint of the object in all its detail, a fixed shadow.

"Shadows," he said. "That's how it's done. The waterfall in your picture. Somewhere it exists. Someone was able to capture its shadow, like the shadows you see on Jocko's wall through the magic lantern."

This work went on for several days. Frankie began to practice with color. He pressed dry green and autumn gold leaves on the surfaces, their membranes stretched so thin that light passed through them. He removed a pane of glass from one of his windows and flattened it against the artifacts. Some of the substances only left grey silhouettes, but after many trials and errors he discovered a potion that cast a perfect colored image, all the nuances of the leaf, the green veins standing out like maps of rivers, the yellow flecks of sunburn, the crackly brown of the edges.

"And now for the big experiment!" he announced one morning. It was a bright, cloudless day, the sunshine glinting blindingly off the snowdrifts in the meadow. Frankie grabbed a painted sheet of parchment and had Johnny walk him to the log house, where they strode through the longhall and he pounded on Jocko's door with his crutch. No answer. He thrust open the door. There was no one inside, but a perfect landscape of snowy billows was glimmering, cast by the magic lantern onto the wall above the shelves.

'Oh, that will never do!" he grumbled. "There's nothing there. We need an image! Johnny, go outside and stand by the wall until I can see your image."

So Johnny went outside and stood by the wall while Frankie called to him from inside. "To the right! To the left! A little higher! There! Now hold it! Hold that position!"

It took a long time, with Johnny standing still and straight as a tree, trying to contain his shivering, while the magic lantern carried his image into the warmth of Jocko's room. But when at last Frankie summoned him back inside he was startled by what he saw.

It was like a mirror hanging from the wall. Or perhaps it was more like a reflecting pool, for there were ripples here and there, distortions of frozen motion. But it was clearly a picture of Johnny's face, upside-down, framed by a background of drifted snow, and the curve of the rounded hill in the distance. Some of the details were sharply defined; each curl of his beard stood out in stark relief, but his eyes were blurred in shadow, a pale yellow halo around the outline of his fuzzy head. Frankie unpinned the parchment, turned it around, and they stared at it for a long time in silence.

"But it's so motionless," said Frankie at last. "If we can transmit a still image through the attractions, we should also be able transmit motion."

These words shook Johnny out of his chilled stupor. Enough of this one-legged man and his relentless obsessions!

"It doesn't matter!" he said out loud. His own voice surprised him. But he was cold, and tired, and lonely.

"What doesn't matter?" asked Frankie.

"It doesn't matter what you can build by harnessing the power of the attractions. What matters was that the waterfall was real, it existed somewhere in space and time, and it was Lucy who gave me the picture."

Lucy! In his mind alone he could conjure up a picture of her slender face; between his fingers he could fell the soft silkiness of her hair, and everywhere his skin tingled with the full force of her hard embrace. Lucy! She was out there beyond the border with the Blackcoats and the waterfalls and the falling scarecrows. She was in peril. She needed him to save her. Ant had said it herself. *Why did you wait so long?* How could he bear to stay in King Corn until the snow melted and the spring returned, and he could set out again on the open road?

Frankie was unfazed by this outbreak. Human temperament did not concern him in his quest for truth. He simply unpinned the picture, mounted his crutches, and started for the longhall.

The musicians gathered that night after supper. It had been weeks since they had played, and Bearclaw and Ant appeared with weary, careworn faces, having been up three nights nursing little Chestnut through a worrisome fever haunted by nightmares. As Jocko slapped out the rhythm, and the melodies poured from their instruments, the lines of trouble slowly smoothed from their eyes, and little smiles turned up the corners of their mouths.

Distracted, Johnny kept turning his face to the table where Frankie sat with the scullery maids. They had his picture spread out on the tabletop and they were leaning over it, laughing, tracing the details with their fingertips.

"Do me!" squealed one of the girls. "I want a picture!"

They helped Frankie up on his crutches and they pinned the picture to the wall by the scullery door. This disturbed Johnny most of all. He didn't want the whole town of King Corn looking at him, thinking about him, not as a fellow townsperson but as some sort of magical apparition, something that came from beyond their comprehension. He barely paid attention to the melodies, so great was the anxiety this stirred in his mind.

It turned out this anxiety was mostly unfounded, for in the days that followed the walls of the longhall filled with pictures. First there were the two scullery maids, and of course this got everyone's attention. For many days Frankie had to leave his research and hole up in Jocko's room, making pictures. He took it cheerfully, though. In the evenings he perfected his potions, and with each successive portrait the details grew finer, the colors richer. Eventually, Mayor Burleyman himself sat for a portrait, and had it framed and hung over the tall chair at the head of the longhall, where he presided over town meetings.

Jocko sat for a picture, but Bearclaw and Ant would have no part of it. One morning, however, little Chestnut, fully recovered from her fever, insisted that she join in the fun. With great patience, Frankie instructed her through the crack in Jocko's wall. They hung the picture next to Jocko's, up near the musicians stage, but it resembled nothing more than a blur of bright gold against a field of white, for of course the little girl could not hold still.

$$\complement$$

Midwinter. In the darkest hour of the coldest night of the season, two strangers appeared in the snowy meadow of King Corn. They pitched their tent at the far end of the clearing, by the grove of walnuts, now empty of leaves. The night might have passed peacefully if it weren't for the cows. In the predawn hours, an alarming sound arose from the meadow, a bellowing, groaning outcry, heavy with distress. The people in the houses awoke, stumbled out of bed and lit their corn lamps. "What is that racket?" They threw on robes and jackets and ventured out, carrying lanterns.

Mayor Burleyman reached the tent first, followed shortly by Bearclaw, Jocko, and Johnny Arcane. Ant stayed behind with Chestnut.

The strangers were cowboys, and they had brought with them two large but sickly beasts. The female lay on her side in the snow, her breath labored, her eyes glazing over. The skinny bull stood and snorted and pawed the ground, his bare ribcage heaving with each thrust of his hooves.

One of the cowboys, the heftier of the two, had his arm slung in a red bandana. "Dagnabbit, Polly Mae!" he cried, "You would pick this time to whelp! And not a blade of grass in sight. What is this world coming to anyways?"

The other cowboy, a scrawny man with a crooked jaw,

shook the larger cowboy by the shoulder. "Climber, turn around. Look behind you."

Climber turned and nearly fell over at the sight of most of the population of King Corn, approaching through the snow with lanterns.

"Well, crack my knuckles, Jack! This isn't supposed to be happening! She could have at least waited till morning. Everybody go back to bed!"

The townspeople drew closer and peered in, curiously, cautiously. Many of them had never seen a cow before, and to them, cowboys were the stuff of legends.

Burleyman stepped forward. "My name's Burleyman. This is the town of King Corn. I'm the mayor here. We don't want to go back to bed. We want to help."

Climber made a sour face. The other cowboy tugged at his arm. "They want to help."

"Oh shut up, Birdleg! It's not my fault this is happening." He turned to the gathering crowd. "I'm sorry. Everything's all turnsy-topsy. We were in the southlands, waiting for the winter, but the winter never came. The cows got confused. She's not supposed to calve until the springtime. And now look at me. Corn damn Blackcoats broke my arm. How'm I sposed to pull a calf out in this condition?"

Burleyman jumped down and touched the cow, stroked behind her ears, then ran his hands down her belly.

"Well, I've delivered puppies before. This couldn't be that much different. Help me now! I need hot water, rags, and some kind of clamp. And a cutting tool!"

People scurried across the meadow. At the longhouse someone rang the dinner bell. Children came out and started playing in the snow, rolling snowballs with mittened hands.

A bucket of warm water appeared, and a bundle of fabric scraps from the seamstery. Burleyman dampened a rag, fell to his knees and began to splay the cow's hind legs with his bare hands. The cow shuddered, then convulsed. One leg kicked out, and a heavy hoof struck Burleyman in the temple. He fell over backwards in the snow.

"Well, she *kicks* harder than a dog," said Birdleg.

The cow shuddered again, rolled herself over on her back, then somehow managed to pull herself up, standing on her spindly, shaky legs. The bull snorted and pawed. Both of them stared down at the man who lay bleeding in the snow between them. The cow nodded. The bull nodded. It was like they were trying to make a decision.

"I can help!" rang out a woman's voice.

It was Maggie Mender, the midwife and village herbalist, wearing the pale green smock of her profession. Johnny remembered her as the woman who tried to climb the silo. She rolled up her sleeves to reveal strong muscular arms. But first she went to Burleyman, who was sitting up rubbing his neck, dabbing his finger gingerly in the blood on his cheek.

"Well, you certainly have a thing about old wounds, don't you? She knocked you open right along the scar line. Myrtle, take the mayor back to the house and patch him up. You! Cowboy! What's the name of your bull?"

Climber stepped back. "We call him Ramrod, ma'am."

"Well, Ramrod oughta notta watch this. Might disturb him. Take him back to the longhall—tell Axel to give him something to eat. He'd probably like some greens."

"Yes, ma'am," said Climber, but he did not move.

"Go on! Git!"

All the way to the log house, leading Ramrod by a bit of

rope, Climber kept stopping, looking back, until eventually the two of them, man and bull, disappeared into the shadows.

Birdleg did not go with him. "The cow's name be Polly Mae," he told Maggie.

It was mostly women who stepped forward, holding up their lanterns so Maggie could do her work. The men stood back, looked at the ground, looked at their feet, looked at their hands, rubbed their hands together, stomped their feet. Johnny did not hold back, though. He worked himself up through the skirts and the sweaters until he found a bare rock at the side of the cow where he could sit quietly and watch the action. He did not have a lantern.

Several women helped Maggie lift Polly Mae and gently lower her back to her side in the snow.

"She does this on her own," said Maggie. "That was Burleyman's problem. You gotta win a girl's trust afore you go spreadin' her legs."

A tableau of women gathered around the cow, like a band of wood sprites, stroking her bulging belly, her heaving sides. Shortly, the birthing began, first the ooze of mucus, and then the hooves appeared.

"Here she comes!"

But soon there was a problem. The legs were turned wrong; the hooves were jamming in the gates. Polly Mae groaned.

"She's gonna need a little help. We be getting' slimy now." Maggie reached up, far inside, a film of pink trailing down her arms. The other women crowded around, blocking Johnny's view. Polly Mae bellowed and howled, but there was another sound as well. The women were singing, a tuneless song, vocal dips and sighs, comfort, encouragement. Suddenly there was a shriek, following by a whooshing sound, and a plume of steam rose from the snow. Johnny shoved his way through the women to see what was happening, Birdleg right behind him.

It looked like an enormous eel, or a lamprey, or just a coagulated glob of moist brown flesh, with a few sprigs of coarse fur tufting out. It looked lifeless and formless.

"What is it?" cried one woman. "It's dead, isn't it? Tell me it's dead."

"It's not dead. Don't touch it. Watch!"

They stepped back and inadvertently formed a perfect circle, Johnny and Birdleg the only men among them. It was as if their fixed attention woke the creature. A spasm of energy rippled through the flesh and out of formlessness, a body emerged. The head bolted up, a mouth appeared, opened, and took in a deep gasp of air. And then there were legs, kicking and thrashing, clumsy with purpose. A tiny cow-shaped being struggled to its feet, took one look at the sky, and toppled back over in the snow.

"It's so wet! Get the towels! We have to dry it!"

"No, no, that's the mama's job. Keep watching."

The little calf made several more attempts at finding its land legs until finally Polly Mae took notice. She clambered to her feet and proceeded to slam the little one back into the snow with a firm butt from her head. Then she covered it with her tongue, dutifully lapping up all the slime and the mucus, all the curds and clots of her own body. The calf arched its back, stood and fell, stood and fell, as it cut a stumbling course toward mama's big, full udders.

"Well, cowboy, looks like you got another bull to worry about," said Maggie. She grabbed one of the damp rags to wipe her arms, and turned to the circle of women. "I think that may be the weirdest thing *I've* ever done."

Birdleg followed Bearclaw and Johnny back to the log house, with Jocko trailing behind. A light dusting of snow was beginning to fall. They found Ramrod tethered to a post, munching on a slop of winter kale, and Burleyman and Climber inside, lolling at a table in the longhall, drunk on corn whiskey. Burleyman's head was bandaged up like a beehive. He rolled it from side to side and flashed a big, sloppy grin.

"Johnny, my boy, I never knew you could make an inebriant outta the very substance after which this town was named. These cowboys know some tricks."

"Ha!" Bearclaw laughed. "This behavior is not befitting a man in your position. Lemme taste that stuff."

Climbed cocked his head at Birdleg. "What'd she drop this time?"

"Another bull. Scrawny lookin' thing."

"Damn!" Climber slammed the palm of his good arm on the table, making the mugs jump. "Well, you better go bring 'em in. The mayor here says he's got some room in the goat shed."

"Climber, I'm not going back out. It's cold. Besides, there's *women* out there." He said this as if he were talking about wolves or horn pigs.

"Well, look at me. I'm in no shape. Somebody's gotta take care of the cows."

"I'll go," said Jocko. Birdleg jumped back in surprise. Jocko had slipped behind them and no one had really noticed he was there.

Bearclaw took a swig of the corn whiskey and grimaced. "Sounds like this be a job for the musicians then. Johnny, you come with us. Let's go see what these cows are all about."

Outside the snow was beginning to fall in flakes, the meadow white and empty, no humans or cows in sight, but back against the trees a warm light glowed from the goat shed where people stood slapping their shoulders and puffing cold clouds of breath.

The three musicians trudged through the deep drifts and stomped the snow off their shoes when they reached the open door. The five remaining goats of King Corn huddled in the shadowed corners of the shed, unsure what to make of these new guests. Polly Mae lay sleeping on her side in a bed of hay, but the little one was standing straight and proud, not a wobble to his knees, staring up into the rafters and the cobwebs with wonder, as if he were beholding the gates of paradise.

There were two women there. One was going over the calf with a soft bristle brush while the other tied little colored ribbons into the longer tufts on his bony back. Johnny recognized these women. They were Frankie's two favorite scullery maids, but tonight they were utterly transformed. Their faces glistened in the corn lamps; their movements conveyed a sense of sureness and calm, as if they had been studying for this moment all their lives. They were both singing little wordless songs, woven from the movements of their fingers.

"Johnny, do you think the cowboys will let us name him? We have a name for him."

"Oh, so you do. And what would that be?"

"We want to name him Johnny, after you."

Johnny didn't answer. He really didn't know what to say. Bearclaw stepped into the light of the shed and found himself a seat on a bale of hay by the door. Not knowing what else to do, Johnny joined him, but Jocko didn't sit. He went straight to the little calf, took its head between both his hands, scratched behind the ears and stared into the face. Something passed between them, Jocko and the calf, something almost visible, a kind of mist, or a flicker from a candle. The girls continued singing, so softly you could hear the snowflakes settling on the roof. This went on for a long time until finally Bearclaw spoke.

"Well," he said, "I think that's a fine name for a cow."

Ɔ

Three days later Polly Mae died. The afterbirth got stuck up inside her and it festered there and poisoned her. The scullery maids, whose names were Misha and Marta, were stricken with grief.

"How will we even bury her?" wailed Marta. "There's no earth anywhere, only snow."

"Bury her?" replied Climber. "We're not going to bury her. We're going to *eat* her."

Marta shrieked in horror. Maggie Mender had to lead her out of the shed or she would have fallen onto the poor cow's carcass.

"It's just the way of things, Marta," said Maggie. "We eat goats. We eat pigs."

But nobody in King Corn had ever eaten a cow. There was much talk among the townspeople that day. Some said they were going to go into their houses and not come out until it was all over. Birdleg coaxed Misha and Marta into the longhouse and Climber gathered four strong men to lift Polly Mae out of the goat shed and carry her into Tom Cleaver's butcher shop. Johnny followed them there.

Tom was curious. He had them spread the cow out on the big marble cutting slab, and he walked around her several times, holding a hacksaw, occasionally stopping to place the blade over this crease or that ripple of the flesh, wondering if this was the place to enter. The cow was too big for the slab. Her legs and head dangled over the sides.

"She's not built like a pig," he said.

"All the meat's gonna be on the haunches," Climber informed him. You gotta go in through the flank lines."

When the saw broke through the uterine lining a great stink rose up—the stench of the putrid afterbirth. Several of the men had to leave the room. But Tom just kept on cutting, a man wholly devoted to his craft.

It wasn't enough meat to feed the whole town of King Corn. The cooks in the scullery filled a cauldron of water and threw in all the root vegetables and winter greens they could find. They cleaned up Polly Mae's bones, and then boiled them for hours so the marrow could permeate the broth. Then they filleted the sinewy muscle from the rump and the round, and chunked up the lean steaks from the ribs, shanks and loins into palm sized cubes, and everything was thrown into the pot, except for the kidneys, which had shriveled into something that resembled two dried apples.

The stew simmered in the cauldron all day, and by late afternoon a strange but alluring aroma was emanating from the log house. People gathered at the door and sniffed. A few came in, but there was still a lot of resistance. When the dinner bell rang, the doors of many houses remained closed, the smoke still rising from the chimneys.

Mayor Burleyman stood up before the gathering of courageous diners and made a speech. He praised the cowboys for providing the town with a unique experience, and he praised the townspeople for their hospitality, and the assistance they had given the cowboys in this, their hour of need.

"New ways are coming to King Corn," he said. "This is only the beginning. The world as we know it has been constant for as long as we can remember. Now it is changing. The borders are breaking down. We should not be afraid. We can work together and make new things happen. By the time summer comes there will be running water in every home and dispensary, thanks to our friend Frankie Fulcrum. This is not the future of legends and prophecies. In that future we were helpless, subject to forces we did not understand and could not control. This future is something we can take in our hands and mold as we wish. This future is ours! We can harvest knowledge and we can partake in its fruit. This is only the beginning!"

A few of the courageous diners whistled, a few stomped their feet. A small chorus in the back of the room shouted "Burleyman!" seven times, the last two disintegrating into something that sounded more like *burley whirly* or *whirly burl*. Obviously, these people did not really get what their mayor was trying to tell them. There was only one common question: *what is this stew going to taste like?*

⊃

Later that evening the musicians gathered on the platform. It was the first time they had played since the cowboys came. Even little Chestnut joined in, banging her tambourine and croaking her joyful singsong. They had all tasted the meat and decided it was good, and that there should be a song written about it. Ant fiddled through a potpourri of familiar dance tunes, stealing a phrase from this one, a cadence from that, until she had patched together a passable little stovepipe, with a key change in the B section.

Bearclaw worked up some chords. "What shall we call it?" he asked.

"Cow in the Kettle!" cried Ant. And the music began.

Johnny's eyes frequented the happy crowd—the *courageous diners*—as the music poured forth. There was a new kind of energy he hadn't felt before. He felt it himself, in his own blood. Mayor Burleyman moved among the crowd, shaking hands, holding court to brief conversations, then moving on to the next, purpose-driven, deliberate. Climber and Birdleg, on their feet in front of the platform, stomped and swayed. A little drunk, they had set aside their corn whiskey and moved on to King Corn's own barley beer, brewed just months ago in Tiller Hogpen's oaken barrels.

But there were those who were conspicuous in their absence. Misha and Marta in the goat shed, tended little Johnny-the-Calf, knitting him scarves and booties, stroking and brushing him, tying ribbons in his tail, singing him songs, telling him stories. Frankie Fulcrum holed up in his workshop, mixing chemicals, brooding over the loss of his two favorite scullery maids. And a good half of the townspeople chose to dine at home on the food from their larders, or what they could glean from the dispensary, afraid of this new meat and what it might do to them, or simply resisting it and all that it symbolized, its intrusion into the predictability of their daily lives.

Later, Jocko sat talking and drinking beer with the cowboys in a dimly lit corner of the longhall. Johnny was curious about this, for it was rare for Jocko to sit still for anything long enough to resemble a conversation. So he sat down with them and listened in.

"Climber, how many cows do think there are in the world?"

"Do you mean the *world*, or the *Known* World? There's a difference, you know."

"That's not necessarily true, Climber," Birdleg chirped in. "The Known World may be all there is."

"Oh, you shut up, Birdleg. You're changing the subject. The boy just wants to know how many cows there are in the world."

"In the Known World," said Jocko. "How many cows have you seen?'

Climber scratched his beard. "Well, once we drove seven cows cross the Ricketyback Bridge. Think that's the most we ever seen in one place."

"Do people always eat the cows?"

"Well, people don't generally eat cows. They eat the bulls and the steers. The cows is for the milk. We just ate Polly Mae because we had to, on account of she was dead."

"What do you see when you're out moving cows around? Do you see mountains?"

"Oh, we stay on the grasslands, mostly. That's the point, so the cows can graze. But sometimes we seen mountains in the distance."

"We saw horses one time," said Birdleg.

"You saw horses, or so you say. I don't think they were horses. I think they were horn pigs. Do you even know what a horse looks like?"

Birdleg forwarded the question. "Do you know what a horse looks like, Jocko?"

"I got a picture of a horse in my room. A mummer at the Cornfest drew it. I made a little horse by looking at the picture."

"What, you made a *horse*?"

"A little horse. I made him out of mud, and dried him in the sun. I like to make little things."

Climber made a sniggering noise through his nose. "Oh

yeah? Well, why don't you just make yourself a little girl sometime, and then drop her down your pants?"

Johnny winced. Jocko was a sensitive boy, especially about his dolls. They were almost a ritual to him, and Johnny feared that he would be offended by this remark. But no. Jocko just laughed. He laughed and laughed.

"Oh yeah?" he said, when he was finally able to catch his breath. "Well, why don't you just make yourself a little crescent moon smoke salamander then drop him in your feedbag?"

Climber scrunched up his face. "Huh?" But Birdleg got it, or at least he got something. Maybe he was just laughing at Climber's perplexity. His laughter started out like a rhythmic wheeze but soon it caught his vocal chords and throated into a full-scale cackle, with subtle notes of giggle and guffaw. Jocko laughed all the more, and it wasn't long before Johnny was laughing too, although he wasn't quite sure what he was laughing at.

"A crescent moon smoke salamander?" howled Birdleg. "Drop it in your feed bag!"

They laughed and laughed into the night, the three of them. Climber never laughed. He just sipped his beer, then folded his good arm across his bad arm and steeled his face, and after a while you could tell his mind had drifted onto other things, and soon he closed his eyes and fell asleep.

CHAPTER TEN

DIVISION

he cowboys left at the next full moon. Winter was giving in to the first probing thrust of spring. Afternoons, beneath the snowpack, a soft voice gurgled, as pale sunlight penetrated the snow and the winter-bound stores of water, free at last, percolated down to seek their hidden courses in the earth. Up sprang the crocuses and the snowbells, first in the deep shadows of the forest, like shy children, then boldly around the rim of the white meadow, laughing at the grey sky with bright colors.

Only a few people saw Climber and Birdleg go. It was early morning. They took the road south around the grassy hill, Ramrod following obediently without a tether. They left little Johnny-the-Calf with Misha and Marta, promising to return one day with some cows for his company.

The next day a squall of warm rain blew in from the east, the wind thrashing the snow from the branches of trees and the water pummeling it on the ground into rivulets that tumbled out of the hills and fanned across the meadow. Soon a lake of muddy slush overtook the meadow, and dirty water scoured the rooftops and gushed out of drainpipes. The townspeople came out in high boots and rain jackets, their collars turned to the wind. They were meeting in the longhall to plan the annual Springfest. No proclamation needed to be issued. It was traditional to do this on the day of the first rain.

There had been no more beef eating since the night *The Cow and the Kettle* was first composed. The Abstainers, as they had come to call themselves, gradually came to realize that Polly Mae had been fully consumed and no one was intending to eat Johnny-the-Calf. Little by little they filtered back to the longhall in the evenings, for meals of goat and cabbage, and games of barn nails, and the dancing of skippers and stovepipes.

Things returned to normal, but there was an underlying sense of tension. It rippled through remarks in conversations, in seating arrangements at suppertime, and in the fact that the Abstainers had singled themselves out by giving themselves a name—the *Abstainers*—a club that you either belonged to or you didn't. The choice was yours.

In the days before the cowboys left, Jocko took to hanging out with Climber and Birdleg most of the time. Daytimes he followed the cowboys around while they did their chores, which were few, mostly making sure Ramrod had something to eat and checking in on little Johnny-the-Calf, who thrived under the doting care of Misha and Marta. Evenings they drank beer and Jocko plied them with questions about cowboy life.

Where do cows come from? Are there wild cows? Are there special songs that cowboys sing? Are there special stories and legends about cowboys? He liked to bait Climber with odd little remarks like the one about the crescent moon smoke salamander. Once he said, *I can understand why dogs sometimes think they are squirrels.*

Climber just grunted and shook his head. The only things

he understood were things that made sense, things he could eat or things he could fasten together. He couldn't get Jocko's method of drawing meaning out of rhymes and rhythms.

But Climber was good for one thing. He knew the cowboy stories, and he could sing the cowboy songs. He told Jocko the most famous tale about a gunfight that took place in the O and K corral between Early Wyman and the Clancy Brothers. And then there was the great Billy Buffalo who used to fight some people he called *Indians* until he learned he could put them to work in a traveling mummer show called the Great Wild West. And he sang all the cowboy songs he knew, *The Mumbling Mumbleweeds, O My Darling Calmerine, The Old Painted Rider, Bury My Hat on the Lone Prairie.* Jocko memorized the melodies and taught them to the band, and they played them in the evenings, much to the cowboys' delight.

There was a deeper side to Jocko's relationship with the cowboys as well. Johnny saw it, even if no one else did. He heard it in the tone of certain things Jocko said. It was an upturn in pitch, a question hiding within the question. And once when the band met in Jocko's room to learn one of the cowboy songs, he noticed two new dolls on the shelf above the bed, a little Climber and a little Birdleg, fashioned of cornhusks, leading a carved wooden replica of Ramrod.

With the signs of spring, Johnny began to realize more things. He realized how invisible he had become in the cold winter days and nights he had spent in King Corn. He had been an observer, following the lives of the townspeople. Immersed in their stories and he had almost forgotten his own. Now with the crocuses and the snowmelt and the chorus of frogs waking in the evenings, his own purpose awoke in him. He had taken off the armband when he first arrived. The blood of his father stirred in his veins. It was time. He would find Lucy and save her from her peril. The thought of travel called him like a fragrance from the distant point where the roadsides converged. He knew which road he would take— the north road out of King Corn, into the mountains and across the northern border, into the unknown.

☽

The meeting went badly from the start. Perhaps it was the particular messiness of the squall that ushered in that spring. Like bears aroused early from their peaceful hibernation, the townspeople gathered, damp and grumpy in the longhall, standing bleary-eyed in line for their bacon and soggy pancakes, grunting greetings with folded arms, while the mayor moved among them, shaking hands and speaking welcome in a voice that scarcely concealed a sense of worry and mistrust.

Plates in hand, the townspeople settled at the tables in an alarmingly ordered pattern. Those who sat on the left-hand side, away from the musician's platform, were mostly Abstainers. Some had even pinned to their uniforms the small yellow ribbon, which had become the Abstainer's insignia. The easternmost tables of the longhall looked like a meadow dotted with early wildflowers. None who sat at the middle table wore the ribbon. These were the undecided. Some had tasted the meat, others had not, but most of those who had tasted it said they did not care for it, or they were unsure of its nutritional value.

Johnny sat in the back with Jocko, Bearclaw and Ant, little Chestnut on Ant's lap, tearing pancakes into the shapes of wild animals. All the musicians had tasted the meat, and even written a song about it, so technically they were on the side of the Non-Abstainers. However, none of them wanted to be allied with either side in the conflict.

"Musicians should always rise above," argued Bearclaw. "Music is the language of reconciliation."

"Music is the language of love." countered Ant.

"Well, I wouldn't take it quite that far." Bearclaw replied.

Burleyman did not sit at his throne. As tradition prescribed, he walked among the tables, carrying a very old scroll, which delineated the components of the annual Springfest.

"Turner, you be fashioning the banner pole?"

"Yes, sir," said a tall man in woodworker's plaid. "It's the summer of the birch. I found her in the north woods, tall and straight she is."

"And have they chosen the banner?"

"Well, there's two in the running. We might take them both, but there's still the issue of which goes on top."

"Tell me more."

"Well, Maggie Mender made one what shows the winter wolves howling on the ridgetop. A lovely thing, but most of us favor the one made by our own fiddler, Antellermarine. She calls it 'The Return of Johnny Arcane.'"

Johnny shook Ant's shoulder. "What's he talking about? What banner?"

"Oh, it's just a silly thing," said Ant. "Part of the Springfest. Every fest they raise a banner pole. Three trees: alder, birch and ash. They rotate them. Then they have a contest. People are supposed to submit banners depicting the most important event of the winter."

Bearclaw chuckled. "Don't let her fool you. She's been working on this every night this past moon. She won't admit that she's proud of what she made. She's still in love with you, Johnny."

Ant blushed. "Oh, you be quiet. That's not it. It *was* the most important event of the winter. And nobody else made a banner about it."

"See what I mean? She's still in love with you."

The discussion turned to food. Pig meat was never eaten at Springfest. The traditional meal was turkey, and this summer many fine toms and hens had been rooted out of the north woods by Sparky Flaxman and his band of metal bangers. They were fattened in the turkey barn by every scrap of food left from the meals in the longhall, and now they were plump as full moons. The scullery maids were already at work on their famous table-long squash cake. And of course there would be honey mead for the grown-ups and apple cider for the children.

For a while it seemed like the subject of cows wasn't going to come up, and a cautious but pleasant camaraderie was spreading among the townspeople at the thought of familiar cuisine. After all, there were no cows to eat in King Corn. There was nothing to discuss.

But then it happened. From the back of the room, while Minnie Bloom was describing the delicate art of sugar-lacing, a voice arose, a man's voice, surprising everyone in its abruptness.

"Well, I made a banner. But nobody wanted to look at it." Minnie stopped talking. All heads turned.

It was Danny Block the sawyer, sitting slouched on his spine, his hands folded over his paunchy belly. "You wanna know what it was called?"

There was a rustle of muffled voices moving from right to left. Then a man spoke out of the cluster of Abstainers.

"We seen your banner, Danny. We just didn't like it."

"It was a good banner, Beetroot. You just didn't like what it was called."

Another roll of voices, this time with a few audible syllables. Beetroot spoke again. "I guess you're right about that, Danny. The banner was well made. But we are not of one mind here on the subject of cow meat. Our banners need to be about something we all believe in."

Now the chorus of voices became more agitated, all from the side of the Abstainers. On the other side the people fidgeted, silent anxiety written on their faces. A woman from the Abstainers stood. "Yeah," she said, "It was hard enough for us to agree on the Return of Johnny Arcane."

Hearing his name, Johnny felt a cold stone drop in the pit of his stomach. Now the tremor was rising on the other side of the room. Several people stood.

"Wait a minute, Foxglove," said a man. "Johnny Arcane did return. Everybody knows that. There's no argument."

"Well, a lot of people returned. Paleface returned from Archer's Bale. Doggy Barker came back from Sputum with a whole new wife and five new children. Nobody made a banner outta that. What's so special about Johnny Arcane?"

Bearclaw glanced down at the discomfort on Johnny's face. He sighed. "Guess I'd better intervene." He jumped up on the platform where everybody could see him. Indeed, he did have the demeanor of a bear as he hunched above the crowd, his hefty, hairy arms poised at his sides, relaxed, but ready to grasp anything that came his way.

"People of King Corn! This bickering is not befitting!" Voices rose to silence him but his was louder and commanded attention. "No! Listen to me! Here me out. I have something to say."

In the momentary silence that followed, Ant, sitting next to Johnny, slipped her hand into his and held it there, firmly, intentionally. Johnny felt equally comforted and confused. It seemed like Bearclaw wasn't doing much better. He stared across the sea of faces with a blank expression, as if words would fail him if he tried to speak. Someone in the back began to mumble. Bearclaw could wait no longer. His words tumbled forth.

"Johnny Arcane is our friend," he began. "He came to us at Cornfest five summers ago. He climbed the silo and he brought down the honey. No one had done this for seven fests. Some of us saw this as a sign. There's hunger, always. There was hunger then and there's hunger now. Sometimes the hunger's for food, sometimes it's for something else. But here's the deal. Johnny Arcane brought us something we were hungry for. It wasn't something to eat. It was a new kind of music. And he showed us how to climb the silo."

A small group of children started banging their plates and chanting, "He climbed the sunbeams and he held onto the birds!" Their parents quickly shushed them.

"Well, he did," Bearclaw continued. "Every Cornfest since then, someone's been able to do it. Johnny Arcane's a good friend. He brought us some good things, and he came back to us this winter. And I...I think that's reason enough to hoist a banner to him."

A general ruckus rose from all sides, but it subsided when a man's voice rang out from the Non-Abstainers. "With all due respect, Bearclaw, someone else came to King Corn this winter, besides just Johnny Arcane. And they brought us something we could really eat."

Bearclaw retorted before the crowd could get out of control. "I have no quarrel with you, Tiller. I ate the meat.

It was good. Just because there's differences doesn't mean there's quarrels."

"Here! Here!" someone shouted. Several heads nodded. From the Non-Abstainers a man spoke in an aggressive voice. "We don't want quarrels!" Then from the Abstainers, a woman said, "It's not just the cow meat, Bearclaw. There's other things. We don't want the water. The water's dangerous. It could bring poison to every home in this town."

Some people standing near this woman distanced themselves from her. "No, we *want* the water, don't we? The water's good!" Others stomped their feet and started chanting, "We don't want the water! We don't want the water!"

Soon there was generalized chaos among the Abstainers, some people standing up, others sitting down, some walking away.

"Quiet! Be quiet!" came a voice, louder than any human should have. People turned their heads. Mayor Burleyman was standing on his throne, holding a large, tapered metal funnel, usually used for sorting grain. "Everybody sit down and shut up! It's not about the water and it's not about the cows. This is about Springfest! There will be no running water and there will be no cows at Springfest. And I hereby decree, there will only be one banner on the banner pole. It will be the Winter Wolves Howling on the Ridgetop by Maggie Mender. We must get along and we must have a Springfest. Anybody doesn't like this they can leave now."

The mayor looked like a wild man standing on his throne with the bandage still on the side of his face where the cow kicked him. He looked like he had been pulling out his hair. It stuck out like spider's legs on all sides of his head. But nobody left, at least not then. Some people mumbled, some people grumbled. There were words of aggravation and words of reconciliation. One by one, everyone sat.

Burleyman himself seemed surprised. Almost sheepish, he stepped down, picked up the old scroll and walked into the crowd. With the scroll unrolled, he approached a group of women at the central table.

"Foxglove, Celandine. How are you doing on the costumes for the petal dance?"

Only the musicians saw the two scullery maids leaving by the service door. Misha had one arm around Marta, who was weeping.

☽

Midafternoon. Tiller Hogpen brought out the beer. It was an oatmeal stout that had just ripened and he said this was as good a time as any to try it. The meeting had dragged on all day. By his proclamation of the Winter Wolves as the only banner, the mayor had inaugurated a tenuous truce. The Abstainers and the Non-Abstainers mingled, but an air of tension remained, forcing every detail of the Springfest through a monotonous funnel of deliberation. *Will the eggs be painted or dyed? Who will spread the cornmeal circle around the silo? What if the full moon is not visible on the eve? Will the banner pole be raised at dawn or dusk? Will the turkey slaughter be public or private?*

Johnny sat at a table playing barn nails with Jocko, Bearclaw and Burleyman. He was not drinking. Jocko had his hand around a single stein of oatmeal stout. Bearclaw had two empties in front of him. The mayor had five, and he was working on a sixth.

"There's too many rules to everything," he said.

"Even to this game?" asked Bearclaw. "Because of the rule of seven, I can take your backstack and add it to my pile." He cupped five nails in his palm and slid them across the table.

"There's too many rules to this festival, for one thing. This is supposed to be about having a good time, welcoming the seasons. People are just superstitious. They think if we don't get every little thing right, it will all go badly. Puttin' cornmeal around the silo. That's the stupidest."

It occurred to Johnny that *stupidest* was a word the mayor would only use if he'd been drinking. "Why do they put cornmeal around the silo?" he asked.

Burleyman didn't answer. Bearclaw tossed three nails onto the grab pile. "The mayor doesn't like to talk about the silo."

"You shut up, old man. You never even tried to climb the silo."

"Nope. And I never will. It's your turn, Johnny. You got a square one there. Don't forget the rule about the square ones."

Burleyman drank some more beer. "We should have more of everything in this town."

"Except rules, of course," interjected Bearclaw.

"We could have more cows. We could raise cows, just like we be raisin' turkeys now. What do they mean, the water's going to bring poison? There's no such thing as poison. People could eat rocks if they wanted to, and it wouldn't hurt 'em. Wouldn't taste good, though."

"Humor the mayor, Johnny. You ever eat anything that was poison?"

"Well, yes, I have. I drank some bad water once, up in the mountains. It made me so sick I thought I was going to die."

"Well, did you die?" asked Burelyman.

"No, I didn't. I just shit and puked for a couple of days, and then I got better."

"Well then, it wasn't poison. It's only poison if it kills you. We're gonna have running water in this town, and we're gonna have cows. And we're gonna have something else. I been talking to Frankie Fulcrum about it. But it's a secret. You wanna know what it is?"

"It's a secret, Burleyman. Don't you be telling Frankie's secrets."

Burleyman was quiet for a while, and they played several rounds. It looked for a moment like he was going to fall asleep. He listed to one side, then he sat up abruptly.

"I can climb the silo if I wanted to. You wanna see me?"

"Just play the game, your honor."

"Don't you be honoring me, Bearclaw. Honor! Honor! It means nothing."

Bearclaw looked at Johnny and shrugged. Jocko spoke in his quiet voice. "He's going to embarrass himself. We should do something."

But it was too late. The mayor stood suddenly, scattering the game pieces across the table. "There's going to be cows in King Corn!" he proclaimed. "And there's going to be water!" Some people at the nearby tables laughed, and a few clapped.

"Sit down, Burley. Don't make a spectacle of yourself."

"I'll make a spectacle out of *you*, Bearclaw. I'll wrestle your arm to the table top."

"All right then, sit down, sit down. Let's wrestle."

Heads turned. Voices whispered, then spoke. "The mayor's going to wrestle Bearclaw!" People gathered around. Burleyman collapsed to his seat, then slammed his elbow down so hard on the table that there was no way it couldn't have hurt. He winced, then he snarled.

"Your corn is shucked, Bearclaw."

Bearclaw grinned. "Your corn is meal, your honor."

And without a bang or a whistle, the match began. The two men, equal of bulk and beard, bore into each other with seething and grunting. Around them the cheers and chanting swelled. "Pulverize him, Bearclaw! Flatten his pancakes!" Nobody was cheering for the mayor. Johnny saw Ant, pushing her way through the crowd, carrying Chestnut. "Bearclaw, stop this! Don't be a fool!"

Bearclaw made an expression with his cheekbones that looked like a shrug. Then he clamped his jaw and pressed harder into his opponent's wrist.

The two men were well matched, and the mayor might have won had he not been drunk. Several times he had Bearclaw nearly pinned, but then he got sloppy and the big man threw him off. Jocko edged in and lowered his head to table level, so he could look up into Bearclaw's face.

"Let it go," he said, almost in a whisper. "Just let him win."

Bearclaw flashed him a look of equal parts ice and fire. Then he made one massive grunt and threw his entire weight into the poor mayor's arm. There was a popping sound. Bearclaw's arm bent in a way no arm should go. His wrist went limp and flopped onto the table and he cried out in pain and tumbled to the floor.

The crowd went wild, hooting and shouting. They tried to raise Bearclaw up into a victory stance but he pushed them away and gaped in horror at what he had done to the man lying on the floor. He squatted down but the mayor leapt to his feet, his arm dangling like a wet rag.

"Don't touch me, Bearclaw! You haven't hurt me. I

can climb the silo!" He staggered to one side, then righted himself. "Watch me!" Then he lunged for the door. People jumped out of his way as if fleeing a charging horn pig; he knocked a few over anyway. Some tried to restrain him, but he pushed through them. Reaching the door he shoved it open with his shoulder and lumbered out into the cold, damp air.

Bearclaw looked at Johnny. "He's going to do it, isn't he?"

"He is," Johnny replied. "We have to stop him."

Outside the rain was slaunching down in earnest, the last muddy drifts of snow surrendering to the rivulets and into the meadow. Burleyman was limping now, and twice he stumbled, pulling himself up out of the mud with his left arm only, his right hand dangling helplessly. Bearclaw ran after him, calling his name, followed by Johnny, Jocko, Ant, and a few others–Maggie Mender, the scullery maids, Tiller Hogpen. But most of the townspeople stayed inside, crowding the doorframe to witness the spectacle.

The mayor reached the silo and grabbed the first hold with his left hand. "You can't stop me, Bearclaw!" he cried, and he was right. By the time Bearclaw arrived, the man had already ascended three notches, his ankles out of reach from the ground. Bearclaw turned, with a helpless look on his face. "I can't climb it," he said. "You have to go after him, Johnny."

A blast of wind threw a handful of rain, scattering like pebbles against the silo's iron wall. Johnny surveyed the ascent. The mayor was trying to climb the segment with conduits and chutes, the same place he had failed in his first attempt, five summers ago. It wouldn't work, even sober with two good hands on a clear sunny day. But there was a thin lip of ledge near the top, where the segments had been welded. Johnny knew only one way to get there.

Burleyman was no longer moving. His feet were jammed in a hatch cleat. He had reached a point where there was nothing to hold, only the curved, round body of the dome itself, and to this he clung, like a child to its mother.

Johnny circled the silo until he found the footholds that led to the sunbeams. The paint was chipped and faded but he could see the birds protruding above. Up he shimmied, while another blast of wind threw rain in his face. When he grabbed the first bird it snapped off in his hands and fell to the ground. No time for fear now! He grasped the next with caution, but it was stable. Bird by bird he pulled himself up until he reached the ledge. There were no handholds from that point on. He had to inch his way with his arms pressed to the wall, until he was directly above the mayor.

"Burleyman!" he called.

Burleyman craned his neck and looked up. "Corn *damn* you, Johnny Arcane! How'd you get up there?"

"I climbed the sunbeams and I held onto the birds. What are you going to do now, Burleyman? Are you going to come up or are you going to go down?"

Burleyman started to cry. "I'm not going up or down, Johnny. I'm going to stay here. Until I die."

Across the meadow, approaching from the log house, Johnny saw a white circle, moving. The hoop girls, bringing the hoop. They stumbled in the puddles, picked themselves up, stumbled again. The hoop listed from side to side as they pulled against each other, shouting, "This way!" "No, this way!" Eventually they reached the foot of the tower and raised the canvass high.

"You can let go now, Burleyman. You don't have to die. The hoop girls will catch you."

Burleyman didn't budge. He pressed his body into the wall like he wanted to pass through it.

A thought crossed Johnny's mind. It made him smile, just to think it.

"There will be running water in King Corn!" he proclaimed.

The mayor looked up. A squall passed over his face; then he suddenly relaxed. His arms opened like wings, and his knees buckled. Just before he fell he let out a holler. "And there will be cows!"

Johnny watched his trajectory until he struck the canvass, bounced three times, and was lowered gently to the ground. Then he felt his own knees buckle, his head begin to spin.

"Hoop girls! Hoop girls!' he called. "I think you might need to catch me too..."

☽

The mayor convalesced at Maggie Mender's. That night she wrapped his broken wrist in plaster and gauze, while he sniffled and wept, and mumbled things like "You can't teach a bird how to fly unless you give it wings," and "It's not poison if it doesn't kill you." When at last his head began to droop and his nose to rattle, she rolled him over into her big four-poster bed and climbed in next to him, which was something she had always wanted to do.

Two days later he woke with a ravenous appetite. She fixed him a tall stack of pancakes, which he devoured in three bites. Then he stood up, knocking over the chair, and said, "I've got to get back to the longhouse. We have a Springfest to plan.

CHAPTER ELEVEN

THE PRINCIPLES OF ELECTRICITY

s it turned out, neither Jocko, nor Johnny Arcane attended the Springfest, and shortly after, Johnny left the town of King Corn. This is how it happened.

Johnny showed up one morning at Frankie Fulcrum's workshop. Frankie had the look of one who had been up all night. In a porcelain crucible under the fume hood, something was burning with a flashing purple flame.

"I have a quest for you, Johnny. This is important. One of my scouts stopped by yesterday. You know her—old Darcy Dinkum, the crazy woman from Hermit Town. Said she'd been trying to reach me all winter. She found something south of here, by Planktown near the river. Some kind of structure, and there was a door into the earth—a vault, a ladder going down, and she said there was something down there that looked like books, but she couldn't get to them. Her knees were too weak."

"What's books?"

"Books? Books are a kind of dolmen. They have information in them, like scrolls, except the words are made with machines, not pencils. And they have pages that are sewed together. I want those books, Johnny. I want you to go down and get them for me. Take Jocko with you. I see his restlessness. He wants to get out of town."

Johnny hesitated. "It's Springfest. We're playing music tonight."

"This is more important than music, Johnny. It's important to Burleyman for a different reason than for me. For Burleyman this may be the one thing that escorts the people of King Corn into his new world of possibilities. He'll let you go. Bearclaw and Ant will just have to play the festival as a duo." Frankie squirmed on his stool and massaged his left fist with his open right hand. "It's important for me too. I'd go with you if I could."

Ɔ

They set out together, Johnny and Jocko, on the misty morning the Springfest was to begin. Tiller Hogpen and Bearclaw were raising the banner pole in the meadow, Maggie Mender's tribute to the winter wolves unfurling itself above the sleeping town. Bearclaw saw them go but he didn't say anything. They had spent the night before making music, untuned and without an audience, by the warmth of Maggie's fire. Now Johnny felt a strangeness in his legs and feet, a tension between resistance and restlessness, to be walking out of King Corn on a spring morning, around the grassy hill on the road heading south.

Jocko was the perfect companion, for he was a man of deep solitude. Comfortably they walked, side by side, each lost in thought. Occasionally, one or the other would voice an observation, but neither seemed to feel burdened by the need to respond to what the other had said.

"Look! Columbines!" said Jocko.

"That hawk has been following us all morning." said Johnny.

Nightfall. In the forest they found a bower of arched branches lashed over a fire circle. Rain was beginning to fall. Jocko gathered wood and kindled a fire. They roasted some turkey Maggie had saved out from the Springfest stores.

"Frankie asked me a question last night," said Johnny as Jocko turned the meat over the fire. "How far outside of your body do you go? Your body gives off heat, but how far outside your body can that heat be measured? I don't think he was just talking about heat, though. He was talking about anything you can feel from a distance."

Jocko nodded and smiled his little half-smile. "Sometimes I can feel the rabbits from across the meadow." He didn't explain this remark so it just floated there for a while.

Eventually, Johnny spoke. "I can feel Lucy. Sometimes when I'm falling asleep I can even feel where she is, which direction, how far away. Like you can feel where your arm is, even when you can't see it."

Jocko's response was immediate. "You must have left something inside of her, then."

For some reason Johnny found this thought disquieting. He remembered something Frankie had told him. For a long time after he lost his leg, Frankie said he could still feel it; he could even feel its pain. Most of the time he felt it where it used to be, below his hip, alongside his other leg. But sometimes, especially at night, he felt it where it actually was, buried in the ground in the graveyard, next to the body of his grandfather. Johnny didn't tell this to Jocko. He contemplated changing the subject. But Jocko spoke first.

"Frankie was in love once."

Johnny startled. It was like Jocko had read his thoughts. "He was? Who?"

"A girl. He never said. We knew. She died."

This sank in, through a season of cricket song and rustling wind. Frankie. *This girl. Lucy. Do you love her? I need to look at everything. Human emotions could send out frequencies.*

"What about these books we're going to look for?" Johnny said suddenly, the human emotion growing too strong for him to bear. "Have you ever seen one?"

"I have one, in my room. Frankie doesn't know. It has pictures of animals in it, and words, but I don't know how to read the words.

☽

Midday, the next day, Johnny and Jocko came down out of the woods into a lush grassland populated with stands of cottonwood. The trees were in bloom; the fluff filled the air, like snow, but lighter, warmer, slower. It rose from the road-bed to dance in circles as they approached, and it settled on their clothing, and in their hair and beards, where it made them sneeze.

At length the path merged with the broad levee road, and the River Only lay shining before them in the sun. They could see the smokestacks of Planktown in the distance, but before them, the watercourse narrowed, clogged with chunks of debris, as if there had once been a bridge, in ancient times, but it had long since collapsed. A strange sort of bridge, though. The remnants were massive and cluttered the river's entire span. Fragments of walkways slouched from the broken pieces, and there were shadowy openings, windows or doors, and things that looked like wheels and threaded columns. The water made rapids here as it swirled around the obstructions, whipping up foam and spray, and sounding a rumble of latent power.

A brick building stood on the shore at a place where the earth had been mounded up like a shoulder for the river. It was clearly an ancient structure, a *dolmen*—the bricks crumbly and aged a dull yellow. There were gaps in the roof tiles, and swallows flitted in and out of the rafters. The door was missing. Above its frame a stone facade was carved with words, but only one of them was legible.

UTILITIES

"I think this is our place," said Johnny. They went inside.

The floor was strewn with shards of sharp metal, spattered with swallow droppings. Under a window against the far wall, stood three cylindrical objects, made of heavy iron. They were each about as tall as a man. They had domed hats, and chimney-like arms. Someone had painted a face on one of them. At a desk nearby, something caught Johnny's attention.

"Perhaps these are the books," he said.

Flat, square objects, rigid boards that framed layers of something that looked like parchment. Three of them. When Johnny lifted one, it crumbled like a wafer in his hands. Carefully he set it down and lifted the top frame. It was hinged on the side like a door. On the plies beneath, there were rows and rows of lines, forming columns, with tiny numbers written between them. Most of the pages had dissolved into a powder by moisture and age, but he recognized two words repeating themselves at the heads of the columns: START. STOP.

"That's not it," said Jocko. "Frankie said it would be in a vault."

They scoured the room until they found a handle in the

floor under a pile of broken bricks. It took the strength of both of them to break the latch and lift the heavy metal hatch. A putrid stench rose. Johnny lit his carbide lamp and lowered it into the hole. Rungs on the wall descended into the darkness. At the threshold of light he saw something moving. It took him a while to recognize what it was. Snakes. Coiled together like intestines they slithered in a ring around the vault walls.

"Phew! Now I see why Darcy Dinkum didn't want to go down there." Jocko took the lamp from him and leaned far down into the hole.

"Those are green well snakes," he said. "They won't hurt you." Johnny hesitated. Jocko looked at him and smiled, gently. "I'm smaller than you. I'll go."

Halfway into the vault, Jocko started talking to the snakes. "Don't wake up for me, you silly tubers. I don't have any bacon." Then there was a snapping sound, followed by a thud, like a body landing in soft dirt. Johnny called into the hole, "Jocko! Are you all right?"

After a while, Jocko's voice reverberated from the depths of the vault. "It gets big in the bottom," he said, "And there are books."

For a long time Jocko scuffled and shuffled in the dark. Johnny could see nothing but the faint glow of his lamp and the silhouetted shadows of the writing snakes. Eventually he heard Jocko's voice again. "I'm coming up now."

The light was extinguished and Jocko began pulling himself up the rungs with one hand, clutching something to his chest with the other. "They were all rotten," he said when he reached the surface. "Except this one."

Johnny took the book. It was thick and heavy, and wholly intact, although there was mold growing on the cover.

He opened it. The pages were full of words, printed more uniformly than any hand could ever do. And there were pictures, sharp and clear, like Lucy's picture of the waterfall, except they were pictures of machines with coils and dials and wires. And there were diagrams with numbers and letters on them. He closed the book and looked at the title.

THE PRINCIPLES OF ELECTRICITY

"Yes, yes. I think this is what Frankie wants. "

Ɔ

Frankie Fulcrum's hands trembled as he turned the pages of the book. At certain passages he gasped. His mouth fell open and he placed the palm of his hand on the page and caressed it as if it were a lover. When at last he closed the book and looked up, his eyes were brimming with tears.

"This is the reason you came, Johnny Arcane. Burleyman was right in the first place. You are the return of Borderbinder. But in a different way than we thought."

They left the laboratory without another word, Johnny and Jocko, Johnny in the lead, his thoughts darkened. So absorbed in the pages of the book, Frankie barely saw them go. Out on the meadow, people were cleaning up the rubble left by Springfest. There were food scraps everywhere, turkey bones and apple cores and the rinds of winter squash. And scraps of clothing, trampled in the mud, especially around the silo. Mud spatters rimmed the base of the silo. At the center of the meadow the banner pole had been snapped in two, as if by a bolt of lightning. Two women were wringing muddy water out of the remnant of the winter wolves.

"Something's wrong." said Johnny.

"It's cold." Jocko pulled on the sleeves of his thin coat.

Breakfast was over, or perhaps it had never been, but smoke was rising from the log house chimney. It was a strong attractor. It pulled them toward the big wooden doors.

There were only three people in the longhall, other than the scullery workers banging pots and pans in the kitchen. The mayor sat at a table, propped up on one side by Bearclaw and on the other by Ant. He was holding a rag to his left eye. The skin around the rag was purple and puffy.

When Ant saw Johnny and Jocko, she jumped up, and Burleyman winced in pain.

"They're back!" she cried. "Johnny! Johnny! There's a message!" She tried to run to them, but Burleyman caught her arm and pulled her back to her seat.

"What happened to him?" Johnny rushed forward.

Bearclaw held up the palm of his hand. "Slow down, Johnny. One thing at a time. You want some barley tea? Jocko, get us all some barley tea."

Jocko went straight to the sideboard by the scullery, where the mugs were stacked. Bearclaw let go of Burleyman's arm and the mayor listed toward Ant.

"He got in a fight with Tiller Hogpen," said Bearclaw. "It was a bit of a strange night — the second of Springfest. Sit down, Johnny. Jocko will bring the tea. This involves you, directly."

Johnny sat. Jocko appeared with five mugs of barley tea on a tray, but Burleyman waved his away. "Never touch the stuff!" he mumbled.

They settled for a while. On the big hearth, the fire crackled.

"A messenger came yesterday," said Bearclaw at last. "He was dressed like a Blackcoat, but he had the arm band.

He scared some people. Tiller and some others went out and got clubs from the woodpile. But the smart ones, they just got close to the man, and sniffed at him. He didn't smell like a Blackcoat, so they relaxed. But after the messenger left, things got strange. It was good until then. Just a regular Springfest. The turkey was good. There was dancing all night, the first night, even without you and Jocko. But after the messenger left, the abstainers got to heckling. *First there's cows, then there's Blackcoats.* That's what they said. Burleyman said..."

Burleyman raised the rag, exposing his swollen eye. "You can leave, I told 'em. Just leave us alone."

"But they didn't leave," continued Bearclaw. "They just kept on. They wanted to fight. Especially Tiller. Tiller wanted to fight even though he says he's not an Abstainer. And now you see the damages. Our woundable mayor. After that, they left. The Abstainers. Tiller went with them. They knocked down the banner pole on the way out."

Burleyman pressed the rag back to his eye and slumped forward. It was then that Johnny saw the parcel on the table, a flattened bundle wrapped in dried leaves and bound with a strand of sedge.

Ant shuffled it toward him with the tips of her fingers. "The message is for you."

Johnny's whole body began to quake, like a cottonwood tree. He grabbed the package and ripped off the leafy cover. The message was written on paper, real paper, like the paper of the book. The handwriting danced on the page. He could not separate the words from each other. He dropped the letter on the table.

"Read it to me."

Ant picked up the paper with steady hands, but as she

scanned the message her eyes pooled. She lowered her lids and blinked away the tears. She raised her eyes, squared Johnny in the face, and read.

My Dear Johnny,
On the morning of the fourth moon they will be moving us to the flesh mills of Ironweed. There we will be killed. Not all at once. The work we do there will kill us. We will be marching on the Onyx Highway with the Blackcoats. You will not recognize us. We will be dressed like them but there will be no other Blackcoats on the road that day. If you must kill someone kill the man they call Glass Darkly. If he is dead the others will have no one to follow and we may be able to escape.

Last night I heard people talking on the other side of the wall. A man said that the time is coming. Johnny Arcane is in King Corn. There's a man that stands outside my cell every morning. He dresses like a Blackcoat but he wears the yellow armband. No one talks to him. Here the only people who know about the armband are from the other side. So I know he is waiting for someone who needs to send a message across the border. Tomorrow on my rounds I will give him this message.

Johnny whatever happens we will be together, in this world or the next.
Lucy.

A silence fell on the longhall. It was like Lucy had been speaking the words as Ant read them, and she ended so abruptly, and there was silence. In all the parts of his body Johnny could feel his life being remolded by a pair of large pair of hands.

"I have to leave. Now. I can't wait another day."

Ant dropped the letter on the table and folded her face

into her hands. Bearclaw reached out and placed his palm on her shoulder. He looked at Johnny. "Come to our house. We can pack you food and supplies. We must send you off in a proper manner."

Ɔ

"But which way will you go? I've never heard of a place called Ironweed."

It was late morning. The day was hastening on with a sense of urgency. The friends had reconvened at Bearclaw and Ant's, even Burleyman, and Frankie Fulcrum, who leaned heavily on his crutches, his back against the wall. Ant was holding a spatula, while griddlecakes sizzled on the stovetop.

"There have to be places we've never heard of," said Johnny. "It's not like there's a wall in every one of the four directions."

"Ah," said Burleyman, "Borderbinder speaks."

"Well, people must realize it," continued Johnny. "How could they not? Just think about the stars, or try to imagine a mountain that has only one side. There has to be a backside to every mountain. Every lake has to have an opposite shore."

"Oh, we realize it all right," said Burleyman, "but we've been taught from birth not to. All the myths and legends. The superstitions. The only place we're allowed to realize it is in our dreams."

"More like our nightmares, I should think!" added Frankie, shifting his weight.

Bearclaw sat with Johnny's map of the Known World in his hands, folded into a quadrant with King Corn at the center. He was tracing a line with his fingers. His thoughts seemed distanced from the conversation.

"Well, listen. The Blackcoats always come down from the north, and they head back north after they've done their mischief. I think north is the direction. Look here on the map. The northernmost town is Cabbage. I been there. What Johnny doesn't know is you don't have to cross the river at Sputum. There's a trail through the north woods. Just before that trail veers west, there's another trail due north. Once when I was coming back from Cabbage I saw some Blackcoats marching north on that trail."

Johnny spoke. "Anyhow, if I was going to cross a border I always thought it would be the northern border. Because it's the closest."

"And the closest attractor," added Frankie.

Ant draped an arm around Johnny's chest from behind, the spatula still in her other hand. "I wish you didn't have to go."

Bearclaw smiled and winked. "I keep telling you she's still in love with you, Johnny."

They settled down to a meal of griddlecakes and grilled onions. Bearclaw spread the map on the table and they studied it together. Each one of them knew towns and roads that Johnny was not aware of, even after five summers of messengering. Using a charcoal pencil, they filled in the blank places with names like Hocker's Falls, Laughing Cat Bridge, Wincherville, Dirty Little Secret, Salivation Pond. The map got denser with lines and drawings, but always, it fanned out into sparseness at the borders.

It was decided that Johnny would take Bearclaw's advice, following the north woods around Sputum and taking the unmarked cutoff just before the switchback to Cabbage. Ant stuffed his backpack with the rest of the griddlecakes, plus some dried meat and apples, some hard bread. Bearclaw gave him several bottles of corn oil, some flints, some charcoal.

Jocko said, "We should make some music before he goes."

"The boy is anxious to be on his way," said Bearclaw. "Perhaps he doesn't have the heart for music."

Johnny knew Bearclaw was right. He could feel the restlessness in his body, as if small legs inside his legs were already treading along the road. But he knew Jocko was right as well.

"Let's play one song. Tuned. Something we know, as a token. What shall it be?"

Ant spoke without hesitation. *"Happy to Meet, Sorry to Part."*

Johnny took out the mandolin and tuned it to the fiddle and the guitar while Jocko thumped the catgut impatiently. They started playing. Before the first verse was over they all had tears in their eyes, even Burleyman, even Frankie, and they played the song again and again, for a long time.

CHAPTER TWELVE

WELCOME TRAVELER

lone again, out on the open road with its freedom and adventure, but this time his heart did not lift; the lonesome tug of what lay behind did not give way to the welcoming pull of what lay ahead. Mostly he felt a kind of dread, for he knew now the real task was beginning.

He recalled his winter in King Corn. It quelled his fear. All its wintry events drifted before him, but especially the faces, the smile lines and the care lines, the ripples of response as he watched each person struggle or surrender to the challenges of everyday life. For it hadn't been an easy winter in King Corn. Burleyman, Bearclaw, Ant, Jocko, Frankie Fulcrum, Maggie Mender, Misha and Marta, the cowboys Birdleg and Climber, each brought a different pile of barn nails to the game. There had been conflict, and even injury, and even *death,* if a cow's death could be counted. Something of all these people flowed through his blood along a course that had once only belonged to Lucy. It was an energy. It moved in waves. He could feel it working its way down his legs and up again, passing through his sex and rising along the roadbed of his spine, warming his heart, flooding his head with color, and when at last it reached his arms, it burst out through his fingers and into the strings of his mandolin.

Yes, he told himself, that's what it was like. But now I must focus on the path before me.

It was not a well-trodden path, and all afternoon walking, he met no one. The woods were mostly summerleaf, maples and birches, just putting out a furze of green. Drifts of muddy snow lay about in the shadowy places. Occasionally he had to ford a streambed of snowmelt crossing the path. In one place a makeshift footbridge had given in to the elements. The water swirling around the broken boards reminded him of the dolmen at Planktown, crossing the River Only, the chunks of chiseled debris and the snake-filled vault from which Jocko had produced the book. How old is this bridge, he wondered, just a few seasons? That fallen structure stared at him with so many ponderous questions, as if a legion of very old ghosts were standing on the levee, asking him, *who were we, and when did we live?*

Past the fallen bridge, he approached an arrowed plank of wood nailed to a tree, carved with one word: STONE-HOUSE. After that, the terrain opened up to low scrub and clumps of oaks, and on the slope above, a line of ancient stumps for as far as the eye could see. This went on monotonously for a long time, until the sun began to dip below the western ridge, and Johnny's thoughts turned to shelter.

Ahead, shadowed in twilight, stood a grove of trees, the likes of which he had never seen before. Evergreens yes, but they were not proud trees like the pines and the cedars. Their branches were gnarled like an old farmer's hands, and there was no symmetry in their silhouettes. They seemed to be leaning over and curling around each other, as if huddled together in fear. Vines connected them like a common shawl.

Rather than trunks, they stood on multiple roots, fingered helter-skelter into the earth, with dark, cavernous places between them.

Something glinted deep within the grove, a flash of light, and it was gone. Johnny drew nearer. In the fading light he made out the shadowed shapes of large boulders, stacked and mortared together to form a sort of dome, like an outdoor kiln, but bigger, big enough for several people to fit inside. The entrance was framed with wood but there was no door, and there were no windows.

Focused as he was on this rough-hewn phantom, at first he failed to notice the sign on the post directly in front of him: STONEHOUSE.

With caution he approached. He was weary, and most times any shelter would serve him, but there was something foreboding about this one. Above the doorframe two words were smudged into the bare stone:

WELCOME TRAVELER.

This calmed him a little. He stepped inside.

It smelled bad, an old smell, not the smell of something that was still there, more like something that had passed through many times over many seasons. There was some light in the center of the room. A smoke hole on the roof admitted a dusty ray of sun, and directly below it, a fire circle of mounded ash. Wild animals had made nests in the corners, but they were long gone. Johnny kicked through the clumps of straw and uncovered piles of clean, dry bones.

"I'll sleep here tonight," he said, despite his foreboding, and went outside to gather kindling for a fire.

$\supset$

Over the fire he roasted the turkey Maggie had spared from Springfest, and brewed himself a cup of spikeweed picked from the forest outside of King Corn. He spread his bedroll against the far wall and pulled the tattered quilt over his shoulders.

The moment his head touched the floor, cats began to howl outside. He could tell by their voices it was the spring mating. He had witnessed this ritual many times as a child. Often he wondered how this act that heralded the spring and filled the world with new life could be conducted with such vehemence and rancor.

Cats were despicable creatures. That's what everyone said. But sometimes, as a child, he would encounter one in the hayloft or the woodshed, and there would be an exchange of essences. A cat would look in his eyes and something would pass between them. *I know you. We share something. We know that beneath all this softness and comfort there runs an undercurrent of struggle, of restlessness, the potential for sorrow.*

This restlessness daunted his efforts to sleep. Every time the dreamy mists of drowsiness closed in and he felt himself slipping under, the cats would resume their angst, and he would have to start the process all over. Finally though, the night settled in earnest, and he descended into a warm dark place where he was caressed by loving fingers.

A sudden, brilliant flash of light awoke him. He sat bolt upright in dense darkness, slowly dispersed by a pale swath of moon flowing in through the smoke hole. He recalled the flash of light that had drawn him from the path to the stonehouse in the first place. He saw something he hadn't noticed before. A tiny red dot was glowing on the opposite wall, like a crimson star. He stood and moved toward it, taking care not to trip on the firestones.

A small, natural enclosure in the rocks held a low table, and on the table, an open book, scored with ledgers and hand scrawls— the kind of book he had first seen in the dolmen chambers at Planktown. And on the wall above the book, a circle, about the size of a dinner plate, lit by the red dot. He touched it. It was paper, and a thin metal arm reached halfway across it. The arm was a pen, leaving a line of ink in concentric rings.

He raised the book to the glow of the red dot, so he could read the words. Each column started with a drawing of a phase of the moon, followed by a number. At the topmost column was a full moon circle, and the number 777. One line over was a single word: *Stubblefield.*

A wave of uneasiness ran down his arm and forced him to set the book back on the table. Stubblefield. The seven-hundred seventy-seventh full moon. Could it be?

He brought the book back to the light and followed the entries down the page. A waning crescent, 777: The Dolmens. Half-moon, 777: Sputum. Waxing crescent, 777: Arden's Plain. Full-moon, 778: Fairheart.

Yes, it was. But to be sure he turned to the last page and read the entries. Four full moon cycles. Sixteen entries. Eight hundred fifty-four to eight hundred seventy: *King Corn.*

The shock was visceral. His head throbbed with it, and before his closed eyelids vein lines pulsed in the dark, like bolts of lightning. It couldn't be denied. For five summers and six winters, beginning with the feast at Stubblefield and ending with the winter in King Corn, someone, or some group of people had been tracking his every move as he cut his convoluted path as a messenger across the map of the Known World. But *how?* He remembered the message he had carried from Burleyman to Mayor Castorbean

I BELIEVE BORDERBINDER HAS RETURNED. HE IS THE ONE WHO BRINGS THIS MESSAGE. HIS NAME IS ARCANE.

He remembered the pictures that had flickered in Burleyman's eyes, five summers later, as he read Darcy Dinkum's message brought back from Hermit Town.

Outside: a sound. Not cats this time. People, definitely people, human voices, stamping of feet. He leapt across the room, grabbed his bedroll, rolled himself into it and curled against the wall. Immediately he sensed a figure in the doorway, and the smell, the latent smell in the room, but present now, emanating.

Some grunting and some rustling and then the tension eased. There was a voice outside.

"Someone's in there. Sleeping."

"Well, shuck my hornpig!" snarled another voice. "We pitch camp in the woods then. Stand watch until he leaves."

More grunting, and some swearing; words like *cat's paw* and *pig's fat*. Johnny heard the voices fade as they rounded the impenetrable backside of the stonehouse. He heard a metallic sound like chains clanking, and someone pounding stakes with a mallet. Then it was quiet.

Of course he couldn't sleep, and there was a good deal of night ahead of him. He reasoned his course. Surely if they meant to hurt him they would just come in and hurt him. He was merely an obstacle to their intentions. They would stand watch until he left and then they would come in and do whatever they meant to do.

Or would they?

What if the stonehouse was some kind of sanctuary in which harm was not allowed, and once outside he was fair game? And an even more penetrating thought: *what if they knew who he was?* For it was becoming more and more clear, he was not an ordinary person.

He was Johnny Arcane.

No! His whole body recoiled at the thought. He was no one! He was no more than a rabbit, or a crow, or a single mummer dancing the old stories to keep the borders intact. He was a person, alive for a while, and then gone. There was no hidden life! There were no side worlds! He could not be something other than what he was, Johnny Arcane, Mother's son, messenger, climber of the silo, sojourner.

He wanted to cry but he dared not make a sound. He closed his eyes and they filled with tears. It was more than he could bear, the weight of this crossing, from the known into the unknown. The shadows drew a cloak around him. He felt his bones soften and his blood go thin. He let the tears wash over him, and in the dark and watery expanse a vision of someone came swimming toward him. Lucy. She was naked, as she had been in the waters of the bathhouse the day they met. She touched him and spoke to him. "Johnny, Johnny, don't worry." She began to remove his clothing. "I will wash you clean."

ↄ

He woke with a start. Light was streaming in through the smoke hole. The day had begun. The only sound was a cackle of crows in the branches outside. His eyes lidded with sleep and a fading vision of sweetness, he rolled up his bedding and gathered his things into the pack. He did this deliberately so as not to disturb the silence. There was a force, a kind of pressure urging him to flee as swiftly and quietly as he could.

The sun was still low in the east when he stepped out the door. He did not look back, but he could feel something like a bundle of heat, or a wriggling of snakes behind him. Then a voice.

"He's leaving."

Another voice. "Be quiet. He'll hear you."

His feet said *run!* He told them *no!* Little arms inside his arms wanted to flail and break free, but he held them in and pressed forward. He clung to the trail, his lungs heaving, while needles of fear pierced his back. He had never known such fear. He walked.

He walked for three days and met no one. For the first day he walked crazily, as one pursued, his legs wobbly, his lungs voicing little yips and yaps, like a frightened coyote. But gradually his fear subsided and he descended into a kind of trance. The troubled thoughts lost their content and rolled like dark clouds behind him.

There were lights in the sky above him. They moved around. He couldn't see them. He just felt them. They disturbed the air. They made the pollens swirl and dance, when there was no breeze. They carved channels between the sky and a power moved along these channels. It descended from the sky and it rose back up from the earth, continuously. It made him think of echoes bouncing back from canyons. It made him think of the magic lantern pictures on Jocko's wall. It made him think of Frankie Fulcrum's concept of the attractions.

And there was something moving beside him, always, some sort of creature, slipping behind the brush and the boulders, keeping pace. He never saw it. He only sensed. Sometimes he thought he glimpsed it out of the corner of his eye, but when he turned, it was gone.

Sometimes he felt his legs penetrate deep into the ground below the trail. He knew this was impossible, but he felt it. And he felt something enter his legs from below the ground, some kind of energy, warm and tingly. It moved upwards through his loins, along his spine. When it reached his heart it spiraled a few times, then sank back down along its route until it emptied itself through his feet into the earth.

The first two nights were warm, and he slept under the stars. He ate most of the provisions that Maggie and Ant had prepared for him in King Corn. On the morning of the third day he came across a field of wild cabbage and he gathered up an armful, hoping to boil it for his supper that night. That day the air grew cold and the trail ascended into a thick, dark forest of firs. As nightfall approached, the path took a sharp bend to the west, but the remnants of another trail continued north. It was overgrown with salal and choke-weed, and riddled with rainwash. At its head, a board was nailed to a tree but there was nothing written on it.

This was it, though. This was right where it should be, the newest feature on his map of the Known World, very near the northern border. Deeper in the woods he glimpsed an opening in the vines, square enough to have been made by a human. He thrashed his way toward it and found a small box-shaped chamber—perhaps once a hunter's blind—now completely covered with thorny blackberries.

He built a fire outside the opening and boiled the cabbage in the last of his fresh water. It was all he had left to eat. In the musty chamber he lit a corn lamp, leaned against the backpack, folded open the map to the present quadrant, and located himself at its topmost edge.

Yes. Beyond here there was no map. The time had come. He was no longer afraid. Tomorrow he would rise and step outside the Known World. In the days since he left King Corn his thoughts had thinned and given way to shapes, like the dimly perceived experiences of dreams. He had been walking in a dream state toward the unknown. Nothing he could think would penetrate this veil, only his forward motion into it.

Yet surely there must be some kind of ritual to make, some rite to mark the pivot of this moment. Rituals were forged by culture and affirmed by community. Here he was alone and unobserved, a mere life form, a weak heartbeat, breathing in a dank, forgotten place.

Something scuffled at the entrance. He looked up. A small animal stood there, a rodent, a marmot perhaps. He didn't know the names of all the animals in the forest. A marmot, he would call it. The creature peered in and saw him, but did not flee. Johnny moved. He waved his arms. Still the marmot did not budge. It ruffled its fur and twitched his nose.

"Hello, little brother," Johnny said at last. "I think I'm in your house. You can come in. There's room for us both. Maybe I can find something for you to eat."

The rodent cocked its ear at the sound of his voice. It stood on its hind legs and scanned the interior of the blind, as if to make sure no one else was in there. Then it entered, but not directly. It slipped in sideways and hugged the wall, trembling a little. It circled the entire enclosure, scratching on bits of leaves, sniffing the scat left by other creatures.

When it had made the full circle it stopped before Johnny's outstretched legs and looked him straight in the eye.

Johnny rummaged in his pack until he found a small chunk of dried cat meat at the bottom. He pulled himself to his knees, very slowly, and held the morsel out for the marmot to inspect. The marmot sniffed at it, wrinkled its nose, and turned its back, intentionally.

It doesn't eat cat.

Johnny shuffled through the pack but there was nothing else to offer. Then he saw on the floor several leaves of cabbage that hadn't fit in the pot. He took one and held it out. The creature perked its ears, twitched its nose, and stood on its hind legs. It snatched the whole leaf out of Johnny's hand and secreted it into a corner of the room, where it gobbled it greedily, like a starving child at a banquet. Then it returned for more.

Johnny fed it the rest of the cabbage, leaf by leaf. When he got to the last leaf he refused to let go. The rodent tugged and tugged, then finally gave in and ate the leaf from his hand, down to the last green vein.

After that they were both tired.

His sleep was punctuated by the sound of the marmot moving about the enclosure, nibbling on dry bits of bark, speaking in little squeaks and whispers. On several occasions it scampered across his back. Toward dawn it settled down in a little hollow it had dug out next to Johnny's reclining ear. He listened to its rapid, rhythmic breathing and a memory crossed his mind.

Once, when he was sick and starving in a dark forest, a weasel had brought him a pheasant to eat.

"Ah," he said out loud. "Perhaps now I have repaid the debt."

CHAPTER THIRTEEN
IN-BETWEEN LAND

e developed a method of counting the passage of days. Every night before he slept he picked up a pebble and dropped it in an empty corn oil jar. It was good to make a ritual, and it served a purpose. He could track the days he had walked, and count the days until the morning of the fourth moon, when Lucy would be marching with the Blackcoats on the Onyx Highway to the flesh mills of Ironweed.

On the day that there were six pebbles in the jar, the terrain changed abruptly. The forest opened up to a rocky rounded slope, dotted with the stumps of fallen trees, devoid of vegetation. The rocks and the stumps were bleached grey, and there was a faint odor of wet, dormant ash. Desolation haunted the place. In the sky overhead, a lone vulture circled.

He was entering the in-between land, the border between the Known World and whatever lay beyond.

Johnny quickened his pace. He preferred the mystery of the forest to this barren hillside with its wounds out in the open, scorched by the sun. At the summit, he looked down. There was almost nothing to see. Below him the land spilled out into nothingness, an impenetrable brown haze, a screen of ancient smoke, obscuring everything, the sky, then sun, the earth. For a moment he began to believe what people said was true. Outside the Known World there was nothing. The Known World was the only world. The fires had destroyed everything else. It filled him with dread. His heart throbbed in his chest. He sat down on a dead stump and stared into the void.

His eyes followed the suggestion of a path, winding down through outcropped rocks and low, scrabbly rabbit brush. The path soon disappeared into the vapors, but the longer he stared into the emptiness the more details emerged. There were shapes in the distance. They could have been tors; they could have been towers. He wasn't sure. But visible as they were from such a distance, they had to be enormous. And there were places where the haze swirled in eddies, and plumes of smoke rose in dreamlike shapes.

He did not tarry. Whatever this new world held in store for him, he was anxious to plunge himself into it. He surrendered to the downhill flow and soon he was walking among boulders and bracken, the valley floor nowhere in sight. There was something in the air, a pervasive odor that did not shift like the other odors, the wood saps, the hidden water, the lingering essence of fire. It smelled a little like corn oil, a little like carbide; it was heavy, the heaviness of rain on the underbellies of dark clouds, thicker than mist, thicker than vapor, suspended only by the stillness of the air.

He came to a colony of burrowing rodents in a grassy field; their fresh dirt mounds everywhere. Sometimes they popped up out of the holes to stand guard on their hind legs, or scamper to another entrance. He sat still in the middle of the field, watching them, considering how easy it might be to catch one, and how it might taste roasted.

But then something else caught his attention. Rising

above a rubble on the other side of the field, a cloud of dust, not a patterned cloud made by wind, more a gathering cloud, stirred up by motion, by trampling, or by large wheels, or by many dancing feet. He forgot his hunger and let his curiosity lead him. The rodents scattered back into their holes as he crossed the field and scaled the rocks, carefully, so as not to be seen by whatever was on the other side.

A broad valley, completely alive with movement, spinning around a central eye. At first he could only discern the shapes in the swirling dust, not the creatures that made them. It was an imperfect circle; it veered wildly, and fractured into rebellious sub-spirals, like ripples in a rocky stream. Eventually he began to see them, shadowy forms in the dust, strong muscular bodies, wild and willful, unrestrained, obedient only to the force of the movement itself, half-crazed, headstrong ...

Horses. Black and brown, glistening coats, flashing manes. He recognized them only from the horse dolls on Jocko's shelf. But he never realized how strong they would be, or how terrifying. The ground under his feet shuddered with the thundering of their hooves. They were singing, voices high and shrill, dissonant angular melodies. Their pace was fast and frantic. Their circle swooned and wobbled, and at any moment he thought it might fly apart and he would be trampled.

Then he saw the woman.

She materialized out of a swirling cloud. She was running with the horses, keeping pace with them. As soon as Johnny saw her, he slipped behind a rock so as not to be seen, even though she was far away. She moved in and out among the horses. She disappeared and reappeared. Her dark hair was as wild as a horse's mane. She was naked, except for something dark tied about her waist.

It was a kind of dance, and the woman was leading. She pressed herself into the fleet of their movements and they shied away. In this manner she created the circles, deliberately. It was a great task, for the herd was large, and those at the edges tried to break away and make for the open range. She ran ahead of their intentions and rounded them in, and the spiral kept drawing closer and more ordered, and the dust itself began to form a funnel.

Then it happened. Briefly the woman vanished behind the screen. When she reappeared she had attached herself to one particular horse, the tallest of the lot, a black beast who shrieked and thrust its ramrod head at her as if it meant to shove her to the ground. But she would not be toppled. She grasped the horse's flying mane. Suddenly her feet were off the ground. The horse reared, but the woman would not be thrown. She rode the upward motion and threw her legs over the creature's back. The horse kicked and bucked, but the woman straddled its body and held on tight, burying her face in its mane, her arms and legs twined like a deep forest vine.

The black horse shrugged and shuddered, then came to a standstill in its tracks as if surrendering to fate. The entire herd was making a sunward circle around it now; horse and rider stood in the eye of a great whirlwind of dust and jostling bodies. Slowly the intention shifted—the movement began to turn inward. Horse by horse, the creatures stilled. Manes flashed and flanks glistened. Eventually, calm fell on the plain, and as the dust settled, the entire herd stood silent in a circle facing the black horse and rider in a stance conveying something that could only be named as reverence.

The woman sat up to her full height on the black horse's

back. She looked around— all around, in all directions, at all the horses. She said something to them but the distance swallowed her voice.

However, her next utterance reached Johnny's ears. It came with a sudden motion, a goading of her legs against the horse's broad flanks. She let out a shrill, horse-like cry: "Hi-yi-yi-yi-yah!"

The black horse took off in a gallop. Immediately a corridor opened in the circle for horse and rider to pass through, and just as immediately, it closed behind them, as every other beast in the herd joined the flight. The gathered creatures moved with one common purpose—to follow their mounted leader forward, thundering across the plain, raising a cloud around them, as if bound to a single thread. The ground trembled and the dust rolled. Soon Johnny could not see the horses at all, only a tumbling amorphous form, racing across the plain into some distant vortex.

He sat on the boulder in stunned silence for a long time, for as long as it took for the dust to settle and the ground to stop trembling—a long time indeed, and during that time his mind began to focus. The sun, a mere blotch of light, hung mid-point in the sky above the gathering dust; the horses had vanished into the west. The trail across the plain had been trampled to oblivion. On the other side of the plain another range of low scrub hills hid the great hazy valley from his sight, but the air above the hills was smoky and discolored, and vaporous plumes rose and flattened against some invisible ceiling.

Path or none, he sensed this was his destiny, to crack the mystery of this formless valley. It was more a premonition than a portent, more an omen than a promise. It placed a discomfort in the pit of his stomach.

But also, he *was* hungry.

☽

The trail resumed on the other side of the plain. It was marked by a cairn of three large boulders, spattered with a flowstone of bird droppings. Some kind of large, raptor-like bird leapt from the top boulder at his approach and lumbered its heavy body into the sky.

As evening approached, Johnny began to see houses and he grew hopeful of finding something to eat. But they were shabby houses, shacks made mostly out of salvaged things, broken down barn walls, cart beds with their axles intact, fence posts, gate metal, mortared field stones. And there were no gardens, and seemingly no people, not at first.

Three children in rags played in a pile of brush, and when they saw him they fled in terror to a sagging sod house built up against the rise of a hill. A man with a rusty shovel dug a hole in an open field while flies swarmed around the carcass of a skinny yellow dog. Johnny stood at the fence and watched until he finally caught the man's eye.

"What happened to your dog?" he asked.

The man stared at him for a time, then returned to his digging without a word.

He came to a small farmhouse with a porch, although the roof was sagging and collapsed in places. There was a garden in front, nothing yet ready to eat, just a froth of green covering the soil, and by the path, an ancient, gnarled pear tree, the last of its wrinkled winter fruit still clinging to its barely budded branches.

Here was food then, and he was hungry. It would do.

He had to climb in the crotch of the tree to reach the

cluster of yellow pears. Just as he was about to grasp them, a noise rang from the house, a popping sound, like two cupped hands clapping. At the same time something whizzed through the branch above him and some leaves wafted down in front of his face.

Then a ragged voice from the house. "You be gettin' down from there right now or I'll shoot you for real!"

Johnny jumped to the ground and instinctively opened his arms to reveal himself to the man. The man stood on the porch. He was very fat and he held some kind of long pole in his hands.

"I mean no harm. I was just hungry and you had fruit."

"Ye'd best turn your back and keep walkin' young man. Ye wouldn't be the first poacher I've kilt."

Johnny stood there, puzzled. The menace in the man's voice was undeniable, but a field stood between them, and the man was fat, and no doubt slow of motion. Surely Johnny could outrun him.

"Please sir, I haven't eaten in days. May I have one of your pears?"

The man raised the stick and he appeared to break it in half, then snap it back together again whole. "Ye don't listen too good, do ye?" He pointed the stick in Johnny's direction.

An unnamed fear rose in Johnny's heart. He turned and started walking away. There was another popping sound, and suddenly he felt his sleeve rip, and a sting in his shoulder.

"Yer lucky I'm drunk!" cried the man behind him. Johnny broke into a trot. He slapped at his shoulder. There was blood, but it was only a graze of the skin. His legs were weak and trembling. He pressed forward.

The path crested a rise and dropped into a narrow valley choked in thorny vines. Four small shacks stood, two on either side of the footway. Two men in grey woolen shirts leaned on a railing, talking. Johnny pressed his hand to his shoulder to hide the wound, and he passed them without turning his head. They glanced at him. "Keep moving, stranger," mumbled one.

Ahead on the trail's crest stood a building. It didn't look like the others. The walls were straight, freshly milled boards, painted a bright clean white. Rows of thin, slender windows, each beveled to a point at the top. From the distance Johnny could see that the glass was opaque and glistened with color from a light within. Steps lead up to an arched doorway. Above the door a tapered steeple, and in its opening hung a bell.

It had to be a roadhouse, and he could tell there were people in it because there were carts outside, and even a few donkeys. And there was music. Drawing closer he could hear voices, many voices, singing in stark, open harmonies.

Where there is singing, surely hearts are good, he told himself. He proceeded.

At the summit some people approached from the opposite direction, a man and a woman. The woman wore a plain grey dress and she had some kind of a white lace napkin tied to her head. The man sported a smart black jacket and a white shirt. When they saw him the woman turned her eyes down but the man lifted his hand to his forehead, as if tipping an invisible hat.

The door swung open and the music swelled out. It drew Johnny forward like one of Frankie Fulcrum's strange attractors. Before he realized it he was inside.

The clamor was deafening. People sat at benches facing the center where a man stood waving his arms wildly. Everyone was dressed like the couple Johnny had seen outside.

The women sat apart from the men. No one seemed to notice him at first, so transported were they by their singing. Some were rocking from side to side, others raising their arms to the ceiling. There were no instruments. The voices surged and veered toward chaos. Johnny strained to make out the words. Many were unfamiliar, as if of a language from long ago and far away, but there was an underlying theme that wove its way through the phrases.

What wondrous worms we mortals be!
In Gimmel's hearth, in Beulah's bower,
When I can read my title clear
So fades the lovely blooming flower.

On the word *flower* a woman stood abruptly, then wilted back to the bench. Others caught her by the arms and lowered her gently. In the precipitous silence, the man in the center flung out his arms. The voices soon resumed.

On Jersey's strong and hearty bowels I stand
And cast a wistful eye to Candy's fangled land
Where my possessions lie...

An agitation spread through the crowd. It started with the women. Another woman stood, raised her arms, and turned slowly sunwise in place. Those around her began a repetitious chant. It sounded something like *Beezle, Beezle, Beezle*. The men raised their voices as if to drown the women out.

The bear to his garden comes
The spices yield their rich perfumes
The glorious stone is rolling on

The gracious work is now begun!

"Who would be *slain*! Who would be *slain*!" cried the man at the center, as the song disintegrated into a babble. Another woman stood up, ripped the bonnet from her head, and rushed forward. "I would be slain!"

The man drew his arm back and thrust it forward. His broad palm struck the woman on the temple and she flew backwards and rattled onto the floor, where she began to thrash convulsively, chanting, *Beezle! Beezle! Beezle!*

Other women resumed the chant. The men again started a song, but one got up, a young, skinny man with no coat, his shirt tails untucked and stained.

"Ezekiel Wheelwright!" cried the man in the center, throwing both his arms in the air. "Rise thy soul and stretch thy wings! Flee the fiery darts of earthly pumice! Bathe thy rod in seas of heavenly rest!"

The young man balked and backed up. "Um, um... my flame flickers." Two of the women grabbed him by his armpits and propelled him toward the center.

A popping sound broke through the clamor, like the crack of a whip. Suddenly people were dropping to the floor all around the room, both men and women, flailing arms and legs and chanting, *Beezle! Beezle! Beezle!* They looked like a mass of writhing insects. The core of the men kept singing, louder and louder, to overtake the din.

Johnny felt the pulsation of the rhythm pulling him by his arms and legs. He felt his warm heartbeat throbbing in the wound on his shoulder. Involuntarily he began to sway.

Broad is the road that leads to death
And thousands walk together

But wisdom shows a narrow path
And here and there a traveler...

His lids began to droop. Suddenly he felt the heat of eyes full upon him. He started and looked up. The man in the center was no longer moving. He was standing stalk straight and staring directly at him.

"Traveler!" boomed the man's voice. "You! Step forth!" With no assent from his mind, Johnny's feet began to twitch. "Traveler, haste! The night comes on. Many the shining hour is gone. Storm is gathering in the west, and you so far from home! While it is day, walk, traveler. While it is day, walk!"

Two women grabbed him by the arms. One of them brushed his wound and pulled her hand back with a shriek, recoiling from the sight of his blood on her palm. That was all it took to break the spell. He wrested himself free from their fingers and turned for the door. But the exit was blocked. Three big men in black jackets and white shirts stood stone-faced with folded arms across their chests. Unlike the others, they did not sing or sway.

"I'm leaving now," he said. They did not push back as he shoved against them. They just stood there, immobile. "You have to let me leave." This time he advanced more forcefully, and when he hit the flank of men he grabbed one of their arms and twisted. The man gave a little, just enough. Johnny thrust himself between the shoulders and broke through.

The door was wide open. He burst out into the light of day and took off running.

He ran for as long as his strength would allow. He felt like he was waking from a troubled dream in which a certain phrase repeated itself over and over.

Traveler haste, the night comes on
Many a shining hour is gone
Storm is gathering in the west
And you so far from home...

CHAPTER FOURTEEN

MARS

t last in the fading twilight he saw the glow of a roadhouse ahead. This time he knew it was a conventional roadhouse with its porch and windows, and its open door. Faded parchment lanterns festooned the linnet. He heard voices inside, and caught the aroma of food. Surely, even in this strange world, certain things were held in common. People still gathered to eat. How could it be otherwise?

As he neared the building, he saw feathers, gnawed bones, and food scraps littered the splintered porch, and the ill-fitted wallboards were bare of paint. Above the open door, chipped glass tubes curled to form words: FOOD, DRINK. Directly below, hand-scrabbled on a board tacked to the doorpost: FREE BEER TONIGHT.

The first thing he noticed when he stepped inside was the smoke. The room was full of it. It wasn't just the smoke of roasting meat, although there was that, too. People at the tables were inhaling smoke through short glowing reeds, blowing it out through their mouths and nostrils. The smoke hung stratified in the air. It smelled like peat fire or the smoldering of wet sagebrush.

There were no longtables. Men, most of them fat, with

beards matted down to their chests, clustered around waist-high slabs of wood. Some wore no shirts, only buckskin vests over bloated bellies. A cacophony of drunken, careless voices and the stench of sweat and spit filled Johnny's nostrils. There wasn't a woman to be seen.

Johnny scanned the gloom for a place where he could sit alone. All the tables were taken. At one table in a shadowy corner, a dark-skinned man sat alone. Dressed in a sashed and rumpled tunic, he looked like someone come from a festival in which there had been a brawl. His eyes followed Johnny's passage across the room.

Men slouched from stools onto a counter. Behind the counter a sloppy man wiped a dish on his greasy apron. Chunks of meat sizzled on a grill, and on a shelf behind the grill: an array of bottles glistened.

Johnny took a stool with no one next to it. The counter man grunted. "What you want?"

"What do you have?" Johnny asked.

The man turned, took a glass tumbler and started filling it from a spigot. "We got sliced beef with taters, or we got corn chowder." He plunked the tumbler down on the counter. "Here's your beer."

"I don't drink beer."

"Well, you'll drink that one. It's free. Now what you eat?"

"Beef, that's...*cow* meat, isn't it?"

The man squinted his eyes and shook his head. "No, it the meat of skunks we finds dead on the roadside. What you think? Course it's cow meat."

"I've eaten cow meat. I'll have that."

The counter man scooped up a few slices of cow meat

and a mound of potatoes onto a metal plate and clanged it onto the counter.

"Could I please have some water?"

"S'water in the beer."

So Johnny ate the meat and potatoes and sipped at the beer. It was only the second time he'd eaten cow meat. It was greasy and grisly and the beer was topped with a head of green scum. He glanced at the men sitting on either side of him. They turned their faces and moved away. The dark-skinned man in the corner was still contemplating him, nodding slowly. Johnny turned away as he had learned to do in such situations. He concentrated on the food.

He didn't drink all the beer but he cleaned his plate. His stomach churned and his feet twitched. He tried his best to sit and savor the nourishment and the faint euphoria of alcohol. Eventually his restlessness grew too strong and he stood from the stool.

"I thank you kind sir, for the vittles," he said.

The counter man looked at him. "Where you going?"

"It's dark. I need to find a place to sleep."

"Aren't you going to pay?"

The word meant nothing to him in this context. He had only heard it used in terms of awareness. *Pay attention to what I'm saying. Pay no mind to that child.*

"I don't know what you mean."

"Pay. You know, *money.* Coins. Bills." The counter man rubbed his thumb under his other four fingers. "Only the beer's free."

This just made him more confused, and now he noticed people were turning their heads to look at him, *paying attention.* He sensed danger. He had to think of something, and he knew he couldn't just flee.

"I have a mandolin. I can play you a song if you'd like."

There was silence at the counter, all clattering spoons brought to a halt, every breath held. One man, his broad back hunched over his beer, began to twitch, his breath voicing a cold, suppressed snicker. Others joined in, snorting through their noses a private, mocking cruelty. The counter man leaned close to the ear of the hunchback.

"He's got a *mandolin.*"

The hunchback smirked and turned his head but not his body.

"I had a mandolin once. Tasted like chicken."

Someone coughed. Someone else slapped a knee. A wave of pig-like laughter began to circle the room. Next to the hunchback another man curled back his lip to reveal a ridge of toothless gum.

"Oh, that weren't no mandolin, Bobster. That were a horn pig."

A man with his head in a bandage stood up and drew his face close to Johnny's, like he was inspecting a piece of meat. His breath smelled liked feces. "Funny lookin' beastie. Where you s'pose he comes from?"

The toothless man scratched his chin. "Morn important, what you s'pose he *tastes* like?"

"Probably tastes like mandolin."

"Probably tastes like horn pig."

Johnny backed up but he didn't dare turn. He heard the sound of chairs moving behind him. He looked down at his backpack on the floor by the counter.

"I'm—just going to take my things and leave now. You won't see me anymore."

A stumble of bodies approached him from all sides and a jolt of panic raced up his spine. He leaned over to grab the pack, but an arm snaked around his belly from behind. It cinched up suddenly with such force a glob of undigested potato spewed from his mouth.

"Horn pig, I think," grunted a voice behind him. "He's kinda soft and squishy."

From the corner, a clatter. A chair knocked over and a blur of color moved across the room. In front of Johnny's face a dark-skinned hand grabbed a light-skinned arm by the wrist.

"Let him go, Blankface. I know this man. He's with me."

"He ain't with you, Mars Daniel. He ain't with nobody. He's a *sojourner.*"

"Oh yeah? Well, maybe then you'd like the taste of my blade on your throat."

Johnny felt his body drop. His knees struck hard on the stone floor. In pain, he rolled over and came face to face with a pair of black leather boots.

The dark-skinned man stood in the gathered crowd. He was darker and browner than Bow Wow; his tunic loose and silky, open at the waist around the sash and spattered with rainbow colors. His hair was enormous—a cloud of dense black curls, like a muffin on top of his head. He stood in a hunched position, and he held a straight blade razor.

There was a momentary hush. A creaking of floorboards. The counter man spoke.

"Well, least you're gonna pay for the food he ate, Daniel. 'Cept maybe that little bit he spit up."

"Course I'll pay." The dark-skinned man lowered the razor. "He's my man. You have no right to be treatin' my man like that. He's comin' with me. You boys sit down."

The boys did sit down, all but one, who hacked his throat and spat at the dark-skinned man's feet. The dark-skinned man quickly flashed his blade within a hair's breadth of the spitter's face.

"You wanna lick that up, Blankface?"

"Don't think I do, Mars. You can't make me."

Mars Daniel moved so quickly for a moment he became invisible. The next moment he was standing behind Blankface with the razor at his throat.

"Course I can, Blankface. Let me show you how." He thrust his arm forcefully and Blankface clattered to his knees, a streak of blood running down his cheek.

"Lick it up, Blankface. You spat it out."

A soft click sounded from the counter, barely audible, but it commanded a fearsome respect. All heads turned. The counter man stood there with a metal object in his hand—some kind of revolving cylinder, with a hollow, rod-like appendage.

"Nobody's gonna be doing any licking here tonight," said the counter man. "Daniel, you and your partner needs to show us your backsides if you know what's good for you."

The dark-skinned man stood upright and a purple flush passed over his face. "Only a coward fights with a gun, Soupbone."

Soupbone raised the metal object. "Well, that don't make you any less dead, do it? Now git!"

Mars scanned the scruffy crowd, and turned to Johnny. "Just a bunch of square heads here, anyhow," he said. "Let's quit this junkyard."

Ɔ

Behind the roadhouse a staved wagon sagged in the shadows. Hitched to it was what at first Johnny thought was a donkey, but drawing closer he saw that it was a horse, although a very small one, with tufts of hair on its hooves, and a shaggy mane.

The dark-skinned man jumped on the buckboard and threw open the tent flap. Johnny had no choice but to enter.

"Mars Daniel," Mars Daniel introduced himself as he lit the matted contents of a corncob pipe with a fiery stick. *Well, that much is obvious,* thought Johnny. It was what they called him at the roadhouse, and on the curved canvass cover of the wagon, among the brightly painted pictures of one-eyed pyramids, roses, flying dragons and naked women with fishtails for feet, sprawled in big, curling letters: MARS DANIEL: POTS, PANS AND KNIVES.

"You want some of this?" Mars held out the pipe. Johnny looked around. Indeed, inside the wagon there were pots and pans hanging everywhere, and rows of shiny knives racked in cases along the walls. A lantern hitched to an overhead stave glowed a dark crimson. The oil did not smell like corn.

"No, I don't smoke."

"Well, this isn't what the boys were smoking in the den. This'll do somethin' to you."

Johnny shook his head. "I smoked something once in the town of Stubblefield. They called it the *illumination.*"

"Never heard of Stubblefield. *The illumination.* I like it. You haven't told me your name yet." Mars took a deep drag from the pipe.

"Johnny."

"Just Johnny?"

"Johnny Arcane."

Mars went suddenly pale, as pale as a dark-skinned man could go. His whole body froze, like a shard of obsidian. His eyes grew big and round. "Oh, sweet mother of Beezle!" he said, and braced his elbows on his knees, cupped both his hands, and folded his face into them.

He shuddered and moaned. He spoke to himself. "Mars Daniel, you and your bleeding purple heart. What in the name of great Zimmerman's ghost have you drugged yourself into now?" He lifted his head and rubbed his eyes with his fist. He looked at Johnny. He glanced at the tent flap as if he intended to escape. He looked back and a kind of determination set in. He clenched his jaws.

"OK, this is what's gonna have to happen." His voice was clipped and rapid. "That's not gonna be your name anymore, you shuck? From now on you're name's gonna be...gonna be...name's gonna be Jimmy...Jimmy *Clearlight*. Got that? Name's *Jimmy Clearlight*."

"But I'm Johnny Arcane. My father was Caspar Arcane."

"I don't care who your father was. Your father was Caspar *Clearlight*, got that? You can't be Johnny Arcane if you're gonna go with me."

"How do you know I'm going to go with you?"

"You have to go with me, Jimmy Clearlight. You won't survive otherwise. They would have killed you in there if I hadn't of come along. I'm your protector, Jimmy Clearlight."

"You don't even know where I'm going."

Mars seemed to be caught off guard. He leaned back on his three-legged stool and frowned.

"Well, where *are* you going?"

"I have to be on the Onyx Highway, heading for the flesh mills of Ironweed on the morning of the fourth moon. The Blackcoats are moving some captives. I have to stop this. One of them is Lucy."

Mars stared off into space for a long time, his jaw ajar. "You want me to die, don't you?" he said at last.

"I don't want you to do anything. This is your idea."

"Lucy. She your wife?"

"No. We were too young."

Mars struck another fire stick and re-lit the pipe. "You sure you don't want some of this? Might change your thinking."

Johnny didn't answer. Mars took a deep drag and savored it for longer than a person should be able to hold his breath. When he exhaled, smoke seemed to issue from his nose, his eyes, even his ears.

"Well, first off, Clearlight, you're not gonna be able to measure time by the moon in Ironweed. She makes herself a stranger there. Do you know the day-count between now and the morning of the fourth moon?"

'I do. I put pebbles in a corn oil jar. I have seventeen days."

"Good. I can make it to Ironweed in fifteen, but they won't let you cross the border. You'll have to hide in the wagon. I have a merchant's pass."

Johnny meshed his hands together and his fingers began intertwining involuntarily, like snakes. In his body he could feel the energy moving in two opposite directions. In the pit of his stomach he felt a great sinking dread, in his arms the rising tingle of hope.

"You can't do this by yourself, Jimmy Clearlight. I'm your only chance. What's a mandolin, anyhow?"

"It's a musical instrument."

"Get it out then. Play it for me. I need music right now."

Mars threw himself backwards from the stool onto a jumble of bedding on a shelf at the back of the wagon. Johnny opened his backpack and took the mandolin from the case. So long ago it seemed, that last morning he played music with Bearclaw, Ant and Jocko, *Happy to Meet, Sorry to Part,* and their eyes were all in tears. Perhaps it was necessary to take on a new name in this strange new place. But it was hard to let go of the past.

He plucked the strings. They were untuned. Then that's how he would play. Untuned. He struck a few chords and ran a bit of untuned melody.

"Break my heart, Jimmy Clearlight," said Mars with a sigh. "Break my heart."

So he played. It was strange to play alone, but it was satisfying too. It seemed to knit together all the fragments of the recent moons and put his mind to the focus of his purpose. His memory connected with certain melodies he had made before, while chasing after the notes that flowed from Ant's nimble fingers, or trying to fit into the dissonant chords of Bearclaw's guitar. He didn't know how long he played. Time seemed contained by the canvass cover of the wagon. It took a while for him to realize that Mars Daniel was sitting up on the bed, staring at him. He stopped playing.

"You got a bullet wound. We need to tie that up."

Mars didn't have any bandages. He washed the wound with a clear fluid from a jar. It wasn't water. It stung like fire and it made the blood go dry and the flesh recoil. He tied up the wound with a black sash and he sewed up the hole in Johnny's shirt with a wooden needle and a fragment of yarn.

"Jimmy Clearlight, " he said, "where do you come from?"

At first Johnny didn't know how to answer. Eventually he reckoned that simplest truth was the best.

"I was born in the village of Aberdeen. I never met my father. Casper Arcane. He was a sojourner, just passing through."

"You come from the other side then."

"What side is *this*?"

"This is neither. This is the fringes. This is where Jupiter comes to make love to Venus. But I just come here to get my wares and sell them across the border, where I live."

"What do you know about the other side, then? The side where I come from."

Mars shook his head. "Nobody knows about the other side. Except the Blackcoats. They guard the borders. We avoid them as much as we can. Our task is just to stay alive."

Where do the Blackcoats come from?"

"The Blackcoats come from the City, where the Thinkers live—the ones who rule this world of chaos and cruelty. Some say the Blackcoats are not people. They're machines. I don't care, though. I just want to survive and thrive and take pleasure in this crazy world. Tell me more about this place you come from. What do you mean, you never heard of money?"

"Never. I still don't know what it is."

"That's crazy. Don't people work where you come from?"

"Of course. Everyone works. You have a job. You have a uniform. There's farmers and millers and metal pounders and thatchers and dressmakers. There's messengers. There's mummers. Mummers. I guess that's a kind of work, but it's mostly just doing dances and keeping the stories alive."

"But don't you get paid to do your job?"

There was that word again. *Paid.* He couldn't wrap his mind around it. He shook his head. "We have *dispensaries.* People bring the food they grow and the things they make, and you can just go there and take things if you need them. There's an old saying, *if it isn't there, you don't need it.*"

"What about houses? Do people build them?"

"Sometimes. Usually they build them out of logs. But most of the buildings have always been there. No one knows how long, or who built them. There's a word for these things, but most people don't know this word. They're called *dolmens.*"

"Do people ever fight?"

"Yes, they fight. Usually arm wrestling. And sometimes they have stick fights. Mostly that happens when two men want to marry the same woman."

"Who marries the woman?"

"The woman makes that decision. Based on who fought the best."

Mars sat for a while with his elbows on his knees, his chin in his hands, staring down at the floor. Outside there were noises, drunken angry voices, the sound of glass breaking. Then it grew quiet. The dark-skinned man threw himself back on the bed.

"Just play me some more music, Jimmy Clearlight. Tomorrow's gonna be a big day for you."

ɔ

For a long time he watched the shapes take form on the ridge, and he wondered what they were. Thicker and more rounded than tree stumps, they stood with the regularity of molars in the mouth of a gap-toothed farmer, and when the morning sun struck them, they reflected back, enamel-white against the brown haze of the distant sky.

Johnny sat next to Mars Daniel on the buckboard of the wagon, the little pony ambling ahead of them as they rattled along the dusty road. Mars held the reins limply; the wagon rolled only a little faster than a man could walk. They talked.

"This Lucy of yours. She a young girl?"

"She was young when I met her. So was I. That was six summers ago."

"So, you must have had other girls since then."

"No. Only Lucy. Others have wanted, but I refused them."

Mars shook his head. "You should never refuse a girl, Jimmy Clearlight. A woman is a carriage that a man rides to glory."

Johnny conjured up an image of Lucy. The words *carriage* and *glory* did not seem to fit. The only word he could think of was *destiny*.

A crow leapt from a dead stump. Mars spoke again. "You say you got mummers, where you come from. We got mummers here, too. I've seen them set up in the streets of Cantankerberg. But they have to be careful. If the Blackcoats see a mummer, they'll kill him."

"Why?"

"Because they tell the truth."

"What truth?"

"The truth isn't something you can tell in words. You have to sing it, or dance it. Your mummers. What truth do they tell?"

"They act out the old stories — the ones we're supposed to remember."

"Tell me one. Tell me a story, Jimmy Clearlight. To pass the time."

Johnny didn't know how to answer. The mummers really only told one story, although there were many variations. Once fire and bandits overran the world. Before that, there was No Time. No one remembers No Time. Borderbinder circled the four directions, laying down a line of cornmeal that the fire and bandits could not cross. But he was captured by Deathbridge and killed. Borderbinder's followers gathered and made a plan. They moved out to spread his teachings, the rituals that must be followed to keep the borders secure. Some people believed that Borderbinder did not die, that he slipped into a side world, and one day he would return. But not everyone believed this. The mummers believed it. In every mummer's show there was a suggestion, a movement, a glimpse not clearly defined.

He couldn't bring himself to tell Mars this story. It made him too uneasy. He told a simple story instead.

"Once there was a messenger who was dispatched to a place he had never heard of. The old man who gave him the message said the place was called *Doorway,* and he drew a map. On the way, the messenger asked everyone he met, have you heard of a place called *Doorway,* and nobody had. When he got there, there was no town, just a small encampment of tents. The people who lived in the tents wore no clothes, and they spoke a language he didn't understand. He only knew he was supposed to give the message to a man named Red, and there was one man there with bright red hair, so he gave that man the message, and left in a hurry. But he wondered about it all summer long. It bothered him so much he returned in the winter and found nothing, no people, no tents, nothing. He told this to a medicine man and the medicine man said, *oh, they must have come here from a side world. That's why the place was called Doorway.*"

Mars stared at him. "Your mummers tell *that* story?"

"No, no, it's just something comes up every now and then, late at night, around the tables, in the roadhouses. Nobody knows if it's true."

"Oh, it's true, it's true, Clearlight. There are doorways

everywhere you look. Sometimes I think there are more side worlds than there are worlds. It will drive you mad, if you let it. *This* is the world we live in."

They moved on. After a while the road folded north and set a switchback course toward the summit, passing between the rows of pillars. Drawing closer, Johnny saw that the pillars were carved of stone, flat like tablets, arched at the top, and some sported stone corbels and gargoyles, and others were crowned with stone-chiseled serpents, crosses, love-knots.

Gravestones. Few burials in the Known World were marked by such extravagance, but he had seen them occasionally, mostly on hillsides outside of factory villages.

Mars reined the pony to a halt at the crest and they stared down into the valley below. The gravestones blanketed the entire slope, all the way down to the floor, and to the west and the east, into the visible distance. Johnny's eyes followed the road as it flowed down through the stones and disappeared into the swirl of vapors that obscured almost everything. But from here he could see more than he had seen before. Structures emerged out of the haze, odd shaped towers, some topped with spires, piercing the muddy sky, others hollowed out in jagged places, pale daylight leaking through. And every now and then he saw flashes of light across the plain, and there were places where there were bands of light, continuously blinking. Small objects were drifting through the sky, like birds, but far away. And there was a sound, one he had never heard before, a little like the sound of the wind but more nuanced, shifting in pitch and pocked with occasional clicks and booms. It was not a loud sound, but it was large. It seemed to come from everywhere at once.

"Well, Jimmy Clearlight, this is where you go into hiding. But first we need to see what you got in your bindle. I don't want to be harboring a smuggler."

They climbed down from the buckboard and Johnny opened up his backpack in the dusty grass by the side of the road. The things he took out most often, the clothing, the tools, the small objects of beauty, these things had gathered at the top, while the heavier, more ponderous items had settled to the bottom. He retrieved the flat metal box and opened it.

"This is a map I made of the world I lived in when I was a messenger." He handed it, still scrolled, to Mars.

Mars showed no interest in the map. He didn't open the scroll. "What else you got in there, Clearlight?" he said, tapping his feet restlessly.

Every item Johnny drew from the pack was infused with memory. It felt like he was bringing objects out of a box of dreams. There was Lucy's letter, written on real paper, wrapped back up in its parcel of green leaves. Frankie had given him one of the smaller attractor poles from his workshop. He had kept it faithfully, even though it no longer did anything. There was a little wooden carving of an owl from Jocko, and a cork he had kept from a wine bottle at Stubblefield, the night of the banquet. He had saved a few iridescent wing-feathers from the pheasant brought to him by the weasel in the wilderness. He held his sharp whittling knife in his hand for a while until the memory filtered back in. His mother had given it to him on the morning he left home.

At the bottom of the pack were two jars of corn oil. He set them on the ground.

"What's in those jars?"

"Corn oil."

"What's it for?"

"Cooking."

"Leave them here. You won't need them. Don't bring anything that can catch on fire."

Johnny took one last look in the pack. There was a small side flap and when he reached into it, his fingers recognized the brown glass vial sealed with wax, given him by the messenger on the road, the first day of his sojourning. *Keep it hid. Only take it if the pain is so strong you can't go on. Powerful medicine, but it don't last forever.*

He released the vial and closed the flap without saying anything. Then he saw something else. A red glow flickered briefly through the translucent inner lining. He blinked his eyes, thinking maybe it was just a trick of daylight. But no. It happened again. He reached in and ran his fingers along the inside. Some small hard thing had been sown into the lining. "What's this?" he said out loud.

"What's what?"

"There's something here that isn't mine." He had no choice but to grab the seam of the lining and rip it open. Inside was a small metal cube with a single, round glass eye. As Johnny lifted it, the eye blinked with a red fluorescence. It called to mind the red blinking eye on the wall of the stonehouse. He held the cube out on his palm in the bright open light of day.

"What is it?"

"I don't know."

Mars snatched the cube and turned it around in his fingers. "Oh, sweet mother of Beezle. You've been tracked. Who gave you this?"

"I don't know." The moment he said it an image flashed

before his mind: the day he left Stubblefield with Mayor Castorbean's message. Old Youngfellow: *Your pack, sir.*

"What do you mean, *tracked*?"

"Don't ask. We have to get rid of it. We can't just throw it away. It has to be buried." Mars scanned the slope of the hill in all directions. His head swerved from side to side until suddenly it stopped at the sight of something far off. "Well, well. Mother Terra has smiled on us. Look!"

In the distance between the graves something was happening. There was a cart and two men and a mound of dirt. One man was shoveling, while the other was standing with his arms folded.

"Come quick. Bring that thing. Hurry!"

They started down the hill at a canter. Johnny had trouble keeping up, but as they drew near the scene, Mars slowed, and when the two men noticed them, he stopped and clasped his hands together respectfully.

There was a body in the hole, wrapped in a plain white sheet. The lower part of the sheet was soaked with blood. Mars nodded.

"Who is it?" he asked.

"That be our brother, Abner Woolcoat," said one of the men.

"Ah. That's what I thought. I knew him."

The man wrinkled his nose. "You knew Abner?"

"Yes, we worked together."

The man gave the other man a puzzled look. "Hell, Abner never done a stitch of work in his life!"

"Ah, but you underestimate your brother. What about that time in the...when he worked in the..."

"In the foundry?"

"Yeah, the foundry. We worked together there. He saved

my life. There was this...this *anvil*. It came loose from the crane and Abner caught it in his bare hands."

The two men looked at each other with identical dumbfounded expressions. It occurred to Johnny that they might be twins, so matched were their faces, or perhaps, with the departed Abner, they had formed a set of triplets.

"I owe the man my life," continued Mars, "But I have nothing to offer. Do you think you could at least allow me to honor him by tossing a handful of dirt in his grave?"

The shovel man sunk his blade into the pile. "Suit yerself, stranger. We're just tryin' to get him in the ground afore the flies come." He scooped a shovelful and dumped it unceremoniously onto the body.

Mars folded his hands behind his back and wriggled his fingers. Johnny understood at once, and quietly slipped him the metal cube. The dark-skinned man knelt before the dirt pile and cupped a large handful around the object. Then he stood and bowed his head.

"Abner, old friend, I'm so sorry it had to be this way," he said as he tossed the heavy dirt into the grave.

CHAPTER FIFTEEN

LADYLAND

nder the platform at the back of the wagon, a compartment, boarded with slats of wood, perched directly over the rear axle. It was packed with costumes—fur-lined robes crazy-quilted with patches of color, deep purples, sky blue and vernal green, belts and sashes and fringed jackets, leather hats with plumed feathers. Into this crammed space Johnny was forced to climb, while Mars nailed the slats back in place. Johnny's knee struck something solid. Along the rear wall he found an array of glass apothecaries, each packed with a dark green herb.

"You find that, Clearlight?" came Mars' voice. "In the jars? That's what you call the *illumination*. Chew on some. It'll keep you quiet." The wagon began to move.

The road was pitted and the axles rocked from side to side, but the clothing cushioned him. He considered Mars' offer of the *illumination*, but decided against it. He must remain clearheaded at this time. Anything could happen.

Perhaps he fell asleep. Suddenly he heard voices—lots of them—a large crowd of people, mumbling, shouting, and singing just outside, in what sounded like many different languages. The wagon was not moving. He realized he'd gotten himself into a position with one arm above his head, the other folded under his belly, and he couldn't move either one. Panic seized him. The thought of being contained like this any longer was unbearable. But no, he must stay calm. He focused on the sounds.

"Seven! Seven! Seven! Seven!" somebody shouted, over and over, and then it sounded like someone said, "Don't step on the snake!" There was a rattling sound, like dice in a cup, but more rhythmic, and it seemed to recede and advance, rhythmically. In the distance women's voices chanted gutturally on four notes.

"Pra-wah-ki-sah. Pra-wah-ki-sah."

Then a voice like a child's threaded through, intoning, "Beezle! Beezle! Beezle!"

"Mr. Mars, you bring any weed?" Johnny felt the wagon lurch and he realized someone had stepped on board.

"Just a little, Sir Duke. Enough for my friends. I didn't renew my license."

"Knives look pretty sharp. Might want to caliber them."

"Caliber away, boss. I got nothing to hide."

"Sokay, sokay. You're a regular. Your papers are in order. Pass on. But stay out of Ladyland this time. That got a little ugly."

"Yessir."

The wagon began to move again. Johnny centered his breathing and tried to bring his focus to his arms. The arm under him was numb. Slowly he managed to roll himself onto his back and the numb arm flopped free and began to tingle. With great effort he brought the other arm down until they were both resting at his sides.

They rattled on through a cavalcade of sounds and smells, intoxicating smells of food cooking, repulsive smells of rotting flesh and singeing hair. Sometimes there was music, mostly percussion, and the rattling of dissonant bells. They passed through a loud argument, many men yelling at each other. He made out a few words. "Castration!" somebody yelled. "Denominator!" cried another. Then there was a woman's voice, screaming, not near but relentless. "Help me!" she cried. No one responded. She continued to scream.

After a while it grew a little quieter. Most of the voices gave in to a low, throbbing hum that rose and fell in pitch. Occasionally there was a crackling noise, like twigs breaking, but it seemed to come from high in the air.

For a while Johnny heard the hoof-clopping of another pony alongside the wagon, and a voice. He couldn't make out the words, but he understood Mars Daniel's reply.

"Yeah, yeah, I got lots; it's good, it's good, but I have to raise the price. No, I can't give it to you here. My license expired. You ride on ahead and meet me at Ladyland."

After that, the sounds returned, especially the sounds of traffic on the road, the rattling of carriages and the whizzing of other moving things. From his confinement Johnny could only guess what they looked like. For a long time there was a mechanical clanging, and the hissing of venting steam. Then the wagon stopped, and there were voices, men speaking rapidly, in a foreign tongue. The floorboards rocked and the voices grew more aggressive. Johnny felt the clunk of footsteps and then the metallic cling of a knife being pulled from a sheath.

"Shuck off, you lousy horn pigs!" barked Mars Daniel's distinctive voice, then a slice through the air and a sharp yelp of pain. The other voices roiled, shouting something like "Canima! Canima!" The wagon pitched wildly as the intruders departed.

Johnny felt the pressure as Mars flopped down on the

platform above him. "Beezle me to death, mother! Dream weavers can't even be alone with their thoughts anymore." There was a knock on the wood. "Clearlight. You OK in there?"

Johnny stirred. "Yes. Are you going to let me out of here?"

"In time. In time. But there's an important lesson for you in this, can you hear me?"

"I can hear you."

"Well, let me make it a little easier for you to hear me." The floor teetered, and then there was a screeching sound as Mars pried some of the slats loose. The garments rustled and Johnny could see his face peering in at him. "This is the lesson, Clearlight. In this place we're going, you gotta choose your battles, you suss? You try to fight 'em all, you be dead in less than a day. Now you and me, we got only one battle to fight. We're gonna save your Lucy, that's all. Everything else, you let it go, you suss?"

Johnny didn't say anything. "You *suss*?" Mars repeated. Still Johnny didn't say anything. He was too overwhelmed to put his thoughts into words. "Well, just think on it then, Clearlight. We'll be there soon."

He left the slats open and the fabric parted. Johnny could see his back as he sat on the buckboard and goaded the pony. He was wearing a fringed buckskin jacket and he had a bright purple scarf tied around his black cloud of hair. But he blocked most of Johnny's view of the road ahead. There were no trees or bushes, or foliage of any kind. Mostly it looked like structures, walls and fences right up to the roadbed, signs everywhere, none of which he could read, windows, occasionally people leaning out of them. Someone threw something at the wagon from a window. It splattered against the canvass. Johnny caught the scent of rotten fruit, but he couldn't see what it was.

Eventually it grew dark. *Well, good,* he thought to himself, *at least there's a constant.* Then suddenly the wagon stopped.

"We're here, Clearlight. Get yourself out of there."

Johnny emerged from his confinement like a moth from a cocoon. His arms felt so light they kept trying to float, and it was all he could do to keep them at his sides. Mars was holding a dark round loaf of unsliced bread. He broke off a crust. "Here, eat this. You're hungry."

Johnny did. He stuffed the crust into his mouth and quickly swallowed the tumbler of water that followed.

"OK, this is what I want you to do. Take this bread in your hands and step out. That's all. Do what I say." Johnny took the bread. His thoughts were too clouded to object to anything. "This is the way out." Mars parted the canvass flap. Clutching the loaf, Johnny stepped down from the wagon.

It was dark, but not the dark of night. It was more the shaded dark of a deep, narrow canyon in late afternoon. The walls were unlike any he had ever seen. Perfectly vertical and only wide enough for the road to pass between them, they were interlaced with a tangle of protuberances so foreign it took him a long time to conceptualize what they might be. His first awakening was a memory—the silo at King Corn with its handholds and hatches and yes, there were pictures on these walls too, but not of graceful birds and mountains; they were odd runes and symbols, blackened by torches, stick figures and geometric patterns. Rails and ladders and metal bars clung to the walls, and further up, fenced ledges and glass windows, many broken.

These canyons were made by the hands of man. It was only then that he realized there were people, high above him, sitting in chairs on the ledges or leaning on the railings. Were they real? They were so motionless. Were they dead people, propped up to look like they were alive, or frozen in place where they had perished?

The questions were answered by a hacking sound, and one man on a balcony far above, spat into the air. His spittle arched in a stray shaft of sunlight, split into three portions, then into a fine mist infused by the accelerating momentum of its descent. Johnny felt its moisture strike his forehead.

Suddenly someone stood in front of him. A child, a small boy, barefoot, dressed in rags, his face smeared with mud. His eyes entreated. He spoke. "Give me some of that bread."

Johnny understood hunger. His heart went out. He ripped a generous handful from the crust and thrust it to the boy.

A shimmering in the air, a rustling in the street, and then out of the cracks and corners of the canyon children poured like cockroaches, little boys and girls, all equally ragged and barefooted; they surrounded Johnny and pressed in on him, yelling and clawing and grasping. One of them snatched the bread from his hands and the others descended upon it, tearing it with fingers, ripping it into shreds, thrusting the crumbs into their mouths, all the while howling and shoving.

Johnny felt a firm hand grasp his shoulder and pull him back. He turned. Mars Daniel took both his arms and thrust him through the upraised flap back into the shelter of the wagon. Johnny stumbled onto the floor, his heart pounding, as Mars closed the flap.

"Object lesson number one, Clearlight. You'll learn soon. You have to pick your battles."

Mars jumped on the buckboard and took the reins. "Sit next to me now. We're gonna see some things." He was restless and alert; his arms moved constantly from the elbows, his eyes darting from side to side.

But Johnny was too stunned to move. The forward jolt of the wagon threw him backwards. He climbed onto the seat and squinted into the darkness. The canyon walls were punctuated with fissures so narrow only a child or a small animal could slip through them. He saw stirring movement and pale rays of colored light high along the walls. Tattered bits of cloth hung like ragged banners, cords were strung from wall to wall, and narrow balconies jutted over the abyss.

Something zoomed past, then another, and another. They were giant hornets ... no! They were people, riding the backs of some kind of flying creature ... no! The creatures weren't flying, they weren't creatures, they were wheeled things and they buzzed like insects and they moved faster than cats, and sometimes two, sometimes even three people rode on their backs. Before he could grasp this, everything changed completely, or maybe nothing changed, maybe he was just allowing his eyes to take in more and more of the overwhelmingly strange detail.

There were people everywhere, more people than he had ever seen in one place, even in the great hall at Stubblefield. The canyons had opened into a broad boulevard and a pale red sun was straining to shine through the hazy skies. A blur of motion filled the street, people moving, no one standing still, each person pressing forward with a sense of purpose, each one alone, locked into himself, noticing the others only enough to avoid a collision. The clothing was mostly drab and colorless, tans and grays, uniforms without embellishment, but the skin pigmentation wildly varied, from chicory brown to rose quartz pink, blue-black like Bow Wow, white as snowdrift.

Mars was talking but his words just floated like some kind of percussive music. Johnny couldn't make any sense out of them. "And this is where you pierce the ear of the sky, and it bleeds, and in that temple they would eat the moon if they could, and they would eat it like a grape. There used to be another moon, you know. It was the blood moon, and when it blew apart, that's how we got the mountains. And, said the owner of the velvet horse, I've tried everything. I've tried cardamom and the silver tipped arrow. The tips are dipped in molten semen, in the semen mines of Mercury..."

Perhaps he wasn't saying any of these things. Johnny couldn't make any sense of it. He looked up and saw things in the sky. They were like letters trying to form words, but then they became birds and flew away. One broad building was completely covered in windows, with vines climbing up it. Someone threw a large square object from a balcony. The crowd parted and it struck the street and shattered. Immediately people rushed forward and began clawing through the fragments.

"Clearlight," said Mars suddenly, as if descending into lucidity. "I have business to conduct not far from here. You'll come with me. They'll take good care of you."

Johnny lowered his eyes to the crowd swirling around the wagon. Mostly women and children, they were obviously attracted to this colorful spectacle. Some of the children tried to climb up on the pony's back. Mars snapped the reins in their faces and they tumbled back into the street.

To the women he was more cordial. One ran alongside the buckboard for a while, stroking Mars' calves with her fingers. Another managed to jump onto the platform and hang on the cover staves long enough to plant a kiss on his lips.

"Mr. Pots and Pans!" she cooed.

"Don't forget knives," replied Mars. The girl lost her grip and fell back into the arms of her giggling friends.

The wagon entered another narrow canyon, darker now, for the sun was lower. In the shadows people moved, slower than the people on the boulevard, shuffling their feet through piles of scraps gathered against the walls, sometimes squatting down, pawing through the trash, pocketing a few choice morsels. If they looked up and saw the wagon approaching they quickly averted their faces.

The canyon ended at a wall of windows, but directly ahead, at street level, an unexpected bloom of flashing pink and purple light created an illusion of motion, illuminating, panel by panel, a mural of sunbursts and ringed orbs and winged raptors with female breasts. A glass door swung open and some people stumbled out, laughing. Above the door, in glowing crimson letters: LADYLAND.

"Our destination, Jimmy Clearlight. This is where we spend the evening."

"But...the wagon. Will it be safe?"

"Now you're thinking. Don't worry about the wagon. I got guardians."

Now you're thinking. Johnny looked around. He didn't think he was thinking, but he saw them, shadowy figures stationed in the chinks in the walls, stone-still, cloaked in black. Guardians.

He found himself propelled through the open glass door. A question flashed through his mind: *Where does all this light come from?* The place was equally dark and light. The light was cast by glowing tubes curved along contours of risers, stairs and ramps, defining shapes and forms but revealing very little, mostly a crimson carpet and a faded floral print on the walls. There were people everywhere, a murmur of voices and the rhythm of drums, but no melody. Slowly he became aware of a low, circular arena, shimmering blue. At first he thought it was a pool, and his memory fleeted over the glowing blue pool in Bow Wow's bathhouse. But it was not a pool. There was no water, and in it a woman, completely naked, was coiling and writhing like a serpent. A crowd of men ringed the enclosure. They were throwing bits of paper onto the naked woman.

"Clearlight, relax." Mars spoke close to his ear. "You're safe here. Leave your mind outside and follow your loins."

"I'm hungry," Johnny said.

"That's all right. You'll be taken care of. Your needs will be met. Listen, this is what's going to happen. I have business to conduct. I'm going to leave you here for a while. Whatever you do, stay in this building. I'm going to give you some money." From somewhere in his clothing he produced a handful of heavy green paper strips, like what the men were throwing at the naked woman. "You're not allowed to leave here until you've spent all this money, you suss? You can have anything you want, but just remember, everything costs money. You suss? And that's a lot of money. Hide it."

A figure approached from the darkness. Out of some newborn instinct Johnny clutched his fist around the paper and thrust it in his pocket. A woman stood there. She was egg-shaped and draped in several layers of shiny black robes that looked like the wing feathers of a raven, her cheeks slathered rouge-red, her eyelashes the legs of small spiders, her hair a nest for rats.

"Mr. Mars, what sort of trouble do you bring us today?"

"No trouble, Honey Mae, only business. Lots of business."

"Legal business?"

"Pots and pans and knives. And I bring you a tender young customer, fully bestowed with spending power."

Honey Mae eyed Johnny up and down. "Tender and young indeed. What's his name?"

"Jimmy Clearlight."

"Jimmy Clearlight? You make up some good ones, Mars. What does he want?"

Johnny felt his will rising in him. He had to assume some kind of control. "I want something to eat."

Honey Mae laughed in a throaty voice. "He speaks! Sit down here, Jimmy Clearlight, before you fall down. Here, this table. Mr. Mars. Take me out and show me what you've got." She lost no time in turning to leave. Mars looked at Johnny and made some gestures that he could not understand. He rubbed his fingers together, then made a flinging motion like he was throwing something away. He passed the back of his hand under his chin, like he was slashing his own throat. Then he just disappeared, leaving Johnny alone, open like a wound, like a bleeding rodent under a sky of circling vultures.

The air rippled, and another woman stood there, holding something wrapped in a soiled cloth. She was older and plumper than his mother and she wore a shiny metallic dress that shimmered in the crimson tubelight.

"Honey Mae says we got a hungry boy over here. Does this look good to you?" She pulled away the cloth, revealing some kind of a roasted bird, the legbone and the breast.

"What is it?"

"It's woodcock. Do you like woodcock?"

Johnny reached in his pocket and grasped the paper bills with his sweaty palm. He pulled them out in one wad and fingered through them. They were all different, different pictures, different colors, different symbols. He had no idea what was what. He selected one with a pyramid and an eye, because he remembered the image from the cover of Mars' wagon.

"Will this be enough?" He handed her the bill. She took it in both hands and held it out, staring at it, her eyes pondering.

"Yeah,' she said casually. "That'll be enough." Johnny saw her make a gesture with her head, a nod beckoning someone across the room, another downward nod indicating Johnny, where he sat at the table. Then she disappeared.

Immediately another woman materialized, this one barely more than a girl, small and breakable; she had fox eyes—there was a wildness in them, and her fox-red hair spilled out over moon-white shoulders. She wore very little, something tied around her waist, and a thin gauzy halter that did nothing to conceal her firm bosom. She slid in next to him on the bench and pressed her body against his side.

"What's *your* name?"

"Johnny..." he stammered. "J-J-Jimmy. Jimmy Clearlight."

"Johnny!" she said with a giggle, "You said Johnny! That's your real name, isn't it?"

"It...it...they called me that when I was a little boy. Sometimes I still use it."

"Well, you can be a little boy here, Johnny Clearlight. Do you like the woodcock?"

"It's good. I was hungry."

She placed her hand on his knee. "You know the wood-cock brings out the man-thing, don't you? It goes right to your man-thing and brings it up, like a broom handle. Is that why you're eating it, Johnny? Do you want to bring up your man-thing? Do you wanna bring it up for me?"

Johnny removed her hand from his knee. He moved away

from her. "I'm eating it because I was hungry and it's what they brought me."

"Oooh, Johnny Clearlight, don't be silly. Nobody comes to Ladyland just to eat. Eat it up, Johnny Clearlight. Bring up your man-thing. I can wait."

Johnny bit into the meat but his stomach was already roiling with anxiety. The meat was greasy and strong-flavored and it yielded itself willingly from the bone. The girl moved closer and started fondling the hair on the back of Johnny's neck.

"I like your hair, Johnny. It excites me. Don't you want to know my name?"

"Wha—what's your name?"

She wrapped her fingers around his neck. "Pleasure. You can call me Pleasure. But that's only part of it. Do you want to know my whole name?"

Johnny didn't answer. He ripped at the meat and swallowed chunks of it whole. His arms and legs were trembling. She was right, and he couldn't do anything about it. His man-thing was rising like a broom handle between his legs.

"Well, I'll tell you anyhow. My other name is Pane. You can call me Pleasurepane."

Sweat broke on his forehead. "You mean pain, like hurt?"

"No, silly. Pane. Like a windowpane. Come on Johnny, you know you want it. You finished your woodcock. Come with me." She grabbed his arms and pulled him to his feet.

He dizzied and stumbled. She took his elbow and ran her hand down his wrists until her fingers laced with his. She led him down a dark, narrow hallway. The walls were painted black and scribbled with white letters and crooked shapes that glowed in some dim recessed lighting along the floor. Even her skin was glowing. No, her skin was not glowing. It was shaded night-black by the darkness of the hall, but the flecks of dust on her bare shoulders and arms glowed like stars in a dark night sky. He heard the echo of Mars' words: *leave your mind outside and follow your loins.* And this he did. The forward thrust of a personal driving force obscured all the weirdness, the menace, the dread that haunted this strange world. The silken softness of flesh. The radiance of desire.

She threw open a door. It was a tiny room, a bed, a table, a lamp glowing under a scarlet shade, a bottle. The sight of the bottle shook loose a distant memory: amber glass, sweet and thick with spirits, the elixir he had shared for seven rainy nights with Lucy. But before he could process this impression she had turned to him, kissing his neck, loosening his buttons, slipping her fingers under his shirt. He pulled away.

"You're tense, Johnny. Do you want to drink?" She reached for the bottle.

"No, no, no drink."

"Lie on the bed, then. On your back. Relax. I will take care of you."

But before he did anything else he reached in his pocket and withdrew the wad of money. "Here," he said, "This?" He tried to toss all the bills onto the table but his hand trembled, and some of them wafted to the floor. She glanced at them briefly, turned away, then glanced at them again, briefly.

"Never mind that. Lie down. You won't regret it." Johnny lay on his back. The bed was deep-cushioned and he sank into it. The girl removed her halter, slipped the cloth off her waist, and climbed on top of him. She straddled his throbbing man-thing between her knees, ripped open his shirt and began licking his chest from the neck down.

Suddenly something came into focus, on the wall across

the room. The recognition jolted him so powerfully he sat up and the girl was thrown sideways into the deep pile of bedding.

"Whoa, Johnny, don't scare me! This was just getting good."

His feet hit the floor and he stumbled across the room. "What's this?" he cried. On the wall, a picture in a frame, hung a little crooked. He recognized it at once but he couldn't understand how it could be here. He thought it was in the metal box, in his backpack, out in Mars Daniel's wagon. How could the same thing be in two different places?

The girl changed into someone else. Her heat vanished. She became someone small and shy and vulnerable. When she spoke, her voice was tiny, troubled, like a deer.

"It's...the waterfall, where the river enters into the other world. We all get one when we start working here. To remember why we're here..."

It was something he hadn't felt in a long time. Pieces of the puzzle, falling into place. *Lucy, a fugitive. A person running from someone who wants to hurt them.* "The flesh mills of Ironweed, the work we will do there will kill us... the fires didn't really burn themselves out. They just moved further away. They're still burning."

"I have to leave," he said firmly.

Her voice changed to something else again, neither siren nor little girl. "You can't leave. We're not done yet."

"Yes, we are. You can leave, too. You don't have to do this. There are other ways to live."

She leapt from the bed and dashed to the door, blocking his exit with her arms spread. "You can't just go now Johnny, not with your man-thing all pumped up like that. It will drive you mad."

"I can take care of my own man-thing." He grabbed her shoulders and tried to force her aside.

"No, don't! Johnny don't! Please!"

The fear in her words disoriented him, but he couldn't stop. He rammed her down with his shoulders, threw open the door and burst into the dark hall. A voice, more machine-like than human, and seeming to come from everywhere at once, pierced the gloom.

"We got a runaway!"

A dark shape appeared in the hall, then another, then another. Bulky men, dressed in black, wearing hoods. He rushed at them, struck the first one, knocked him down. A familiar stench lingered from the impact. The second one grabbed at his jacket. Johnny pulled away. The third took a dive at his feet and Johnny leapt over him and broke out into the big room where a cloud of blue smoke hung over the arena, and the naked serpent girl was now coiled on the floor with a naked serpent man.

There was a blast of sound, like the caw of a huge crow caught in a deafening loop. Commotion everywhere, people jumping up out of the darkness, scrambling for the door.

"Runaway!" someone yelled. "Stop him!"

But he got to the door first and slammed into the glass pane. It did not give. He struck it again. It was solid. He looked around in desperation. A heavy pottery vase, the height of a man's legs. He grabbed it in his arms, swung his body, and hurled it into the glass. The door buckled and the shards fell like hailstones. Without hesitation he leapt through the opening, into the dank, dark night.

The cover of the wagon was lit with some inner glow, and the wagon itself seemed to be rocking from side to side. The pony was asleep on her feet, but when she heard the ruckus approaching from Ladyland, she woke and became agitated. Johnny bolted. He saw the tent flap open and Mars appeared, bare-chested, buckling his pants. One voice, louder than the others, rose above the din.

"That's it, Mars Daniel! I knew I never should have let you back in here. Look at what your little boy has done! He busted my front door and he woke up the Blackcoats. We don't want any dealing with the Blackcoats here."

Mars rubbed his eyes and scanned the scene. Then he reached out, grabbed Johnny by the wrist and pulled him up on the buckboard. "What have you done, Jimmy Clearlight? I told you, you weren't allowed to leave."

"Oh, he left, all right!" cried Honey Mae. "He hoofed it like a horn pig. And what are you doing in there anyhow? You're dealing the weed. I know it! You can't be trusted. You're no more than a common ground snake."

Mars looked down at Johnny who was curled up and shivering on the floorboard. "Where's the money I gave you, Jimmy Clearlight?"

Johnny gasped. He could barely form words. "Inside. In the room."

"All of it?"

"All of it."

Mars slammed his fist on the buckboard. "Well, did she *do* you?"

"Did she do me *what*?"

"You know, did she *do* you? Did she exercise your man-thing? Did she drain your love juice?"

Johnny started to cry. "No. I ran."

"Oh, for the love of Beezle!"

"Listen here, Daniel," barked Honey Mae. "I'm gonna

turn my back on you now, and when I turn again I want to see you gone for good. Do you know what I mean?"

Mars scratched his chin. "Not gonna happen, Honey Mae."

"What?"

"The boy wasn't serviced. He didn't get what he paid for. I want that money back."

For a long time the two just stared at each other, caught in some weird impasse of will. Honey Mae seethed through her teeth. Mars sat with his arms folded, his jaw firm. Finally Honey Mae turned.

"Duckworth, run into Flora's room and fetch that money. I'd hock my whole business never to see this man again."

A small boy turned and hurried through the broken glass into the building. The wagon rocked slightly, the flap parted and two girls jumped out, naked, clutching their dresses against their bodies. They cowered and disappeared into the crowd of silent, standing figures. Everyone seemed to be frozen in a time-locked moment, unable to move or speak, paralyzed by the visage of the three Blackcoats, hooded and ominous by the shattered door.

In time the boy returned with a cloth sack and handed it to Honey Mae. She peered into it, nodded, and handed it up to Mars.

"That's the price of your soul, Mars, all in that little bag. You got the cash. You left your soul. Hope you can live with it."

Mars adjusted his belt and gathered his shirt from the seatbed. He smiled. "Pleasure doing business with you, Honey Mae." Then he shook the reins and the wagon began to move.

A while later, the wagon rattling through some dark alley where the only residents were rats, Mars glanced down at Johnny who still lay shivering and sobbing on the floor-boards.

"Oh, Jimmy Clearlight," he moaned. "You're gonna be the death of me. I can feel it. You're gonna be the cause of my death."

CHAPTER SIXTEEN
BADLANDS

While the wagon rolled on over cobbles and chuckholes, Johnny lay on the floorboard under swaying pots, pans and knives, watching his own thoughts sift back through recent events. He grasped at certain things, moments in which his will had overcome his weakness, and slowly these glints of memory soothed the hollow in his stomach and the wizened desolation of his sex. He had been placed in an impossible situation, and he had done the right thing. He had not been armed for this. *Choose your battles,* Mars told him, but this battle had chosen him. The girl was like Lucy. She was no different than Lucy. Perhaps Lucy had once been in that very room, slave to the very same degradations. And now she was a captive, driven toward further degradations—*the work we do there will kill us.* These were not multiple battles. This was all one battle, and he had chosen it.

He felt his strength return. He sat up, stood, braced himself against the wagon's veering motions, lifted the tent flap and stepped out onto the buckboard.

They were rattling through a dark place of weathered walls and dense fog. Mars was almost asleep at the reins, the pony trotting ahead on her own volition. He startled as Johnny's weight sagged into the seat.

"Clearlight. Are you feeling better?"

"I'm feeling good. I did the right thing."

Mars looked him up and down. "You did what you did, Clearlight. We're just gonna go with it from here."

"Where are we?"

"Don't worry about it. I know a place we'll be able to finish out the night safely."

They rolled on in silence, and each wall was more dilapidated than the one before. Cornerstones were crumbled, some lay in piles of rubble on the ground. Some lone ramparts stood thin and meaningless, supporting no roof, enclosing nothing. Bats flew in and out of freestanding chimneys. An owl regarded them from a sagging doorframe.

Eventually the walls disappeared entirely and they came into an open place where small fires freckled a range of rounded hills. Drawing closer, Johnny saw that they were not hills at all, but mounds of debris, broken things, wheels, boxes, piles of rags, scraps of rotting food, the dry skeletons of large animals. Here and there shacks were built of boards and bedsprings, and people gathered around the fires, warming their hands, roasting things on sticks, or just sitting, staring into the flames.

"These are the gentle people of the badlands," said Mars. "They can't protect you, but they won't hurt you. We can rest here."

They found a smoldering fire with no one sitting by it, and there was a little grassy patch where the pony could graze. The wind was chilly and they welcomed the warmth that Mars kindled from some old barn boards. The sparks disappeared in the darkness to join the invisible stars.

Neither spoke. There was too much to say, and no place to start. Sounds echoed from the distant fires, voices, the snapping of sticks, someone singing, someone crying, perhaps the wail of a far-off coyote, Johnny wasn't sure. His eyelids grew heavy. He started to sway on his feet.

Suddenly he spooked. There was someone else standing next to him, a thin shadow swaying with him, leaning toward the fire. He glanced at Mars at the same time Mars noticed the stranger. "Whoa! We have company."

Johnny looked at the boy—just a boy, no older than he himself had been when he first left home. Perhaps younger. He was little more than skin and bone. His hair was cropped short and his eyes were sunk in two dark blue craters. A one-piece jump suit hung loosely from his shoulders. It was ripped in places and spattered with blood. He wore no shoes.

"Are you all right?"

The boy leaned forward and spoke, but his voice was but a soft and wordless mumble.

Johnny pressed his ear closer. "I can't hear you. Say it again."

"I got away. They hurt me."

Johnny turned to Mars. "Can we give him something to eat?"

Mars grumbled. "Yeah, yeah, go ahead. In the wagon. Bread and cheese."

Johnny went inside to fetch the food, all the while thinking, there's something familiar about that boy, something from the past. When he turned from the counter with the bread in hand, the recognition flooded in.

Jocko. The vulnerability. The slightness of build. The quiet, almost disembodied voice. This would be Jocko if he were to be thrust unexpectedly into this strange and hostile world.

The boy ate the food dutifully, but without attention or appetite. "Water," he whispered. Johnny let him drink from his own canteen.

"Take me with you."

Mars' voice was firm. "*No*. No riders."

The boy was silent. He bowed his head and his chest began to heave.

"But can we give him something else to wear? He's hurt, and his clothes are bloody."

"This isn't your battle, Clearlight."

"He's not a battle. He's a person."

Mars groaned in exasperation. "You really want me to die, don't you? Inside, where you were hiding. Just get something. Be quick about it."

When Johnny returned he had a floral print tunic with a fringed collar, and a pair of red, flared corduroys. There were no plain clothes in the trailer. He handed them to the boy. "Here, put these on."

The boy took them, but he just stood there clutching them to his chest, staring at the fire.

"You heard him, captain," said Mars. "Change your clothes."

Absently, the boy undid a few buttons on his jumpsuit. It was all he needed to do. The garment fell off him like a cornhusk and he stood there naked. His body was covered with puffy bruises, and the blood was just beginning to coagulate on a deep gash in his abdomen.

Mars sighed. "Well, don't be showing off for us. Come on, get dressed." Still the boy did not move. Mars looked at Johnny. "Oh, for the love of Beezle! All right then, let's do this."

They lowered the boy's bare butt onto a stump. Johnny

lifted his arms and poured the tunic over his head while Mars struggled to pull the pants up onto his legs. Finally the boy was dressed and seated. He looked ridiculous, like a rooster who had lost a cockfight.

"That's it," said Mars. "We got an appointment in dreamland now. Let's hope you're gone by the time the sun is up." He turned and started wearily for the wagon.

$$\mathrm{O}$$

Voices and the insistent rattling of the wagon staves woke them.

"Pots and pans!"

Dawn had broken. A dozen or so ragged people were gathered around the wagon—men, women and children. Some of them were carrying things. A man held a long-handled pitchfork. A small goat struggled in the arms of a young girl. A woman had a wardrobe of soiled dresses draped over her arm. Another cradled a stack of what Johnny recognized were books, although he had only seen one before.

Mars rubbed his eyes. "I'm not trading," he said. "I only take money."

A man held up a fistful of bills. "We got money."

Mars jumped down and took one of the bills between his fingers. "This is highland money. You can't spend that here."

Johnny looked around at the fire circle, the stump. The boy was nowhere to be seen. People started jumping up on the buckboard.

"Clearlight, go in there and don't let them take anything without paying for it. Any money, I don't care. Higland, lowland. Don't worry about it."

The wagon was choked with people. Woman were taking

pots and pans down from the hooks and running their fingers along the handles and lids, while men stroked the blades of knives. Johnny planted his legs firmly and stood in front of the canvass flap. He was a little afraid, especially of the men with the knives, but soon he relaxed. There was a gentle murmur in the voices, and a spirit of respect in the way the patrons brought the wares to him and offered up their paper bills. He had no idea what anything should cost. He took the money and the customers left with happy smiles on their faces.

The woman with the stack of books approached with a skillet in her free hand.

"May I see your books?" he asked.

She turned and shrugged the books his way. There was no place to set them down. Five books. He took the stack in his hands and pawed through them. The first four were in a strange alphabet, annotated with odd shapes and symbols. But at the bottom, a thin volume with a tattered blue cover: THE COLLECTED POEMS OF THE KNOWN WORLD

The title startled him and filled him with curiosity. "I want this one," he said.

"Yes, yes, you may have. I want this pan. Very good for fish." She reached her hand awkwardly into her sleeve, but he shook his head.

"No, no money, we will trade."

The woman stared at him, a wad of paper money in her hand. Then she clutched the pan to her chest, turned and fled from the wagon like she had committed some great offense, leaving Johnny holding all five books. The first four he let drop. The book of poetry he shuffled under the buckboard seat.

Later, when all the ragged people had completed their purchases and drifted on their way, Mars roused the pony and they started on the path through the trash hills. The pony seemed happy to be moving. After a while, Mars shook the reins and handed them to Johnny.

"You take her, Clearlight. I wanna count the earnings."

At first Johnny didn't think he was up to the task. His heart and mind were wracked with a panorama of thoughts and emotions. But the pony just continued as long as the reins were slack, and eventually the reins themselves anchored him to the realities and responsibilities of this strange world.

"You did fine, Clearlight." Mars turned the bills over in his hands. "Lots of money. Where'd you get that book?"

Johnny laid his hand on the book in his lap, feeling foolish and embarrassed.

"You traded it, didn't you? Thought we said there'd be no trades."

Johnny tightened his fingers on the book's four corners. "I didn't—I didn't think it was something you would want."

"Well, let me see it."

Mars pried the book from Johnny's hands. He held it up like an offering to the sky and flipped through the pages one by one. He stopped at a certain page and stared at it until a smile curled his lips, then a chuckle.

"Holy Beezle, my mother used to read this to me back when I was her little love child. I could recite it by heart. This is why she named me Mars. Did your mother ever read to you, Clearlight?"

"No. There were no books. Sometimes we sang songs together."

"Well, this one's for you, then. This can be your medicine. This can be your daydream. Listen." Mars read the poem in a playful chanted rhythm, the way a mother would read to a child.

*Now the four-way lodge is opened, now the hunting
winds are loose
Now the smokes of spring go up to clear the brain
Now the young man's heart is troubled,
Now the Red Gods make their medicine again
He must go, he must go, he must go away from here
See, your road is clear before you,
When the old spring-fret comes o'er you
And the Red Gods call for you!*

A drum seemed to beat in the air for a while after Mars
stopped reading. The pony was dancing and the wagon was
swaying in time. The bleak edges of the landscape softened,
like a watercolor. Then Mars closed the book with a pop.

"It's okay you traded, Clearlight. I don't mind. I traded
too. Look at this."

Johnny looked. Mars was holding a large and formidable
knife. It looked older than a dolmen, a single shaft of heavy
dark metal pounded out in an age before no time, unhilted,
unserrated, unadorned, a weapon with a simple purpose. Its
coarse texture reflected nothing of the pale, overhead sun.
It stirred something like dread in the caldron of Johnny's
stomach.

"Beautiful, isn't it? Someday one of us will have use for
this."

☽

They traveled all morning under a continually hazy sky,
through a landscape of strange abandoned buildings, mills
of some sort perhaps, silos, smokestacks, cables, chutes,
ladders. Not as ancient as dolmens, they were still in the

process of collapse. Metal awnings sagged precariously, bits of machinery hung from snapped cords, rusty gates soughed in the wind.

Mars took the reins again. The first thing Johnny did was locate his corn oil jar and drop in another pebble. There were fifteen days left until the morning of the fourth moon. Johnny asked Mars about the people of the trash hills. Why did they have money? Why were they so able to part with it?

"Money doesn't serve them well there. The currency is merchandise. It's a vicious cycle. Every now and then the junk men come along and buy the things they salvage. But merchants hardly ever go there anymore. I'm one of a dying breed. They get tired of looking at the same old garbage. They want to see something new and shiny."

Mid-afternoon, the scenery changed again. There were no buildings ahead, no structures, no foliage, no features of any sort. The earth was flat and dry with cracks big enough to hide a man's fist, the road itself nothing but two tamped wheel ruts. A great white cloud of dust gathered behind them. If they slowed, it would overtake them. Every now and then one of the buzzing machines Johnny first saw when they entered the city crossed their path. Wild-maned, half-naked men banked their machines in sharp hairpins, laughing crazily, and disappeared into their own dust.

The air grew warmer. The pony's hooves copped monotonously and the wagon staves creaked a hypnotic repetition. Johnny grew silent. Mars sang some modal melody, something about a girl on another planet, about making love to her while she slept. His voice grew dusty and the song trailed off into a mumble of moans. Time stretched out into longer and longer segments, and every now and then a segment would break off, and Johnny woke with a start to find nothing had changed, and the pattern began again.

Then there was a buzz, like grasshoppers. It rose in pitch, then stopped abruptly. A sense of presence startled Johnny—a person sitting next to him—between him and Mars on the buckboard. He turned. Mars turned.

It was the boy.

He was still wearing the floral tunic with the fringed collar, although its color had faded with the dust.

Mars looked at Johnny. "Holy sweet Beezle. How did he get here?"

The boy looked straight ahead. "I hid. Under the bed," he whispered.

Mars shook the reins sharply. The pony halted and immediately the cloud of dust overtook them. "Well, you can just get out, right now."

The boy didn't move

Johnny said, "You can't throw him off here. He would die."

"Well, that's not my problem. I told him no riders."

Johnny felt his will rising. This was not how people were treated in the world he grew up in. "Keep him for a while. There must be a safer place than this. And besides, maybe he can help us, somehow."

Mars stared off into the distance, pondering. He nodded his head several times, then rolled it from side to side and nodded it again. "You might have a point there, Clearlight," he said at last. "The Blackcoats surely want the boy back. They'd probably pay a pretty good price for him."

The boy let out a cry and his body began to shiver, like he was sitting on a block of ice. "No, no, no, no, no—" He sprang from the buckboard but his knees buckled and he folded into a pile of bones in the dust.

"You heard what Clearlight said. You'll just die out here. Now, get back on the wagon."

"No, Mars." Johnny's resolve was now fully awake. "You can't do this. You can't be saving one person from the Black-coats if you're just going to be selling another one back to them."

"Be quiet, Clearlight. This is no time for sentiment. Help the boy back on the wagon."

Johnny jumped down and lifted the boy up from under his arms. There were fresh clots of blood foaming on the tunic. "I won't let him do this to you," he whispered. "Just come with us now."

Back in the wagon the boy did not stay on the buck-board. He stumbled inside and threw himself onto the bed, sobbing. Johnny climbed up next to Mars. He could feel the hair bristling on his arms. "Don't talk to me about love if you're going to do something like this."

Mars looked straight ahead, reins in hand. "There's smart love and there's stupid love, Clearlight. You'll come around. Giddy-up, Angel."

The Pony began to move. Johnny folded his arms across his chest. Anger was coursing through his blood, down his legs, up his spine, but it kept meeting up with something else, something softer, something that spoke of a connection to home, to music, to friends, and all the sweetness he had left behind.

He has a name for his pony. He calls her Angel.

Even so, he couldn't stay on the buckboard with the man. He went in the back of the wagon where the boy lay on the bed, no longer sobbing, just whimpering softly. He poured a tumbler full of water from his canteen. He found the bread and some dried meat. These things he offered to the boy. He sat on the floor below the bed while the boy ate.

"What's your name?"

The boy didn't say anything.

"Where are you going?" He thought the boy wouldn't answer this question either, but eventually there was a muffled reply. "Sascutchen. My mother."

Johnny folded his hands in his lap. "Yeah, I got a mother, too."

The wagon rolled and rattled on for a long time, and the buzz of insects came and went. Mars' voice could be heard singing softly from the buckboard. Johnny grew sleepy. He had completely forgotten that he had mentioned his mother, when the boy spoke again.

"What's her name?"

A picture flashed through Johnny's mind: Mother, fingering a pinch of fire grate ash into the northernmost wall sconce. "Well, I called her Mother, but her name was Calendula."

"Calendula Clearlight," the boy whispered. It was not so much a question; it was more like a pair of words he wanted to taste.

Johnny didn't know why he said what he said next. It just tumbled out of his mouth. "No." he said. "Arcane. Calendula Arcane. My father wasn't with her long, but she kept the name."

The boy let this sink in. "Jimmy Arcane," he said.

Johnny didn't answer. There was another silence, then the boy spoke again, his voice now infused with lucidity. "*Johnny* Arcane," he said, conclusively.

Neither of them spoke after that. The boy fell asleep. Perhaps Johnny fell asleep too. The next thing he knew it was dark. The wagon had stopped and Mars was inside, rattling his pots and pans.

"I'm gonna fix us some supper now," he said. "We're staying here for the night. And we're not going to talk about it, you suss?"

"About what?"

"You know what. The place where we disagree."

Mars had a little stove that burned with a strange blue flame, hotter than corn flame. He cooked up some kind of stew in one of his pots, chunks of dried meat and some unnamable dehydrated vegetables. He took a lantern and they ate out on the buckboard, the two of them. The boy stayed on the bed but he accepted the bowl of stew between his cupped hands.

Outside it was so dark the only visible feature was the line of the horizon, circling them in all directions. The sky yielded up no stars and Johnny knew from his pebbles there would be no moon. After eating, Mars stuffed his pipe with the *illumination* and lit it with a fire stick. Johnny's heart was as dark as the night. *The place where they disagree.* But if he couldn't talk about this place, what could he talk about? It was crucial. He was alone with this man in the place where they disagreed.

"Why don't you smoke this, Clearlight?"

"It makes me do bad things." Johnny's voice was flat and cold.

"No it doesn't. It's the illumination. It opens up your mind. It lights your way. When you got a hard problem to solve, you just smoke some and the question is answered. You drink whisky?"

"No."

Mars chuckled. "Now there's something that'll make you do bad things." He took a deep drag on the pipe. "But I miss it some. I been clean now for over three summers."

Clean. The word did not fit with Johnny's conception of the man, and he wished he could express this, but he didn't know how. Finally he just repeated it. "Clean."

"Oh, yeah. I became a drunkard when I turned thirteen, just like my daddy, or so we think. I lost my soul completely. It was Beezle that found it and brought it back to me. You got drunkards where you come from, Clearlight?"

"What's a drunkard?"

"You know, a drunkard. A drunkard is a little lamb that loses his way. He falls in a well of whisky and he can't get out. A drop of whisky lands on his skin, it sinks through the pores and drives him so mad he has to break the jar to drink the rest. I traded in my desire for whisky. I traded it in for the golden light of love. Don't people drink whisky where you come from, Clearlight?"

"Everybody drinks where I come from. Whisky, beer, brandy. They drink when they get together and it warms their hearts. It's not a problem for anybody. Except it was for me. It made me do something I regret."

"Oh yeah? And what was that?"

"I ... broke a code. A code of honor."

Mars thought about this for a while. "Honor?" he said at last. "Honor is weak. Desire conquers honor every time."

CHAPTER SEVENTEEN

THE MINES OF PERPETUA

n the middle of the night he woke with a restlessness gnawing at the pit of his stomach. Mars lay flopped across the bed, snoring like a bullfrog. The boy curled against the wall on the other side. The confines of the wagon seemed to be pressing in from all six directions. It was hot and stuffy. He went out on the buckboard.

There was just enough light in the sky to lend some contrast to the dark shadow of the earth. Still no stars, but a pale luminescence in the east suggested the rising of a new moon. The air outside was as still and close as it was inside.

Out of the blackness he saw movement, a darker shadow scurrying across the dark ground. He could barely make out the form—a creature, shorter than a man, running on its hind legs, hunched over, its forearms reaching almost to its feet, a long thin tail. It vanished in the darkness, and then another crossed its path from the opposite direction, and then another. Johnny heard the dry earth crunching under foot. One of them stopped, looked at the wagon, and let out a sound, like laughter, almost human, but with an edge of craziness. A glint of red flashed from its eyes. In the distance, more movement—these beasts were everywhere, covering the entire plain. Johnny felt a mixture of sadness and dread. The safest place was back in the wagon, but he stayed a little longer on the buckboard, pondering.

Everything was confinement. The Known World with its four sealed borders was confinement, and here, outside those borders, there was a great confinement of spirit, a pressing down of the sky, like the fingers of a widespread hand, always pressing down. And the body itself was a kind of prison, repressing the proclivities of the mind with its boundary of skin and bone, with its yearning for distant things—*desire conquers honor, every time.*

He could not think these thoughts. They were not useful. He went back inside to seek the oblivion of sleep.

Midafternoon, the next day, a gauzy grey dome materialized over the northern horizon. It didn't rise like smoke and it didn't drift like a cloud. It just hung there, a smudge from an inky thumb, and there was a sound, a continuous rushing at first, but after a while there were individual modulations, screeching and growling and the clanking of metal. Mars watched with a placid face. Johnny sensed he knew what it was, but he wouldn't say.

The boy hadn't spoken. He slept, mostly, his face pressed against the back wall. A few times he got up and drank some water. Once he lifted the flap and urinated off the sideboard into the dust.

Except for the dark dome, the scenery was relentlessly static, but the dome grew larger with every rattle of the wheels. And the horizon drew no nearer. The ruts of the road merely dovetailed to a vortex where the earth meets the sky.

Then, in the span of an indrawn breath, it changed. With the dome nearly overhead, a feature appeared in the earth, the slightest of rises, no taller than a man's knees. The wagon rattled toward it. The sounds swelled. The earth seemed to give way. Angel the pony pulled back her mane, whinnied, and shuddered to a halt.

Before them, the earth opened out into a great round pit, as deep as a mountain is high. Clouds of black dust rose from its depths, and there were things moving, far away, enormous creatures with hinged jaws, taking great bites of rock and spewing them onto the backs of what looked like massive, lumbering tortoises. There was growling and snorting everywhere, and puffs of smoke escaped from flared nostrils. The walls of the pit were terraced and the roadbed itself followed the terraces down into the yawning abyss.

Mars' smile was flushed with pride, as if he had dug the whole thing himself. "There you have it, Clearlight. The belly of the beast."

"What is it?"

"The black rock mines of Perpetua. This is where the blood comes from, the blood that runs through the veins of the world, even *your* world, Clearlight. This is also the shortest route to Ironweed, if you still want to go to Ironweed."

"What are those animals?"

"Those are not animals. Those are machines. They use the power of the black rock itself to dig the black rock out of the ground. Everything runs on the power of the black rock. Mills melt it down to oil and the oil fuels the machines. It's a cycle, like the cycle of the trees. It replaces the cycle of the trees."

"Are we going to go down there?"

"Yes, but not till dark. Everything stops then. We can pass through."

They watched and waited. Mars grew disinterested. He

jumped from the buckboard and started turning over the wafers of cracked earth, examining their backsides, crumbling them to dust between his fingers. The more Johnny watched, the more he saw. Indeed, the animals were machines. They did not have feet. They perambulated on broad looped tracks that gripped the earth so the machines could do their work while hugging the slopes. The tortoises were wheeled vehicles, and once filled, they rumbled away and up the terraces out of the pit on the opposite side. And there were people, lots of them, so far away they were mere specks, marching in flanks, carrying heavy objects, lifting and lowering, digging and shoveling.

After a while Johnny began to hear a rumbling, like thunder, behind him to the south. He turned toward it. There seemed to be a storm brewing in the southern sky, a dark cloud billowing from the horizon.

"Mars, look. What's that?"

Mars straightened and turned his gaze southward. He spoke under his breath. "Oh sweet Beezle." He jumped back up on the buckboard. "We'd better start moving now. We don't want to be seen here on the rim."

"But what is it?"

"I don't know yet, but it may be an old acquaintance I'd rather remain forgotten."

It was hard to convince Angel to venture down the terraced trail. She shied and whinnied and pulled toward the rock wall. The drop was nearly vertical and the roadbed was barely wider than the wagon's wheels. Chunks of stone, loosened by their passing, tumbled to the tier below. Aroused by the movement, the boy lifted the tent flap and his face froze in terror.

"Get back inside, kid," barked Mars, "It's a long way down."

Soon they were in the shade of the overhanging cliffs where mud nest villages clung to the cornices, swallows flitting in and out.

"But what about the people down there? Won't they see us?"

"They won't care," replied Mars. "We're just merchants passing through. Perhaps they'd like to buy some pots and pans."

The road wound through a series of tight switchbacks and their passage set up a continuous landslide of gravel that followed them to the bottom. They reached a level place where their path cut a course toward the center of the pit. The rattling of falling rock subsided and the sound of machines filled the air. Johnny craned his neck. It was strange to be standing at the bottom of a bowl, staring up at its rim. It made him uncomfortable, as if at any moment the earth could swallow him up. And there was something happening up there on the first terrace. A cloud was swarming in the darkening sky, and now it was curling over the rim, slowly pouring itself into the pit, along the roadbed. He did not mention this to Mars. Perhaps it was nothing. Perhaps it was just the shadow of their dust. He wasn't sure. Dust was everywhere.

They continued. There were machines on the lower terraces. People were in the machines, controlling them. The rocks they dug from the cliffs were pitch black and shiny. There were piles of rocks and piles of soot, and the soot-grey dust hung sluggishly in the air.

Further from the walls the sun reappeared but the shadows were long and the light pale. They came to a squared basin of grey water and Mars let the pony drink from it. Pebbles scattered from a slag pile and a small brown rabbit scampered. Mars made a sudden leap and caught the creature in his fist before it could make it across the road. With a swift thrust of his free hand he slipped a knife from its belted sheath and pulled it across the rabbit's throat.

"Look! We got ourselves some dinner!"

They moved on. They came to a place where there were fewer machines and the road passed through a complex of low buildings made of large stones. There were no doors, just open square portals into darkness. An odor wafted from these openings, a stench that hardened into a knot of dread in Johnny's stomach. He glanced at Mars. The man was oblivious to it. He was talking, and had been for some time.

"They'll be stopping their ruckus soon. The power gods are afraid of the dark. The spirit children come out when they leave. We'll be in good company. Around this bend here. A good place to settle down for the night."

A rock wall, higher than the wagon staves, marked the border of the complex of buildings. In the darkened hollows Johnny heard scuffling sounds, rats perhaps, but it wasn't rats he smelled. Around the wall they came to an open paved area flanked by a row of wizened and nearly leafless willows, the first living foliage they had seen in a long time.

The rim shadows were moving in and the air was growing cold. Mars built a fire at the center of the paved area. Indeed, the grumblings of the machines grew softer and receded into the northern distance. Crickets began to trill softly. Darkness moved like a cloak over the world, but soon another kind of light appeared, a ghostly white illumination diffused from globes hanging from poles at the corners of the clearing.

Mars skinned the rabbit and wiped the knife blade on its fur. He filleted the haunches and skewered them on a stiff metal rod.

"Come on out kid and warm your bones, we're gonna cook up this rabbit."

The boy was so weak he couldn't hop down from the buckboard. He had to sit and lower himself to his feet. The hem of the tunic was wet with fresh blood, but he managed to shuffle to the fire and stand there with his hands out, his head bent down.

Something whistled from the shadows, a bird perhaps, or some other unnamed creature. The boy glanced about, his breath making little fearful gasps. A distant wail echoed from the canyon rim. Then there was a sound from behind the wall, three sharp raps, like a stick on a metal plate. It was not random. Its intention was evident. *We're here. Are you there?*

Mars stood to his full height. "Who goes?" he called.

A short silence, then a whizzing sound. A rock flew over the wall and landed on the pavement. Mars picked it up. There was writing on it, but Johnny couldn't read it.

"Ah, so you want to play a game." Mars unsheathed his knife and made a scratch on the rock; then he lobbed it back over the wall.

The boy's eyes bulged. "No!" He cried. "No! No! No! No!" He turned from the fire.

"You shut up and be quiet! Do you want to die?"

As soon as he said that, figures appeared from behind the wall. Blackcoats. They leapt over the rim and poured from the sides. The boy screamed. He stumbled, then lurched, struck the wagon with his shoulder, but managed to drag himself up onto the buckboard. He rolled onto the seat, grabbed the reins and shook them wildly. Angel woke, looked around, whinnied, and then started to run.

"Clearlight! Stop him! He's taking the wagon!"

Johnny didn't move. His heart jumped with hope. But it fell, and his blood froze in his veins when he heard the terrible pop he had come to recognize as the mocking bark of death. The pony screamed like a woman. Her knees buckled, she staggered sideways and fell, blood spurting from her belly.

"Angel!" Mars threw himself forward and fell upon the pony, flung his arm around her neck and buried his face in her mane. "Angel!"

The boy tumbled from the wagon, picked himself up, and set off running, his legs tapping some mysterious source of energy. But he didn't get far. There was another pop and he was lifted up, his arms flying, a crimson fountain bursting from his chest. He landed face first in the dirt.

The Blackcoats swarmed past, leaping over the fire, over the fallen pony and the weeping man. They grabbed the boy under his arms and dragged him forward. It didn't take long. They had gotten what they came for, and in their departure their voices set up a low murmur, eerie, rhythmic, chant-like, strange syllables, almost the singsong of children. And then they were gone, only the trampling of their receding footfall, the vibration of their voices.

Mars looked up. His arms and chest were soaked with the pony's blood. "Cowards!" he cried in a ragged voice. "Cowards! Only a coward will fight with a gun!" He turned and looked at Johnny. "We'll never get to Ironweed by the fourth moon now!"

A change crossed Mars' face. For a moment all emotion drained out of his eyes, and then suddenly something else flooded in, something like astonishment, or perhaps total surrender. At the same time a sound, a thundering rumble approaching with great velocity from behind the wall of the complex of buildings.

Johnny spun around just in time to see the hooves of the first horse appear. Then another, then another—horses, enormous and terrifying, pouring out from behind the wall. Some shrieked and reared, others lowered their heads and pressed forward with fierce intent. They fanned out and filled the open space, yet still more and more arrived. Mars screamed and fell prostrate on the pavement, his hands extended in supplication. Johnny edged closer to the wagon.

A human voice rose above the rumble, a string of trills, yelps and ululations. Flanks and manes parted for the entrance of the great black steed and its rider. She was as Johnny remembered her from the distance, but now she was here before them. Her hair was a kind of liquid power that poured in braided locks across her shoulders. Concentric auras of color encircled her bare breasts, and tattooed briars, resplendent with rosebuds, draped her shoulders and wound around her strong, sinewy arms. In one hand she held a heavy wooden staff twined with vines and small green buds. Her face was fierce and fearsome, yet softened with tenderness and an indescribable beauty.

The spiral of horses slowly subsided around her and over them fell a circle of hush, all faces turned inward to the elements at its center, the wagon, Johnny pressed against the canvass, the dead pony, Mars, lying prone on the pavement. The woman goaded the steed forward at a sauntering pace until its hooves straddled Mars' outstretched arms. Between these arms she planted the blunt end of her staff.

"Why do you grovel, Mars Beacon? Get up and show me your sorry face."

Mars pulled his arms in toward his body until he was able to lift himself up. For a moment he knelt before the horse, his bloody hands clasped, his face a mixture of reverence and despair. But then his expression changed, his eyes hardened, his jaw set. He dropped his arms and stood shakily to his feet.

"We don't have any more business together, Mab. Our paths have diverged."

The woman eyed him. "Well, at least you've got one part right. Our paths have diverged. But we still have business. Who is this man you've brought along?"

Mars spoke without turning in Johnny's direction. "His name's Jimmy Clearlight. His woman has been captured by the Blackcoats. I'm going to help him save her."

Mab coaxed the horse toward Johnny. Her eyes pierced him. He knew only one thing. If he had to speak to her, his voice would permit him nothing but the truth.

She turned back to Mars. "I heard what happened at Ladyland. I went there. I talked to a girl. Her name was Flora. She said your friend was hiding something, but not very well." The woman turned again to Johnny and he felt a chill rise from the base of his spine to the back of his neck. "What's your name, young man?"

"Johnny."

"And your other name?"

"Arcane."

She was quiet for a while, her face closed inward. She spoke softly. "As I thought." Then suddenly her body snapped to attention and she leapt from the horse's back, her feet striking the pavement with barely a sound.

"We've got to sweat. All of us. Johnny Arcane, help me move this fire." Johnny gasped in disbelief as the woman threw wide her arms and scooped up the fire into them, cradling the glowing coals and the flaming logs against her bare skin as if they were no more than a bouquet of roses. A few embers slipped and fell to the ground. "Get those, Arcane," she commanded.

Johnny glanced around and caught sight of one of Mars' deep pans hanging from a peg on the sideboard. He grabbed it and started sweeping the coals into it with his hands. He couldn't move fast enough to keep his fingers from being burned.

On the other side of the willows was a low, rounded, brick structure, like a pottery kiln or a slow roasting oven. Mab threw open the door and hurled her fiery load inside. Johnny did the same.

"Take off your clothes," she commanded. "All of them."

CHAPTER EIGHTEEN

SWEAT

The three sat naked in the close, hot darkness of the oven. It was impossible to stand. The woman, Mab, had raked the coals to the center and set the cooking pot filled with water. The only light was from the embers and the quick darting tongues of flame, and the air was heavy with moisture. To Johnny's eyes the figures of Mars and Mab were mere shadows, distinguished only by the voices.

Despite his first protestations, Mars had not put up a fight. His only concession to pride was to assume an air of authority. "Do what she tells you, Clearlight," he said as he stripped off his shirt and poured the water over his blood-stained arms.

Now out of the silence and the penetrating heat of the kiln, Mab responded. "Why don't you call him by his real name, Mars?"

The other shadow did not speak. In the dim light Johnny perceived that Mars was not sitting. He was lying on his back, his arms to his sides, his head resting on a pillow of stone. Mab sat straight-backed, her legs folded, her spine erect, her hands resting on her knees, palms upturned. The heat was both an elixir and an oppressor. Johnny felt his flesh sagging from his bones like molten wax. Streams of sweat poured from his skin. His mind was lucid, but moving slowly, like a river in late summer.

"It was for his protection. If they knew who he was, he would be killed."

"You knew who he was. Why didn't you kill him?"

Mars winced. "What you take me for, Mab? You know I've sworn the oath of love."

"What happened to the pony?"

"The Blackcoats shot her."

"Why?"

Mars was silent. The fire crackled. A drop of water slid down the side of the pot and hissed on the coals.

"He doesn't want to answer that question," said Mab. "Johnny Arcane, perhaps you can."

Johnny knew he was helpless against her power. She would use him as a conduit for the truth.

"The boy was trying to get away in the wagon, so they shot the pony, then they shot the boy."

Mab shifted the weight of her hands, ever so slightly. "And who is the boy?"

"He joined us at the trash hills. He hid in the wagon. He didn't talk much. I didn't know him, but he knew me. He knew my name."

For a long time there was only the sound of Mab breathing through her mouth, deliberately, filling her lungs with air, releasing it slowly. With each exhalation a brightness seemed to enter the kiln. Shadows waltzed on the walls. The flame danced.

"I'll tell you a story, Johnny Arcane," she said at last. "This man you travel with, Mars Daniel. We used to call him Beacon. Mars Beacon. We were lovers. We lived in a place called Freeland. There were seers in Freeland, women and men, who learned to capture the powers of the mind. They built an invisible wall of protection to the extent that their power could reach. Outside this wall there was nothing but chaos and cruelty, so strong that the seer's power could go no further. So within these boundaries was Freeland, and the chaos and the cruelty could not penetrate it.

"The seers learned to expand their perception beyond the limits of space and time. They could not cross these limits, but they could perceive what lay there. They learned that the world is very old, and many cycles of creatures have lived on it. People are only the most recent, but there have been many cycles of people. Cycles that vanish leave things behind, and those that follow use these things without knowing anything about them, including their dangers.

"At the end of the last cycle of people, before chaos and cruelty overtook the world, there was a seer. His power was great. He saw the chaos and cruelty coming, and he built a border as large as he could with the power of his mind. That border still exists, to this day, and the people within it live in peace and freedom from chaos and cruelty. But the seer was killed and the people lost all their connection to his power. Although the border still holds, in places it is crumbling, and the people within it stumble in ignorance. They cling to half-truths told as legends, and they practice empty rituals, on which they do not agree. That is how it is today."

Her words trailed off, but not into silence. Beneath the crackling of the fire and the hissing of the steam a quiet, steady lament was heard, almost melodious, and the words chanted, barely audible, "I'm sorry. I'm sorry."

Mab moved. She rolled to her knees and crawled across the center of the oven floor, resting one hand briefly on the fiery coals. She settled her back against the wall and Mars flung his head into her lap, weeping like a child. With the hand that had touched the coals, she stroked the back of his neck and ran her fingers through his wiry locks.

"This is why he cries. When Mars and I were lovers in Freeland, we made a vow. The seers told us they could see the future, but it's not the same as seeing the past or the present. The future is not fixed. Every living thing has a destiny there, but not every living thing fulfills its destiny. A spider begins to spin an orb. But then a strong wind blows, or a headstrong child passes through, and the orb is not completed. Our vow was to strengthen the power in Freeland, to protect its borders and to help the seers push them, ever outward. Perhaps one day they would overrun all the chaos and cruelty, and a new cycle would begin."

Mars stopped his sniffling and whimpering and he turned his head to rest his cheek on Mab's knee, his arms around her calves. "I haven't forgotten the vow, Mab."

Mab ran her fingers down his arms, from shoulder to elbow, again and again. "You have, to some measure. You have acquired skills to navigate the world of chaos and cruelty. You have learned to partake in its pleasures. Your strength has grown but your spirit has diminished."

Mars shrugged his arms and Mab stopped stroking. "It's the way I bring love to the world."

Mab shook her head. "It can't be done. The pleasures of chaos and cruelty are too seductive. Tell me this. What were you going to do with the boy?"

There was silence. Mars' body seemed to wilt in her lap. Mab lifted her head. "You can tell me, Johnny. What was he going to do with the boy?"

Again, the inevitability of truth. He was helpless against it. "He was going to sell him to the Blackcoats."

For a while there was the sound of Mars sobbing, while the woman stroked his hair. Little by little, she joined her voice with his, a low murmur, barely audible, wordless, soothing. But Johnny's heart was not soothed. As the heavy heat lengthened his muscles and sinews, he began to hear the melody of the distance he had traveled to this point, a dominant cadence, yearning for resolution. He didn't know there were words for it until the words rose spontaneously from his mouth.

"Who *am* I?"

Mab let her song go still, then she replied. "Who do you think you are?"

"I don't know. I know what I'm not. I'm not a seer—what you call them. I'm a sojourner. I follow the road because I don't know where it will lead."

"Then you follow your destiny, Johnny Arcane. Remember what I said. The future is not fixed."

"But why do people want to kill me?"

Mab made a wordless sound, perhaps a continuation of the melody she had been singing to Mars. "Not everyone wants to kill you, but there does seem to be something moving in the path in front of you. A story is being told, one that hasn't happened yet."

"Where I come from they tell a story of something that hasn't happened yet. They say Borderbinder will return and re-open the borders."

"And you think this has something to do with you?"

Johnny hung his head. A memory of shame rushed in upon him. "When I was a messenger, once I read a message I was carrying. It was an accident, I didn't intend to, but what

I read intoxicated me. 'Borderbinder has returned. He is the one carrying this message. His name is Arcane.'"

Mab hummed again. It seemed like this was the way she processed information. "You're not the only foolish one, Johnny Arcane. Seers should be quiet about what they see, especially what they see in the future. The future is not unbreakable. There is great danger in stirring the waters of destiny. You must be calm and follow the road before you. Don't ask too many questions. What is your goal right now? What star is fixed in your mind?"

"I have to save Lucy."

Again, the wordless voice, this time for a long time. Finally Mab moved. Gently she lifted the dark-skinned man's head from her lap and rose to her knees. "Tomorrow, I will give you my steed. His name is Trespasser. He can run fast, much faster than the poor pony. You will be able to reach Ironweed by the fourth moon, and you will save your Lucy, although there will be a price. Don't think of anything beyond that goal. That is your current destiny. And now we have finished this sweat. We should sleep."

She shoved open the door and the bracing chill of the night rushed into the kiln.

CHAPTER NINETEEN

CANTANKERBERG

In the morning they buried the pony in a soft sandy area under the withered willows. It was the only place nearby where the earth was not made of hard, black rock, impenetrable with a shovel. Standing knee-deep in the hole, Mars sunk the blade and it struck a solid object. He uncovered a segment of the ribcage of some long-forgotten creature.

"Well, at least she'll have some company," he said.

They lowered Angel in the grave and Mars covered her with his blood-soiled tunic.

All the horses gathered around as Mars and Johnny took turns shoveling dirt onto the body. They bowed their heads, hoofed the ground, and sang a dirge together, antiphonally, a murmuration of snorts and whinnies, sung in a round, circling the final resting place of their equine sister. In the distance the machine-beasts were already clearing their throats for the day's work.

Mab said she was taking the horses back the way they had come, but the crusaders must hasten on to their destiny. She helped hitch Trespasser to the wagon. The harness had to be retooled to fit his broad shoulders. The horse had a fire in his eyes. He seemed fully cognizant of the adventure ahead.

In place of Trespasser, Mab chose a young, shy mare to ride on her return. Before mounting, she kissed Mars full on the mouth with a passion that seemed part portent. Without another word she leapt on the mare's bare back and disappeared around the wall, the herd following her, obediently, single file.

Trespasser's power was almost too great for the little wagon. The staves rocked wildly and in a very short time, all the pots and pans had loosened from their hooks and clattered to the floorboards. The axles creaked and the wheels wobbled. Johnny grasped the sideboard tightly to keep from being thrown to the ground.

Mars, however, held the reins loosely and stared straight ahead, lost in thought, silent. In any case, it wasn't long before conversation was impossible, for they were passing through the heart of the mine; the machine-beasts were everywhere, and the din was deafening.

It took all day to cross the pit, but by late afternoon there was more dust than noise, for the road had diverged from the course of the haulers, and here the earth had been wasted of its usefulness. On both sides, deep gouged scars lay open, some of them bleeding a black, fluid tar, and in places, fires smoldered, the very earth blistering in its own heat.

But in time the smoke cleared and they could see the other side, a low ridge, nothing like the cliffs they had descended, with a gentle notch for the road to pass through. Mars spoke the first words he had uttered since Mab and her horses had disappeared around the wall.

"Jimmy Clearlight. I've never been fed anything that tasted so bad."

Johnny sighed. "Why don't you call me by my real name?"

Mars didn't answer. He was silent for so long that Johnny was afraid he wouldn't speak again, from here to Ironweed. But that didn't happen. "A woman who travels with seventy-five wild horses carries a lot of weight," said Mars at last. "But she doesn't know everything. I call you Clearlight for your protection. I told you that."

Johnny pondered for a while, and he remembered something that troubled him. "Once I slept in a shelter that was used by the Blackcoats. They had some kind of device in there, and a book where they wrote things. They were keeping record of all the places I had traveled since I left King Corn."

Mars frowned. "Ah, Clearlight, you're not supposed to think about that. Don't you remember the day we buried the box in the graveyard? I told you, you were being tracked."

Johnny could feel the puzzle quivering, another piece about to fall in place. "How do they do it?" he asked.

"Do you remember what Mab said—how the people today use things that were made by the old ones, even though they don't understand them?"

"The dolmens."

"Yeah, whatever. Well, the old ones left things in the sky. They circle the earth. I guess maybe you don't know that either. The earth is round, but that's another story. Anyhow, the Men of Knowledge figured out how to talk to these things in the sky. That's what we buried in the graveyard. The things in the sky were watching you."

"The blinkers..."

"These aren't children playing with toys, Jimmy Clearlight. If we really are going to fulfill this destiny, we have to be very careful."

◯

They rolled out of the pit at dusk. The sun was a visible ball of orange sinking in the west, and ahead of them lay a city, a word Johnny had never even heard before crossing the border. It shimmered through layers of haze, a maze of towers as tall as mountains, but most of them were frayed at the top, as if they had been eaten by flames and battered by fierce winds. Light glowed from the lower windows. Further up there was darkness, the glass shattered, the walls crumbled and stained with soot. On the streets life teemed. Lights flashed, vehicles bustled; crowds of people flowed here and there, like water.

"Cantankerberg," announced Mars. "The first stop on the power chain. It will take all day tomorrow to get through it. On the other side is the Onyx Highway to Ironweed."

The entrance to the city was abrupt. No shantytown or abandoned factories lined the road down from the ridge above the mines. Two enormous rusty iron gates slouched open, and a tattered banner sagged between the towers: CANTANKERBERG.

Nobody seemed to be leaving or arriving, but the moment the wagon crossed the threshold, the travelers found themselves engulfed in a turgid sea of humanity. Trespasser snorted and stomped his hooves. He had braved the machine-beasts of Perpetua without balking, and now he pressed into the crowd with a fierce valor. Men, women, and children, mostly wearing dingy browns and greys, crowded around carts and tables where vendors sold their wares. The air was filled with a succession of shifting smells—greasy meat fat, weighty spices, wafts of incense and smoke, mold and decay. Whole carcasses hung from hooks. Johnny could not always identify the animal, and some looked disturbingly human. A man jostled past, carrying a tray of pig's heads. A woman was stacking sheaves of some bright green foliage. Shouts and chants and the clang of hammers, the whine of belts, the throb of pistons.

A few people rode on the backs of the buzzing insects Johnny had seen in the previous city. They wove their way impatiently through the dense crowds. A vehicle approached, a large green wheeled tortoise with a man on its back. The man was armored and carried what Johnny had learned was called a rifle. He spoke into a cone that amplified his voice. "Step to the left and keep moving!"

They passed an alley where the crowd had formed a circle. Two young boys, completely naked, were fighting with broken bottles while voices goaded them on. Each had one leg chained to a rung in the street so they could not make full frontal contact. They swung their shards wildly at each other, their arms shredded and bloody. A pot of money stood on a nearby table.

Mars pulled the wagon up to a vendor, jumped down, and returned with an armload of puffy baked things. "Here, eat this." He handed one to Johnny. It was flakey and filled with some kind of meat. It tasted rancid, but Johnny was too hungry to complain.

In the falling dark, people around them were setting out colored lamps and the sound of drums reverberated from somewhere above. A pretty girl with a dirty face walked across the street carrying an armload of roses and someone on a balcony whistled. Two dogs broke out of an alley, fighting over the pelt of a rabbit. In a brightly lit kitchen, old men were playing a game with ceramic tiles clacking on a metal table.

"I know she's right," said Mars with a sigh. "This world has been given over to chaos and cruelty. But it's hard for me to let it go. It's a beautiful chaos, and there's a sweet sadness in the cruelty. I wish I played an instrument like you, Jimmy Clearlight. It's music that bridges the worlds." He gummed the last bit of his pastry and spat out a bone. "Let's keep moving. I know a place we can spend the night. I have some business there."

When the light had completely faded from the visible patches of the sky, they entered a short, narrow canyon that ended at a wall on which was painted a huge eye with a delta-shaped iris, squiggly lines of color emanating from its orb. Mars pressed a button on a post and the eye began to move. The wall shuddered and rolled up, revealing a dark, cavernous space.

Back on the buckboard Mars goaded Trespasser and they entered. Shapes appeared out of the gloom. There were animals in stalls, some bearded goats reclining on a padded pallet, a cluck of chickens scratching in a pen, a small donkey munching on a pile of straw. Light burst from an opening door. A man appeared, a young man, dressed in white robes, like a mummer, his face cleanly shaven, long straight hair flowing over his shoulders.

"Holy Beezle, Mars Daniel! When did your pony get so big?"

"Pony died. What you see there is a horse. How you been, Jason?"

Mars and the young man embraced with their arms clasped. "Just countin' the days. We knew you'd come, but we didn't know when. What you bring us?"

"Something brand new, my friend. It grows on the southern slopes. They call it the *illumination*."

Jason laughed. "Well, good. It gets pretty dark around here. Who's your friend?"

"Clearlight, jump down. Meet the host. Jimmy Clearlight, Jason Argonite. First child born in Freeland."

Jason shook Johnny's hand. "Any friend of Mars. Just leave the horse here. I'll have Bambi take care of him. Isobel will be so surprised!"

They entered the bottom of a well. Johnny looked up. Flights of stairs ascending in a spiral. He counted eight landings before the stairs disappeared into darkness. They started up, their footsteps reverberating in the hollows above.

On the seventh landing Jason threw open a door. A cool breeze rushed out of the room, redolent with the aroma of evergreens. The room was full of trees, miniature pines and cedars thriving under a bank of soft white light along the ceiling. The floor was spongy mulch, like the floor of a forest. A girl sat at a table. She had long blonde hair and she wore a robe like Jason's, except hers was cornflower blue. When she saw Mars she gasped, then laughed, jumped up and threw her arms around his neck.

"Of course you'd come today. I dreamed you last night."

Introductions were made. From somewhere among the trees the girl produced four large, slightly soiled cushions. In the higher branches tiny birds flitted, and the walls and ceilings were painted sky, with shades of distant mountains. The artifice was so effective Johnny found himself drawn into the illusion, as if he were sitting in the woods above King Corn on a sunny afternoon with Bearclaw, Ant and Jocko.

The girl's name was Isobel. She passed around mugs full of clear, cold water, and the four of them settled into the cushions with the birds chirping overhead. The girl began to speak. Her voice commanded full attention. It drew all the focus in the room toward her, like a northernmost attractor. "This must seem very strange to you, Jimmy. It's a long, strange story, but we have all night. Sit deep and I will tell you."

Jason leaned into her and stroked her arm. "She tells it well, Jimmy. Listen closely."

Isobel closed her eyes and pressed her fingertips together, conjuring the words. The birds hushed and the light seemed to dim. She separated her fingers, opened her eyes, and began.

"We were born in Freeland. We knew nothing else. When I was fifteen and Jason was seventeen, we grew restless and began to plot our escape. Not that escape was forbidden, it was simply not done. That was when Mars and Mab arrived and the evening councils began. Mab told tales of a great devastation and the changes to come. She told us of the thread of destiny that each person must follow as the power of love was pushed gradually outward against the forces of chaos and cruelty. Her tales did not dissuade us. We wanted to experience this chaos and cruelty for ourselves. We wanted to learn its ways so we could more effectively combat it.

"One spring morning we left Freeland and never returned. What we did not know was that on that same morning, Mars left Freeland as well, commissioned by Mab to follow us, watch over us, protect us from harm.

"Dangers beset us at once, from bandits, beasts and bands of renegade Blackcoats. Mars was able to remain incognito for a while, ambushing marauders and making deals with other protectors in dark smoky taverns. But in a lonely field outside of Kidney Stone, he had to reveal himself, or I would have been captured into the slave trade, and the knife the Blackcoat held at Jason's throat would have entered the flesh."

There was a pause in the narrative. The pause itself seemed as deliberate as the story, like this whole telling was something they had done countless times before, a kind of mummer's tale. Jason laid his head on Isobel's lap. "I love you, sweetheart," he said, his voice like a child's. But Mars stirred, restlessly.

"Get to the good stuff, Isobel."

Isobel closed her eyes, consulted her eyelids, and continued. "We traveled together then, for many seasons, and Mars and Jason learned something about each other. As repulsed as they both were by the ugliness and depravity of the world, they had, each in his own way, developed a fascination for it, for its garish colors, its cacophonous rhythms, the relentless pace with which it hastened the flow of blood through the body, and also the way that small moments of tenderness, those that would have gone unnoticed in Freeland, stood out in bold contrast with the terror and bitterness of the world of chaos and cruelty."

Jason sat up, with one hand on Isobel's knee. "Isobel didn't share our fascination," he said. "I get to tell this part. She said it was a sign we had learned what we came to learn, we had overstayed our welcome, and it was time to return."

"But we couldn't return." Isobel picked up the thread. "A great fire had broken out on the plains of Ableman, the entire city of Kidney Stone had been destroyed, and bands of flesh-eating hominids, roused from their caves, were migrating east.

"We sought the relative safety of the crowded underbelly of Cantankerberg, and Mars left us to build his business of pots and pans, and to glean the mind-bending herbs that grow wild on the southern foothills just across the border. We hunted wild cats in the alleys and sold their meat in the night market until Blackcoats destroyed our stand."

Jason spoke. "I had to kill one of them, or I would have lost Isobel."

"He was deeply grieved," Isobel continued. "We fled to the catacombs within the walls of the city, and eventually we discovered the flight of stairs and this empty room on the seventh floor of Solomon's Tower. It has a generator that burns the blackstone and there was a goodly supply of the ore in the bin. With what money we had, we hired the child, Bambi to bring us the things we would need to survive here. We made a pact in blood that if the changes did not come in our lifetime, we would die in this place. The world outside was no longer an attraction."

Isobel left another pause then, even longer than the first, and in it Mars stood, stretched, coughed, and sat back down. Jason sat up straight-spined, took a long draught of air and expelled it slowly. Isobel allowed the silence to gather.

"One day Bambi arrived with her entire body wrapped in a string of frosted glass tubes. The inscription read Magic Grow. We plugged them into the generator and suddenly it was a warm summer afternoon. A moon later and things began to grow from the cracks in the walls, little vines that ran down and curled across the floor, and, after a while, little pink and purple blossoms."

"Our spirits were lifted," said Jason.

"We developed a plan," continued Isobel. "Bambi enlisted some of her friends. Daily they brought up buckets full of fertile soil from a small wooded area near the river. It wasn't long before foliage began to sprout from the floor, first the mushrooms, then the scrub brush, and finally the sweet little arms of tender young trees.

"Bambi brought paint and brushes. I painted a blue sky and hazy distant mountains. Birds that had been lost for generations in the hollow caverns of the building found the young trees and made them their home.

"One day Mars Daniel appeared. He wouldn't say how he found us, but he brought money and food, and smoking herbs from the southern foothills. Since then, he has come regularly, whenever he passes this way. He is our connection to the world outside."

"We've created a little bit of Freeland here," Jason said. "We made a pact and sealed it in blood. If the changes don't come in our lifetimes, we will die here. But since we made that pact, all this has happened. It feels like Beezle has smiled on our actions and blessed us."

Jason had finished the story that Isobel had started. He turned to Mars. "So tell me my friend, what about this *illumination* you brought us?"

☊

In the night Johnny got up to pee, but he didn't know where to do it. Had this been a regular forest, outdoors, he would have just peed on the first tree he found, but that didn't seem right, here. Mars was slumped out on a pile of dry leaves and Jason and Isobel were hidden somewhere in the shadows. The magic grow lights were dimmed to simulate the glow of the moon. Johnny felt his way through the branches until he came to a wall. He followed the wall until he reached a door. It had no handle. He pushed it gently and it swung open. The hot, fetid reek of the street rushed into his nostrils. There was a dark, narrow hall littered with unidentifiable scraps, some hard and sharp, others soft and squishy—at the end of the hall, a pale undulating glow, and the muffled clamor of the city.

He found himself on a tiny iron balcony no wider than his own stance, looking down on the tremulous streets of Cantankerberg, still teeming with life at this late hour, the lanterns glowing, the patterns of moving bodies, the hum of voices, quarreling, coaxing, exuberant, mournful, the buzz and rumble of vehicles, the barking of dogs.

On the opposite tower he saw lights glowing in some of the lower windows, but from the eighth floor up, all was dark, the higher panes shattered, and at the top the building disintegrated into a mass of crumbled walls and splintered metal shards, like flame frozen in mid-flicker.

Above him from the higher floors of Solomon's Tower, he heard a cry. It could have been a wolf or it could have been a woman. A volley of other voices followed: wails, yips and barks from all directions, above and below. Then another sound, the repeated report of gunfire—more than one gun—then more voices, rhythmic, pulsating, and a woman's scream. From many floors above, glass shattered. Johnny saw the fragments raining down; then, soundlessly, a naked body, twisting slowly in obedient descent.

From the street grew a disturbance of voices, first a minor chord, then a scattering of phrases rising to a chorus of screams. But it quickly subsided, washed over by a wave of other sounds, the whine of engines, a heated argument in another alley, the throb of drums.

Johnny felt his body go limp. If it hadn't been for the railing he too would have tumbled to the streets below. Then he remembered. *I came out here to pee.* With hands trembling he dropped his pants and released his bladder into the abyss.

CHAPTER TWENTY

AMBUSH ON
THE ONYX HIGHWAY

arly morning, Mars shook Johnny awake. "Better to get moving while the town still sleeps. We got two days to get to Ironweed."

They tried to rouse Jason and Isobel but the couple remained motionless, Isobel's head on Jason's chest, Jason's head resting on a pillow of sand. Mars placed his hand on Jason's forehead. "The time is soon, old friend. You can't hide much longer."

Down in the bay, the child, Bambi was feeding Trespasser bunches of collard greens by hand. She couldn't have been more than seven, but her arms were strong and steady. Hens clucked and pecked around her bare feet. "He lay down and I slept on his tummy," she said. "He sang me songs."

Mars hitched the horse to the wagon. He gave Bambi some money, and a kiss on the top of her head.

Out on the street, the first thing he did was to buy a long leather whip from one of the vending tables. "We'll be needing this."

The streets were quiet, but not empty. People slept huddled in the alleys. Vendors rolling back their awnings gazed up pensively at the small patch of sky above the black-ened, burnt out scalps of the tall buildings. Slabs of meat and crates of vegetables appeared, and all the little figurines, like Jocko's dolls, fat-bellied pranksters carved in stone, corn husk girls dancing, bird replicas, fully feathered. Johnny counted the windows until he located what was surely the balcony from which he had urinated the night before. By then, Trespasser was guiding them through the maze and they were sitting on the buckboard.

"I got up in the night. I stood on that balcony. There were gunshots above, and a body fell."

Mars sighed. "I have to get Jason out of that place. One floor above there, a summer ago, a couple moved in. They weren't from Freeland, but they were starry-eyed. Cecil. He used to get drummers together and they played in the under-ground, to drive away the demons. But thugs stole his drums and broke his fingers. They went back in the room and they never came out. Bambi brings them their needs. The eighth floor is as high as she will go. Above that, it just gets crazier and crazier. People who don't even look like people anymore. Near the top, people who eat people."

Johnny remembered something. "I saw a carcass in the meat market yesterday that looked like a person."

"Oh, that was just a hominid. You'd know it wasn't a person if you saw it with its skin on. Hey yah! Get down! Get down!" A gang of unruly boys had jumped onto the sideboard, laughing and taunting. Mars cracked the whip and picked them off one by one. A few pulled themselves from the dirt and ran after the wagon. "Get off there, you dirty barnacles!"

Further in, things got bleaker. No more tall buildings, only the rubble of their collapse, and no more commerce, no more the cries of the vendors or the greasy aroma of fried meat, only a few workshops where old men banged on metal objects and skinny women hung out strips of cloth to dry.

But occasionally there were gardens, squared-off plots where green things were growing out of the hard-packed earth, tall tasseled stalks of corn and young squash just putting out blossoms, and sentries of scruffy marigolds between the rows of beans and peas. The people tending these gardens were mostly young, and their clothing more colorful than the others. When the wagon passed they did not avert their eyes, but stared openly, curious, wondering.

The travelers moved on steadily for two days straight, day and night, stopping only briefly to rest. As the city thinned out, the road attached itself to the shores of a broad river. Johnny asked if the river had a name.

"They call it the Separation. The land on the other side has been given over to fire." Indeed, on the other side, Johnny could see nothing but a scarred and rubbled desolation. He recalled the burnt-out summit over which he crossed out of the Known World. The near shore was cluttered with shanties, some built on shaky stilts directly over the water, connected by rickety catwalks with no railings, and in the water, makeshift boats of all sizes and shapes, tarpaper patched and creaking at berth, and people on the decks, mostly sitting or reclining, stupefied expressions on their faces.

"Where does it go?"

"Takes a westward bend past Angel's Gate. We'll be leaving it before then. It winds its way to the ocean, but very few people go there anymore."

"What's the ocean?"

Mars chuckled. "That would be something too big for me to describe, if you don't know already."

Johnny fell into thought. He thought of the picture of the waterfall cascading out of the cave — the River Only entering the Known World. He wondered if the Separation and the Only were the same river, one water passing through both the unknown and the known worlds. But he said nothing.

Nightfall. They spent a little time in a riverside road-house where the main attraction was a fight pitted between a possum and a skunk, each creature chained, the possum spitting, the skunk reeking. The food was terrible. Mars speculated they were eating the loser of the previous battle, and he hoped it was the possum. A skirmish with knives broke out and they escaped out the back door and into the night.

They rolled for a long time through total darkness, trusting that Trespasser could follow the lay of the road by its feel under his hooves. They took turns at the reins while the other dozed. Sometime before dawn they came upon a grassy place where the horse could graze. They stopped there, chocked the wheels and took the bit out of the tired beast's mouth. They slept.

The morning light woke them to a strange and fearsome landscape. At some point in their darkened night journey, the road had arched away from the river, just as Mars had predicted. Now they found themselves at the entrance of a different kind of forest, not made of trees but of jet black stone, jutting out of the ground at all angles, like forks, or fisted fingers chiseled to razor-sharp points, fractured into fragments that mirrored the dazzling light back from the rising sun. The big ones were as large as the silo at King Corn, but there were all sizes, down to the tiny petaled crystals that crowded the cracks and seams of the larger formations. The road was wider here, its bed paved with shards of black stone. It descended into a broad canyon, the walls steep and slick as glass.

"The Onyx Highway," announced Mars. "If your girl is right, we'll find her down there, after a day's travel."

They drank some water and ate some dried meat. They hitched Trespasser to the wagon and started down.

There was a heat in the canyon that did not emanate from the sun. In places, steam vented from the rock, and there was an odor of bad eggs. For most of the morning, a lone vulture circled high above their heads, always following.

Midday they rounded a corner and came upon a man hanging by his neck from an out-jutting rock. Trespasser whinnied and reared back.

"Whoa, boy," said Mars. "You've seen dead men before. This one's no different." He jumped off the buckboard, scrambled up the rock, unsheathed his knife and cut the rope. When the body struck the ground it broke into pieces, releasing a billow of dust.

"Poor old traveler, he's been there a long time. Can you imagine what he's seen?"

"Who did this?"

"Could have been the Blackcoats, but the Blackcoats don't usually go in for hangings. Most likely he did it to himself. It gets pretty lonely out here. Jump down, Clearlight. We'll build him a little monument."

They made a cairn of seven concentric stones and swept the fragments of the dead man into a pile at its base. Mars chanted some words. The only one Johnny recognized was *Beezle*. They continued.

"Blackcoats have caves in this canyon where they keep

tracking devices like the one they used to follow you. They could be watching us right now."

"Will they attack?"

"No, I don't think so. Not if they're transporting slaves to Ironweed. They don't want to attract attention."

Further in, the formations grew more twisted, like writhing snakes or the gnarled branches of ancient trees, the small clustered crystals mimicking leaves. At one point they passed under a wide stone bridge, its underbelly nippled with black stalactites. As the sun grew low, bats appeared, diving from the cornices and eddying around the columns, echoing tiny bell tones against the walls. Far below, at the road's vortex, Johnny saw an opening, and a glimpse of a flat plain.

"That's the Ironweed Prairie," Mars told him. "Look above you. See that ledge? We'll spend the night there. We'll be able to see them coming in the morning. The Blackcoats won't march after dark. Too easy for the captives to escape."

In a short time they reached the bluff, following a steep side road through a narrow fissure in the rock. The view was sweeping. Every detail of the canyon was etched out before them, all the stone-hewn chasms and the hairpins of the highway, and even the distant speck of the lone vulture still circling. And to the west, on the other side of a flat plain, the fiery ball of the setting sun was hovering over the skyline of the strangest city Johnny had ever seen in his short history of seeing cities. No conventional buildings, only the silhouettes of enormous black tubes strafing the horizon, piercing the clouds, bent and angled in all directions like crooked fingers. On the ground below, multiple mounded domes, each riddled with circular openings out of which issued colored vapors, grey, blue, pink and magenta, the mists merging and seeking the lower places, oozing along the ground and away from the city, flowing like spilt cream over the plain.

"The flesh mills of Ironweed," said Mars. "Nobody really knows what happens there. It's where the Thinkers live, the ones that conduct the experiments and devise the plans that keep this world rolling on as it does. We have to get some rest now. We can't destroy that place, but the work we do tomorrow will be a gesture. We may save some lives." He gave Johnny a piercing look. "One in particular."

There was nothing to eat but dried kale and a little bit of cat meat. Trespasser had to eat dried kale also, as there was no grass to graze. Their supply of water was running low. Mars measured it out in mugs and a bucketful for the horse, but after they ate, he sat on the buckboard and fired up some of the *illumination,* as the sun dropped beneath the strange skyline of Ironweed.

"You oughta smoke this, Clearlight. It'll give you the courage."

Johnny shook his head. "I have the courage." Indeed, he did feel something like courage racing through his blood, but it was blended with many other substances. He felt a bit like he was waking from a dream. From the moment he had first crossed the border and tried to give his bread to the child in the street, each taste of cruelty and violence and sorrow and death had driven him ever deeper into a place of numbness, conspiring to steel him against the next shock. He remembered what Mars told Trespasser. "You've seen dead men before. This one is no different." It was like that.

Now he found himself on the precipice of decisive action. No more was he a mere spectator. He would participate in the horrors. The worst thing that could happen, could happen. His blood rose to the surface of his skin. Every hair on his head, his arms, his legs stood upright. His man-thing was engorged and his nipples tingled, his legs restless.

Suddenly, a rumble rose from below. The wagon staves were rocking and creaking. The whole wagon dipped, swayed and rattled, as if rolling down a gravely road. Small rocks began to break loose and tumble down the cliff, and from across the canyon came a shuddering moan, as streams of dirt and stone rippled down the slopes.

"Earthquake!" cried Mars. "Holy mother of Beezle, don't let it take us!"

Inside the wagon, pots and pans were crashing, and some of the tools hanging from the sideboards clattered to the ground. Trespasser pawed and stamped and neighed, and then one quick sideways jolt knocked the horse over onto his side. It also threw Johnny off the buckboard into the hard-packed earth.

But then it was over, only the creaking wagon wheels relaxing into stillness, and the snorting of the horse as he tried to upright himself. Mars reached out with shaky hands and helped Johnny back up.

"I thought we were gonna die, Clearlight. I thought this was gonna be the big one."

"Why does that happen?"

"Oh, Clearlight, Clearlight, it's the power under the ground. It's the mother of Beezle herself. She sleeps beneath the mountains, but we have disturbed her. It's a race against time. If she wakes completely she will throw off the mountains like bed sheets, and we will all be destroyed. Then the young flower of love will sprout anew, but we will not be there, or our children. Oh, Jimmy Clearlight, do you still have that book, the book of poems? I'm so in need of poetry right now."

Johnny found the book in the wagon under the rubble. A falling knife had made a gash across the front cover.

"What do you want to hear?"

"Anything. Anything. Just poetry."

Johnny thumbed through the pages until a short verse caught his eye. He did not hesitate. He read.

"I will arise and go now, and go to Innisfree,
And a small cabin build there, of clay and wattles made;
Nine bean rows will I have there, a hive for the honey bee,
And live alone in the bee-loud glade.
And I shall have some peace there, for peace comes
dropping slow,
Dropping from the veils of the morning to where the
cricket sings;
There midnight's all a glimmer, and noon a purple glow,
And evening full of the linnet's wings
I will arise and go now, for always night and day
I hear lake water lapping with low sounds by the shore;
While I stand on the roadway, or on the pavements gray,
I hear it in the deep heart's core. "

In the silence, a breeze ruffled the canvass and Trespasser sighed, as if he too had been listening. Mars had his face buried in his hands. When he looked up, his eyes were blurred with tears. "Give me," he said.

Johnny handed him the book. He stared at the words for a long time, breathing heavily. Then he lifted the book up as if he were handing it to the sky.

"I will arise..." he began, his voice rich and vibrant:

"I will arise and go now, and go to Freeland

And enter the house that from childhood stood
Uninhabited, ruinous. And I shall have peace there
I shall float in liquid gardens from the veils of morning
Where the caravans gather in the purple glow
I shall taste the honey from a flower named Blue.
I will arise and go now, and go to Freeland
And stand by the gate of the lapping shore
And sing the call, bold as love from the deep heart's
core ..."

His voice broke and fragmented into moans and murmurs, then suddenly he stopped himself, like he was reining in a horse, and he pulled his open hands across his face from scalp to chin. He looked at Johnny, his eyes shining.

"Clearlight, this is how it will happen. Tomorrow we will save your girl. And then we will return to Cantankerberg and save Jason and Isobel from what they have become. The girl can come if she wants. We will arise and go to Freeland. The wind will remember the names it has blown in the past. We will return. We will be free. This will happen ..."

Then he raised his hands above his head and poured something invisible down over him, like the *dough*. Just at that moment the wind changed. It did seem to be blowing a name, but not one that could be spoken with human words.

ɔ

In Johnny's dream Lucy is riding a pony across a narrow bridge with no railing. A lone vulture is circling overhead. Lucy's hair is longer now. It falls across the pony's flank, and a bright purple scarf is tied around her forehead. The vulture drops something from its beak. It looks like a fiery ring, like the sun if its center were blackened. It falls, spiraling, disappears into a roiling caldron of clouds below. At that moment the bridge begins to sway and tremble. "Earthquake!" cries Mars. The pony stumbles to its knees and Lucy is thrown from its back.

Johnny felt a tug, then a shove. He opened his eyes. He was lying on the platform in the back of the wagon. Mars was standing over him, dressed in an outfit that he hadn't seen before. The sleeves hung open like drapes and the fabric was embroidered with eyes, animal eyes of many shapes, round, almond, some compound, like insects, some irises slit, like reptiles. A collar of brown feathers ringed his neck and a leather belt slung around his waist, hanging with knives. He had removed his headband and teased his hair into a shiny black bristle.

"Clearlight. Get up. They're coming."

Johnny and Mars stood on the bluff, facing east. A cloud of dust hung over the canyon, and they could see the distant figures moving along the roadbed like an army of black ants, marching.

"We don't have a plan." Johnny said.

"We don't need a plan. We have the power of love. You take the big knife—the one I got for trade in the trash hills. I'll hitch up the horse. We'll go down and meet them where the road comes out into the plain."

They started down. Trespasser could sense the excitement and smell the danger. His nostrils flared and his gait was brisk. Johnny sat on the buckboard holding the big knife in both hands. It had no sheath and the cold of its blade entered his fingers and traveled up his arms. His entire awareness was focused sharply on the present moment. Everywhere he turned he experienced color and detail, the jagged outlines of boulders, the dry smell of dust, the dizzying sensation of descent as the road dropped steadily toward the plain.

Where the Onyx Highway spilled out of the canyon it cut a straight line to the spires of Ironweed. Someone had planted a makeshift wooden placard here with the painted warning: TURN BACK NOW. At the center of a clearing, directly behind the sign, they parked the wagon. There was grass growing, so Mars unbridled Trespasser and let him graze.

Johnny took a position beside the wagon, his back to the canvass, his eyes fixed on the canyon's opening. "She said if I have to kill anyone, kill the man they call Glass Darkly. But how will I know him?"

Mars shifted his weight. "That's easy. He'll be the only one on a horse. A white horse. He stole it from Mab back in Domination."

One thought turned over three times in Johnny's mind. *I am going to kill a man.* On the third turn, the words changed. *I am going to kill a bird.* He had killed birds before. Out of necessity.

It wasn't long before they could hear them, a sound somewhere between the rumble of wildfire and the peal of distant thunder. Soon the dust began to roll out of the canyon.

Certain images flowed unchecked, each briefly, one following the other. Lucy singing, *begone, begone the mud of sorrow!* The amber glass bottle under the mattress and the first night they made untuned music, and the many nights that followed, and the sweet deep tuning of their bodies together each night when the music fell silent. Lucy moving the dough through the air, assigning each movement a name, *rocking the baby, sending out the lambs, calling the falcons.* Lucy. The blue ceramic bowl behind the cabin: FOR

RACCOONS ONLY. The ladles singing in the continuous rain, singing her name.

Lucy. Lucy.

The memories soothed him. His heart softened. He settled into a place of peace and pleasure so deep that he almost missed the moment the figures first emerged from the canyon, thrusting him violently back into the here and now.

At first they didn't appear as individuals. It was more like a black tar oozing out of the screen of brown dust. The pointed hoods were the first features to manifest. The figures marched so close their shoulders touched, their pace swift and relentless, pressing forward, blindly obedient. But then something happened. Some in the forefront caught sight of a disturbance in the way things should be: a horse grazing, a wagon, two men, holding knives.

The frontline faltered. Those that followed, still oblivious, stumbled into them. From behind, rows of marchers, propelled by momentum and unable to pass through the obstruction, poured around the sides. There were shouts and grumbles, and a new movement at the front. Another phalanx of Blackcoats broke through. Smaller, spryer, their hoods covering their heads, their faces to the ground, they poured out into the clearing a good distance before realizing they had broken from the flow. There was confusion. Some stopped and tried to press back, others began waving their arms, a few sat on the ground. But one leaned forward, stared straight at the wagon and screamed.

"Johnny!"

Johnny felt the earth dissolve under his feet. "Lucy!" He took a step forward and Mars' strong arm grasped his shoulder.

"Don't!"

Commotion, voices raised, the rustling of bodies. Then another sound, the high, wild scream of a horse and the stomping of hooves. Blackcoats cringed and scattered. Some fell to the ground as the great white stallion pounded through their ranks, thrashing and writhing and baring its yellow teeth.

The rider wore no hood. His hair and beard were as dark and shiny as the blackrock, and his eyes were piercing. At the sight of the wagon, the stallion balked and the rider jabbed at it with his ankles. There were blades on his boots and the horse's flanks were scarred and bloody.

Johnny felt a poke in the small of his back. He thought it might be the tip of Mars' knife, but that didn't matter. What it felt like was the urgent prick of courage, borne not of vanity but of sheer necessity. He stepped forward and stared the rider straight in the face.

"I know you, Glass Darkly."

The rider's face ruptured into a contemptuous grin. "I know you too, Johnny Arcane." Almost friendly, the voice was surprisingly thin, empty of resonance. "The girl just confirmed my suspicions."

The words flew unbidden from Johnny's mouth. "The girl also told me that if I were to kill you, the others would have no one to follow, and the captives would escape."

Glass Darkly raised his eyebrows and a shadow crossed his face. "That's not true," he said sharply, and he reined the horse in a full circle, to scan the panorama of faces behind him. "My men are loyal. And anyway, you can't kill me. I'll kill you first."

"Let's find out. Come down. Show me your weapon."

A disturbance of voices rippled through the crowd behind the horse and rider. Johnny couldn't clearly discern the mood. Fists were clenched, but at whom? Provocation, encouragement, resentment, anxiety. Bodies began to jostle erratically. A few people shoved. Some tried to flee, but others restrained them.

All fell still when Glass Darkly slipped from the horse, landed softly on his boots, and opened wide his two bare hands. "These are my weapons," he said. "Your childish dagger cannot touch them."

Johnny felt the pressure of a hand between his shoulder blades. Mars whispered in his ear. "Weak spot: left side of the neck, from behind. Don't let him touch your legs."

Glass Darkly advanced, his arms spread wide, his fingers splayed. Johnny saw the flow of black-robed bodies fanning out, circling around. Some had thrown off their hoods. Others were gesturing inexplicably, and shouting words he did not recognize. He sensed Mars had moved away, behind him, and he heard the clink of the reins. But mostly Johnny focused on the man who stood before him-his *combatant*. He shifted his weight toward the man. He gathered his arms inward, *moving the dough*.

Johnny thought, *I don't know this man. I have no feelings for him. I have no rage, no resentment, no anger. I have only a duty to carry out.* He ducked swiftly, even before the arm was swung, then dropped to the ground, scrambled to his feet and found himself at the man's back. Glass Darkly spun around with both arms swinging. One fist struck Johnny's ear. There was a moment of darkness, followed by a flash of light and a film of blood across his eyes. He raised the knife above his head.

They had traded places. Behind Darkly's approaching bulk, Johnny caught a glimpse of the wagon and Mars, cinching the reins on Trespasser's bridle.

Johnny brought the knife down full force and felt the hand grasp his arm so tightly his wrist went limp and the dagger fell to the ground. He slammed his foot on its blade and an image flashed through him—the silo at King Corn, his arms around the beehive, releasing himself into the hoop. He willed his body to fold. Kicking blows pummeled him on the way down but he clamped the hilt in one hand. With the other he made a fist and slammed it full bore into Glass Darkly's knee cap. The knee buckled, the man staggered. Johnny took the opportunity to jump behind his left side, and slung the blade swiftly at the flesh below the man's left ear.

It was like sinking an axe into a soft green log. The blade stuck, lodged horizontally in the man's neck. Johnny couldn't pull it out, and around its point of entry a trickle of blood began to form. One scream, then another, then another, and soon the air was filled with voices, howling and screaming like a pack of wolves. Darkly's eyes bulged. His arms swung loosely, like empty sleeves in a wind. He opened his mouth and his tongue moved, trying to form a word. Then suddenly he sagged and became unbearably heavy, all of his weight hanging from Johnny's grasp on the knife. Johnny let go. As the body struck the ground there was a rush of air from the lungs, shaping a single, throatless word.

"Beezle!"

Johnny's stomach turned. The sensation of the knife entering the flesh repeated itself in an endless loop until it forced a mass of bile up through his torso and out his mouth. He fell to his knees, retching violently. His arms became eels; they tried to wrench themselves from their sockets. He fell on his face and the earth pitched forward. He thought he might fall into the sky.

"Clearlight! Get up!" He lifted his head but he could not support his body on his elbows. Everywhere Blackcoats were running, fleeing in all directions with ululations of excitement and terror.

Lucy was right. *If he killed the man, the others would have no one to follow, and the captives might escape.*

"Lucy!" he tried to cry, but his voice would form no more than a gagging whimper.

"Clearlight! Get up! Get on the wagon!"

He turned to look. Mars was on the buckboard. Trespasser was reined and stamping restlessly, thrashing his head. Johnny managed to sit and raise his arm feebly toward the wagon.

"But ... *Lucy!*"

"Find her then. Hurry!"

Another wave of strength enabled him to his knees and he managed to get one leg up. But then there was a searing passage of heat, and he saw flames. A Blackcoat ran by, still hooded, carrying a fiery torch and intoning a long, modulated wail. He flung his arm and released the torch into the air. It struck the wagon and immediately the canvass bloomed into a rose of flame. The petals overtook the one-eyed pyramids; the flying dragons fishtailed into the naked women.

"Mars!" Johnny cried, his voice now fully formed. Mars was not on the buckboard, but he emerged suddenly and hurled something into the air. It was Johnny's backpack, and when it struck the ground, the mandolin case broke off and rolled across the dirt.

"Find her, Clearlight! Find your girl!" Mars shook the reins and the horse bolted. The wagon lurched on two wheels, spitting sparks and smoke. A flaming tongue lapped down the rear axle and one wheel shuddered and jammed.

For a while it was dragged by the other three; it bounced and snapped and fell, and the floorboard slumped to a halt.

There was a moment of silence, like an inheld breath. Then a great ball of fire ripped from the belly of the carriage, followed by a deafening roar. Bits of flaming debris filled the air and the staves collapsed. From the buckboard leapt Mars Daniel, completely engulfed in fire. He ran, screaming wildly into the clearing. Trespasser, freed from his grasp, galloped off in the other direction, dragging the reins.

Johnny's strength rushed back into him. He leapt to his feet and tackled Mars, throwing him to the ground and rolling him in the dirt, smothering the flames with his own body.

Mars did not stop screaming. It was as if he could not inhale. He thrashed the ground and a steady stream of agony poured from his mouth. His clothes were charred and clung to his flesh. His face was covered with blisters and his hair was completely gone, his blackened scalp smoldering.

Johnny thrust his arms under Mars' back and knees and lifted him from the ground. His skin was still hot to the touch. The lifting made him scream all the louder. Johnny looked around. Blackcoats were still scurrying about the clearing, but fewer, many had fled in one direction or another.

There was a ridge and a line of green. Green meant water. Around some boulders, a swale, bedded with moss and cattails. The stream was barely a trickle flowing beneath the moss. The good thing was that the boulders provided some shade from the morning sun already burning harsh in the hazy eastern sky.

He laid Mars down in the cool moss. Mars winced. "It hurts! It hurts! Make it stop!" His words turned to more screaming. Johnny remembered something.

"Just lie still," he said. "Breathe. Stay."

He ran back to the clearing. Little fires of the wagon's remnant still flickered but its structure was completely gone. Glass Darkly's body lay on its back. The head was completely gone, as was the knife. The rest of the body had been stripped naked. The genitals had been removed. All the Blackcoats had scattered. Johnny could see their tiny shapes disappearing up the canyon, into the arroyos, across the prairie, and up along the Onyx Highway. For a moment only, he wondered, which one was Lucy. But there wasn't time to think about it. He snatched the backpack and started for the swale. Then in afterthought he returned and retrieved the mandolin as well.

Mars was still screaming. Johnny dug into the backpack and found the tiny glass vial in the deep pocket.

"Stay with me. I have something that might help you." He sat on a rock and cradled Mars' tortured head in his lap. "Open, open." Johnny pried open his lips and emptied the elixir into the parched mouth, followed by a sip of cold water from his canteen.

For a while, Mars continued shrieking while Johnny cradled his head and hovered his hands a breath above his face, because it hurt too much to touch him. Little by little the screams grew less urgent, and there were pauses, longer and longer pauses, punctuated at first by gasps and sobs, giving away slowly to studied breathing, finally relaxing into a calm and steady cadence.

Mars opened his eyes. "What did you *give* me, Jimmy Clearlight?"

Johnny sighed. "Some strong medicine a traveler gave me, long ago. He said someday I might need it."

"Like to get me some more of that." Mars' voice was a

grasshopper's rasp. He lifted one hand to his face and studied the blisters. He winced.

"Do I look terrible?"

"Yes, you look terrible."

Mars lowered his hand. "It doesn't matter. I can see all the way now. I can see all the way through, to the other side. I can see all the planets, and God is moving them about with his stick. I can see the gates of Freeland, and they're singing, the little wolverines, and the mermaids, and the hummingbirds so loud. Music! I want music! Clearlight, where's your mandolin?"

"I've got it. I've got it right here."

"Play me. Play me, Clearlight, bring me to the moon."

Johnny took off his shirt and pillowed it under Mars' head. He opened the case and strummed the strings. They were in perfect tune, which was impossible, but there it was. Perfect tune. He took it to his chest and began to play the only song he could still remember. *Happy to Meet, Sorry to Part.*

"Oh Clearlight, you send me home. You send me home to Freeland."

He played the song, over and over.

"Oh, Clearlight, Clearlight!" Suddenly Mars drew a sharp breath. He tried to sit up but fell back. "I can see it coming, like a great golden star, falling from the moon. It's moving now. It's breaking free. Clearlight! Clearlight! I'll see you again in the next world, Jimmy Clearlight!"

His head fell back and his eyes glazed over. He took one long inbreath, one long outbreath. There was silence. Out of the silence he sat up once more, reached out his charred hand and pressed his fingers against Johnny's chest.

"I'll see you again," he said, "In the next world, *Johnny Arcane*."

Then he sank back down and his spirit left his body. Johnny felt it pouring out of his own chest and racing for the sky. His eyes were tearless. His mind was hushed.

But the hush was broken by a voice, sharp, intrusive.

"There he is! There's the man who killed Glass Darkly! Get him!"

CHAPTER TWENTY-ONE

FREELAND

hree Blackcoats stood on the bank. They wore no hoods. Two had weathered faces with ragged beards. The third was a young boy with long blonde hair. The old ones held daggers. The boy was empty-handed. One of the old ones looked back and gestured. "We got him! Go around so he doesn't get away!"

A dissonant chorus sounded from the clearing. Johnny jumped to his feet, his heart already broken, now racing. He scanned the surroundings. Maybe he could escape along the bed of the swale. The two older Blackcoats were already scrambling down the boulders. The boy held back.

Overhead a sound like wind in a funnel, and a dark shadow swept the earth. For a moment a black shape obscured the sky; then the thud of heavy hooves shook the ground. The stallion reared, wailed and pawed the air. The two Blackcoats froze. One drew his dagger. The horse's hoof came down and dashed the dagger from his hand, and the man screamed in pain.

A band of Blackcoats appeared over the horizon. At the sight of the great horse thrashing its weight in the swale, some of them cried out, some fled, others fell to their knees. Johnny stepped back, and without knowing why, he grabbed some invisible substance from the air and held an open hand out toward the creature.

"Trespasser."

Trespasser pawed the ground and thrashed his muzzle. He pivoted, caught sight of Mars' body, and jumped back, startled. Then he stilled and whimpered, like a child. He straddled the charred corpse, bent his long neck, and sniffed the crackled skin. His big tongue came out and made one pass across the dead man's blistered face. Then he looked at Johnny's outstretched hand. He stepped carefully away from the body and approached with caution and curiosity, his nostrils flared. He parted his lips, bared his teeth, inhaled and swallowed the invisible thing from Johnny's palm. His eyes grew wide. His head reared back. He danced a quick circle and presented Johnny his side. The message was clear. *Get on! Let's go!*

More Blackcoats were swarming over the rise. They held clubs and long knives and they shrieked with fury. Johnny leapt, grabbed the mane, and swung his leg over the horse's bare back.

A gunshot rang out, then another. Johnny sunk his face into the mane and clenched his arms and legs around the body. He counted three muffled hoof beats, then he felt a sensation like falling, only upward. He dared not raise his head. The wails of the Blackcoats were receding in the distance. Something brushed his hand. The reins were still dangling from the horse's bridle. He curled his fingers around them loosely.

He saw nothing. All sensation was motion and air, the rushing wind, the long slow arcs, and the measured impacts, like a stone skipping on water. He felt objects flying from his body, tiny things dislodged by the wind, vanishing in the distance behind; teacups no larger than a speck of dust, shirts and bedsheets as gossamer as a gnat's wing, little red armbands, the pressure of miniature fingers, grains of cornmeal, flakes of glass, bits of music and the bawling songs of cows, coyotes, knitting needles, hoops. All these things sloughed from his skin as more and more oozed from the pores, took form, and flew away.

This went on for a long time. Perhaps he slept but he did not lose his grip. He learned to embrace the rise and fall of the rhythm and willed his body into it, the kneading of dough, the chopping of wood, the in and out of breathing, the thrust and release of sex.

He heard music, a continuous drone intoning a complex harmony. It was blown by the wind but it wasn't just the wind. He could feel his body vibrating from a resonant point between his shoulder blades. Then he realized what it was.

The mandolin. Still strapped around his neck and riding his back, it was singing to the rush of wind and the freedom of escape.

Freedom! His lungs filled with wonder and the terror of it. So much grief, so much had been lost in such a short time. Mars was dead, his head resting on the backpack which contained everything Johnny had carried or acquired since he left home so many moons ago, the box of maps, the picture of the waterfall, Lucy's letter, Jocko's sculptures, his canteens, corn lamps, jackets, and every other tool he needed for survival. He had heard Lucy's voice, but he had not seen her face, and now she too was free, freedom in all its terror and wonder, and he did not know where she was.

And yet he felt the great and familiar elation, the lightness he remembered every time he left a place and set out alone on the open road. The music of the wind across the strings sung its song, transforming all the sorrow into sweetness. But he could not lift his head. He could only trust in the wisdom of the horse. Trespasser had tasted something invisible from the palm of his hand, and it had infused him with knowledge. A course was set. A purpose was determined. There was nothing to do but to hang on tightly for as long as it took, to surrender to the forward motion while the wind continuously inhaled sorrow and exhaled sweetness through the singing of the strings.

At some point he became aware that he was no longer moving. For how long, he could not tell. He felt the sun, low on the horizon, its warmth on his shoulders. It must be late then, and he remembered it was early morning when he had climbed on Trespasser's back. Then the realization sunk in. *The sun in the sky!* He had not actually seen its orb since he first crossed the border three full moons ago. He sat up abruptly.

He was still on the horse. Trespasser was standing knee-high in a field of green, grazing contentedly. Johnny scanned the western horizon. Indeed, the fiery ball of the sun was just now dipping, evening-orange, into a ridge of pointed firs. There was a cool breeze ushering in a scent of verdant promise. The green meadow rolled on to a darkening eastern horizon befouled with grey vapors. But directly before him stood a forest of strong and stately evergreens, and a road welcoming into it, and a carved wooden sign hanging above the road with one word: FREELAND. And below this sign a portly, dark-skinned and bearded man, standing, smiling, wrapped in a pumpkin-orange robe.

Johnny burst into tears. Every emotion that had been hiding in his cloistered heart broke out at once and the world disappeared in a blur. He cried openly, loudly. He bawled like a baby. He mopped his face with his hands. Snot poured out of his nose. His convulsions settled into sobs. His vision cleared. He looked at the orange-robed man, still standing, still smiling. He found his voice.

"Bow Wow."

Bow Wow chuckled, pressed his fingers together, and bowed, ever so slightly. "Welcome to Freeland, Johnny Arcane. We've been expecting you. Come down and walk with me now. The horse needs a rest."

Johnny felt another wave of tears rushing toward his eyes, but he fought them back. "Bow Wow," he said in a tattered voice. "I killed a man. Lucy is free, but I let her get away. And Mars is dead."

"What did I say, Johnny Arcane? Walk with me. We can talk about it."

Johnny slipped off the horse. When his feet hit the ground his knees buckled and he collapsed in a heap. His legs had gone completely numb from the long ride. Bow Wow helped him up and took Trespasser by the reins. They entered the cool deepening shade of the forest.

"It makes me sad about Mars, but I'm not surprised. It was his destiny. But Lucy—*that* is very good news. You have a destiny too, Johnny, and you are fulfilling it. I will send out scouts. They will bring her back here. And you will stay with us for a while, to rest and recover, but it can't be for long. The dark ones will come looking for you, and our power is not yet strong enough to resist them. But don't worry. You'll be safe. We will give you protection along your way. Look!"

Bow Wow raised his hands to the sky. Johnny looked up. Between the branches above the road, a cord was suspended, and another sign hung there, the same as the sign at the entrance to the forest, but the wood was more weathered, the letters more obscured:

FREELAND.

"This used to be the entrance, but the forest has grown. Our work presses outward, always, but it is very slow, as slow as the growth of new trees. You'll see what I mean."

They passed under the sign. Johnny began to see build-ings nestled among the trees, moss-covered and thatch-roofed, blending so well into the glade that he discerned them mostly by the glint of light from the windows.

"I returned to the bathhouse some time later," he said. "It had been destroyed completely. I was told it was the Blackcoats."

Bow Wow did not answer right away. They walked for a while. "It was meant to happen. Sometimes I think our time there was for only one purpose: so that you could come to us, and you did. You keep your promises, Johnny."

"I don't remember making a promise."

"You don't have to remember them to keep them."

They arrived at a green meadow, framed by a ring of blue flowers. Another sign hung above the entrance to the meadow but the writing on it was gone.

"This was the original entrance to Freeland." Bow Wow said.

In the clearing, people, gathered in a cluster, were moving the dough—men and women, all dressed in identical orange robes. Their movements were perfectly synchronized. They scooped up invisible things from the air, rolled them into balls, stretched them into ribbons, flung them skyward, and then scooped up more.

"You are tired. A meal and a bed tonight. Tomorrow you will see what we are about."

They cut a course directly across the meadow. The dough-movers, enrapt by their own movements, did not seem to notice. On the other side, the forest resumed, but here there were oaks, ancient and stately, gracefully gnarled. A village had been carved into the hillside, founded with stones and wattled with wood and straw so that everything blended into everything else. The entrances arched, resembling caves—perhaps they were caves, and the structures were merely conformed to their meanderings. People in robes were walking about. Some carried things, bundles of firewood, bunches of carrots, crates of apples. They smiled at Bow Wow but they did not speak.

They came to a complex of wooden stalls where ponies and donkeys were stabled. The young boy who took Trespasser's reins was awestruck to behold something as magnificent as a horse.

They entered a labyrinth of tunnels. Candles flickered, and flecks of crystal in the rounded walls sparkled in the light. There were wonderful smells of good things cooking, and faint traces of soft music.

Bow Wow led him to a room. The ceiling curled over a small bed covered with a colorful quilt. On the bedside table stood an amber bottle and a mug. Across from the bed, a pool, steaming slightly, glowed faintly blue from within.

"Take off your clothes and leave them outside the door. Bathe. We will bring you supper and a robe to wear. Don't worry. You won't have to wear the robe into the world. We will wash your clothes. Sleep well now, Johnny Arcane. Your journey is not finished."

He did as he was told. His clothes were stained with blood and the mud of blood mixed with dust. There were flecks of vomit in his beard and a stain of bile on his skin. This had been his condition when he first came to the bathhouse and Lucy had bathed him and given him back his voice.

He lowered himself into the warm waters of the pool. His own hands were her hands, washing him clean. He sang her song to himself:

Be gone! Be gone! The mud of sorrow
Be gone! Be gone! The filth of sorrow
Be gone! Be gone! The stink of sorrow
Come on! Come on! Into the pool!
Into the pool! Be clean!

Out of the bath, he fingered the orange robe, but he did not put it on. There was a knock on the door. Naked, he opened it. As always, there was no one there. As always. As if nothing else had taken place between those seven sweet and distant days and nights and this deep and mysterious moment, redolent with the aromas of the past. Johnny lifted the tureen and inhaled its fragrance. So familiar! The blend of cardamom and clove, the sweetness of honey. Just before he ducked back into the room he heard footsteps down the hall. Two orange robes disappeared through a doorway, girlish voices giggling at the ridiculous sight of a naked man.

Naked he sat at the table and ate the soup, savoring every bite. For a long time afterward he contemplated the amber bottle and the empty mug. Surely it was permissible. This was Freeland. He could do no harm. He poured a small amount in the bottom of the mug and sipped it. Yes. It was the same. The woodruff and the damiana and the bracing heat of the spirits. He filled the mug, set it on the table, and slipped into the bed. The sheets were velvet soft and there were two big, plumpy pillows. A candle danced from a wall sconce. Johnny took a long, slow draft from the mug, then another.

How persistent had become the ragged discomforts of life on the road, sleeping uncovered on hard rocks under a storm-filled sky, trudging soaked and bitter-cold through dark forests, or parched and famished under a blazing sun. The misery of illness, the cruelty of men and women. And still arrives this interlude of comfort, like a smile from some unnamed benevolence. Lucy! The room disappeared in the candleglow and he was there again, in the little cabin above the bathhouse, the last discords of the music still ringing, and their naked bodies aglow with the warmth of the elixir, merging into a seamless union that laughed in the face of sorrow and pressed its sure and steady hand toward the heart of pleasure.

In the morning, all the citizens of Freeland gathered in the meadow to sing to the rising sun. Johnny was awakened by the sound, soft and reverberant, through the walls. He got up and put on the orange robe. His mind was clear and curious. His legs wanted to be moving; his hands to be doing.

The sky above the meadow arched a brilliant blue, the meadow grass green, turning to gold, glistening with dewdrops. The breeze carried the scent of bay laurel and alder berries. The old oaks were sporting their young leaves like new spring dresses. The orange robed singers moved with a loosely knit precision, weaving in and out, strands forming and dissolving, forming again. Some held hands, other moved dough. Johnny felt at home in his robe, entering the meadow and the flow of moving bodies. There were plenty of other bearded men his age. There were old men and women, young girls, children. Some were fat; some were thin, some tall, some short. There were all shades of skin, from night-sky black to peony pink. No one's energy was stronger than anyone else's. There was relaxation, and a sense of active peace.

He joined the singing. The melodies were simple and there were no words, just open vocalizations. If he met someone's eyes they merely smiled in recognition, and only turned away when the flow pulled them on.

At some point the singing stopped and everyone sat on the ground. A formation of orange-robed people moved through the crowd, handing out cups and some kind of round loaf. Bow Wow was among them. When he saw Johnny, he knelt beside him, poured something from a pitcher into a cup, and handed it to him. It was warm and spicy.

"Did you sleep well, young sojourner?"

"I slept wonderfully well. I am comfortable here."

Bow Wow smiled. "Don't become so comfortable that you cannot leave at a moment's notice." He tore off large piece of the loaf and handed it to Johnny. "Come. I will show you our garden."

A footbridge across a tree-lined creek led to another sunlit clearing. A round building, made of what appeared to be dried mud, stood before a forested background. Its graceful curves and lines suggested it had been fashioned lovingly by a single hand, although its highest spires were as tall as the tops of the trees. The garden poured from its doors. Purple grapes hung from the arbor over a path through cultivated rows, beans climbing poles, corn already tasseling so early, yellow blossoms emerging from the open hands of squash plants, tender green raspberries dancing on a fence. Here and there, orange robed people were working, hoeing new rows, trimming vines, raking mulch over fresh-turned earth where inquisitive blackbirds hopped about, watching for worms. Some people stood among the rows, moving the dough, scooping it from the air, releasing it from their fingers over the crops.

At the side of the garden was a row of beehives. Bow Wow led Johnny there. A man was pulling out trays of honeycomb and allowing the amber honey to flow down through a funnel into a glass jar. He wore no hood on his head or gloves on his hands. Bees were swarming around his face and climbing up his neck and around the curve of his ears. He nuzzled the cluster of bees on the back of his hand with his bushy moustache.

"They like to be touched," he said. He looked into Johnny's face. "You're Johnny Arcane."

"I am."

The bee man dipped a finger into the honey and touched it to his tongue. "There are bees where you come from." he said.

"There are. My mother kept bees, and once I brought down a hive of bees from the silo, at the Cornfest in King Corn."

The bee man nodded; then he carefully slipped the comb back into the hive and closed the jar. "There were no bees outside Freeland," he said, "Until just recently. The trees stopped making fruit and most of them died. The cornfields and the wheat fields dried up. Many of the meat animals starved. But now we hear from our scouts. The pears outside our borders are blooming again. The mustard fields are yellow. Our bees have flown beyond the forest. This is how it happens."

Bow Wow walked Johnny through the arbor and back into the garden.

"Nothing comes in from the outside," he said. "Except a

few souls like yours, who are guided by destiny. At the heart of Freeland is a well of living water. Our task is to prepare the soil so that water can percolate out into the world. It can't be pushed. It has to flow. This is what Mars Daniel did not understand."

Johnny knelt and ran his fingers along the fuzzy leaf of a young tomato plant. He stood. "Lucy told me that Freeland was founded by seers. Are you a seer?"

Bow Wow held up his hand with the fingers splayed. "What do you see here, Johnny Arcane?"

"I see your hand."

"Ah! So you see. You must be a seer."

"But I thought a seer was someone who could see the invisible, the past, the future, things far away. Things that other people can't see."

"There is no distinction between the visible and the invisible. Start with anything. A hand, a leaf, a turd by the side of the road. Soon you will see everything. We are all seers here, and so are you. Abigail! We must find some work for our young sojourner, Johnny Arcane. He thinks too much."

A young woman looked up from a plot of freshly sprouted greens. "I'm thinning," she said. "He can help me thin."

So Johnny spent the morning thinning greens in the gardens of Freeland. Abigail told him that the seeds were tiny, and no one had the eyesight or the patience to sow them each, four fingers apart, as required. Instead they would sprinkle the seeds as they fell along the rows, and now the rows were verdant with sprouts, crowding each other for space. For each sprout that remained, a dozen had to be pulled, and you had to choose carefully, determining which were most likely to grow into strong, healthy heads of vigorous, life-giving leaves. And then of course you had to apologize to the ones you

pulled, all of them, each one, one at a time. I'm sorry. I'm
sorry. I'm sorry. It wasn't your destiny.

"Sometimes after a morning thinning, I just have to go
someplace and cry," she said.

When the sun reached center-sky a bell rang from the
round building and everyone gathered at a stone pool to
wash for the meal. Children splashed in the water and threw
it in each other's faces. There were ladles in troughs, and
some people scooped water over their heads and down the
folds of their robes.

Inside the building was a single room, like a longhall,
but it was round, not long, and flooded with natural light
from openings in the vaulted ceiling. At the center stood a
large, round stone table with cushions all about, food on the
table, piles of fruit and vegetables, rounds of cheese, loaves
of bread. People helped themselves and sat on the cushions.

Bow Wow beckoned Johnny from his cushion. A child sat
next to him, a boy no more than six summers old, shy and
clinging to Bow Wow's arm.

"I told you about the few souls who come here from the
outside. This is Timothy. He showed up one rainy night last
winter, speaking a language that none of us understood. It
was a wondrous thing to discover there are languages we
don't know about. He has learned a few of our words, but
we have yet to learn a single one of his."

Timothy shied behind Bow Wow's orange robe, peeked
out with sun-round eyes, then hid behind the robe again.
Johnny empathized his discomfort and left to find something
to eat. There were no plates at the table, and many of the
fruits and vegetables were unknown to him. He tried this; he
tried that. All the while, the child, Timothy, eyed him with
caution and curiosity.

After the meal was finished and cleared, some, mostly children, gathered in the open space, while the others went out to resume their chores.

"Watch closely, Johnny," said Bow Wow. "This is when the young people learn the movements, what Lucy called *moving the dough*. It may serve you to know this."

The teacher was a woman with long, white hair. Her words were not direct. She simply stood before the loosely gathered collection of children and announced, "Form One." Then she began to move. She spoke of each movement in fanciful terms. Leaning over and scooping from the floor, she said, "Here we gather the gifts of the morning dew, and here we roll them into the warm ball of the sun," as her hands curved around a sphere of invisible substance. "Here we knead the dough and shape the loaf," her fingers extending and contracting with each thrust and release. Her hands scooping high above her head down to the caldron of her belly, she intoned, "Here we harvest the stars to give them to the earth." With sweeping arcs up and away from her body, "Here we fling the flowers of the morning over the tops of the trees."

The smaller children, earnest and clumsy, stumbled through the movements with awkward sincerity. The older ones performed with grace and confidence, and a bit of pride, especially the girls who scoffed at the missteps of the boys. And the youth plodded along grudgingly, listless and distracted, their minds on other things, the boys stealing glances at the girls, the girls at the boys.

"Form One, again!"

The second time Johnny joined in. The movements were simple. They flowed naturally and it wasn't long before he began to feel the substance in his hands, its weight when he lifted it, its shape changing when he rolled and stretched and molded it, the sudden lightness in his fingers when he hurled it into the air. It balanced him through the swoons and pivots of the form. It lent him grace.

There were three forms, each completed twice. The second had to do with the effect of the substance on the body of the mover. Feel it radiating from your palms to your face. Draw one handful from the cold well, the other from the warm. Feel the difference. Gather as much as you can in your arms at one time; feel it escape through your fingers.

The third form was interactive. They played catch with the substance. They pulled it into ribbons, like taffy, in pairs, two people stretching and compacting a single ball. Abigail from the garden approached Johnny with her arms cradled around something invisible. They worked it between their fingers. When she pulled, he could feel his body shifting toward her. He pulled back and she leaned his way. This made her giggle and the substance immediately became weightless. They had to gather some more to continue.

In the long shadows of evening, Johnny found Bow Wow strolling through the rose garden on the hillside behind the roundhouse. Young Timothy was walking beside him. The roses were sorted by color into beds, and each variety had a metal placard with its name. Bow Wow was reading the names of the roses to the child, and the child was repeating them.

The Shy Maiden's Blush, The Plowman's Pride, Welcome Home, Meet Me On The Bridge, The Lover's Knot, Safe at Anchor, Summer Wine, A Friend for Life. They sounded like the names of fiddle tunes, and if there weren't fiddle tune with those names, he could surely make some up.

"And how was your day in Freeland, young sojourner?"

Johnny sighed. "I don't know if I can help it. I feel like I belong here."

"You are here, Johnny Arcane, but there is still work for you to do. It is the nature of this work that does not allow you to stay."

Johnny scanned the roses and the placards until his eyes focused on one:

BITTER CUP.

"A man came to the bathhouse while I was there. He bothered Lucy. She said you sent him away by erasing his memory. Mars said that's how you keep Freeland safe. You can erase the memory of anyone who attacks, and they forget why they came."

"I know what you're thinking," Bow Wow replied. "Our power is greater than the powers of chaos and cruelty, and we are destined to triumph. But it isn't that simple. If there is a battle, we will always lose. Battle is the crowning triumph of chaos and cruelty. Our victory is always in the slow, outward growth of the forest, the flight of the bees, and the way we send out the dough to catch the wind and sail it into the world."

The bell at the roundhouse began to ring. Young Timothy perked up his ears. He tugged at Bow Wow's robe and said something in another language.

"You go ahead," said Bow Wow. "We'll catch up."

The boy did a quick dance and scampered off. As he ran he chirped a little birdsong made of trills and syllables. Johnny felt a startle of recognition. It was Lucy's language, clear and bright as the bell tones of the rain ladles. Lucy! Was it possible Bow Wow did not know?

"We're going to sing the sun down now," said Bow Wow. "Will you join us?"

☽

That night he sat at the table in his room, eating the meal that had been left at his door. The amber bottle was empty. Tonight he drank cold water. His clothes were clean and folded neatly at the foot of the bed. He had no wish to put them on. The orange robe was so comfortable on his skin. His heart was troubled. His memory would only skip lightly over the events of the recent days. He had broken the glass door in Ladyland. He had watched a body fall from the upper levels of Solomon's Tower. He had killed a man, and Mars was dead, and Trespasser had brought him safely to Freeland. *Where he belonged.* Where he felt in every pore of his skin, in every breath through his lungs, in every melody in his ears, and in the feel of the dough between his fingers, he belonged in Freeland. But he must leave. Battles are only won by the powers of chaos and cruelty. He still had work to do, but the nature of the work was not disclosed.

Why were there so many mysteries? But of course, there are always mysteries. Most people ignore them. His mother would simply sprinkle a pinch of fire grate ash into the wall sconces, and the mysteries would leave her alone. It was his fate as a sojourner to be troubled by the mysteries. Driven to wandering the roads alone, he had made a map of the Known World, and finally crossed over into the unknown world. But the mysteries only compounded, mystery upon mystery. These thoughts did no good!

He got up and paced the room. Where was Lucy? She wasn't here tonight, as she had been last night, conjured by the elixir and the bath's warm waters. But the boy, Timothy, had spoken her language. What did that mean? What did anything mean?

Too restless to sleep, he left the room and entered the hall. It was pitch dark. He had to feel his way out through the labyrinth and into the open air. It must be very late. There were no lights anywhere, but the stars shimmered over the meadow and the waning moon was rising above the trees.

Suddenly he saw sparks, quick little dances of light that flashed and faded, here and there in the clearing.

Fireflies! He recognized them at once. How many summer nights as a child he had sat on the porch with mother, watching the fireflies sparkle over the garden. He entered the meadow. The sprightly spirits leapt and cavorted around him. He stopped at the center and stood stone still. Something was gradually dawning on him.

They weren't fireflies. There were people in the meadow, orange-robed, slowly moving the dough, and at certain pivots in the form, the substance caught a glint of some hidden light and reflected it back, briefly, like the flash of a firefly. Stunned, he sat on the ground, slowly and quietly as possible, not to be seen.

For a long time he sat there, watching the graceful shadowed movements, watching the bursts of illumination as they traced the form, marveling at the occasional rebellious spirits of light that escaped from their confines and streaked up above the treetops into the starlit sky.

Ↄ

Early morning, a quiet rap on the door awakened him. Bow Wow stood there with two others. One of them was the white-haired leader of the movement class. The other was a thin, elderly man with a gentle face.

"Johnny, we have found Lucy."

Johnny's heart jumped. "Is she alive?"

"She is moving toward Freeland. We have not seen her. We have just detected her movements. Today we will send out protectors to surround her, and assure she arrives safely. She will not be aware of them."

Johnny sat on the bed. His mind was dancing. "Then I'll see her again."

Bow Wow laid a hand on his shoulder. "I'm afraid that is not so, Johnny Arcane. It is too dangerous. They do not know you are here now. If they find out, they will attack. People will be killed, maybe even Lucy."

Johnny couldn't believe what he was hearing. "But ... where will I go?"

"That has been arranged. We will erase your memory, then give you instructions. When your memory returns, you will be far from here, on a long journey that will bring you home." He held up his hand to the woman behind him. "Beatrice."

The white-haired woman came forward holding something. "This was made for you, Johnny Arcane," she said. "Sandyman worked on it all night. This morning we stocked it with provisions."

She held out a leather bag with straps, filled with parcels, packets, cloth sacks with drawstrings, boxes wrapped in parchment, bottles and jars, and at the bottom, something that looked like a book. The leather of the pack was burnished to a reddish hue and tooled with flaps and pockets, and a webbed holster had been sown in one side, for the mandolin in its new cloth case.

"I'm sorry," said Bow Wow. "Today we must be like the wind and not the tree. We have provided everything you need. You will not know who you are, but you will know how to survive, and where to go. You will be given a guide. You may not recognize the guide at first. Come. We will demonstrate how we protect ourselves in Freeland."

It happened so quickly. Johnny didn't have time to speculate what it would be like. The two others entered the room. The woman sat at his right side on the bed, Bow Wow at his left. The other man pulled up the chair and faced them. Bow Wow reached out and they formed a circle of hands. Suddenly Johnny remembered what he was wearing.

"But—the robe."

"Don't worry," said Bow Wow. "We will take the robe."

Then they closed their eyes.

CHAPTER TWENTY-TWO

REMEMBERING

Walking. Feet on the path. The familiar cadence that puts distance between things.

As the day moves on, the road begins to ascend, continuously, circling the mountain, like a whirl-wind. The man senses his place on it by the feel of the air. Time is metered in the change of light. Even in the fog there are shadows and shifts in color. You can measure the passage across the breast of a day by observing these things ...

The *breast* of a day ...

Women. Soft, rounded, deep, compassionate, plea-sure-giving.

Men. Hard, boisterous, brawny, bearded, clumsy, companionable.

Near the top, the fog thins, the air cools, and the man's breathing becomes labored. At the top, a clearing and a clear sky, and a view into great distances of cloud. The sun is down, the sky is darkening blue, peppered with young, fresh stars, and a thin, waxing, crescent moon over the western horizon.

If I leave something, a cairn of stones, a rag tied to a tree, others following will know I have been here. If I find some-thing, I will know others have come before me.

The man sits on the granite and removes his pack. He

will sleep here. He takes out some of the food. The *food*. Several of the packets have been opened and consumed. One of the three bottles is empty. He chews on the nugget, wondering what it is, and who made it.

He drinks some water. He stands and urinates. Then he finds a hollow place where the curve of the rock can make a pillow. He lies on his back, pulls the warm coat over him, and watches the sky turn black and fill with stars. Just before he sleeps he notices one star moving, blinking, plowing through the fields of night. "I wonder what that is?" he says. Then he sleeps, awakened once, briefly, by the song of a single, distant creature, a soaring, mournful tune that he recognizes, but cannot remember its name.

Morning, he wakes, remembering falling asleep the night before, and the song of the wolf in the dark. A *wolf*, then. It has a name. Behind that, there is nothing, only the evidence of time having passed, the waning moon, the food eaten. But below him the fog has cleared; he can see the rising sun shining on forests, meadows, mountains, except to the west, where the horizon flattens into a line of gray.

So. He looks for something reflective to give him some clues about who he is. The metal water bottle. Its curvature distorts, but he learns some things from it. His beard is brown, his eyes blue. There's a small wedge-shaped scar on his cheek.

But who am I? The question does not raise much anxiety. More anxious he would be if he knew who he was. There is bliss in ignorance.

He eats some food. He drinks some water. He hoists his pack and starts back down the way he came. Seven circles gird the mountain, and at its foot another road continues to the west. He had missed this before, or perhaps it simply had not been there. This seems to be a time when things come and go, and their meanings are obscured. For now he simply must continue.

He begins to remember the names of certain things along the way. That tree is called a white spruce, and those are foxgloves growing wild on the roadside. *"Don't eat them!"* a scrub jay scolds him from an alder branch. When he comes to a stream splashing down the mountainside, he thinks, *I should fill my bottles. One needs water.* He knows the road is winding steadily westward—*sunward*—and this feels right to him. If it veers one way or another, to circumvent some obstacle, or to follow some natural contour, he feels uncomfortable, reassured only when it realigns itself with the westward trajectory of the sun.

The sun is sky-center, the road meets a river and attaches itself to its course. The river soon winds out of the forest and spills onto an open plain where it slows and disperses into marsh and wetland.

The fog returns. First it swallows the sun, turns the sky gray, and then begins to close its fist around every landmark, every tree, bush, stone, the still and the flowing bodies of water, the waterbirds, the flying things. Much of what he had remembered he begins to forget. He's knows he's moving. He feels the treadle of his feet, but everything else is standing still.

He falls into a kind of walking trance. His mind, unable to comprehend nothingness, supplies him with images. A great fire rages across a prairie. A long fire-lit hall throbs with moving bodies, a murmuring of voices. A torrent of water bursts from the mouth of a cave and cascades into a pool. A sky is filled with so many birds, they block the sun, their wingsounds like wind. He catches himself slipping into unconsciousness, straying from the path. Shaken, he stops and allows his heartbeat to settle.

In the stilling, he begins to hear a sound, a real sound, not one of his mind's making. It sounds like the breath of some great creature as large as the sky. It breathes from the west in cycles longer and slower than the capacity of any human lung. It frightens him, yet it draws him. He moves toward it, quickly.

The road ends here, abruptly, like a long life, ending. Clouds of white birds circle over a grey horizon, asking mournful questions. The scent of rust and sphagnum, and the taste of salt on the mist, and everywhere, the constant murmuring chant of some great voice, or chorus of voices thundering from behind the veil of the western horizon.

A bluff of fine, loose sand where tufts of coarse grass tenaciously cling. He scrambles over, falling several times. Bleached bone-white, the gnarled corpses of trees mock him. Heedless, he plunges into the maze. The sand drags at his feet. Wooden fingers claw his arms. He slams into the open and skids to a halt, dumbstruck and senseless, numbed with astonishment.

A single immense living being, made entirely out of water. It breathes and sings and dances. He cannot take it in. His knees become butter and he melts to the sand. All the fluid drains from his mind. Empty of knowing, he waits, silently watching.

From beyond the range of the eye, rolling swells move in until they can no longer contain themselves. They tumble over headlong and explode into blossoms of white light, slowly subsiding across the slick, reflecting sand. The creature draws a breath; something rattles in its throat, a harvest of pebbles, a gathering in.

But it isn't that simple. Everywhere, the inbreath and outbreath are happening at once, forces dancing and wrestling playfully. And out there on the horizon's edge, dark shadows, jagged rocks, greyed by fog. Beyond them the waves are marching from the edge of the world, row upon row, crashing into the rocks, throwing spray into the air.

He sits on the sand for a long time, and ponders, to the extent that a mind as vacant as his can ponder. *Why this? I know the names of things. Trees. The names of trees. Birches. Oaks. Cedars. Mountains and birds—the names of birds. Jays. Sparrows. Wrens. And water, water takes different forms. Rivers. Lakes. Springs and creeks. Tumblers and canteens. But never this ...*

He stands and moves toward the water. A wave rushes to greet him. He drops to his knees, lowers his face to its surface, drinks, and spits it out at once. Undrinkable, saltier than tears or blood. This is a creature with no flesh or bone, only blood and tears.

He sits for a while and soon another wave advances to cover his shoes, and he has to move back.

Just before it disappears, the sun becomes visible, a wedge of orange between the strata of cloud and the line of the horizon. For a time, there are birds everywhere, white birds that swoop and dive, little fat long-legged birds that run around on the sand in circles, large elegant birds with enormous pocketed beaks moving in slow formation along the line of the shore. As the dark moves in, the birds move on, except for the little waders who scatter about with skittering voices as they court the incoming waves.

His thoughts grow still as the darkness surrounds him. With less to see, he focuses on the sounds. He counts the wave sounds—he still remembers numbers. He counts the timespan between waves, and he takes note of the small sounds, the clicks and rumbles, the birds. He observes patterns: the longer silence after each seventh wave, the gurglesome warble of certain inhalations, the occasional doubled boom, and the even more occasional trebled boom—is there a pattern here? The pattern eludes him, but there is a pattern to everything else.

At some point the insistence of the sound acts as a calmative. He relaxes. He molds the sand into the contours of his body. He rolls his coat under his head. He sleeps.

He wakes, surrounded by water. The Great Being has ambushed him in his sleep, one of its many hands curving its salty finger around him, carving out the sand from under him. The water is very cold. He jumps up and grabs the pack. The fabric is wet but the contents are dry. His backside is drenched.

He stumbles inland where the sand is dry and shifting. He looks around. The sky is black and brilliant with stars, except for the west where the fingernail of the moon sinks into a clouded horizon. But there is light coming out of the waves. Every time they curl and burst, they flash bright blue and fade. This happens all the way to the horizon—wherever there is spray, there is light. When his feet kick the sand it bursts into particles of light.

He pulls the coat around his shoulders and walks south. *Why south?* He doesn't know. He just does. He must have dreamed. There are people walking in his head, men and women. Some are wearing robes; others are shrouded in black, with hoods pulled over their faces. Some are dancing, singing. A young man with wild curly hair is plucking music from a single string. A dark-skinned man in a purple shirt is reading to him from a book. Hands, lifting him in the air, are carrying him across a field. A small creature approaches with a large bird in its mouth.

But the cold and the damp are insistent. He must keep moving to stay warm. He cannot pursue these phantoms. When he does, they run away from him like shy deer. Deer. Coyotes. Cats. Raccoons. All the beasts and the buildings, longhalls and towers, houses, wells, a man with a knife, a wagon, a horse. Silence, wind. The fading of forms.

He wants to cry, "I can't remember!" For the first time, he regards the loss as something to mourn.

He hears dogs barking in the water, which is strange. They are barking from the big rocks offshore where the waves crash into short, bright blue flames. He has been walking for a long time now, almost all night. The moon is gone and a pale golden glow is stranding through the foggy east. It has been a long night chasing shadows, but his clothes are dry now, and perhaps he can get some rest.

Ahead, on the bluff side of the shore, is some kind of structure. He sees it a long way coming. It doesn't look like a building. Its shape is too irregular, rounded and knobby, more like a beaver's lodge or a very large bird nest. Drawing closer, he sees something else. A thin line of smoke rises from a circle in the sand. *Someone else is there, then, or has been recently.* He slows his pace. He's not sure if he's ready to encounter another person. Encountering himself has been work enough.

Closer. Making out the details, he stops. Yes, it is a house, but the walls have been hobbled together from the dry bones of trees, water-weathered boards, tin plates, iron springs, mortared with mud and leaves. One segment is embedded with a mosaic of shells and glass. A round metal wheel serves as a window. Colored stones are strung between the spokes on wires, like dew drops in a spider's orb. The door is shingled with broken shell, and above, the shape swirls to a focal point where a purple windsock hangs from a long forked limb. Before the fire circle a heavy log has been worn smooth and contoured to fit the shape of a human body. A corked green bottle sits in the sand at the foot of the bench. But there is no one there. The door is open. He looks inside. A table top. Dishes. Cups. Bottles. Jars of food. A lantern. An unmade bed. Something hangs from a peg. He cups it in his hand. On a string, a flat medallion; a face conveying two emotions. The mouth laughs. The eyes weep.

He sits on the bench and watches the waves. Perhaps whoever lives here will return. He is not tired, except for his feet—it's good to be off them. But his mind is sharp, focused on the things before him, curious about the things unseen. There is something nagging at him. Perhaps it is just hunger. There is food in the house but he is not sure of the generosity of his host. There's food in the pack. He opens it, peers in. Something in the bottom, under the parcels and the jars. Something that has always been there but he's never thought about it before. He takes it by its hard-soft edge and draws it out. He drops the pack on the sand. His fingers tremble.

A book. The cover is leather-bound, with nothing on it. The spine is rigid. He opens it at the center and the pages flip through his hands. It's full of words, painstakingly written, tiny, elegant letters in rows as straight as the surface of a still lake. So many words! Can he read them? He's not sure. He thumbs through and picks out a word here and there. *Musician. Mayor. Hornpig. Cornmeal. Springfest. Lucy...*

He stops.

Lucy.

A face bursts before him. A girl. Her dancing eyes, her thin cheeks, her sleek black hair, her sprightly voice, her slender waist, her arms around him. She is surrounded by others, children laughing and twirling, a bow pulled across a string, a cow, a silo; but these shapes materialize out of the smoke and disappear into the air, and with them the girl disappears, only her name and her face, and the soft pressure of her body against his, Lucy, receding, Lucy—

The vision drowns in the crashing of the waves. Birds drift above the water, their wings gold-tipped with sunrise. He is empty again. Only here and now. But he holds the book in his hands. He can recognize the words. He opens to the first page. He reads.

A messenger appeared on the afternoon of the owl moon in Johnny Arcane's seventeenth summer. Johnny was out working the garden, thinning the carrots, when he saw the stranger round the crest of the western ridge, no more than a speck from that distance, like an oak tree walking ...

CHAPTER TWENTY-THREE

INTERSECTION

nce again, the sun eased her way down into the bed of clouds above the western horizon. An entire day had passed. Johnny Arcane sat, resting against the smooth contour of the sitting log, watching the waves roll in, the book closed in his lap.

So. It was all there then. Everything had returned. Every word from the book had been a simple act of remembering. He sat, hushed and amazed, brimming with the wonder of himself.

In his seventeenth summer a messenger brought the news of his father's death. The separation from mother had been quarrelsome, and his earliest wanderings as a sojourner were cursed with a kind of loneliness felt most strongly when he was not alone. He escaped into the forest. He ate the food offered to the gods. He drank the poison water. He got sick, and fell, and a weasel saved his life. He came to the bathhouse where Lucy washed him clean, gave him back his voice, and they spent seven rainy days and nights in the little cabin, making music, making love.

But he had to leave. He came to King Corn in time for the Cornfest; he climbed the silo and brought down the honey. He was lifted up as a hero, and he taught the untuned music to Bearclaw, Jocko and Ant. He put on the armband of messenger.

At the feast in Stubblefield, he tasted the Illumination. At the Dolmens on the road to Sputum, he broke the code of the messenger by reading the words he was carrying. For five summers he served his profession, and during that time he made a map of the Known World, following his travels.

In time, the road led him back to the bathhouse, but it had been destroyed; Lucy and Bow Wow were gone. He returned to King Corn where he spent the winter apprenticed to Frankie Fulcrum, unlocking the mysteries of the attractions, seeking ways to harness their powers.

Lucy's message arrived in the early spring. He set out once more on the open road to rescue her from the Blackcoats. At a roadhouse near the border, Mars Daniel saved his life—Mars Daniel, who became his protector in the unknown lands. In Ladyland, he smashed the door and they escaped to the trash hills where the boy became their burden. Blackcoats overtook them in the black rock mines of Perpetua. They killed the boy and the pony. Mab arrived with her herd of great horses and she gave them Trespasser to complete their task.

The task was completed but at great loss. Mars was killed and Lucy disappeared. Trespasser carried him to Freeland where he learned from Bow Wow of the greater mysteries. The seers had to erase his memory so he could escape Freeland in safety.

The last words in the book:

Then they closed their eyes.

He opened his eyes. He opened the book. It was just as he thought. Every page was blank, not a word. He had sensed this as it was happening. With each memory firmed and fixed, the words had faded from the paper. He was barely aware of it happening, so intent was he on the unfolding of the path. And now they were gone, pages white, clean and empty, like the future spread out, open and empty before him.

In the distance, wreathed in fog, a person was approaching along the sand. Johnny sat and watched, calmly. *This is the deliverer,* he told himself.

Close enough to see and be seen, the man stopped. He peered at the cabin, one hand above his brow, then made a slow, circular wave. Johnny waved back. The man continued.

He wasn't a young man. His hair, not long, was spiked and matted. He wore tan pants and a brown shirt with a hole in the pocket. He had something slung over his shoulder. Johnny recognized it at once—a squeezebox, like his mother used to play. The old tunes. The stovepipes, the strathspeys.

"Evenin' stranger," said the man. "You come to see me, or are you just sittin' for a spell?"

Johnny smiled. "A little bit of both." He felt comfortable with the man at once.

"What's your name?"

"Johnny Arcane. Yours?"

"Wilbo Hoegarden. You like to share a mug of tawny port?"

Johnny glanced at the bottle in the sand. "Sure. Why not?"

"*Why not* is not really a question." Wilbo uncorked the bottle. "A question is something more like *whyfor* do you come down to this sandy beach on this warm April night?"

Johnny looked out on the waves. April. An unfamiliar word. "So it's called a beach. What do you call *that*, then?"

"What do I call *what*?"

"*That.*" Johnny pointed.

"You mean the ocean?"

He suddenly remembered asking this same question of Mars Daniel, and Mars' reply. *That would be something too big for me to describe, if you don't know already.*

"Yeah, the oh—shun."

Wilbo made a funny face. "You're not from around here, are you?" He went in the cabin and came out with two heavy stone mugs, which he filled with the remaining contents of the bottle, carefully, doled out, checking the levels to assure they were even.

It was sweet wine, and strong. Its taste somehow matched the rumbling of the waves, the gathering of the fog, the cries of the birds. Wilbo stirred the fire until he got some sparks. He threw on some twigs.

"So where'd you wake up this morning, Johnny Arcane?"

Johnny laughed. "I don't know. I don't think I woke up this morning. I think I was up all night, walking. I came here when the sun was rising. There was no one around."

"Ah. You're like me, then. Prone to ponder. I left early this morning. I had to meet my friend Carl at six thirty."

"What's six thirty?"

Wilbo gave Johnny a long, puzzled look. "I'm serious, Johnny Arcane. Where *do* you come from?"

"Well, I was born in Aberdeen."

"Aberdeen...Scotland, or Mississippi?"

"Aberdeen. In the Known World."

Wilbo sat, sipped from his mug, nodded his head up and down. "So, if you come from the known world, where are we right now?"

"I don't know. You tell me."

"Hmm. Well, the first thing that comes to my mind is a time warp. You come from far in my future, I come from far in your past. Most people who hear this story for the first time, that's what they would think. Tell me. In your world. What year is this?"

"What's years?"

"Years. A year. Three hundred sixty five days. Approximately."

"Oh. We just count the moons—and summers. What year is it in yours?"

Wilbo chuckled. "One thousand nine hundred and seventy-three. So there you go. But I'm still not convinced."

"Of what?"

"Of the time warp theory. My friend Carl, he says there are parallel worlds. Lots of worlds, side by side, right now, and sometimes they intersect. I think maybe you come from a parallel world. You know why I don't think you come from the future?"

"No. Why?"

"Because you talk like we do here. In the future, language would have evolved."

"Oh. Where I come from we call them side worlds. Once Mars told me he thought there were more side worlds than there are worlds."

"You mean Mars, the God of War, or Mars the Red Planet?"

"Neither. Mars Daniel. The merchant. He sold pots and pans, and knives. But he died."

Wilbo held his palm over the rim of his mug for a while, as if he were taking in the fumes. Then he looked up. "I've never met anyone who died, actually. Although I've heard it happens. My father, although I didn't see him die. Once I almost died. Out on the ocean. But I was saved."

"Who saved you?"

"Don't really know. It's a … It's a private joke. Between

me and myself. What you got in that case there? That an instrument?"

"Mandolin."

"Mandolin! Excellent! Do you know any fiddle tunes?"

"I know *all* the fiddle tunes."

"All right. Let's play some fiddle tunes, then. A language we can both speak." Wilbo picked up the squeezebox and tugged the bellows. "Here's an A."

Johnny tuned and launched into the first thing he could think of.

"Don't know it. What's it called?"

"*Ants in the Cornmeal.* You try something."

Wilbo wheezed out a melody. It had the lilt of a stovepipe, but the intervals were unfamiliar. "*The Boys of Bluehill,*" he insisted.

"Don't know it."

"I thought you said you know *all* the fiddle tunes."

"A figure of speech. I know lots. How about this?" He played a round of *The Cabbage Moth.*

"I like it. Don't know it. What about this... *King of the Fairies!*"

Back and forth they went, but quite soon it became clear they were working out of two completely separate songbags. Johnny tried to follow a jig called *Smash the Windows*, but he lost the cadence. Wilbo chased after *The Dairyman's Daughter,* but the progression was too foreign for him. Finally he just let the bellows dangle, wheezing and squawking. "There must be *something* we both know."

"Maybe this," suggested Johnny, and he started in the melody he usually saved for last, the one that always seemed to come at the end of things.

"Ah. It's about time." Wilbo lifted the squeezebox and

rattled into the opening strains of *Happy to Meet, Sorry to Part*. They played and played. They took the song apart and put it back together. They made the seabirds dance and the dogs on the rocks offshore began to bark, and tears came to Johnny's eyes. They played for about forty-seven verses and Johnny was the first one to stop. Wilbo laughed and laughed.

"It's a very old song." Johnny said.

"That convinces me then." said Wilbo when he caught his breath. "Where you come from—the known world. The known world must be a place in time, very, very long ago. Let's go again!"

CHAPTER TWENTY-FOUR

SPIRIT GUIDE

ohnny Arcane no longer knew how many days and nights passed. He continued south along the coast. After leaving Wilbo and his little house in the sand, he saw no one. He saw no buildings. He saw no human footprints. He saw no smoke curling from a fire. The days were fogbound, the nights lit with the flashing waves, the twinkling stars, and the occasional blinker crossing the sky. The constant murmur of waves, the cries of birds, the barking of the seadogs on the rocks offshore, these things lulled him into a kind of undifferentiated forward motion in which he could lose himself in his thoughts. Over and over he relived the story, lingering on the clues as they appeared before him, linking them with others, seeking connections.

The cornmeal sealed the Known World. The trees that formed the border of Freeland grew steadily outward into the realm of chaos and cruelty. The knife that killed Glass Darkly was pounded out in No Time, in the Known World, before the fires, before the borders were sealed. Bow Wow said, *battle is the crowning triumph of chaos and cruelty. Our victory is always in the slow, outward growth of the forest.* On Pleasurepane's wall in Ladyland hung the picture of the waterfall, the same image Lucy had given him. Frankie said,

"Burleyman wants me to harness the attractions, to make our lives more comfortable. That doesn't interest me. It only keeps us here." One upon one, each phantom danced before him, then dissolved into another, helter-skelter, forward and backward, across the spectrum of time.

At some point he realized he had left the ocean. He was still walking on sand but the sound of the surf had faded. There were channels of water and tall stands of flatgrass and cattails. Birds he recognized, big white egrets; sometimes they startled him with their loud, flapping wings. And little ducks and round black mudhens swam in the shallows.

He stopped to rest on a drifted log. Something moved outside his vision. He turned quickly, but there was nothing. A grassy knoll. Fog.

His feet were too restless to remain still. He got up, shouldered his pack and continued; south, maybe, he couldn't be sure. There was no sun. He followed the footprint of the sand in what could have been a southerly direction.

Again, movement, just outside his vision, on the left. This time, when he turned, he saw the grass closing over something that had entered it, but he did not see what it was. A flutter of birds took to the sky from a willow branch. A small breeze brought him the scent of fennel. He continued.

Little by little, a trail was being formed, although not the sort made by men. Perhaps a hunting route for certain animals, or a long dried up watercourse. Evening was approaching. He decided to sleep. He found a sheltered place where a dune coved him from the wind, and the sand was as soft as a feather bed. He drank some water and ate one of the wafers from the pack. Only a few left. He would have to find some food soon.

Just before his eyes closed he heard a sound in the tall

grass. A slow rustling and a few soft snaps, like twigs breaking. It reminded him of Rug Chomper, his childhood dog, how she used to circle three times around her cushion before settling down for the night.

In the morning the fog persisted but he could see by the pale glow of sun that he was still traveling south. There was water everywhere—standing water, blanketed in mists, held captive in beaver dams and log jams, completely overgrown with berry brambles. He ate all the berries he could. They were sweet and juicy, but they made him feel a little drunk. A flood of blackbirds swarmed in and scolded him so severely he had to move on.

Three times that day his hidden companion made herself known. The first was a sound, a crackling in the bracken, heavier than a bird or a small mammal. The second was the simple flicker of movement out of the corner of his eye. The third time he was ready. For a while he had been watching as he walked, and suddenly it happened. The grass quivered, and a patch of grey fur slipped between the fronds.

He called out to her. "Hey!" He heard the scamper of her hasty retreat.

"Don't go! I want to see you! What do you want?" But she was gone, and there was no more from her for the rest of the day.

C

Evening. On the far foggy horizon a red light flickered. Closer, he saw that it was a fire, leaping and dancing. Still closer, he saw that there were people at the fire, tossing things into it. Even closer than that, he began to wonder if they *were* people. They stood on their hind legs but they hunched over, and their movements were skittery and somewhat beastlike. And they were naked, but it was hard to tell at first because their bodies were covered with hair.

The words of Mars Daniel echoed in his head: *Those aren't people. Those are hominids. You'd know they weren't people if you saw them with their skin on.* He sat against a rock, concealed by its shadow, watching. They had some kind of stick structure, and a large dark skewered object was roasting over coals. He remembered something else, something Jason had narrated in Solomon's Tower: *A great fire had broken out on the plains of Ableman, the entire city of Kidney Stone had been destroyed, and bands of flesh-eating hominids, roused from their caves, were migrating east.*

What was the secret of this place? Layer upon layer, the mysteries only deepened. Words, disappearing from books, became memories, and memories, poured into words, were lost in the oblivion of death and chaos. The wanderer has no real map. A guide appears just when you think you're lost, and you follow. It's a gift bestowed upon you by the whim of chance, but it only leads you deeper into chaos and mystery, layer upon layer.

He grew sleepy. He closed his eyes. It didn't really surprise him when he heard the sound at a distance in the under-brush, the crackling, the rustling, the ritual of some creature circling three times before settling down for the night.

In the morning he walked over to inspect the campfire, now cold and abandoned. A bit of meat still clung to the skewer. He broke off a piece. It wasn't meat at all. It was some kind of fungus. He sniffed at it. It smelled clean and food-worthy. He tasted it. It was good. He ate it all.

"We are not different," he said out loud.

Before he left, he built a cairn of three small stones by

the fire, and beside it he placed one of the packets of food given him by Bow Wow. He continued on his way.

He did not count the days that followed. There was so little to see—fog, grass, wetlands, birds. The markers in the sky, the sun, moon and stars, made but brief appearances, not long enough to establish any real sense of time. He could have counted the passages from light to dark, and back to light again, but he chose not to. What did it matter? He was lost in his thoughts, reading the book of memory over and over, from beginning to the present, looking to shed some new light on the course of events. But no light came, only the story itself, the twist of the plot, one thing moving into another, a ribbon unrolling into the darkness, a river rolling across a plain, a blinker drifting slowly through the sky.

And always, and more and more, he sensed the presence of his companion. He heard the rustling of grass and sometimes the splash of soft paws in shallow waters. She was always a little ahead of him, and whenever he slept, whether it was day or night, she stopped, circled three times, and settled down, not beside him, but close enough to keep watch over him.

Eventually the food ran out and he knew he would have to find himself something to eat. He considered the birds. There were always birds, long-legged wading birds, fat little black coots, colorful larks and finches that circled in formation, throaty scolding jays. He knew how to catch birds. He had relied on this often on the long treks between messages. It just took stillness and patience. He knew how to pluck them, gut them, and roast them.

He built a blind by suspending his coat between two short willows, and he wove a disguise of green rushes to cover it. It was a warm afternoon with a weak sun shining in the sky, so he set out his metal water can at an angle to glint its light as an attractor. Then he waited.

For a long time a pod of little black coots sputtered about in the bog. No, he wasn't hungry enough for such mealy tidbits. Soon they were driven out by a family of young ducks, all too skinny to offer up much food value. He watched the shadow of the blind creep across the grass. An elegant white egret swooped down and the ducks scattered. He was excited by the grace of her plumed white breastfeathers but he didn't think this was hunger. He had never eaten an egret before. She stabbed the water and came up with a fat squirming bullfrog. Frogs, maybe. He had tasted frogs.

But there was a disturbance in the grass behind him. The egret cocked her beak and exercised her wings several times before she became airborne. Johnny held his breath and stilled his heartbeat so not to startle whatever it was that was approaching.

A chuckling sound, like a woman laughing at a silly joke—he knew it at once. It brought back a memory: Springfest at King Corn, the fattening of the wild turkeys. The hen hobbled into the open. She was indeed fat. Her ringed feathers wrapped her belly and her dewlap flapped like a pancake as the sunlight off the metal reflected in her sidelong eye. Two steps and she pecked at the can. It rolled over. She ran after it. Johnny made his move. He grabbed the coat by the sleeves, lunged and covered the now panicked and squawking turkey. She was strong and desperate and almost broke free. But Johnny located her neck in the squirming mound of feathers, and he snapped it with a quick, sure twist of his wrist.

He spent the twilight hours plucking and cleaning, and marveling at the great elation he felt at the act of taking a life so that he may continue to live his own. He found a sandy place, dug a circle, and built a fire with twigs and bracken. He laid the clean carcass directly on the coals. It was dark and there were stars in the moonless sky, by the time she was ready to eat.

How good it felt, full of wild meat, reclining on a soft dune, and able to see the stars after so many dark and starless nights! This was the joy of the road as he remembered it. This was the destination of the sojourner, peace and contentment at the center of the unknown. He glanced across the rippling disturbance of the rising flames. There was something there. It moved, then stilled. A thrill of recognition coursed up his spine.

She was the skinniest wolf he had ever seen. She sat on her haunches, her legs like candlesticks, her ribs like barrel staves. But she was not small. Her sinews rippled and her head slouched between bony shoulders almost as tall as a man's.

She was watching him. She had been for a while, and she knew what he had been eating. Her moist pink tongue quivered and dribbled from her mouth. They sat, eye-locked, man and wolf, for a long time.

He was not afraid, not after the initial shock wore off. But she was. He could tell. Yet more than afraid, she was hungry. He knew what he had to do.

Without moving his head, he looked at his hands, holding the bone, still heavy with flesh. He took his time. He imagined raising his arm before he actually did it.

But still he was too fast. With a whimper she shied and turned, but not for long. Still within the fire's glow she turned back, her head low, her eyes darting. He held out his arm full length.

"Here," he said, "You can have it, and there's more. I want to thank you."

His voice startled her, but she approached, sniffing. Her teeth, sharp and white, closed around the meat and bone. Then she vanished, the broken rushes closing behind her. She did not go far. He heard her crunching on the cartilage in the bushes, her voice worrying the flesh from the gristle.

He pulled more meat from the carcass, boneless white meat from the breast. It wasn't long before she returned. She was calmer, less desperate. She ate in his presence, her head bowed, glancing up at him, inquisitively. He spoke to her.

"I hope you don't leave me. I want to go home. To the Known World, to Aberdeen, and King Corn. I hope you can guide me there. Whatever I catch, I'll share with you. Please stay with me."

She listened, her head on the ground between her paws. He couldn't think of anything else to say. He thought, *maybe I could sing. Maybe I could play the mandolin.* But she startled suddenly, as if in realization. *He is man. I am beast.* With one wary eye on him, she backed out of the circle of firelight. Then she disappeared into the night.

Later, as he prepared for sleep, he heard the familiar sound, not far away, a wolf, circling three times before settling for the night.

Ɔ

She stayed hidden most of the time. Only once or twice a day did he catch a glimpse of her moving through the reeds, always on his left side, always a few paces ahead. It was all he needed. He had a guide. It made a difference. He walked with certainty, trusting his feet, trusting the journey, confident of the destination. The unknowable was unimportant. He thought of something Bow Wow told him. *You don't have to remember your promises to keep them.*

The terrain changed very little, flat grassland, shrouded in fog—small clusters of trees, mostly cottonwoods. One thing that did change was the water. There was less of it. Whenever he came upon even the smallest of streams he always filled all the bottles.

He didn't eat every day. Occasionally there were berries, but little else in the vegetation. Once, he caught a lone, fat mallard in a small pond. In a field riddled with burrows, he set a trap before he fell asleep, waking to find a meaty, frightened groundhog shivering in the wooden cage. Once, an unsuspecting jackrabbit jaunted out of a spinney of willows. He was able to snatch it up by its long, lanky legs. He snared a few blackbirds and he caught one small, but tasty quail out of a family of five, scurrying from the berry bushes.

Whenever he had meat, he waited until nightfall, and built a fire. It wasn't long before the wolf appeared: always shy, but always hungry, sitting on her haunches across from the coals, head slightly bowed, eyes darting, cautious. The first few times she snatched the meat and dashed away quickly into the grass. Slowly she grew bolder, carrying it to a place outside the firelight, but still in full view. Eventually she let down her guard, remaining where she was, relaxing into a reclining position, experiencing for the first time the pleasure of sharing a meal with a friend.

It was then he began to talk to her. He told her about his childhood home, the little cabin outside Aberdeen. He told her about his mother, how she made pancakes, how she churned the cream into butter, how she saved the fireplace ash for the wall sconces. He described the garden in late summer, the bean vines so heavy they dragged down the poles, and the melon vines crept low along the ground until they invaded every corner of the plot; melons the size of a man's head would be found hiding among the collard greens, and huge red tomatoes lay on the ground under the squash blossoms, their stems too weak to sustain their weight. He told her about the rabbits, Huxley and Vermillion, and Rug Chomper the dog, and how they died — how one morning he found the remains of Huxley and Vermillion in the wire pen, devoured by wild pigs, only their ears and entrails left in the dust. He couldn't remember how Rug Chomper died. It was too long ago.

That was all he said the first time, for after she had licked all the grease from the bones, she looked up suddenly, startled. Reverting to her instincts, she backed away with a worried snarl and disappeared, leaving him in silence until he heard her circling motions settling her full belly down for the night.

Over other meals he told her other things. He told her of the farms and the orchards of the Known World, of the longhalls and the roadhouses where people gathered to eat, drink, dance and make music. And the festivals—every town had its festivals, the Springfest and the Cornfest and the Hopfest and the Festival of the Migrating Tarantulas and the Festival of the Crazy Old Men. He told her of the silo in King Corn and how he had climbed it and brought down the honey and people carried him in their arms above their heads. He told her about music, about how when a string is plucked, and then halved and plucked again, it produces a mysterious thing called an octave. But when a string is trebled it produces the even more mysterious interval of the open fifth, in which if you listen very closely you can hear countless hidden overtones. He told her how Jocko could coax melodies from a single catgut string tied to a metal washbucket, tensing and loosening it with a broomstick.

"I'm trusting you," he told her. "Bow Wow said the path would lead me home and I would be given a guide. I'm trusting you will guide me home."

The nights grew cold, and one morning he woke to find his jacket rimed with frost. For several days there was no food, and he did not see the wolf, he only heard her off the trail, ahead of him. Vegetation thinned and water grew scarce. The land became flat, like a sheet of glass, and in the mornings it was icy and slick. With no bushes to hide behind, the wolf still kept her distance, but she was always visible. If there had been an observer, he would have seen only three things: a flat, cold, fogbound expanse, and a man following a wolf across it.

One afternoon they happened upon a field of ring-necked geese, a hundred or more, scattered all the way to the horizon. The wolf saw them first. From the distance they looked like no more than freckles on the face of the plain. She took off running. He couldn't keep up with her. Ahead he saw a mass of motion and he heard the squawking and the fluttering of wings. They filled the sky, ordered themselves into formations, and took off for nowhere. In no time they were gone.

Across the blank page, the wolf approached. The bird in her jaws was still alive, flapping and screaming. The wolf dropped the goose at Johnny's feet and bit it once, hard in the neck. Its protestations ceased.

They had nothing to build a fire with. Johnny plucked the bird and sliced it open. The wolf took one wingbone, Johnny the other, and they pulled it apart. He scooped out the guts and they settled down to their portions. The wolf devoured hers whole, but Johnny didn't have the stomach for that. He rinsed the flesh with a little of their precious water, then he sliced it into strips. He lit a corn lamp and seared each strip briefly before he ate it.

Darkness closed in, a deep darkness, void of stars. The wolf lingered. Johnny realized he had not been telling her stories as had become the custom during a meal. He felt awkward and desolate. The night was bitter cold. The wolf began to pace. She did not go far. Several times he heard her circle and settle, but she did not stay settled. She got up, paced, circled and settled again, over and over.

He pulled his coat over his shoulders and tried to sleep. Perhaps he slept, for he woke in the deepest, coldest part of the night feeling strangely warm, like he remembered feeling on cold nights as a child, when his mother warmed a blanket over the coals and spread it over him while he slept.

He startled, but only for a moment, as he realized what was happening. The wolf was lying against him, her forelegs across his shoulders, her furry belly pressed against his side, her muzzle nuzzled into the crook of his neck. She grizzled softly in her sleep and snuggled in closer.

He was wide-awake now. He was warm. He was afraid, but there was something hushed and wondrous in his fear. He was Johnny Arcane, returning from the land of chaos and cruelty. He was keeping promises he could not remember making, and fulfilling his destiny.

"I haven't told you about Lucy yet," he said. The wolf stirred and sighed. "Let me tell you about Lucy ..."

But his story was broken by a far, distant sound, echoing from a range of moonlit hills on the northern horizon, a mournful, lovelorn howl rising and falling on the wind. The wolf heard it too. She lifted her head, sniffed the air, whimpered, then went back to sleep.

In the morning she was gone. Her paw prints cut a track from the cold ashes of the campfire through the loose sand toward the low-lying hills in the north. At Johnny's feet lay the feathers and bones of last night's goose. He squinted and scanned the horizon in all directions. To the south and the east there was only fog and the flat salty plain over which they had traveled. But north and west the mists were clearing, and there was something vaguely familiar about the scrubby hills. He followed the footprints as far as his eyesight would allow. There was nothing moving. She was long gone.

But there was something. A dark frame of a house, unpainted, leaning. A scraggly palm tree. The silhouette of a windmill, its blades turning slowly. The memory was not complete, but it was there, like a taste in the mouth. He gathered his tools into the pack, shouldered the pack, and set out. The closer he got, the sharper the focus. A long time ago—had this even been mentioned in the book? But he was there once. There was a place in his memory for this. His heartbeat quickened as he drew near.

The house was so abandoned there was scarcely a membrane of life left in it. He had to step over the rotten porch boards to enter, and inside there was no floor, just splinters and sand, and the tunnels left by termites. Doorless cupboards with no dishes, the cracked iron corpse of a woodstove, but one bittersweet remnant—in the split and paneless window frame, the tatters of a pink curtain hung.

He went outside and walked to the windmill. There was a hand pump to draw water from the well, but it was rusted shut. He sat on the wellstone and stared at the house until the memory fully congealed.

As a child he had wandered the four directions around the home he shared with mother, watching, wondering. He remembered an argument they had had, after the messenger brought the news of father's death. *"You don't even know the four directions, Mother. You only know the four walls of this house. Let me tell you what I know about the four directions. I've been outside. I've wandered the four directions. There's a house on the southern horizon, with a palm tree and a windmill. On a hot afternoon in appears to be shimmering in a lake of shallow water. I walked there once. There was no water. The house was deserted, falling down. The ground was dry and barren."*

This was that house. He had returned to the Known World.

The wolf had brought him home.

CHAPTER TWENTY-FIVE

MOTHER

It was a half-day trek from the abandoned house to Aberdeen. He approached his childhood home from the south, fearing what he would find. The first thing he noticed was the garden. Clearly it had not been put to bed before the onset of winter. Rain-rotted vines hugged the stalks of dried cornrows, and here and there misshapen melons lay broken open, their seeded intestines spilling out. Hardy mustard survivors had already bolted in spring's warmth, yellow blossoms rising triumphant above the sad and sagging bush beans. On the porch, the tinderbox was empty and only an armful of small pine logs lay scattered across the boards. No smoke rose from the chimney.

Anxiety seized him. He dashed up the steps, almost tripping on a broken plank, and grasped at the doorknob. The door was locked. *Locked!* Whoever heard of locking a door? He pounded. Only silence answered. He pulled back the shutters and peered in through the window to the parlor.

Mother was sitting in the soft armchair by the cold woodstove, where she often sat. Her hands were gnarled around the nine-patch quilt on her lap, her eyes focused on nothing. Her face was thinner than he remembered. He rapped on the glass. She did not move.

The back door, then, by the root cellar. He hastened around the side of the house. This, too, was locked, but only with a hook-and-eye, and he was able to rattle the knob up and down until the hook jumped out. He stilled his breathing before he entered.

The old rocker sat as it always had, facing the woodstove. Johnny lowered himself into it. Mother raised her eyes and looked at him. She did not speak. Neither did he. They sat that way for a long time, eye-locked, like a locked door. He thought maybe she couldn't really see him, but her eyes were clear and focused. Her hair, however, was disheveled, with streaks of grey that hadn't been there before. And her arms were thin, her bony hands knit together. He looked away, to the kitchen. There were opened jars, tomatoes perhaps, the fruit separated from the broth. In that moment he heard her voice, brittle, like a twig.

"Who *are* you?"

A lump rose to his throat. "Mother. I'm your son. I'm *Johnny*. I've come home."

She did not move. She did not blink. Her expression did not change, but her eyes grew reflective, like pools, deeper, bluer, and deeper, until from one, a bead fell and ran down her cheek.

"Where have you been?"

"I've been outside, Mother. Outside the four directions. I've been to the land of chaos and cruelty. I killed a man. I had to. I've been to Freeland."

He didn't know if she understood any of this. He almost hoped she didn't. He barely understood it himself. He watched her as she moved. She seemed to be waking from a trance. She looked around, pulled the quilt to her chin.

"I'm cold. Johnny. Build me a fire."

On the porch, he tindered a clutch of kindling from some of the loose logs, and gathered the rest in a bundle under his arm. The sun was getting low and the shadows were long. Back in the house he found her standing on shaky legs. She watched him silently as he built the fire and fanned it into flames. There was something solid and steadying about the task, an imprint of layered memories insisting themselves with a strength greater than anything that had come after. Countless times he had built a fire with Mother watching. Soon she would say something, as she always did, some remark about the garden, or the weather, or the phase of the moon. Even so, he was startled when he heard her voice behind him.

"Everyone's gone, Johnny."

With a thumping heart he made his reply without turning.

"Where did they go?"

"Stubblefield. All of them. To work at the mill. I'm the only one left."

He closed the firebox and adjusted the back vents until he heard the air whooshing up the chimney flue. He stood and faced her.

"The garden hasn't been tilled. What have you been eating?"

"What I can find." she replied.

"Have you been sick?"

"I don't know. I haven't been well."

"What about the doctor? Doesn't he visit?"

"He went to Stubblefield. All of them. There is no Aberdeen anymore."

Johnny grew agitated. He went to the kitchen and threw open the cupboard door. Nothing but a few jars with rusted lids. White flies hovered over the residue in the flour bin. On the tiles, a plate with something that might have once been a potato, now green with mold. When he turned back to her he noticed behind her, the window by the door. A jigsaw crack was forming just below the crossbeam.

He did not ponder his words before he spoke them. "Mother, I'll stay here with you. I'll find help. There must be someone. I'll plant the garden and cut the wood. I'll cook for you. I'll stay with you until you are better."

She sat back down on the armchair, not deeply, only on the very edge, like a fragile bird on a perch. A small smile creased her lips.

"Yes, Johnny," she said, "That would be nice."

ɔ

So Johnny Arcane stayed with Mother through the summer, and through the winter that followed, and into the spring after that.

That very night he went out in the back woods and snared a fat brown rabbit. He boiled up a stew, and into the pot he tossed the bolted, woody winter's greens from the ruined garden. The next morning he dug out the garden and mounded up the refuse into a moldering heap, after first separating out the viable seeds, corms and fingerlings. With a shovel he turned the patch over and over, breaking the loam from the clay until the worms appeared and the blackbirds gathered to pluck the worms from the turned soil. Then he dug rows and strung strings over them, and planted all the harvested seeds, corn, cabbage, mustard, beans, kale, melons, potatoes, eggplant, ground cherries, onions, shallots and leeks, beets and radishes, carrots, cucumbers. In the afternoon he gathered as much downed dry wood as he could find, and the next day he went out with the single-handled band saw and brought down four skinny pines, which he logged up and stacked for the beginning of the winter store.

In a deep part of the woods he found three beehives, abandoned, but still rich with crystallized honey. The next morning he baked the last of the winter pears in a honey glaze and set them before Mother at the table.

"I'm going out today to explore," he told her. "I'll be back before sundown."

Just as she had said, he found the small town of Aberdeen deserted and in ruins, but in the granary cellar there were two sacks of wheat flour unmolested by weevils, and another of coarse-cut oats. And next to them, a flatbed cart with two metal wheels, one of them bent, as if left by some grudging but benevolent providence, to further his purpose.

Mother got better. Color returned to her cheeks, and her conversation became more coherent. She talked of inconsequential things. It had always been this way. It's easy to tell a tree frog from a pond frog. Old Mr. Walker used to bring his grindstone over and sharpen these knives. But he died. The knives had belonged to her mother and no one knows where she got them. This house itself was her own mother's, and she could remember a time as a child when there was no glass in the windows.

"No one in the Known World knows how to make glass," he said, when she told him that. "All the glass there is, comes from the time before, and no one knows who made it."

"Nonsense, Johnny. There was no time before glass."

A full moon after he arrived, he found her one morning emptying the water from the wall sconces and depositing the fire grate ash. "You have to honor the four directions, Johnny," she said. "It's about time you learned that." That day she went outside for the first time. She examined the garden, running her fingers over the sprouted melon vines and the bean leaves, caressing the tender young corn tassels. When she walked to the edge of the forest, Johnny watched her closely from the porch. She never left his sight. After a while she came back with a smile on her face.

"The robins have hatched in the Graham oak," she said, and she held out a palm full of blue eggshells.

"We have to get some chickens," one day he told her. "Don't you know anybody?"

"The Carlyles left their chickens behind when they moved to Stubblefield. Maybe they are still there."

So that day Johnny took a burlap sack and walked to the old Carlyle house, or at least where the Carlyle house used to be. It was completely gone, not like it had burned, more like it had been disassembled and the boards carried off. But sure enough, there were seven red hens clucking and pecking about in the grass grown over the foundation. He bagged them all, and that night they ate one. The rest they put in the chicken pen, and within another moon, they were laying.

The days passed, uncounted, and summer rolled in. Johnny set his mind to the task at hand. He needed this. It was like returning to a timeless place before there was anything, a time before glass, when the seasons rolled in and out of the window of the sky, and there were days and nights, and there was food from the garden, and the henhouse, and the occasional wild creature from the forest. And sometimes there were games in the parlor, at the table, with barn nails or shells, or the charcoaled scribblings of runes on bark.

And yes, there was music. One evening toward midsummer, Mother brought out the accordion, a bit shyly, or so he thought. "Do you still play, Johnny?" she asked.

They played late that night, all the strathspeys and cotillions, slip jigs and stovepipes. Mother was surprised he remembered them. "I never stopped playing," he told her. He remembered them better than she did, and for good reason, he thought, as he watched her wipe the layer of dust off the accordion with her apron. As always. Mother played with a focus more on form than pleasure, concentrating on the placement of the mordents, the fermatas, the appoggiaturas. But as the night moved on, her stance relaxed, she leaned into the music, and several times she chuckled at the conclusion of a lively coda.

On other nights they didn't play as late, and many nights they didn't play at all. But on nights they did play, afterwards, when she was sleeping, he left the house and climbed by lamplight to the top of Gravestone Hill where Huxley, Vermillion and Rug Chomper were buried, and there he sat and wept. For there was no way the music could not reopen the memories the work had kept at bay, the nights in the little cabin behind the bathhouse playing untuned with Lucy, and all the melodies, tuned and untuned, with Bearclaw, Jocko and Ant, the times when the music tapped the sorrow of life and turned it to sweetness, and how did he know, back then, anything at all of the sorrow that was yet to come? In those moments he saw beyond the borders of the four walls of the house, the four directions of the Known World, the curved boundaries of Freeland pushing slowly, gently, insistently, into the world of chaos and cruelty.

Eventually, in time, as it always happened, the inheld breath of summer was released, the summer sprites fell in streaks of light from the dark night sky, the leaves of the oaks turned brown, the alders yellow, and a spidery web covered the last of the summer blackberries.

Johnny grew restless. It was always this season that made him restless, always; the turning leaves and the morning chill stirred the sojourner in his blood, and it ran through his arms into his legs, and propelled him to wander the hills in all the four directions, a curve in the road ahead, always disappearing, always beckoning. Mother was well now. She had taken on most of the cooking and some of the gardening while Johnny occupied himself with felling fresh green logs and bringing home the occasional meat from the forest. This gave him much time to roam and ponder. There had been no one else since he had arrived, only Mother. He knew within a day's walking he could find a roadhouse, friendly faces, conversation, but he chose not to. He needed to be close to Mother, to protect her. He feared leaving her, even for one night, with the darkness hovering so close outside. So he was alone with these things, and it fueled the fire of his restlessness.

Ɔ

The first winter storm rolled in unexpectedly over the wooded hills from the north, following a day of golden sun and the last harvest of corn. Johnny didn't have time to put the garden to bed. He woke in the dark to the wind howling and the shutters slamming against the upstairs windows. In the morning the fire had blown out and the wind was whirling circles of snow and hurling darts of ice against the windows. The garden could not be seen, and the dress Mother had hung on the clothesline the day before had vanished.

Seven days later Mother got sick and took to her bed.

"Don't fuss over me, Johnny. It's been like this for a

spell. In the winter I fade. It really wasn't you that saved me. It just happens."

Her words angered him. "It *was* me, Mother! If I had not come, you would have died. It was already spring and you were barely breathing."

She reached over and patted his hand. "You were a good son. You did well. But there is a time for everything. This time is mine."

In the days that followed it was all he could do to keep the house warm. The storm did not let up, and the garden lay hidden under a blanket of snow. The chicken pen had blown over. He found one hen huddled in the woodshed. The rest were gone. He brought the hen in the house. Mother rose from the bed, her face in terror.

"Take her out! Quickly! *A chicken in the house disturbs the south wind!*"

"Mother, we need her. We need food. Surely you still don't believe those foolish superstitions."

"They aren't foolish. Those are the words of Borderbinder. This is how we have lived in plenty so long."

"There was no Borderbinder. He was a myth!"

"Don't say that, Johnny! Don't say that! I can't die knowing that's how you feel." She rolled back into the bed and turned her face to the wall. Her voice was weak. She kept saying, over and over, "Don't say that. Don't say that."

After that they quarreled incessantly. Although she was weak with illness, Mother's will was still strong. They did not quarrel about small things, as they had done before he first left home. Now everything was on the table. The borders of the Known World were crumbling.

He commanded her to tell him. Why had everyone left

Aberdeen to work the mills in Stubblefield? And why was there a lock on her door?

"Because I have no more neighbors," she said, "And there have been Blackcoats on these roads."

"There, you see! Your rituals have done nothing to stop what's coming. The Blackcoats are descendants of the bandits. They bring chaos and cruelty into the Known World."

"The Blackcoats are not bandits," she retorted. "The Blackcoats are just rascals who weren't raised right. Their mischief is petty."

"The Blackcoats are the servants of chaos and cruelty. I know. I killed one of them. And now, look at this storm coming down from the north! They have even changed the weather. Your borders won't stop it."

"Don't give in to gloom, Johnny. Honor the four directions. You will be safe."

Her protestations never lasted long, though. Her efforts weakened her and she would take to her bed. Then Johnny would go down and sit in the parlor, his thoughts dark and clouded. Why was he telling her these things? She had provoked him. It would be better if she didn't know. Perhaps she was right. Perhaps he hadn't saved her, and perhaps now she would die in spite of his attempts to save her. Everything in its place and everything in its time. It would be better for her to die content with her illusions. But he had shattered them. It would have been better if he had not told her.

Once he tried to explain to her about Freeland. "Freeland is our only hope. They follow a path truer than Borderbinder's. They do not try to seal the Known World in. They expand outward, slowly. Slowly. If there was a battle, they would lose. The only thing they have on their side is time."

She did not raise an argument to this. Perhaps she didn't

understand it. For a long time she lay so still he thought she was sleeping, but then she spoke.

"Your father willed his own departure," she said. It took Johnny a while to connect the thread. It had been so long ago.

"I'm not sure I believe that. He was killed by fire."

"It doesn't matter how. It is possible to will your own departure."

Then she fell asleep in earnest, leaving him speechless, perched on the brink of a great mystery.

☽

On the coldest day of winter Mother refused to eat. Johnny pleaded with her. "You owe it to me, Mother. I don't care what you say. I came back and saved your life."

"All the more reason, son. How could I leave this world with the thought of never seeing you again?"

He contemplated the things she loved the most. He used the last of the precious wheat flour to make her a stack of salted pancakes slathered with the honey he'd stolen from the hive in the woods. She waved it away. "You eat that, Johnny. You need to keep your strength up. There's still work for you to do."

She asked for tea. He brought her a brew of strong chicory, and she spat it out. "I said tea, not blood. Something thin to moisten my tongue."

He brought her a brew of dried linden flowers with a half-spoon of honey. She spat this out, too. "No sweetness, Johnny. Just tea."

He told her he would also stop eating then; if she did not change her mind, they would die together. "No, you won't,

Johnny. This isn't your time. Very soon you will realize that."
And he knew she was right, even then. He ate the pancakes,
and on the nights after that he always fixed a supper, dished
it onto two plates, and took it to her bedside, where he ate
one and she refused the other.

One evening, after Johnny had finished his portion of
cabbage and grits and set the plate on the end table, Mother
rolled over, reached out, and placed a bony hand on his
knee. When she spoke, it was only a whisper, a mere sibilance. He had to lean his ear to her lips to hear the words.

"You're a good boy. You'll grow up and be strong.
You'll plant your seed. Death isn't the end of everything,
Johnny. It's just the end of you. If you've planted a seed,
this shouldn't bother you. I can go now. I've planted a seed.
You are the seed I planted, Johnny Arcane."

When the moon rose full, it had been ten days. On
that night he entered her room and found her wide-awake
and staring wild-eyed at the moonshadows on the wall. He
rushed to her and stroked her face. She was burning with
fever. She recoiled from his touch and began to thrash and
tie herself in the bedsheets. He ran downstairs and returned
with a damp cloth from the kitchen. She screamed when it
touched her forehead and she threw it across the room. She
sat up on the bed, then stood screaming and collapsed on
the floor. He scooped her up and lifted her back to the bed
while she wriggled in his arms like a newborn goat. When
she spoke, her voice was as dry as a grasshopper's.

"It hurts," she rasped. "It hurts so much, Johnny.

"Where? Where does it hurt?"

"Everywhere. It hurts here." She folded her arms and
closed them across her chest. "I didn't know. I didn't know
it would be so hard to die."

She began to cough convulsively, grasping the bed frame while her body rose and fell. She urinated, drenching her thin cotton nightgown. When he rolled her over to pull the soaked sheets out from under her, she began beating her head against the wall so hard the curtain rod slipped from the window and a film of blood appeared on the plaster.

It was then he remembered the messenger's vial he had given to Mars Daniel just before he died. He had carried it so many days he had forgotten it until the time came when it was needed. Oh, why didn't he have it now!

Mysteriously, the thought seemed to have the effect of the medicine. Mother turned from the wall. She calmed. She lay on her back, her eyes closed, breathing heavily, rapidly, then slower, slower. Her hand released their clutched fists and opened into petals, and the pain seemed to drain out of her fingers. Soon there were moments of stillness between the outbreath and the inbreath, each moment a little longer than the one before.

Johnny sat. He took her hand. He marveled at these silences, so empty and yet so deep. And then she would draw another breath; something like color would spread across her face, and she smiled slightly, like someone savoring some wonderful food. *This breath, this miracle of breath,* and she crossed its summit and fell back into silence.

The silences grew so long, many times he thought this would be the last. But then again another draught would rise, another taste of what was departing, given back to stillness, and another moment of waiting.

The morning sun was just breaking into a cold, cloudless sky when Mother surrendered her final breath.

꙯

On the first night after his mother's death, Johnny heard the winter wolves howling on the ridge, reminding him he couldn't take her outside in the snow, and in the house she would soon begin to decay. So the next day he tore down the henhouse and used the boards to build a sturdy box that no wolves could defile. He dressed Mother in a clean cotton dress and carried her outside in his arms. He sealed her in the box and dragged it to a sheltered place behind the woodshed.

Winter slowly released her icy grip. Johnny did what he needed to do to keep himself alive and alert. He stoked the fire and prepared himself meals from the stores that remained. He melted a can of resin and patched the crack in the parlor window. He nailed down the loose shutter boards and braced up the sagging drainpipe. He went through Mother's things. She had very little, the kitchen supplies, the tools, a few vases for flowers, the barn nails and the shells and the charcoal for games. In her closet hung five dresses. A dresser drawer held some clean and neatly folded quilts, and underneath the quilts, in its envelope with the broken wax seal, the letter the messenger had brought from father, foretelling his death.

The rains came. The snow melted and the ruins of the garden revealed themselves. On the first clear day he walked up to the top of Gravestone Hill and tested the soil. Yes, it was ready. He dug a deep hole in the shade of an elm, away from the stones of Huxley, Vermillion and Rug-Chomper, so not to disturb their bones.

But the next day it rained again and the grave filled with water. He had to wait five more days to complete his task. On a morning when the sky was eggshell blue and the crocuses were nosing up around the woodshed, he pried the lid off the wooden box. Inside was what looked like a cornhusk doll with a porcelain face, and she weighed nothing when he lifted her. He hefted her over his shoulder like a sleeping child and carried her effortlessly to the top of Gravestone Hill. All the while the emotion hovered in the sky above the event, a swirling vapor that would not descend into his heart. He lowered her into the grave, caressed her cold face, straightened her collar, then climbed out. It was when he began shoveling that it entered and passed through him, a flight of butterflies perhaps, or very tiny birds, or maybe just the substance of sorrow without form, descending, descending, piercing his shoulders, through his arms, and into each portion of earth, covering the remnant of his bloodline, his *mother.* He wept clean tears, almost saltless, and when the ground was level he sat on the grave and wept himself clean, all the sorrow passed through him and vanished, and he sat there whole and empty—*Begone! Begone! The filth of sorrow, into the pool, be clean!*

But there was still work to do. In the days that followed, spring roared in like a wild boar, and with it, all its tasks. The garden was as he had found it the first time, wasted by winter, with its dark and soggy matter intact. He dug out the vines and the rotted fruit and mounded them into the moldering heap, then tilled the soil deeply with the shovel until the worms appeared to greet the air and the blackbirds appeared to pluck the worms. But he did not glean the seeds and corms and fingerlings for replanting. *Before harvest,* he told himself, *I will be gone.*

In the evenings he sat by the fire with Mother's quilt spread across his knees, sipping some warm brew, trying to penetrate the dense shrouds of forgetting that hung about his mind. Perhaps Bow Wow's spell had left something permanent there. Yes, in fact, that had happened, the seers in Freeland, gathered around holding hands. But then he would find himself thinking of something else, some bit of work he left unfinished that day, the disorder in the root cellar, the loose porch board, the squeaky pump handle. Yes, it was like Bow Wow's spell had left a residue. So much of the story slept, and only woke in drifted, formless dreams.

Two moons passed and summer moved in to fulfill the promise of spring. A stranger appeared on a warm afternoon. Johnny was out digging weeds from the garden plot when he saw the man round the crest of the western ridge, no more than a speck from that distance, like an oak tree walking.

The stranger stomped the road dust off his boots when he reached the house. He was mostly dressed in rags, but he had the distinguishing red armband of a messenger, and he wore a fine leather hat. Johnny recognized him at once. A few new wrinkles, some sprinkled grey in his beard, he was the same messenger who brought the news of Father's death in Johnny's seventeenth summer. "If you be looking for my mother, she has passed."

The messenger shook his head. "I be looking for Johnny Arcane. Believe that be you."

He went inside and sat at the table. Johnny gave him a tall glass of water and an oat cake from the morning's breakfast. The messenger reached in his pocket and produced a tattered envelope. Johnny glanced at the wax seal. It was broken.

"A woman of interest in King Corn," said the messenger. "If ye like, I'll step outside while ye read."

Johnny waved his hand. "No, no, stay. It's cool in here." His fingers trembled as he pulled the letter from the envelope. It was written on linen paper with an amber shade and the faint scent of lavender. The words were few and scrawled in large letters.

JOHNNY
WE HAVE FOUND YOU. YOU ARE ALIVE
CORNFEST IS NEXT MOON. PLEASE COME.
BEARCLAW WILL TELL YOU. I AM

The last two words were crossed out. The letter continued.

WE ARE BOTH STILL IN LOVE WITH YOU
ANT.

The messenger waited long enough for Johnny to read the letter three times.

"If ye wish to return a greeting, I can wait till ye write it."

Johnny set the letter down on the table. "No, no. Stay with me awhile." He looked around at the sconces, the curtains, the cluster of lilac he had placed in the vase on the counter the night before. "This house," he said. "Tomorrow I will leave it. It will be empty. You can live here if you want."

The messenger chuckled. "Ah! No, I not be needin' a house. I been a sojourner for too many seasons to stop now. But I be sure to inform others along the way."

CHAPTER TWENTY-SIX

THE KNOWN WORLD, KNOWN AGAIN

n the ridge, he stood and gazed down over the blue-green and gold valley that rolled and rippled to the smoky grey mountains in the north—supple fields of tasseled corn framed by vineyards and amber round hills, elegantly gridded with orchard of apple, plum and pear, meanders of riparian vine following ancient streambeds, and here and there, a bleached white house, a brown weathered barn, a garden fenced from the deer, a dog running; and on the distant ridges, stately rows of pitchy pine and sweet cedar. His eyes welled with tears. Such unbearable beauty, which had once simply been life as it was, everyday life, the life you were given, from which you yearned desperately, to escape. Oh, people! If you only knew, outside of this, there is only chaos and cruelty...

No, there is something else. *There is Freeland.*

He followed the road into the valley, heartbroken and enraptured. He examined every leaf on every tree. He caressed the bark of trees and he listened to the barking of dogs and the trills of birds as if they were fiddle tunes. A flicker hammered out a rhythm from the top of a mighty oak, and squirrels chased each other amorously around its trunk. Sweet smoke rose straight up from chimneys, to join the blue sky. He plucked a low hanging pear from a roadside tree. It tasted sweet and sorrowful. A woman, pinning white sheets to a clothesline, smiled at him.

"Where you heading, traveler?"

"North," he replied. "King Corn."

"That be seven days walking. Ye'll make it by Cornfest."

Nightfall. He came across a roadhouse nestled in a stand of willows on the shore of a river. There was music from within, fiddles and guitars, and the sound of drunken voices. Two separate herds of goats milled about untethered on the grounds. He knew there were two because there were two different brands, one the trident, the other the hourglass. Shoving open the heavy wooden slab of a door, he was met with a redolence of spices, especially coriander, and he remembered.

This was the roadhouse where he stopped to eat on the very first night of his wanderings, when he first lost his voice, but he knew he would not lose his voice tonight. He eased his way in and moved among the long heavy tables where the same people as years before sat—goat people wearing colorful rags, along with potters in clay-grey shirts, farmer in bib overalls, woodcarvers with sawdust in their hair, mummers—both men and women—in white robes. The sight of beer steins, full and empty, and heavy stone bowls ladled with stew, the sound of hearty voices and boisterous laughter—these things filled him with warmth and tenderness. Sweet people, innocent people, people free of the sorrow of chaos and cruelty. He wanted to join them, but he had to go slow. He was still a stranger here.

He sought out the only single table in the house. He

remembered sitting here before. A stout woman appeared with a tray. "You'd be wantin' some supper I suppose," she said. "Tonight we be servin' beef brisket with parsnips and rutabagas. And a fine pale ale."

He sat up suddenly with a start. "You eat *cow?*"

She eyed him suspiciously. "Ye not be one of them *abstainers*, be ye?"

"Oh, no, no, not at all. Yes, I'll have the brisket. But just water please, no ale."

The brisket was warm and flavorful and the water cold and clean. He put aside all inclination for a stronger beverage and settled back to listen to the conversations that surrounded him.

"Dropped a whole load a onions on the road to Sputum this morning." The speaker was a farmer in a broad straw hat. "Something scared the donkey. Don't know what."

"Where's the onions now?" asked a woman in a dressmaker's smock. "Still in the road? I need me some onions."

"Just the bruised ones. A messenger stopped by to help me pick 'em up. I never saw him coming and I never saw him going. It were strange."

"Probably a greenman," said the woman. "Also what scared the donkey. You give him something? Your sposed to give greenmen something made out of dirt. Keeps 'em down."

"No, it weren't no greenman. Had the armband. You know there's no such thing as greenmen, Millie. Don't believe in 'em."

"Well, that's why you keep dropping onions."

Across the table a man in a mummer's robe lifted his stein as if to make a toast. "There's things outside of what we know or believe in." he said.

"Spoken like a true mummer," Millie replied. "If there

really are things outside a what we believe in, why don't we just believe in them?"

The mummer only laughed, and the farmer raised his stein. "Well, I only believe in the things I can see, and right now, what I believe in is this fine pale ale. Here's to you, mummer." The mummer and the farmer clinked their steins and drank.

But Millie persisted. "That's not what the mummer said. He said there's things *outside* of what you believe in. That's why you leave them things alone. You give the greenmen something made out of dirt if they helps you. Ask the mummer. That's what the mummers are allus tryin' to tell us with their stories and their dances."

The mummer beamed a big smile and waved his stein in a wobbly manner. "Silly Millie! We just want to make you laugh."

A burst of laughter broke from an adjacent table where a group of metal bangers were drinking. "To the mummers! They make us laugh!"

Drawn by the mirth and camaraderie, Johnny found himself rising from his solitary table, stein in hand, and approaching the talkers. "Evening, friends," he said, "Mind if I join your conversation?"

Millie's grin displayed a jumble of crooked teeth. "Welcome, stranger. What you be drinkin'?"

"Similar to what you're drinking," said Johnny as he took the proffered chair.

"Weigh in your thoughts, stranger. Farmer Levon here says he don't believe in greenmen cause he's never seen 'em. Mummer Cade says there's things outside a what we know and what we believe in. But then he says mummers are only here to make us laugh. I say, if you see things you don't believe in, you gotta appease them, so they leave you alone. That's my approach. What be your thoughts?"

As Johnny settled in the chair he could feel his heart rising up into his head. How good it was to join a warm circle of lost and friendly souls, to sit down for a while in the comfort of strangers, to breathe new life into old ideas! "Well," he said, after a suitable season of ponderment. "Here's my thoughts on the matter. Here's my money's worth."

Millie gave him a puzzled look. "What's *moneysworth?*"

For a moment it felt like there was no earth beneath him, and he was falling, but he caught himself. "Oh, that's just— an expression—where I come from. Here's my *thoughts* on the matter." He tried to pull his ideas together but they were going everywhere at once, so he just jumped in.

"I think mummer Cade is mostly right, only more so. There are more things to see than your eyes could ever see. If your eyes could see everything that there was to see, they would explode right out of your face. If your ears could hear everything there was to hear, they would explode right out of the side of your head. So Millie's right, too, when she says you have to appease the things you see, but you don't believe in. But consider this. Imagine a beautiful forest, surrounded on all sides by a world of chaos and cruelty. That could be us, right now. Green and peaceful, everybody's happy. They know they can't leave because it's too dangerous, so they stay there, and they love each other and they make each other laugh and they make each other happy. And that laughter and that happiness moves outward, to the edge of the forest, and it makes new trees to start to grow. You know how long it takes a tree to grow. Sometimes it takes longer even than a person. So the forest is growing out, always, slowly, slowly, into the world of chaos and cruelty. Because of laughter and happiness. Never mind the rituals. And where it grows, chaos and cruelty are pushed back, slowly, slowly. If those people in the forest stay true, and teach their children, and teach their children to teach their children to stay true, someday, in the endless supply of time, that forest will overtake the world of chaos and cruelty."

There was a long silence after Johnny's words ran out. He hadn't expected it, and he didn't like it. He thought he was just going to blend in to the talk with some ideas of his own. Millie sat with her nose wrinkled, her lip pulled up, her jagged teeth shining in the corn lamp. A glob of drool was slowly rolling out of farmer Levon's mouth. The mummer looked like he was asleep.

"Darndest thing I've ever heard," said Millie at last.

But then the mummer, Cade, spoke. "No. No, I think I know what he's saying. It's like the stories we always act out at the festivals. The borders are sealed with cornmeal. Then Borderbinder returns and opens them up again. Maybe Borderbinder doesn't return all at once. Maybe he's like that forest, growing outward, a little at a time."

Now Johnny was getting really uncomfortable. He wished he could change the subject. He wished somebody would change the subject. He wished they would start talking about how to fatten spring turkeys, or which way to raise the banner pole at the harvest festival. But then a ruckus broke out at a nearby table. An arm wrestling match was going on, and people were gathering, rooting and cheering. Skirting around them, a man approached. Johnny recognized him as the fiddler in the band. He was still holding his instrument, and he stepped directly up to their table.

"Evenin', stranger," he said. "Couldn't help but notice

you were carrying a turtlebox on your backpack. Maybe you know some fiddle tunes. You might like to join us."

A broad smile of relief broke over Johnny's face. "I know *all* the fiddle tunes, and a few others."

"Well, what you waitin' for, then? Go get your box. What be your name, young man?"

"Jimmy," replied Johnny Arcane. "Jimmy Clearlight."

Ɔ

From Arden's Plain northwest to the Ricketyback Bridge, two days walking through wooded hill country, interspersed with fields made fertile with the drifted sphagnum of the Only River Delta; crossing the bridge, the road hugs the west side of the river north past Chokeberry, Footbalm and starting its grand wide bend at the Dolmens. The snowy mountain is visible to the northeast on clear, sunny afternoons. The road to King Corn leaves the river just before Stubblefield and dives into the deep woods of the northeast hills, past Fairheart, Belltone, and Hermit Town, the round bare hill proclaiming King Corn in two days walking, seven altogether, just as the woman at her clothesline told him.

The map, long gone, remained printed in his mind. He had taken every step of this journey more times than he could count. He knew all the roadhouses and he knew the haylofts and the woodsheds and the duck blinds that offered shelter where no roadhouses could be found. Not much had changed, but a few things had. Some houses had been abandoned, their garden plots lying fallow. Crops had been rotated. The immense cornfield east of Sputum had been given over to a kind of green he didn't recognize, shorter than corn, tasseled, but not eared.

When there was music at a roadhouse he was often asked to join in, and when he wasn't, he would invite himself. His pseudonym soon came to precede him. At a roadhouse outside of Fairheart he recognized a fiddler from his former travels, so he held back, not wishing to attract attention to himself. But the fiddler drew him out. "I know who you are!" he called from across the room. "You're Jimmy Clearlight! They say you play a pretty mean turtleback. Come up and join us."

Through all this his heart rose and fell, through tenderness and sorrow, and the beauty of everything; the clouds that rolled like horse's manes in the blue morning sky, the way the veins of leaves reflected in the dewdrops on the curves of round, red apples; the mound of blackberries engulfing an ancient brick ruin at the center of the freshly plowed field just east of the Dolmens, a single tree on a ridge silhouetted black by the setting sun, children playing with acorns, the tired eyes of farmers who rose from the roadhouse tables to shake the stiffness from their bones and dance to melodies that cadenced between the major and the minor keys.

At the mouth of the road that broke from the river's course and cut a line toward the northern hills, a new, freshly painted sign had been planted.

KING CORN. TWO DAYS WALKING.

He quickened his pace. Faces of friends appeared in the leaves of trees—Jocko, Bearclaw, Ant, even Burleyman with his awkward, troubled ways. He remembered Frankie Fulcrum's devotion to the study of the attractions. Indeed, the meadow, the silo, the log house, the people of King Corn were the attractors, and he was the attracted. An invisible cord of affection drew him steadily forward. *Perhaps,* he thought, *if I do not sleep, I can be there in a single day.*

But he slept. Nightfall, he wearied, and there was a roadhouse in Belltone. There was no band and the food was bad. He shared quarters with two old men who snored and farted like horn pigs. His sleep was fitful. Much of the time he lay awake, staring at the ceiling, while invisible legs inside his legs trudged steadily forward on invisible paths. He left before sunrise and continued along the road, his mind disturbed by unremembered dreams.

Midmorning he came upon a side path and a sign he had never seen before. A painted arrow and a single word: ABSTINENCE. Curiosity compelled him, and collided with a murmuring dread. But he had to see for himself.

A short jaunt through the forest opened out into a round, clear space. It was surely not a natural space, for it was blanketed with the flat rings of trees sawed off at near ground level. Around the clearing, rough log cabins presided, all facing the center. At the center, a covered platform. A ladder leaned against the canopy and a man stood on the ladder. He wore a straw hat and sported a long beard, impeccably trimmed. There was no moustache on his upper lip. Across the broad face of the canopy he was nailing a clean white banner on which words were neatly blocked.

NO CORNFEST. NO COWS.

The man glanced down briefly when Johnny entered the clearing, but he continued hammering. He had a mouthful of nails, their round heads protruding from his lips.

Johnny stood at the foot of the structure for a while, as the man kept hammering. Finally his curiosity got the better of him.

"What do you mean, no Cornfest?"

The man scowled at him, then set down his hammer on the canopy ledge. One by one he removed all the nails from his mouth and cupped them in the palm of his hand.

"If ye be goin' to the Cornfest, ye not be comin' here," he said.

"Why is that?"

"Because we don't shuck with the eatin' of cows, that's why. They is unclean, just like all the other unclean things they do in King Corn."

"What other things?"

The man sighed, like he wished he didn't have to go into this. "Well, they got a woman what plays the fiddle, for one thing. And they got running water what spreads poison throughout all the houses. And now I hear they figgered out how to catch the lightning from the sky and light up a room. It's that one-legged man what started it all." He squinted at Johnny through his right eye. "Who be ye, anyhow? Ye look familiar."

Johnny felt something grab him from the inside of his stomach. Suddenly it seemed like the clearing he was standing in was immeasurably large, and he wanted nothing more than to get out of it without being seen by anyone. A crow cawed overhead and then, from one of the cabins a door was flung open with a bang.

He wheeled around to see a child running across the field, a little girl, barefoot, dressed in rags. "Papa!" she cried. "Papa!" She stopped and caught her breath. "Papa, Sugaree threw up on the floor again!"

The man groaned and flung his handful of nails to the ground. "Damn it, Cappy! You know where the slop bucket is!" He started down the ladder. "Ye better get back in there and clean it up afore I take the switch to ye!" The little girl turned to run, the man after her.

Johnny took the opportunity to make a hasty retreat.

Ɔ

In the evening shadows, people in festive costumes gathered along the road. Children in layered, colored skirts, boys and girls alike, skipped and sang and chased metal hoops down hills. Men wore laced leggings, garlanded vests, jaunty feathered hats. One man carried a long bow and a full quiver of arrows. Women sported lace vests with buckskin fringe, layered petticoats, long conical hats with tassels, wreaths of roses around their necks, and bells on their ankles. People transported ducks and chickens, and live beehives rode on donkey carts. And of course there were mummers. They walked, dancing in circles, their robes flaring. Johnny recognized Mummer Cade from the roadhouse out of Arden's Plain. They stuck up a conversation.

"You opened a bag of bees the other night, Jimmy Clearlight," said the mummer. "Silly Millie wouldn't leave me alone. She wanted to know if you were a mummer in disguise, if we had initiated you into our secrets. *Ask him yourself*, I told her."

"She never did."

"Of course not. Millie would never want to learn something she didn't already know. Ah! I must run! We'll see you at Cornfest!"

The other mummers were spinning on ahead. Mummer Cade kicked his heels and leapt into their movement. Dust rose from their twirling feet and hung over the road as they disappeared around a bend. The fading sunlight turned it into a golden cloud.

Johnny slowed his steps. The road was empty after the mummer's departure. The brief spate of solitude made him pensive. Returning to King Corn for Cornfest after all the darkness he had been through, all the chaos and cruelty—what would it be like? The simplicity of life before was gone, gone from his heart, yes, but even more so; he sensed something troublesome had also entered the Known World, across its borders. There were suggestions of this, everywhere. The change in the weather. The disappearance of Aberdeen. Abstinence. The lock on Mother's door.

His feet stopped of their own accord, and he stood, watching the mummer's dust settle. Something was emerging from the shadows at the road's bend, in the clearing of the haze. It looked like a face growing out of a tree. He squinted to make it out, but reluctance kept him from drawing nearer. It was intrinsically familiar. It was the face of someone he knew. It mocked him. *Why did it mock him?* His heart jumped into his throat.

It was his own face.

It was a picture of himself. His nerves went cold. The memory flooded in. Frankie Fulcrum. The magic lantern in Jocko's room. A sunny, snow-covered morning, not so long ago. All the pictures that day, hung on the wall of the longhall, by the scullery door.

Why was it here?

His feet began to move. He approached the image. It was thin and crinkled, tacked to the trunk of the tree. Hand-scrawled in large letters above the face: *JOHNNY ARCANE*. In equally large letters at the bottom:

KILL THIS MAN.

At that moment, there were voices behind him, and the creaking of wagon wheels. Johnny dizzied. His arms trembled. He knew what he had to do but he didn't know if his hands would allow him to do it. The voices drew nearer. It must be done. At once. He hefted his pack, ran to the tree, grasped the poster by its corners and ripped it down. It was not parchment. It was made of thin paper, thinner than the paper of books. It was not the original. He folded it eight times, slipped it in his pack just as the travelers came in sight.

There were two of them, a man and a woman, pulling a handcart laden with colored glass bottles, plainly dressed, but the woman had a pink camellia in her hair. The man wore black suspenders and sported a neatly trimmed beard, no moustache.

"Greetings," said the man. "Is this the road to King Corn?"

Johnny did his best to calm his heartbeat and bring a warm smile to his face. "It is. Is it your first time to Cornfest?"

"Indeed. We will have no more to do with those abstainers. Such a dour lot!"

Johnny stilled his breathing and brought his attention to the man's face. The eyes were straightforward and honest, yet sad, and the wrinkles reminded him of dry riverbeds. Something about the face calmed his thoughts.

"If you ask my opinion, you have made the right choice. You will find much to please you at the Cornfest. I will be there myself, shortly."

"Much obliged for your words," said the man. "It's been a long and winding road. We shall proceed along it." He tipped his hat as they passed. The woman cast her eyes down. It looked like she had been crying.

CHAPTER TWENTY-SEVEN

AN UNEASY ARRIVAL

he stars were breaking through the veil, and the golden glow of the moon, still hidden, was cresting the eastern tree line by the time he reached the rounded hill that served as the gateway to King Corn. The road thrummed with echoes and dust, all the travelers having reached their destination and settled in. This gave Johnny some relief, but there was a dark worry in his thoughts, and a pressing urgency to find out what was behind it. His pulse throbbed and his stomach churned as he rounded the bluff and the town came into view.

King Corn was not as he remembered it. Lights hung everywhere, golden globes from trees and poles, illumination from the windows of houses. And the silo was gone. In its place stood a complex of low stables, lit by lamps, indistinct forms moving slowly within, and a sound he had heard only once before—the mournful lowing of cows. Tents clustered in the meadow, and tables, some of them already spread with wares. Lantern glow, the quiet murmur of people settling down for the night. Johnny headed straight for the stables. There were voices there, and he thought he recognized one.

He entered the cowshed quietly. A pale glow fell on the stalls from glass globes. He had seen this kind of light often in the other world, but never before in this one. There were seven cows, each in a separate stall. All but one were lying on plush carpets of hay. At the farthest stall, a young black and white bull stood, and a man and a woman were tending him. The man, with his back turned, was brushing him. The woman was tying little ribbons in his short hair. The woman looked up. Their eyes met. It was Misha, the scullery maid. Her eyes grew large and her mouth dropped open. She tugged the man's sleeve. "Burley! *Look!*"

Burleyman stood and turned. A quick breath rushed into his nostrils. He steadied himself on the cow stall.

"Come closer," he said. "Step into the light."

Johnny stepped into the light. For a long time they just stood there, staring at each other, the attractions of memory flowing between them. Finally Burleyman spoke.

"So you *are* alive. We weren't sure."

Johnny had no time for warm greetings. He took off his pack, opened it, pulled out the notice he had ripped from the tree, and handed it over.

"What does this mean?"

Burleyman grasped the paper. He made a long, drawn-out sound somewhere between a groan and a sigh. "Oh. Oh." He shook his head. "A crazy world. What a crazy, crazy world! I thought for sure we got them all."

"Who put them there?"

"We don't know. We can guess. Midsummer, some Blackcoats came in the middle of the night. Frankie was the only one to see them. He was drunk, as usual, at the tables. He said they ignored him. They went straight to your picture, hanging by the kitchen. They took nothing else, and they were gone before their smell could leave their bodies. Within a moon, these signs began to appear everywhere, on trees, barns, fences, even houses. We went out every day, took them down, burned them. Finally they stopped. We thought we had them all."

"Who wants to kill me? And why?"

Burleymen let the picture drop to the ground. His face relaxed and he almost smiled. "Maybe you know the answer to that better than me. I only know the stories that are told, and you can't believe every story. What have you done, Johnny Arcane?"

It was like Burleyman had dreamt this question for countless sleepless nights, but only now was he able to ask it. Johnny didn't have to rake through his memories for the answer. He had done many things, but only one pertained.

"The letter," he said. "Lucy. She wanted me to rescue her. She wrote, *if you have to kill anyone, kill the one they call Glass Darkly.*" He paused, pondering the best words to form. At last he said, "I did as I was told."

'Waaaaah!" The mayor made a sound like he'd been hit in the stomach. He dragged his hands over his face. "We have to *protect* you."

Johnny shook his head. "I'm not sure that you can. You have to protect yourself. Maybe I shouldn't have come."

"No, no. This is meant to be. Stay here. With us. Cornfest is tomorrow. You'll be safe. Much has changed."

"The silo is gone. What happened?"

"There was an explosion last summer. The cornmeal caught on fire. It was under great pressure and the walls blew apart. We think it was intentional. There was no Cornfest last summer. This will be the first Cornfest since the abstainers left."

Johnny felt a shifting in his balance, like the earth settling under his feet. The events of last summer appeared through a crack in his memory. Warm sun shining on the garden, Mother alive, resting on the porch in the rocker brought out from the parlor while Johnny hoed the bean rows and harvested the long yellow carrots. He had thought nothing of Cornfest then. It was buried under layers of memory and forgetting. And now here he was, at Cornfest again, and everything so different.

"Johnny, do you remember Maggie Mender, the midwife?"

"Yes. Maggie. She took you in. When you fell."

"We were married, just shortly after you left. She's expecting our first child any day."

Johnny felt obliged to congratulate the mayor, but he couldn't find the words. He leaned against a post. His eyes scanned the lamplit meadow. Everything was so unfamiliar. "The other changes," he said. "The cows. The lights."

Burleyman took a deep breath and held it in his chest. His smile glimmered with something like pride. "Ah, Johnny, where to begin? The cows. Last summer Climber and Birdleg brought us five more cows, plus two steers and one bull. The bull gets all the fun. They return tomorrow with two more steers. Soon we will be the main supplier of beef for all the nearby towns. We slaughtered one of the steers for the feast tomorrow."

"But we will never kill little Johnny Arcane," said Misha, patting the young bull with the ribboned locks. "He is our pet."

"Someday he will be the Boss." said Burleyman.

"And the lights?"

Burleyman raised his finger. "The principles of electricity. You should remember. You were the one who found the book. Frankie showed us how to build a generator. There are many other things you can do with electricity, Johnny.

Wondrous things. Frankie is going to create miracles here in King Corn. But he could do a lot more if he wouldn't drink himself blind every evening. It gets worse and worse. Don't go in the longhall right now. It isn't pretty."

Burleyman's voice trailed off and he looked into Johnny's eyes. His face flushed with an old familiar tenderness. "You've come back, Johnny Arcane. You didn't die. And you're tired. You've had a long journey. Go over to Bearclaw and Ant's. They've been waiting for you. I don't know how they know it, but they told me you were coming. Go there now. Tomorrow will be a big day."

☽

It was a short walk across the meadow to Bearclaw and Ant's little house, past the tables and the tents where the light from the globes was slowly fading. Johnny wrestled under the weight of his thoughts. A summer had passed and the silo was gone. Blackcoats had entered the town, stolen the picture, and posted warrants for his death. Burleyman had said he was safe here, but he knew that wasn't true. No one is safe here, least of all Johnny Arcane. Where was this leading? He felt a gathering wind, heavy with portent, rolling his way.

The house was dark. He knocked softly at the door. There were muffled footsteps from within. The door opened. Ant stood there tall, slim, and bleary-eyed. Lovely as ever. She wore a flimsy cotton nightgown. Her voice was heavy with sleep.

"We thought you'd come earlier, Johnny. We set a place for you at the table. But now we're asleep. Come join us. We can talk in the morning." She took his hand and led him to the bedroom. Bearclaw rolled over in the bed and looked at him through lidded eyes.

"Welcome stranger. We've been expecting you. Chestnut, you'll have to get in your own bed, now. Johnny Arcane's here."

The blankets rustled and Chestnut's sun-bright head emerged. She rubbed her eyes. "I wanna sleep with Johnny Arcane!"

Bearclaw laughed. "That's what all the girls say. Not tonight, though. Your bed's too small. Up! Up! Quick before the moon dog gets you!"

Chestnut threw back the covers and rolled out of bed onto the floor where she leapt to her feet and landed with one bounce in her soft little pallet in the corner.

"Come on, Johnny. Get in before we wake up and start talking."

Bearclaw threw aside the covers. Immediately Johnny felt himself collapsing inward in exhaustion. He climbed into the bed, into the soft warm depression Chestnut had made between Bearclaw and Ant. Bearclaw rolled his back away from him. Ant turned toward him. He spent the night riding the peaceful waves of slumber with Ant's face and body pressed against him, and the rolling surf of Bearclaw snoring at his back.

CHAPTER TWENTY-EIGHT

MAGIC LANTERN

The morning of Cornfest dawned, warm and birdful. Johnny sat in Ant and Bearclaw's kitchen with his hands wrapped around a cup of steaming chicory. Sleep had refreshed him, but trouble still lurked in the quiet of his mind.

"Burleyman thought I was dead, and you knew the exact day I would return. You set a place for me at the table. How could that be?"

Ant flapped two more pancakes onto Johnny's plate while Chestnut danced pirouettes to the yellow sun streaming in the window. On the stove, the kettle began to whistle.

"Burleyman has more things he wants to know than things he knows." said Bearclaw. "Don't get me wrong, the man's heart is good. But he's driven by something that won't let him relax. You've seen it. You know what I mean."

"That doesn't tell me how you knew I was coming."

Ant sat down and rested her head on Johnny's shoulder. "We heard it in the strings."

"In the strings?"

"Jocko heard it first. We were playing the harvest in Archer's Bale and he stopped right in the middle of *The Old Red Hen* and said 'Johnny's coming. I can hear it.' After that, we started hearing it, too, a little louder every night. And last night when we finished practicing, we all looked at each other and we said it at the same time. *Tomorrow*. He's coming tomorrow."

Bearclaw picked up the story. "When we told Frankie, he started talking about wavelengths, something he read in the electricity book. He said the air is full of all these different wavelengths vibrating at different frequencies, like the strings of a guitar. You can't see them and you can't feel them, but he thinks you can tap into them if you have the right kind of instrument. Our instruments. They picked up your wavelength."

"Of course he was drunk." said Ant.

"That he was." replied Bearclaw. "He was in the longhall last night when we left, asleep at the table. I suppose we should go there now and see if he's still alive."

They finished up the pancakes and Ant cleared the dishes. Bearclaw asked Ant to stay with Chestnut while they went to check on Frankie. Chestnut threw herself on the floor.

"I want to go see Frankie!"

"No, baby," said Ant. "You need to stay here and help mommy sew the birds on the bonnets."

Bearclaw and Johnny walked out on the meadow, toward the log house. Already, people were gathering, milling about, setting out their wares. Mummers were practicing their mummering, jugglers their juggling.

"Frankie's not the same man anymore." said Bearclaw. "He hardly even lives in his house. He calls it a *laboratory* now. He learned that word from a book. We found him three more books, me and Jocko. He sends us out on missions, and we scour the vaults of abandoned ruins. One on engineering, another on chemistry. But the third, he never reads. It's called *A Critique of Pure Reason.*"

The doors to the log house were open. Inside was commotion. Big kettles were set out on almost all the tables, and a cauldron of water boiled over the blazing fire in the massive fireplace. Scullery workers were bustling about. Tom Cleaver, the butcher, stood in the open scullery door, rasping a knife on a sharpening rod with such vigor that sparks leapt from the blade. The air was close and moist, and smelled of blood.

Frankie was the only person sitting at a table. He was propped upright with a wool blanket pulled across his shoulders, staring blankly at the light through the open door when Bearclaw and Johnny entered. Bearclaw advanced with caution.

"I've been here all night." Frankie's voice was hoarse and rumblesome. "Why didn't somebody carry me home?"

"We were tired, Frankie. It was late. Besides, you're a grown man. You can carry your own self home."

Frankie's eyes were swollen. He was barely able to open them. "Who is this *man* you brought here?"

"Don't you recognize him? It's Johnny Arcane! We told you he was coming."

Frankie squinted. He was able to lift only one eyelid, while the other remained fixed. "That's not Johnny Arcane. Johnny Arcane is a boy. This is a grown man I see before me."

Johnny couldn't tell if it was a smile that broke through the distortion of Frankie's face. He felt a wave of sadness, seeing his friend in such a state of disrepair. He sat at the table and covered Frankie's clasped hands with his own. "I've grown a bit." he said.

Frankie nodded. "I see. And I have sacrificed some. But for a cause. *Your* cause."

"I have no cause. My cause was to save Lucy. I saved Lucy."

Frankie ran his tongue over his gums as if to find words there. He stared into Johnny's face. Several times he shaped his lips as if he meant to speak. But finally his mouth sagged in resignation. He turned to Bearclaw.

"Pull me up now. Take me home. I have something to tell Johnny."

The man was heavy, and he hung limp as they held him under his arms, Johnny and Bearclaw on either side. His crutches were nowhere to be seen. He smelled terrible. Outside, with the sun shining on his face, he began to mumble incoherently. "Yesterday," he said, "We broke through. Level seventeen. Trebled energy. No time."

On the meadow the party was starting up. Banners were being raised and drummers were drumming. Scullery workers had carried one of the big kettles out onto a table piled with flowers. From the cow stables Mayor Burleyman looked up to see the two men dragging the one-legged man through the crowd. He raised a leafy wooden staff in salute, just as they disappeared around the stalls.

The first thing Johnny noticed on entering the laboratory was a low, steady hum, like a string continuously vibrating. All the shutters were drawn and the room was dark but for numerous small glowing objects here and there. The air was warm and heavy with vapors, especially the esters of alcohol.

"Put me down! *There* they are!" growled Frankie. His crutches were leaning against a counter.

Details emerged as Johnny's eyes grew accustomed to the dark. The workshop had, indeed, become a laboratory. Suspended cupboards had been built above all the countertops. They were jammed with jars and instruments with protruding coils and knobs. There was motion everywhere. Tiny flames danced from burners, colored lights blinked on panels, a group of little pennant-shaped objects spun on needle-thin shafts. One wall was covered with flat paper wheels like the one Johnny had seen in the Blackcoat's hideout. They turned slowly while pens left squiggly lines. In the far corner a miniature jag of lightning leapt between two metal rods.

Frankie pulled himself up on both crutches. "I am tired, Johnny." he said.

"We'll get you into your bed." Bearclaw replied.

"No. No. Johnny. I want to talk to Johnny." He maneuvered one crutch to the side and wiped a ball of slobber from his mouth onto his sleeve. "Where's your instrument? The mandolin."

"The mandolin? Here, in my pack."

"Give it to me."

Frankie snatched the mandolin from Johnny's hands and laid it flat on the counter. From an overhead hook he grabbed a hand drill with a thick iron bit and leveled it over the instrument's tailpiece.

"Wait! What are you doing? Don't do that!"

Bearclaw took Johnny's arm and squeezed it.

"This won't hurt it." said Frankie as he turned the handle and the bit began digging into the wood. "Ask Bearclaw. It's a small thing. Compared to...It's what the people want. At the fest tonight you will play *electric*."

He handed back the mandolin. Johnny felt shocked, violated. But Bearclaw patted his shoulder. "It doesn't matter," he said quietly. "It will be all right."

"Waves, Johnny." Frankie seemed exhausted from the work of drilling. But he thrust himself from the counter and grasped both of Johnny's hands in a vice-like grip. "I need to tell you this. You will see this sooner than you know. Waves are everywhere. Sunlight is waves. Sound is waves. Heat. Cold. Your thoughts are waves. Every living thing sends out waves. Trees. Animals. People. Waves are passing through your body right now, as you stand there. Stand there!" Frankie pulled himself upright on his crutch. "If you stay still you can feel them. Stay still! Feel the waves, Johnny!"

It was an awkward moment. Johnny and Bearclaw stood still with perplexity in their faces while Frankie's body began to sway. His eyes were closed and it looked like he was going to topple. But then his lids popped open and he lifted his arms. "We can tap into the frequency of a wave!" he declared. "We can use waves to send messages to distant places. I have done this. Johnny! Catch me!"

Frankie folded at the middle and keeled forward. His crutch rattled to the floor. Both Johnny and Bearclaw rushed to him, but his weight was too great. Bearclaw's knees buckled and Johnny was knocked off his feet by the momentum of the two stumbling men. A row of beakers flew across the room. Bearclaw hit the floor first and Johnny rolled the one-legged man sideways to keep the guitarist from being crushed.

Frankie moaned. Bearclaw crawled to his knees.

"OK, old man, that's it! We're putting you to bed!"

"Wavelength," blubbered Frankie as they dragged him by the arms to the cot in the corner of the laboratory. "I've found the wavelength. Level seventeen. *Tonight* ..."

◡

Bearclaw and Johnny stumbled out of Frankie's darkened laboratory into the bright light of morning. They had to squint their eyes. There was color everywhere, and buoyant objects drifting on the layers of the air, like leaves, or pages ripped from a book. Bearclaw started to cough. His lungs filled with phlegm and he coughed and coughed until finally he had to squat down on his haunches to stop himself.

"I don't know, Johnny," he said, standing. "I just don't know what's happening anymore."

They walked into the meadow, past the stalls and the bright canopies, the jostling, colorfully dressed revelers, the smoky smell of roasting flesh. Johnny could barely take any of this in. He tried to slow his thoughts to a pace where he could make words and say something.

"This ... this *electric* music. What does it sound like?"

"It just sounds like music, only louder. Chestnut hates it. It makes her scream. We haven't tried it untuned yet. Oh, Johnny, everything is moving so fast. It started when Frankie first opened that book you brought him. The Principles of Electricity. I think he has to get drunk every night to stop himself from catching fire and burning down to a crisp."

Johnny raked his mind for the pieces of the puzzle. "On the road, on my way here," he said, "I came across a town. Abstinence. The Abstainers."

Bearclaw took out a handkerchief and wiped the sweat off his forehead. "The Abstainers are a crude and ignorant people," he said. "I don't shuck any corn with them. But this thing Burleyman calls progress—it worries me. It worries Frankie, too, but he goes along with it. I think that's why he drinks. He didn't want the generators. He says we can make electricity by blocking up the streams that run down the mountain, and we can send electricity on wires to other towns. But Burleyman couldn't wait for that. So Frankie had us build the generators. The first night they put electric lights in the log house kitchen, Custer and Brank stayed up all night making cakes and pies. They were so excited they didn't want to stop. The next day Brank came down with a fever from lack of sleep and there were so many pies nobody knew what to do with them. Chestnut can't sleep when the lights are on in the meadow. The owls stopped nesting in the hayloft because the balers keep the lights on so they can work late. Frankie told Burleyman he's going to make an electric saw that can cut straight boards out of logs. We can build new houses. Burleyman likes that kind of thing. He wants to build a dome on top of Round Hill so he can sit up there and watch who's coming on the roads. It's just happening so fast, Johnny. All this in the summer since you've been gone."

"These generators," said Johnny, "What fuels them?"

"It's something called black rock. It's a rock that burns. A merchant brought it to Frankie in a wagon. In the middle of the night. He brings more from time to time. Always in the night. We've never met him. "

Johnny shivered. His memory rolled back over the shadowy forms of things he had seen, from the deep canyons of cities to the hungry mechanical beasts in the mines of Perpetua. In the frayed and splintered towers of Cantankerberg mad people lived like animals and fed off of human flesh while in the streets below children were chained, armed, and pitted against each other for money. *Money.* Nothing could be exchanged without it. He was given money to pay Pleasurepane in Ladyland. Mars wanted to trade the boy back to the Blackcoats for *money.* Because of money the Blackcoats killed the boy with a gun. A gun which money probably bought.

For a moment Johnny glimpsed a vision of a long chain of

cause and effect. He wanted to tell Bearclaw. Words began to gather and connect. He almost spoke. *The place I have been. It may be where you are going.* But the opportunity passed. Bearclaw looked up and a smile bloomed on his face.

"Look!" he cried. "The cowboys have returned. And there's Jocko!"

Four small brown cows were standing in front of the barn. There was Climber's bulk and Birdleg's bones, and Burleyman in his blue robe, trying to pry open the mouth of one young beast. But when Jocko saw Johnny, he turned at once and started running toward him, if you could call it running. It was more like a crazy bird dance, his arms flapping like chicken wings, his legs wobbling in a heron's waddle, his head bobbing like a mountain jay.

"Johnny! Johnny! Johnny!" he sang in a chickadee's warble, and when he arrived he shoved Johnny so hard on the chest he almost knocked him down. "Johnny Arcane!" he proclaimed. "Kill this man!"

Bearclaw laughed and laughed. "He doesn't mean that. We've just taken down so many posters, it's become his slogan."

"I heard him first! I heard him so loud we had to stop the music, didn't we, Bearclaw?"

"Yes, we did, Jocko. We stopped the music."

"Let's go find Ant! Let's tell her Johnny's here."

"Ant already knows, but yeah. Let's go find her. I'm tired of this Cornfest already."

They worked their way back through the gathering crowd. Contests were beginning to form, leg wrestling, ring toss, hoop jump. Already, grown men were carrying steins of beer, and young girls were walking arm in arm.

Back at the house, Ant greeted Bearclaw with a kiss, and

Jocko with a knuckle on the head. "Together at last!" she said. "And I made muffins. Let's play."

So they played. At first Johnny was bothered by the hole Frankie had made in his turtle box, but then he noticed similar holes in Jocko's washtub, in Ant's fiddle, in Bearclaw's guitar. It didn't seem to affect the sound. They played tuned. They played all the fiddle tunes, and Johnny taught them the few he had learned from Wilbo. They stopped and ate muffins and laughed and told stories about the past. Jocko spoke of the travels of the cowboys and Ant spoke of the antics of Chestnut. They did not tell stories about the future and Johnny did not tell stories about the places he had been or the things he had seen. They picked up their instruments and played again, while the midday sun crossed the meadow and shone down on the revelers, increasingly sloppy in their cups, and while Frankie Fulcrum slept in his laboratory, dreaming of sounds and moving pictures, streaming toward King Corn on wavelengths from somewhere far away.

Ɔ

Eventually the orange ball of the sun dipped below the western ridge, and Chestnut, weary of weaving pine needle baskets, began pulling pots and pans out of the cupboard onto the floor.

The music fell apart. Bearclaw set down his guitar and scratched his beard.

"I guess we should go out there," he said. "It *is* Cornfest."

"Oh, Cornfest!" sighed Ant. "It isn't the same without the silo."

"Well, anyhow, we have to eat. No point cooking supper

with all that cow meat going around. Besides, tonight we're playing *electric*."

Out in the meadow the crowd was growing more boisterous. Several spirals of dancers had formed, and another line was weaving in and out between them. Without a shared center, each group was singing a different song, and the result was cacophony, bordering on chaos. Some of the stalls had been knocked over, their wares scattered on the ground.

The four musicians wove their way through the crowd. Ant carried Chestnut in her arms. They elbowed through the rowdy gathering at the log house door, where the harried scullery workers were busy dishing up the meat and pouring out the beer. On the platform some musicians were already performing, if you could call them musicians. They had no instruments. They were old men, pounding out rhythms on kettles and buckets, and tunelessly warbling the words to a song about a young girl who gets stuck upside down in a tree with her petticoats falling down above her head. Nearby, a few people were stomping their feet and clapping their hands to no particular rhythm.

Across the room, Johnny caught sight of Frankie, sitting at the very same table where they had found him that morning. He had slept. He was upright and clear-eyed. There was a stein of beer and a plate of meat before him. Their eyes met, and Frankie nodded, but Bearclaw looked down.

"I think I've had enough of the old doctor for one day. Let's go see what these fools are up to on the platform."

The fools on the platform were not from King Corn. They were farmers by their uniforms, but one wore the three-cornered hat of a tent maker, and another had his overalls on backwards. Evidently they did not recognize the approaching musicians.

"Her feet were pink and her knees were red," sang the man in the three-cornered hat.

"Her bum was as bald as a baker's head," sang the man in the backwards overalls.

"You boys shut up!" hollered a voice from the crowd. "Show some respect for the ladies!"

Some people started to boo. Some started to cheer. Someone said, "No, look! Here's the real musicians! Show some respect for the real musicians!"

There was stomping and clapping. Johnny felt several palms slapping his back.

"Bearclaw, where's yer gitter? We want some real music."

"On the stage, Tucker. Come on out. We're going to play *electric.*"

"Johnny Arcane!" yelled several men at once, and behind them, a chorus of women and children sang, *"He climbed the sunbeams and held onto the birds!"* Chestnut picked up her head and laughed.

"Where you boys from?" asked Bearclaw.

"We be from Sputum!" said the man in the three-cornered hat.

"Sputum? That's a long way to walk, just for the Cornfest."

"We didn't walk. We came on a cycable."

"Cycable? What's a cycable?"

"It's the new thing. They makes 'em in Stubblefield. Got wheels, and chains!"

The man in the backwards overalls leaned forward. "Hell, you watch. Next fest we be flyin' into Cornfest on the back of a *skypig!*"

A scullery man came around with a tray full of meat and steins of ale. The musicians settled down at a table near the platform.

"You boys keep singing," said Bearclaw. "We like to hear what they sing about in Sputum."

"*She shook her arms and she cleared her throat,*" crooned the three-cornered hat.

"*Up jumped the fat little man in the boat!*" replied the backwards overalls.

A round of sloppy laughter rolled from the other side of the longhall, and then a sound, like porcelain tiles slapped on a tabletop. Very few people were sitting at the tables, although the room was crowded to overflowing. A restlessness pervaded. In the din, there were more proclamations than conversations. Men touched men, backslaps, handshakes, a punch on the shoulder, while women evaded the touch of men, and children scampered about underfoot. There seemed to be a great anticipation of something about to happen.

But Frankie sat, stone still and resolute, his eyes fixed on the musicians at the table by the platform, where the fools from Sputum continued to reel out their vulgarities. He had been alone at first, but now Marta, the scullery maid, was with him. From time to time he leaned over and whispered something in her ear.

"He wants something from you, Johnny," said Bearclaw. "What do you suppose it is?"

"I don't know."

Someone threw an apple core. It landed at the feet of the backward overall man and he kicked it back into the crowd. From the scullery there was a metallic crash, and a woman let out an oath. Then Marta detached herself from Frankie's side and began weaving her way through the crowd toward the platform.

She seemed awkward and shy, like she was uncertain of the message she was bringing. She stood by the table.

"Johnny. Frankie wants you to fetch him his crutches out of Jocko's room."

There was a moment of silence. Jocko blinked and shook back his head. "What was Frankie doing in my room?" Another moment of silence. Bearclaw spoke. "Marta, you've got two good strong legs. Can't you fetch Frankie's crutches yourself?"

Marta stammered. "He...he wants Johnny."

A tremor fluttered in Johnny's heart, like a wavelength passing through. There was more here than meets the eye. He stood up. His legs were shaky. "I'll go."

Immediately Marta sat down in Johnny's chair and laid her head on the tabletop. Jocko reached out and touched her hair. Johnny turned and started into the crowd.

A group of drunken men had formed a chain with their elbows locked, and they were swaying back and forth. Johnny had to make a long circle around them. Someone had spilled a bowl of beef stew on the floor and children were running and skidding through it. A dog was barking, continuously. Two girls were playing patty cake with their palms and chanting rhythmically, "*Climb the sunbeams! Hold onto the birds!*" As Johnny passed the hearth, a skein of flame burst out of the embers with a roar, as if saying hello. He felt the waves of heat passing through him. He felt the sound of the voices around him, passing through his head like waves. He felt the tide of his own blood rushing through his body. Waves. Everything was made of waves. His face flushed. He thought he might fall. He shoved himself into Jocko's room and slammed the door behind him.

Quiet. Still and cool. He stood for as long as it took for his heartbeat to settle and his eyes adjust to the darkness. On the mat in the corner, Jocko's quilt lay, rumpled. A candle flickered on a small table. On the shelves, Jocko's little dolls, everywhere, as they had always been. On the wall, across from the mat, above a shelf of dolls, shadows moved in a patch of blue light. It must be the moonlight through the magic lantern. He watched the patterns move. For a while they soothed him, and conjured up the sweetness of unseen memories. But the forms began to take shapes, and in his heart he felt a constriction, some kind of barrier to the flow of waves, a longing perhaps—*yes*!

A longing.

Fiddle tunes. Orange robes. Horses. The ocean.

The curve of a face, like the bowl of the night sky. Two bright stars. Eyes. Wind-blown leaves. A formation of birds, encircling a globe. Arms. Water flowing over hills. Hair. Shoulders. A mouth. A voice.

"Hello, Johnny."

Her image was like a reflection in a pool, distorted by ripples. His heart broke, and salty seawater flooded his body.

"Lucy!"

The image breathed. Her chest heaved. A tress of black hair fell across her cheek.

"Johnny. Can you see me?"

Johnny flung himself at the wall, knocking the dolls off the shelf. But immediately his shadow blocked the image and obscured it in darkness. He reached out his hand but all he felt was the dry plaster of a bare wall. He fell back on the floor and she returned, slowly, like a reflection returns after the troubling of the water.

"Lucy. Lucy. I can see you. But I can't feel you. Can you see me?"

"I can't see you or feel you. We haven't worked that out yet. I can only hear you."

"What do you mean, *we*? Who has done this?"

"Bow Wow. And Frankie. Bow Wow told Frankie you can't just use machines to do this. You have to move the dough. Johnny, what do I look like?"

Johnny stood back and looked into her face. "Your hair. You cut off your beautiful hair."

"The Blackcoats did it. It was long ago. I'm growing it back."

Johnny drank in the image. It shifted and shimmered, and frequently threatened to disappear entirely. It was Lucy, but it was not Lucy. He couldn't tell what she was wearing. The movement of her lips was not in time with the sound of her words.

"Where are you?"

"In Freeland. We got away. All of us. You saved all of us. When you killed that man."

"Freeland!" Tears swelled in Johnny's eyes. "I want to go back! I want to be there with you. Lucy! Lucy, I love you!" The longing in his arms was unbearable. If only he could throw them around her. She wasn't there. She was far away. He couldn't touch her. She was so far away.

"I love you, too, Johnny," she said, but her voice sounded empty and sad. "I love you so much. But things are different now. "

"Different?"

Lucy didn't say anything for a while. She kept her eyes down so that Johnny could only see the lids. Finally she looked up.

"Johnny, you have a son. You've already met him." She turned her face to the side. "Come, Timothy. Say hello."

The boy appeared, a blurred shadow, shy, fearful. He didn't seem to know where to rest his eyes. "He can see you," Lucy told him, "Even if you can't see him. Say hello."

"Hello."

"Johnny Arcane is your papa. You can call him Papa."

"Hello, Papa. Welcome Home. *Meet Me on the Bridge. The Lover's Knot. Safe at Anchor ...*"

Johnny's eyes overflowed. These were the names of the roses in the garden at Freeland. The memory was clear and vivid, clearer than the moving picture before him. Bow Wow reading the placards. The boy repeating the words in his high and wistful voice. And then suddenly, Mother's voice, weak and straining. *Death shouldn't bother you if you've planted a seed...*

"Lucy! Lucy, wait for me! I'll come back to Freeland. We can be together. We can raise him together. We will be a family!"

Lucy was crying openly now; he heard her sobs but the teardrops were nothing but smudges on the grainy screen. She kept her head up and shook it slowly from side to side. "Johnny, I can't. I can't." She stopped. Her body became still. She took a deep breath. "I'm married now."

There was a popping sound. The image jumped and began to fade. Johnny felt like he was falling into an abyss. His stomach flipped and a volley of sparks crackled through his head.

"Married...?"

"His name is Erik. He was a Blackcoat. He escaped when you killed Glass Darkly. He helped me get to Freeland. Bow Wow took him in. Bow Wow says we can never be together, you and me. It isn't our destiny. Erik is kind. He takes good care of me." In the distortion there was a sound like the fluttering of a bird's wing. Then Lucy's voice again, jumping and jerking. "He isn't you, Johnny. You're the one I love. I'll always love you—*Johnny!*"

A jagged line ripped across the screen followed by a harsh, stuttering noise. Lucy's voice shattered into fragments. A burst of light, a crack of sound, and then darkness, silence, save for the guttering of the candle and the distant clamor of agitated voices in the longhall.

A thumping sound and the door flew open. Johnny turned. Frankie stood there, leaning on his crutch. His voice was uncommonly subdued. "I'm so sorry, Johnny. We don't have enough power to sustain it for very long."

There was a pause, like a momentary halt of the wheel of time, like a breath held, inhaled, holding, like a fist clamped around a great heart, to prevent its next beat. Then there was a commotion at the door. Bearclaw burst in.

"Johnny!" he cried. "Johnny, I'm sorry. You have to come. We need you. They're going crazy out there. It's getting dangerous. They want the band. We have to play!"

CHAPTER TWENTY-NINE

CHAOS COMES
TO KING CORN

falcon holds something precious in its talons, a great, silvery fish snatched from the waters of a deep lake. The falcon flies above a sea of clouds with a bright yellow sun overhead. Out of nowhere comes a gust of wind. The falcon falters. The fish slips from its claws. The great bird lets out a cry of dismay and watches helplessly as the treasure disappears into the mantle of clouds.

Urgency rushed in to clear Johnny's thoughts. "Where's my mandolin?"

"It's on the stage. It's plugged in." Bearclaw looked at Frankie and his face darkened. He pointed an accusing finger. "This is what happens..." he began, but he did not finish his thought. He turned, and they were out into the clamoring crowd.

The mood in the meadow had lost all the gentle mirth of a festival, the voices now rolling, drunken, and sloppy—many voices at once, but few in unison, at least not for very long. From a distance, the glow of the lamps seemed to be panning and throbbing, like sheet lightning. Drawing closer, Johnny could see that men had shimmied up the poles and were deliberately swinging the lamps. People had climbed onto the roof of the cow barn and were jumping off into the crowd. The hoop girls dashed from side to side, trying to catch the falling bodies in their hoop. Mummers who ordinarily performed their rites in rings, were now scattered about, their robes soiled, each one twirling to some private rhythm. All the tables had been knocked over, garments, pottery, produce, trampled in the mud. And through the crowd strode the mayor, still in his shiny blue robe and starry wizard's hat, now wielding his wooden staff, taller than his head, and spiraled round with painted green vines.

"May there be cows!" he bellowed, thrusting his wand into the air. "Honor the principles of electricity!" He was drunk. People were grabbing his pole and trying to wrestle it to the ground, the ragged chant swelling from their voices. "Burleyman! Burleyman!"

When the musicians jumped on the stage, the focus of the crowd shifted. All faces turned forward, and the din of voices pulled together in unison. No words were distinguishable above the roar, save for the mayor's voice weaving through the bodies, "Cows! Electricity!" and the crowd's chanted echo, "Burleyman!" Fists were raised. Smaller people climbed on the shoulders of larger people, to get a better view.

A black box stood in the corner, a bank of red lights glowing. Wires, like vines, spilled across the floor. All eyes were on Bearclaw as he snatched one of the wires and thrust the metal plug into the hole in his guitar. A deafening squawk blasted from the box. People screamed. Women covered their ears.

Bearclaw strummed the strings. The sound was like a full toolbox being dropped on a metal plate. Jocko plugged in the washboard and plucked the catgut once. The floor shook like thunder.

"Are we tuned?" Jocko asked.

"We are not." Bearclaw answered.

"All right then." Jocko lit into his single string with purpose and intention. The floorboards began throbbing a rhythm, more vibration than sound. Johnny felt it in the pit of his stomach and the hollow cavity of his chest. Jocko himself looked surprised. The power of the sound almost threw him backwards, but he kept going.

Bearclaw joined in. The dissonance of the six untuned strings exploded with a ferocity that startled everyone, no less Bearclaw himself. His whole body puffed up, like a cat in a fight, and a sly smile curled to his lips. His fingers slammed into the rhythm that Jocko had established, and the crowd went wild. With a backbeat to connect them, everybody started moving in unison, and the shouts and the hoots began to assume the regularity of music.

Ant lifted her bow and touched it to the strings. A single, clear tone penetrated the frenzy of Bearclaw's fretwork. It seemed to frighten her. She stared, wide-eyed, at her bow arm, as if it were a thing possessed. But as he watched her, Johnny saw her reserve crumble. It started with her hips. They began to sway, and her shoulders relaxed. She closed her eyes. The notes that poured forth were long, strong, and screaming. They ascended like birds with wings on fire, like leaves and branches in a spiraled wind.

Johnny knew it was time. He strummed the strings just before he sank the plug into the opening. A cathedral of sound burst fully constructed into the air, and immediately he heard the voices.

"Arcane! Arcane! Johnny Arcane!"

So. This, then. This was it. This was what he had been told by Mab, by Bow Wow, the secret in the stories, destiny in her relentless pursuit, overriding all the longings and sorrows of the individual heart, like a storm rolling over a mountain, like the relentless waves of the sea. Like a cow giving birth in the snow. Like a forest slowly growing its boundaries outward, into the land of chaos and cruelty. There was no choice to be made. With tears streaming, Johnny flung himself into the music.

Riding Jocko's resilient heartbeat, the instruments clashed and bickered, and sought common ground. Harmonies were forged from dissonance. Counterpoint emerged from cacophony. Across the meadow, arms were raised and swaying from side to side. Faces beamed with wonder. This was like nothing they had ever heard before, and its sheer power swept them up. Bodies writhed and reeled. One man in front fell on his face. Others lifted him up and passed him, flailing, over their heads into the mass of the crowd. People screamed and hollered with something close to defiance, as if they meant to drown out the noise with their own voices, to no avail.

At the back, near the cow barn, Johnny saw something happen. Two men, vigorously thrashing to the rhythm, collided, and each fell to the ground. One, his neighbors had to help up; the other stood on his own, whereupon they immediately rushed each other and collided again. Johnny couldn't tell if it was a playful dance or an angry tussle, but it caught on at once. Others around them began throwing themselves at each other, knocking each other down, picking each other up. One man started swinging his arms about wildly, striking anyone who came within arm's length. A cloud of dust swelled above the small patch of revelers and the crowd shifted, hiding the incident from view. But then it began in another place. In another part of the crowd a small cluster of people began hurling themselves at each other, ramming their bodies together, tumbling into a heap.

From the cow barn a spinning motion began, a single mummer, twirling wildly, trailing a stream of colored ribbons, oblivious to anyone in his path. A few people were knocked down. Others saw him coming and threw up their arms as a barricade. One man grabbed him by the robe, drew him back and thrust him forward like a stone from a slingshot. The mummer lost his balance and pummeled headlong, knocking several people down before he rolled against a broken flower stand.

Johnny glanced at Bearclaw whose eyes were already fixed firmly upon him. There was panic in those eyes. They said *what do we do now?* But he kept playing. He tried to modulate the sound to something less aggressive, more stately. Johnny lit into the melody of *Sweet Garnet's Reel*, but it sounded more like *The Horn Pig's Revenge* on his untuned strings.

Out on the meadow, more and more zones of disturbance broke out, and everywhere, the moving bodies were losing their sense of unity. Some swayed right, some swayed left, and the torsos collided with intention. Two women, each astraddle the shoulders of a man, engaged in a thrusting match. Hoop girls moved through the crowd with their hoop taut, and people were jumping into it and bouncing out onto the ground. A shoe went flying through the air, then another, then another. Soon other things were thrown. Food, mostly potatoes. From an overturned produce stand, perhaps. For a moment, the air was full of potatoes. A potato struck the back of the head of a shirtless man and he wheeled around, fists clenched. There was a short scuffle, quickly swallowed by the surging crowd.

Then from the front of the crowd, Johnny heard a shout that chilled him with its menace. A swarthy hunchback with long shaggy hair and a grizzled chin was brandishing a rusty dagger. His words were fierce but unintelligible. They sounded something like "*Ginnas hurly mannee oof ooly full-amuckle.*"

A skinny mummer in a soiled robe stood back and held his hands up to his sides. He said something like "*Hurly mannee nolo wolo.*" The hunchback leapt at him, knife first, twirling it between his beefy fingers.

The mummer fell backwards and the knife swiped sloppily over the top of his head. Someone grabbed the hunchback by both arms, and another man stepped out of the crowd. This one was huge, barrel-chested, shirtless and bearded.

"Gimme him!" he growled and raised a serrated fillet knife, clearly taken from the scullery. The hunchback broke loose and tossed his dagger from one hand to the other.

"I'll have you blobbled!" he uttered.

Some of the people nearby started chanting, "Woof! Woof!" and raising their fists. The two combatants faced each other and began circling, each making little jabs in the air with his blade.

Out of nowhere, Mayor Burleyman appeared and jumped between them. He was still carrying his staff, but his wizard's hat was missing. It sounded like he said, "You'll have to cow me first!"

Someone stumbled forward and tackled the mayor to the ground. The combatants set upon each other at once, but the big man quickly wrested the dagger from hunchback, whereupon someone jumped on the big man's back, and the hunchback threw a grazing sidelong punch across the big man's face. The big man started writhing arms around as if they were snakes with knives in their mouths, while behind him, more and more people swarmed in to see the fight.

There was an enormous amplified crash. Johnny looked up at Bearclaw. Bearclaw had pulled the plug from his guitar. "Let's get out of here!" he urged. The music pummeled to a halt. Ant had already stopped, and as soon as Jocko damped his last deep tone, it was like the bottom fell out of the Known World.

All across the meadow, bodies were falling, rolling, scuffling, throwing punches, but in the sudden disappearance of amplified sound, the crowd's voices seemed weak and puny, like flies buzzing around a corn lamp.

"Bring your instruments!" cried Bearclaw. "Follow me!"

Ant swept Chestnut up into her arms. They ducked through the small opening at the back of the stage. Jocko could barely fit with his wash bucket. Just as Johnny broke through, he caught the sound of the mayor's voice above the chaos.

"There will be cows! There will be electricity!"

CHAPTER THIRTY

SORROW INTO SWEETNESS

ehind the stage it was dark and quiet, and smelled of moss. This was the entrance to the deep forest, where children often played, but were warned not to stray too far. The ruins of the goat shed stood there. It had fallen into disuse since the building of the cow barn. Out of the darkness came the braying of a goat, and a white shadow slipped between the trees. Maggie Mender's remaining herd still roamed about untethered here, simply because they preferred the place to anywhere else.

"Does anyone have a light?" asked Bearclaw.

"I do!" came a voice.

It was Marta, the scullery maid and keeper of the cows. She held up a small corn lamp with a glass mantle. "Take me with you."

They set out into the dark, the four musicians, with Chestnut and Marta. The trail skirted the slope of the little green mountain commonly known as the Hunter's Horn. Attaining some elevation, they began to hear the distant, agitated voices from the meadow through the muffling of the trees. The sound was not unlike the call of a flock of northbound geese, or the crackling of a fresh fire, or the patter of spring rain. Over the path ahead, owls fled deeper into the forest, away from the approaching light.

Suddenly there was more light, glowing from behind them. Johnny and Bearclaw turned at the same moment.

Several more lamps were moving among the trees, following the convolutions of the trail, and there were shadowy human forms and the sound of labored breathing.

"Who goes?" called out Bearclaw.

"Friends," came a soft voice. Another voice added, "And lovers."

As the figures gathered in a circle of illumination, Johnny scanned the faces. He recognized some of them. There were Chamomile and Celandine, two of the hoop girls, Celandine in a blue hooded cape and Chamomile with a lace shawl across her shoulders. Tom Cleaver stood there, still wearing his bloodstained apron. Turner the woodworker was leaning against a tree. And Johnny recognized the plain-dressed man and woman he had encountered on the road, entering town. *We will have no more to do with those abstainers. Such a dour lot!* Behind these people there were others, maybe thirty, maybe forty people, some children, some elderly. Some carried lamps. Others huddled in the darkness.

"We want music," said Tom Cleaver. "We don't like what's happening back there."

Bearclaw stood still for a while, his eyes studying the gathered crowd.

"Follow us, then," he said at last. "I know a place."

ↄ

The trail grew steep after that, the trees larger, closer

together, and bearded with shaggy moss. Strands of silvery moonlight slanted through the branches. Overhead they heard the skittering of bats. The hoop girls began to sing, a wordless duet based on one of the fiddle tunes, Johnny couldn't place which. They came to a place where a tree had fallen across the path. Jocko stayed behind to help each person over it. Johnny held back so he could listen to the string of curious words and phrases Jocko delivered to the comrades as they scaled the log.

"Keep your blue eye in your pocket and your brown eye in your hand."

"A rabbit is always behind you."

"Give me your seven fingers."

"It gets bigger at the bottom."

Just below the summit of Hunter's Horn, the forest opened to accommodate a large, sloped clearing, oval shaped, indented, as if some giant childbearing woman had rested her enormous belly there. The full moon hung directly overhead in a dome of stars, its golden light pouring like cream over the clearing and over the layers of treetops rolling down to the plain of King Corn and the bald knob of Grassy Hill, which stood as her gate.

There seemed to be a collective sigh of relief as the people spilled out of the confines of the forest into the freedom of the clearing. They fanned out into it with laughter and soft conversation. Children began to twirl. The hoop girls formed an invisible hoop with their clasped hands and began spinning it sun-wise, gathering up the children with each turn. Short phrases of melody rose from voices and rippled through the crowd.

Gradually people began to find their places and settle down. The musicians, accustomed to performing on a stage, gravitated to a flat slab of rock near the treewall at the top of the clearing, where they could survey the entire scene, and the moonlit vista that lay beyond. Ant set Chestnut down. The little girl sat on the edge of the rock, clutching her quilt, staring out at the settling crowd.

Some people gathered close. Others clustered at distances all the way to the lower line of trees. Some brought blankets, cloaks, bedsheets, to spread on the ground. Others remained standing. A quiet cradled in. First the singing, then the conversations grew silent, until there was nothing left but a rustling expectation.

"We should be tuned," whispered Bearclaw.

"Yes, we should," affirmed Ant.

Bearclaw cocked his ear to the strings and twisted the pegs until he was able to produce a ringing major chord. Ant and Johnny quickly followed. Murmurs of approval echoed from the audience, and a smattering of gentle applause.

Jocko started playing. The notes were free of the invasive edge of amplification. They were more a suggestion of rhythm, a relaxed amble, like a dog on a walk. A few heads began to nod. Bearclaw rapped his knuckles on the fretboard, looking for the downbeat. He glanced up.

"You call it, Johnny Arcane," he said.

"*Woodpecker's Dream!*" called Johnny Arcane.

And they were off.

The moment the music started, Johnny knew this time would be different. The harmonic sweetness of the very first chord snapped his heart in two. Images gushed into his mind, and all of them bore the name of *Lucy*. He remembered how she had once told him it wasn't always her name. Bow Wow gave it to her. It means *morning light*. How many seasons had he carried her in his body? How many nights had the sweet softness of her skin been pressed against his in the illumination of memory? And through the dark lands he had pushed on to save her, and he had saved her, but only by taking the life of another, and others perhaps, considering Mars, the boy, the pony.

Bearclaw called the next tune. *Up the Misty Mountain.* It was easy to follow. Johnny's fingers knew the way. He looked out on the crowd spread across the clearing. They all looked like mummers, quietly performing the passion play of life. Everyone was moving: some almost imperceptibly, gently swaying, just the arms, the shoulders, the fingers thrumming rhythms on knees, heads nodding like nestling robins. Others, especially women, especially in the distance, spun and swooned, weaving filaments of moonlight between their fingers, eyes closed, drawing the music inward, into a shared but private place.

"The Cabbage Moth!" called out Ant. The key shifted.

How did it turn out this way? How did Bow Wow know it was not their destiny to be together? The ache struck him so hard he pounded it into the strings of his mandolin, but the music just continued. Every memory stung him with sadness, even the good ones. The first warm welcome of the open road and the deep dark isolation that followed. The first Cornfest at King Corn, when he climbed the silo and brought down the honey. The seasons wandering as a messenger; the drawing of the map of the Known World. The return to King Corn for the winter of the wolves and the cows.

A conversation played itself in its entirety. He was talking to Jocko on the eve of the discovery of The Principles of Electricity.

I can feel Lucy, he said. *I can feel where she is, which direction, how far away. Like how you can feel where your arm is, even when you can't see it.*

Jocko's response was immediate. *You must have left something inside of her, then.*

"The Boatman's Daughter!" called Jocko as he pulled back the broom handle and steered the rhythm in a new direction.

It was then Johnny realized that all of them—Jocko, Bearclaw, Ant—all of them had come with their hearts ripped from their bodies and splayed on the strings. *Happy to meet* always meant *sorry to part.* And now the borders of the Known World were crumbling, the corn meal had blown away, and the forces of chaos and cruelty were closing in. The people before him knew it too. He could tell. They had fled the chaos of Cornfest and followed the four musicians, seeking the peace and beauty they felt slipping from their lives. He turned from his strings and focused on the faces, lit by moonlight, some young and smooth, some old and weathered, some standing, some seated, some lying flat on their backs, staring at the starry sky. Some moved with grace, some with awkward clumsiness, but they were all moving now, even the ones who appeared to be still. There was a rippling motion circling sunwise, shifting, elusive, hypnotic.

At the back of the crowd, a man stood. Johnny recognized him at once. It was the stranger who had escaped with his wife from Abstinence. *Such a dour lot!* He was still wearing his plain, brown farmer's clothes but there seemed to be a glow coming from him. Perhaps it was just a trick of the moon. The moment he found his feet, his arms began to rise, like a heron opening its wings. With the ascent of his arms, his head lifted from his shoulders, his mouth an O of wonder. His eyes turned upward and his hands went out ahead and upward, reaching, reaching.

Then for a moment his body began to rise from the ground, slowly, like a plume of smoke. A few people nearby turned and gasped. A sound, like a cote of doves, passed outward through the crowd. A look of astonishment dawned on the man's face, and he let out a tiny cry.

Suddenly he went dark, all the glow of his body fading, and he collapsed on the ground. Everyone in the band saw it happen. Distracted, but driven by the music, they kept playing, until a commotion rose around the fallen man.

"No! No!" a woman cried.

"What happened?"

"What happened to him?"

"Oh Percival, no! Please, Percival, don't do this to me!"

"What's wrong with him?"

"He's dead!"

"He's dead!"

"Percival!"

The music fell apart. Bearclaw set down his guitar and jumped from the stone. The others followed.

So deep had been the peace that a calm prevailed, in spite of the urgency of the moment. People stepped aside to let the musicians pass. The voices conveyed curiosity and concern, but very little fear.

They gathered around the fallen man—Johnny, Jocko, Bearclaw and Ant, with Chestnut in arm. Someone lit a corn lamp. The woman was sitting on the ground, weeping, the man's head in her lap. Bearclaw knelt, tilted the man's head, listened for breathing, and felt for a pulse. Finally he looked up into the woman's face.

"He's gone."

The woman began to wail, and soon a wall of wailing and shrieking moved outward from the center of the circle. But still there was a sense of calm that would not be broken, emanating from the man. People drew closer. Some laid their hands on the woman's shoulders, her head, her arms, speaking in soothing, comforting tones. Some reached out to touch the man himself.

"He was floating. Did you see? He rose up in the air!"

"Look at his face...his smile..."

When the news reached the boundary of the crowd, an ululation of women's voices rang out and moved back toward the center.

"Percival," sobbed the woman, "Why?"

"We should take him to Maggie's," said Bearclaw. "She's a safe distance from the meadow. I'll need some help."

Eight men gathered around. Someone brought a heavy wool blanket. They made a bed out of it and hoisted the man into the air. All the while his face retained the sweet smile of a sleeping infant. The woman clung to her husband's arms as the bearers began to move. People started singing. It was an old melody that Johnny recognized at once. *The Soft Light of Dawn*. Ant recognized it as well. She set Chestnut down on her wobbly feet and joined in on the fiddle. Bearclaw couldn't play it on his guitar, though. He was one of the men bearing the body.

Johnny stayed behind, his heart pensive, both troubled and calm. The singers and the twirlers and the body bearers lumbered forward in a procession toward the opening, where the trail led into the dark forest and back to the town. The singing continued, accompanied by the fiddle. With weeping and chanting and tender embraces they disappeared, lamp by lamp, into the screen of trees, the lights flickering like fireflies, the voices fading vanishing dreams.

Johnny found himself alone in the moonlit clearing. His face was flushed and his heart throbbing. Behind him, someone spoke.

"Johnny." He turned. It was Jocko.

"Jocko," he said," Come with me. Let's take a walk."

Ɔ

Johnny Arcane and Jocko sat on a rock at the summit of Hunter's Horn, their backs to the town of King Corn, their faces north, to the moon now sinking toward the dark rolling forested hills and the distant snow-capped cone of the Misty Mountain. A pack of agitated coyotes was making its way through the ravines below them, all yips and yaps, none of the long, soulful melodies coyotes are capable of when they are at peace. Yet, there was a sort of peace here, temporary as it was, on this high, windy vantage, far above the rushing of waters, the mooing of cows, the clanging of bells, the shouts of men and the cries of women. They had said nothing since they arrived, accepting the cradled seat that the stone had offered, settling in, content with the sharing of solitude, of breathing and of human warmth.

But there was something on Jocko's mind. Johnny could tell. That was why he brought him here, and he knew Jocko well enough not to be the first to speak. How strange it was to know these things about someone over the brief passage of time. How short were the moments of human companionship! How long the wanderings in between!

The coyotes quieted. Perhaps they found what they were looking for. At that moment, Jocko inhaled deeply.

"I don't understand," he said. "Why did he have to die?"

It was what Johnny thought he might say. Indeed, it was something he had been pondering himself, and already the thread of a reply was binding in his thoughts. But he struggled for a way to say it. Perhaps a story. Stories often worked better than concepts. Especially with Jocko.

"I never met my father," he said at last. "But he sent a message to my mother just before he died. Part of what he said—he said it is possible to choose the time of one's own departure."

Jocko thought about this for a while. He folded his hands in his lap.

"Why would someone choose death?"

Below, the coyotes grew restless again, briefly, then settled into a tenuous calm. Above, the moon paled behind a thin stratum of cloud.

"It might be he didn't choose death. Did you see the look on his face? He might have just gone into a kind of bliss that was too strong for his body."

"Death is bliss?"

"No, no. I don't think death is bliss. Look at it this way, maybe. You saw him. You saw his face before he fell. He was looking at something—something that can't be contained ..." Johnny grasped at the words.

"By time?" Jocko suggested.

"Yes, by time. Yes, that's it. If you go to that place it doesn't matter what's next. Nothing is next. It doesn't matter if you die. Maybe the body is just too small to hold that feeling."

That's good, he thought, *I've said the right thing. I've said what he needs to hear.* But suddenly Jocko started shivering, uncontrollably. He pulled his arms around his shoulders as if he were clutching a blanket.

"I can't help it. I just can't. I'm afraid to die." Jocko began to sob, quiet little sobs with no breath in them. Johnny was at a complete loss. He thought, maybe a hand on the shoulder, a pat on the back. But he did nothing. He waited. Eventually Jocko's breath went quiet. He stared down at his hands. He looked up.

"I want to show you something," he said. From somewhere in the rumples of his coat he produced a crinkly bundle, roughly folded, many times. His hands trembled as he opened it and opened it, until at last he held the corners of a battered document, about the size of the magic lantern projection in his bedroom. Illuminated by the moonlight, it was a picture of himself, a *photo-graph*, the very one that had once hung on the wall outside the scullery door in the longhouse. Above the face, in large, ink-blocked letters: *JOCKO MOTO.* Below the face: *KILL THIS MAN.*

Johnny winced through clenched teeth. "Oh, *Jocko!* Where did you find it?"

"On a tree. North road. Facing north."

"When?"

"Two days ago."

"Do you know why?"

Jocko took a moment to respond. "Me and Bearclaw, we were always taking down your posters. One day I was out by myself, looking for acorn hats. I saw your poster on a barn wall. I took it down. There were Blackcoats hiding in the barn. They grabbed me. They cut me." He held up his left hand. The stubbly tip of his smallest finger was missing. "They said, *we'll take the rest of you next time*. And they let me go. "

Johnny felt like he was going to cry. Jocko. So sweet. So vulnerable. How could this be happening?

"You have to leave King Corn. At once."

"Why?"

Indeed, why? The answer to that question was almost too strong, too strange to be spoken. "Things are changing, Jocko. Believe me, I've seen it. You've seen it too. The borders have collapsed. It's going to start happening very quickly now. It will be better if you're moving. You'd be safer as a sojourner. Change your name. Cut your hair. So they won't be able to find you. Trust me, Jocko. You don't have to die yet."

Jocko took a deep breath and let it out slowly. He took another, and folded his arms, his hands grasping his shoulders.

"I want to go with the cowboys. Birdleg and Climber."

"Then you should do that. Yes, that's what you should do."

Jocko shifted his weight, unclasped his arms. "What about cows, though? Isn't that when it all started? When the cows came to King Corn."

"No, it started long before that. I don't know about cows. You can go with the cows, for now. I don't know what's good, what's bad. The change just has to happen. It can't be stopped. There will be chaos and cruelty, and it might go on for a long time—but not forever. There is something stronger than all this. It is growing, slowly, like a forest, growing slowly, outward from the center. It will take a long time—maybe longer than we will live—but it will prevail."

They didn't say anything for a while. It was like something in Johnny's words had brought the details of the moment closer, and they had to pay attention to them. A warm, gentle wind was blowing. There was a rustling sound coming from all directions, all the trees for as far as the eye could see were swaying gently in the moonlight. A blinker had just risen over the peak of Misty Mountain, and was starting its lazy climb into the starry skies. Below them there was a clear strip of land where one of the tiered hills had been denuded of trees to fuel the fires for the textile mills in Stubblefield. Some kind of mottled shadow was rolling across this space. Johnny noticed it, but he didn't think much of it. The forest was always full of moving shadows.

He turned his gaze upward to the stars, to the moon, to the rising blinker. He had always wanted to see a blinker cross the moon. Would it pass in front or would it pass behind? That would tell him something about the blinkers. He fixed his eye on the moon's orb, but as always the blinker arced and moved away, to lose itself in the river of stars. The mystery remained unsolved. He returned his attention to the treeless patch of the forest.

There was definitely something moving down there. Less abstract now, distinct shapes were entering the clear space from the north, and disappearing into the forest in the south. Animals, perhaps. He remembered the restless yipping of the coyotes. But coyotes did not move like this, in such large numbers, with such deliberate intention. He recalled once coming across a migration of salamanders, moving over the forest floor like a living carpet, bound for the spawning marshes of the river. But these were not salamanders. They were far too large. A cold stone of dread began to harden in his stomach. At that same moment, Jocko spoke.

"What *is* that?"

Johnny knew. This was far too familiar a feeling. It was not what he wanted to feel at this time.

"Oh, no," he said. "Please, no. Not yet."

"Johnny?"

"It's the Blackcoats, Jocko. They're coming for me."

Jocko stiffened, and his back became straight as a tree. "Then they're coming for me, too."

"No. Just for me. It's not your time. This isn't your destiny."

"I won't leave you, Johnny."

"You will. You must. There is more for you to do. Go back down. Hurry. Find Climber and Birdleg. Tell them you want to go with them. Change your name. Cut your hair. Take to the open road. Do it."

"Johnny—"

"*Do* it!"

Jocko stood. "I'll go down and distract them. You can escape."

"Don't! They will kill us both. Don't argue. This is part of its plan."

"No!" Jocko threw himself at Johnny. He grasped at his shoulders and tried to pull him into an embrace. But something happened. Johnny felt a surge rush outward from the core of his body, down his arms, out through his hands. Jocko was thrown backwards. He landed with his back on the ground, his eyes wide with terror, no less than the terror Johnny felt at his own sudden power.

"I'm sorry, Jocko!" Johnny cried as the force drained from his limbs. "Save yourself. Go quickly."

For a moment the two men stood staring at each other. Johnny could only imagine what Jocko was thinking. From the forest below he heard sounds, bodies breaking through bracken, the chant of muffled voices. Out of nowhere he remembered the last words of Mars Daniel.

"Jocko," he said. "Jocko Moto. I'll see you again, Jocko Moto. In the next world, if not in this."

Jocko turned and fled. Johnny heard him hurtling through the trees along the trail, down to the open bowl where the music had been played, down through the dark forest that opened out into the valley of King Corn. As he ran, he cried and wailed, and the further away he got, the more his cries resembled a melody, a familiar fiddle tune fading in the distance, happy to meet, sorry to part.

Johnny stood on the stone where they had been sitting. He stood as tall as he could. He put his hands on his hips. *So this is it*, he told himself. But then, this is always it. With his mind clear and his heart pure, released from the chains of the world, known and unknown, Johnny Arcane rose to greet his destiny.

EPILOGUE

n a lonesome prairie, three cowboys are gathered around a dying fire, picking the last meat off the bones of a roasted cat. In the distance the restless coyotes are settling down for the night, and the pungent aroma of sage permeates the warm air. The cows, eight of them this drove, are lowing quietly in a copse of straggly madrone. Overhead, a blinker works its way slowly between the stars and through the wisps of cloud. There is no moon.

"Well, he's a good kid," says Climber, "He just gets this way some times. We should keep him on."

"Course we should," replies Birdleg. "He works hard. "Sides, I like his little carvings. Other day he made a wooden apple so real I was like to eat it."

Aramis, the youngest cowboy, lifts his head from his bedroll. "You're *talking* about me."

"Thought you was asleep."

"I was. But you started talking about me."

Climber stirs the fire with a stick and makes the sparks dance. "Go back to sleep, Aramis. We'll stop talking about you. Just don't you be crying anymore. Disturbs the cows."

There is silence for a time, until Aramis makes a loud snuffling sound with his nose.

"What'd I say?" barks Climber.

The young cowboy lies very still.

"You know the old song," continues Climber. *"He loved to laugh but he did not laugh when Frankie took the photograph…"*

Aramis lets out a puff of air. His thin voice follows the trace of an old melody.

"He climbed the sunbeams, and he held onto the birds…"

Slowly Climber pulls himself up from the log where he sits, stretches, and lumbers over to the bedroll where Aramis lies. There he kneels down laboriously.

"Sit up, boy. Look me in the face." The boy sits up, looks him the face.

"It weren't Johnny Arcane, you hear? You knew Johnny Arcane. You played music with him. You saw that man. That were no Johnny Arcane."

Aramis sniffs. His lower lip quivers. "It was a long time ago. Almost two summers. People change."

"Not when they're dead they don't."

"He didn't die. He moved sideways. Sometimes people can do that. He told me once. Like the people at the camp."

"Well, that didn't happen neither. Just because people say things, don't mean they're true. It's like horn pigs. Unless I sees it, it didn't happen. That's what I allus say. Now you stop crying and get some sleep. We got a long drove tomorrow."

Climber gets up, returns to the fire. He sits back down on his log. "We do got a long drove," he says. "That cow's gonna calve in three days. We gotta get to Stubblefield afore she does."

"What's left of Stubblefield … " says Birdleg.

They don't say anything else for a while. An owl hoots in the madrones, and the cows complain about it. Coyotes on the ridge hear the cows and set up a chorus of wailing. In the distance there's the bang of a gun, and the coyotes and the cows go still. An ember in the fire pops, like a shy reply.

Birdleg looks like he wants to say something. He moves his mouth, silently trying on words. "Well, there was *somebody*," he says at last. "You did see somebody standing there. It could have been Johnny Arcane."

Climber cracks the stick he's holding and throws it on the ground. "Oh shut up!" he yells. "Don't *you* start! I'm gonna go check on the cows. You better be asleep when I get back." He pulls himself to his feet and moves away from the fire, muttering, "Corn damn horn pigs!"

Then it's quiet again. Birdleg gets up from his hard, jagged rock and sits down on Climber's soft mossy log. He picks up the broken stick, breaks each half in two, and tosses the four twigs into the fire. They immediately spark to life, and an orange glow illuminates his face.

"It *was* Johnny Arcane," says Aramis softly. "He's not dead."

"I dunno. Maybe." Birdleg stirs the fire.

"It *was*. Johnny Arcane's not dead. I know it. Johnny Arcane is *alive!*"

The cows moo. The grass rustles. Out of the blue-black sky the blinker sinks into the shimmering red glow behind the northern ridge.

A NOTE FROM THE AUTHOR

o begin with, thank you. I hope you enjoyed reading my book as much as I enjoyed writing it.

The Ballad of Johnny Arcane started with a song I composed in 1973. The song was later recorded by David West and released on his CD called *Arcane* in 1992. That CD is still available from Taxim Records : (https://www.taxim.com/items_de/tx3003.htm).

It's a beautiful piece of work and it never got the attention it deserved. What a hoot it would be if my publishing this book would ignite a resurgence of interest in that album! Please do what you can to make this happen.

The song is just a skeleton of the story—no real flesh. Over the years I wondered, what is this really about? Finally I decided to find out. I did so by taking long walks through Wilsonville's Memorial Park, calling the story down and reciting it into a hand-held digital voice recorder. What I was given was the first draft of *The Ballad of Johnny Arcane*. Subsequent rewrites have not changed the basic structure much.

Once a book is published it is neither the responsibility nor the privilege of the author to interpret the story. That dubious task lies entirely with the reader. Having said that, I would love to hear and discuss your take on what I have written. And please, if you like my book, encourage your friends to get their own copy.

And who am I? I am a songwriter, author, father, husband. I have written the first draft of several other novels but this is the first one I have polished. At the time of this publishing,

I live in Oregon with my wife Claire. We have two fine grown sons, Brendan and Devin. And may I take this opportunity to promote a gripping and ultimately redemptive novel written by my wife? It's called *Saint Sullivan's Daughter*, by Claire Germain Nail, and information about it is available from Abbott Press: (http://bookstore.abbottpress.com/Products/SKU-000529426/Saint-Sullivans-Daughter.aspx).

Love you all,

Jim

CPSIA information can be obtained
at www.ICGtesting.com
Printed in the USA
FSOW02n1839100216
16709FS